The DeLuca Furlough Brides

Book 1: The Ones They Left Behind

a novel by
Alan Simon

author of
The First Christmas After the War

and
the forthcoming sequel to this novel:
The DeLuca War Brides

Book 2: The Ones They Brought Home

The DeLuca Furlough Brides
Book 1: The Ones They Left Behind

First Print Edition

ISBN: 978-0-9994665-1-3

Author's Note About the Terms "Furlough Bride" and "War Bride"

The term "war bride" is likely to be more familiar to most readers than "furlough bride." Today, most readers will likely think of a World War II-era *war bride* as a woman from a country other than the United States who 1) married an American serviceman during or shortly after that war, 2) and then came to live in the United States with her new husband.

However, over the years, I had also heard the term "war bride" occasionally used to refer to a young *American* woman who hastily married her sweetheart shortly before he left for World War II military service. While conducting primary research for this novel and its sequel, though, only a handful of references to these rapid marriages being termed "war brides" could be located: for example, an article in *Independent Woman* from January 1942 entitled "War Brides."

More commonly, American women who married their war-bound sweethearts on short notice were referred to at the time as *furlough brides*. A *Life* magazine article from June 22, 1942, entitled "Furlough Brides" noted that "Wedding bells are ringing more frequently than ever before in U.S. history. Estimates are that 1,600,000 couples will be married this year...because so many of their bridegrooms are service men, most brides will marry in haste but with formal ceremony." (*Life*, June 22, 1942, Page 37.)

I explored this theme of a hasty early 1942 wedding in *Unfinished Business* as well as the alternative – becoming engaged but then waiting for one's fiancé to return from the war before getting married – in *Thanksgiving, 1942* and continuing into *The First Christmas After the War.*

Originally for this two-book series, I had planned to use "war bride" to refer to both 1) the two young women who hastily marry into the DeLuca family in early 1942; as well as, in the second novel, 2) the two young women from other countries who wind up marrying the other two DeLuca brothers and then return with those brothers to Pittsburgh after the war.

However, based on my research I decided to adopt the term that is lesser known today – "furlough bride" – for this first book's title, especially since both of the DeLuca brothers who marry at the beginning of our story are indeed on furlough.

A final disclaimer: the explanation above, like this book itself and its sequel, is a distinctly American perspective on our subject matter. Someone from England, for example, might think of a war bride as a British woman in the early 1940s residing and working in London, Birmingham, Manchester, or another British city or town while her husband was off at war.

Author's Note About Newspaper Headlines and Stories

For the most part, headlines and stories from various Pittsburgh newspapers are genuine and were published on the exact date mentioned in the story. Occasionally, a headline or story has been slightly shifted to a different date, or a different time of day (morning vs. evening), or credited to a different newspaper for purposes of story development.

Likewise, for the most part the movies and other wartime distractions cited in our story were playing on the exact dates and in the same neighborhood theaters referenced. Some train schedules in the story are exactly as they were in real life, while others have been shifted for purposes of the story.

Dedication

In this story, I place one of my supporting characters in a job at a war plant called the Dravo Shipyard, just downriver from downtown Pittsburgh; on Neville Island, which happens to be in the middle of the Ohio River. In real life, the Dravo Shipyard built a large number of LSTs ("Landing Ships, Tank") that participated in the D-Day invasion of Normandy in 1944 and other amphibious assaults during the war.

Even though I was born in Pittsburgh and have been interested in World War II-era history since I was young, I only recently learned about the Dravo Shipyard when I visited my 88-year-old father while I was writing this book. My dad asked me about this latest novel that I was writing, and I outlined the World War II homefront story line for him. He then began telling me how his own father, along with his two older brothers and also his sister's husband, worked at the Dravo Shipyard building LSTs during World War II. He had never shared this information with me before; or if he had, long ago, I had forgotten.

I decided to add this long-gone piece of Pittsburgh history to my story, even though the novel was already underway, for one reason. That visit with my father took place in a hospice facility in Tucson, Arizona, late one Saturday afternoon. I saw him again later that evening, and again the next morning before driving back to Phoenix. I made plans for another visit as soon as possible, but he passed away three days later.

Beginning with my novel *The First Christmas of the War*, my father read every word of each of my novels. He eagerly contributed tidbits of wartime and postwar Pittsburgh history and culture to the stories set during those time periods. Even as his health deteriorated, he would ask me for details about my current and upcoming writing projects. He was particularly intrigued with the Coleman family members in my "An American Family's Wartime Saga" series, and frequently asked questions about the characters' fates as if they were real-life people rather than my own creations.

Actually, maybe my characters do have a touch of the real world in them. The patriarch of the Coleman family was a Pittsburgh shoemaker who later worked in a war plant (Gerald Coleman, who makes a small appearance in this novel), deliberately modeled after one of my grandfathers: my father's father. The characters in those novels all went to the same high school that my father had attended. One of the sons was roughly the same age as my father had been during the war years, and perhaps reading about Tommy Coleman took my father back to his own wartime teen years.

I used to look forward to printing off a completed manuscript of each novel to take down to Tucson for my father to read, and I eagerly awaited his thoughts about the story, the characters, and the setting. I'm sad that this tradition has now ended.

Perhaps in some way, in some place, my father's spirit will find a way to enjoy this novel and (hopefully) many more that will follow. For now, I am dedicating this novel to my father, Bernard Simon: to his life (1928-2016), to his service (US Army Air Forces, 1946-1947), and to his memory.

Prologue – Saturday Morning, April 25, 1942

Katherine Buchanan forced a smile to her face. After all, the mother of the bride was expected to be exultant at her daughter's wedding.

For a brief moment Katherine feared that if any of her friends sitting elsewhere inside Saint Alban's happened to notice her smiling they would think of her as a weak-willed woman, one who had surrendered her principles merely because her daughter had just begun to walk down the aisle on her father's arm. But those fleeting thoughts passed as quickly as they appeared. Katherine Buchanan's friends – her true friends – would know very well what thoughts were in her head at this very moment, and of course understand that the concocted smile was merely for show.

Even as her duplicitous smile remained fixed in place, Katherine's eyes narrowed as they shifted from her daughter Elizabeth to her husband. This whole fiasco was Spencer Buchanan's fault, Katherine told herself for perhaps the hundredth time since the beginning of the month, when Elizabeth had broken the shocking news of her engagement and this hasty wedding to her parents. Well, perhaps not directly his fault; after all, the unfortunate melting pot of Peabody High School had put Elizabeth in close proximity to this Italian boy, Carlo DeLuca. But Spencer Buchanan had been the one who had legitimized these Italians when he began doing business with them back in 1930.

True, three years of bootlegging alongside some of Pittsburgh's shadier characters had restored the inherited Buchanan wealth that had evaporated with the stock market crash. And during those final three years of Prohibition, if at any moment Katherine had been forced to testify under oath, she would not have raised an objection to her husband taking whatever previously abhorrent actions he could to keep his family in their stately Highland Park home and to get their bank accounts back to where they had been before the crash. After all, throughout the twenties Spencer and Katherine had spent many of their evenings at one speakeasy or another, the Prohibition laws notwithstanding. So what if Spencer Buchanan's involvement with illegal liquor shifted from consumption to production and distribution? And so what if his good Scotch-Irish name came to be spoken around the city in hushed tones, often in the same sentence alongside other names that had long carried a seedier connotation? Desperate times called for desperate measures, as the saying went.

But even after Prohibition was repealed, and after the Buchanan bank accounts had been refilled with liquor money, Spencer had insisted on maintaining acquaintances with those Italians. He could have simply washed his hands of every single one of those associations and left those...those *men* behind in the past. But to Katherine's dismay, her husband insisted that it was a matter of principle for him to continue occasional social contact with those men rather than callously abandon those relationships. Why else would any of those Italian former bootleggers, each one now involved in new murky illegal dealings, have ever been guests in the Buchanan home along with their wives throughout the 1930s? And if those men had never been presented as acceptable guests and thus seemingly legitimized the idea of Buchanans socializing with Italians, then Katherine had no doubt in her mind at all that Elizabeth would never have begun dating Carlo DeLuca.

And now, that dating had led to this shameful wedding!

Katherine's strained smile began to fade, so she forced it back into place as her daughter approached. The Lord knew that Katherine had not held back one bit in private, loudly and persistently expressing her dismay to her daughter about this hurried wedding. But Elizabeth had been adamant, insisting that with Carlo home for a very short furlough following Marine Corps boot camp and soon leaving for infantry training in less than two weeks, a wedding *now* was the only sensible alternative for the two of them.

As Spencer Buchanan delivered his nineteen-year-old daughter into the hands of Carlo DeLuca, standing ramrod straight in his Marine Corps uniform yet beaming at his bride, Katherine began to quiver with disappointment. Shifting her gaze away from the horrific sight in front of her, Katherine noticed several young men in attendance wearing Air Corps uniforms, which quickly shifted her thoughts to the events of a week earlier. Colonel Doolittle's planes had shocked the enemy with their surprise aerial attack on the Japanese islands!

To Katherine's way of thinking, this first aerial assault on Japan indicated that the United States was serious about fighting the Japanese every bit as much as they would take on the Germans. Many people had conjectured that with Japan's relentless invasions and conquests during the past four and a half months all across the Pacific, that theater of the war was now thought to be unwinnable for the United States. As a result, the thinking went, Roosevelt would be forced to negotiate some sort of peace treaty with this hated enemy so that the Americans could concentrate their efforts on helping England defeat the Nazis.

But if that were truly the case, then most likely the effort to bomb the Japanese islands would never have been expended. And if American forces were to be committed to a campaign in the Pacific, then first among those forces would be the United States Marine Corps.

Katherine Buchanan's gaze shifted back to her daughter who was now standing next to Carlo DeLuca. Maybe – just maybe – this Italian boy would go off to Marine Corps infantry training and then to the Pacific, where he would soon become a casualty at the hands of the fearsome Japanese army.

And if that happened, then this tragedy unfolding in front of her at this very moment would essentially evolve into an unpleasant dream from which they all would awake. Elizabeth would become a war widow, and after a brief period of mourning she could put this tragic lapse of judgment behind her and find an acceptable husband.

This time, Katherine Buchanan's smile was genuine.

*   *   *

On the other side of the center aisle at Saint Alban's, Rosalia DeLuca smiled as she watched her son's wedding ceremony begin. Rosalia felt the joy a mother feels when watching her son about to become a married man, even though the ceremony was taking place in an Episcopalian church rather than a Catholic one. Yet those joyous thoughts tussled with the trepidation that her son, only nineteen years old, might never come back from whatever battlefields he would soon be forced to endure.

Her smile began to fade as her eyes filled with tears, and she hoped that anyone in Saint Alban's who noticed her crying would think that these were tears of joy rather than fear and sorrow.

1942

Chapter 1

Saturday, May 2, 1942

"Can I get one of those?"

Elizabeth DeLuca's head quickly pivoted to the right at the sound of the girl's voice. Even before she had fully turned she knew that the words had come from her brand-new sister-in-law Angela. Barely three hours earlier Angela Antolini had married twenty-three-year-old Tony DeLuca, the oldest of the four DeLuca brothers, with the wedding taking place exactly one week after Elizabeth's wedding to nineteen-year-old Carlo.

"Sure," Elizabeth nodded as she fished into her dress purse for the pack of Pall Malls. The delicate purse was barely large enough to hold the cigarettes, so she had no difficulty locating it. She flicked the half-empty pack in Angela's direction, and the new bride reached for one of the two cigarettes that had settled halfway out of the paper package.

"Here," Elizabeth reached back into the purse for a pack of matches that she handed to Angela. After lighting the cigarette and inhaling deeply, Angela released the smoke along with a huge sigh.

"Tired?" Elizabeth asked, knowing the answer.

Angela rolled her eyes, looking back toward the front door of Saint Michael's.

"This is *so-o-o-o* exhausting," Angela replied, exaggerating her tone to indicate just how tired she actually felt. It was barely past four o'clock this Saturday afternoon of her wedding day, but the non-stop frenzy of activities that began hours ago with the lengthy Catholic wedding Mass had worn Angela to a frazzle. After dancing with what seemed like a thousand DeLuca cousins in a row, she was finally able to slip away from the church basement, up the stairs, and outside for some fresh air on this glorious early May Saturday afternoon.

"Mine also," Elizabeth nodded, thinking back to her own wedding a week earlier, the memories and sensations still vividly fresh yet paradoxically already starting to fade. "By nighttime I was ready to drop from exhaustion I was so tired; all I wanted to do was go right to sleep."

"But you didn't, I'll bet," Angela countered, her voice heavy with salacious innuendo that caused Elizabeth to instantly blush.

"She didn't what?" A new voice, coming from behind the two recent additions to the DeLuca family, was the source of the question. Both Elizabeth and Angela pivoted and saw their new sister-in-law Carmela approaching them. Carmela was the only girl among the five children of Giuseppe and Rosalia DeLuca. At twenty and recently married herself, Carmela – now Carmela DeMarco – was squarely in the middle of her brothers by age. Besides Elizabeth's and Angela's new husbands, the other two were twenty-one-year-old Vinnie, who had enlisted in the U.S. Army Air Forces only two days after Pearl Harbor, and eighteen-year-old Michael. Vinnie was already gone and most likely on his way to England, or maybe even over there already; none of the DeLucas knew for certain because of wartime secrecy. Michael was still in high school for a few more weeks, but of course headed for one service or another very shortly after his upcoming graduation.

"We were talking about her wedding night," Angela continued unabashedly, her tones louder than Elizabeth would have preferred, given that the three women were gathered on the sidewalk right outside of Saint Michael's. The occasional person strolled by in one direction or the other, so to Elizabeth's way of thinking this was hardly the venue for the type of girl talk that typically occurred when cloistered with close friends behind a closed bedroom door.

A lascivious look, so very similar to the one on Angela's face at the moment, immediately came to Carmela. Elizabeth was struck by the physical similarities between these two girls: the jet black hair; the olive complexion so common among the Italian girls Elizabeth had known at Peabody High School; and an overall aura of sensuality radiating from each one's attractive facial features. Both Angela and Carmela were the same height: a shade under five feet, three inches tall. Both were slender. In fact, one might look at the two of them and not be faulted for presuming that they were blood sisters rather than sisters-in-law.

The strong similarities between these other two girls naturally drew Elizabeth's thoughts to how different from them that she looked...in fact, how different Elizabeth looked than probably a hundred other twenty-ish Italian girls back inside the basement of Saint Michael's at this very moment. Elizabeth was only an inch taller than these other girls and equally as slender; but she was blonde and fair-skinned, clearly marking her as a Scotch-Irish

Protestant. Still, Elizabeth rightfully thought of herself as equally attractive as these Italian girls, just in different ways.

Besides, before she began dating Carlo DeLuca halfway through their junior year at Peabody High, Elizabeth Buchanan had never lacked for beaus and had gone steady with three different boys for around six months each. Of course each of those steadies had been from Scotch-Irish families who lived on the same Highland Park block as the Buchanan family, which was why her beginning to date Carlo and then getting serious with him had come as such a shock to Elizabeth's mother.

"So was it your first time?" Carmela interjected and Elizabeth was immediately struck by the brazen words coming from her new husband's very own sister!

Elizabeth could only blush in response, which in fact gave Carmela her answer. The truth was, though, that ever since Carlo had enlisted in the Marines, their necking had progressed on more than one occasion into something more heated, more titillating. After all, they were now engaged. Carlo had abruptly asked Elizabeth to marry him back in early January, the day after he joined up, and from that point on she no longer felt obligated by propriety to put a halt to his roving hands.

Despite Carlo's best efforts during the days leading up to their wedding, though, they still hadn't "done it," even after Carlo had returned to Pittsburgh from Marine Corps boot camp. Elizabeth had insisted that despite the war, the homefront chaos, and even Carlo's impending departure, they would hold off until they were actually married. Still, Elizabeth was certain that if Katherine Buchanan had known what her daughter was doing in the back rows of various movie theaters around Pittsburgh or in the back seat of a parked Packard Six – especially with an Italian boy, engaged or not – the always proper older woman would have been shocked and scandalized.

"How about you?" Carmela turned to Angela. "You and Tony been doin' it before today?"

To Elizabeth's astonishment, Angela just shrugged.

"There's a war on, ya know?" was her casual declaration that followed the shrug.

Elizabeth shouldn't have been so shocked at the unanticipated revelation. Anthony DeLuca was now twenty-three years old, and had been going steady with his bride-to-be during Angela's entire senior year at Peabody High and through the many months that followed. There had been whispers in the Peabody hallways about Angela's brazen behavior with that older boy – older man, actually – from the very beginning. But once Angela and Elizabeth both graduated nearly a year ago and daily high school gossip slipped into the past, ideas about Angela Antolini's possible or even likely indiscretions never again made their way into Elizabeth Buchanan's thoughts, even though the two girls were dating two of the DeLuca brothers. Tony and Carlo DeLuca weren't particularly close, and the two couples rarely double-dated or did much of anything together. Until the outbreak of war and both girls' rapid engagements, Angela Antolini was little more to Elizabeth than just another girl from her recent Peabody High past whom she now rarely saw or thought of.

Maybe Angela had it exactly right when she said "there's a war on, ya know?" Not even five months had passed since the surprise attack on Pearl Harbor, and it already seemed that *nothing* was the same in America anymore. From blackouts to rationing to the nonstop news of nearly every boy Elizabeth knew enlisting in one service or another, Pittsburgh had changed over the past few months into a city that was so very different than it had been in 1940 or early '41. All the old rules seemed to have flown right out the window.

And the engagements! One after another! Carmela had been one of the first, becoming engaged to Tony DeMarco this past Christmas Eve, only weeks after the Pearl Harbor attacks. Unlike both Elizabeth and Angela, though, Carmela's wedding had taken place while Tony DeMarco was still a civilian, before he headed off to Fort Dix and basic training. They had gotten married in mid-January, only three weeks after becoming engaged…the most rushed of all of the neighborhood weddings.

All across Pittsburgh – indeed, all across Pennsylvania and also throughout the rest of the country – the flurry of engagements not only continued but actually accelerated as 1941 gave way to 1942. Some of those rapid engagements came with a deferred wedding date to take place after the war, whenever that might eventually be. But even more engaged couples, fully cognizant that this new war would almost certainly be a long one, set their wedding dates for as soon as possible. Carmela DeLuca and Tony DeMarco may have been among the first; now the two new additions to the DeLuca family standing on the sidewalk this Saturday afternoon alongside Carmela were among so many others who had opted for the "sooner rather than much, much later" choice.

"Make sure he wears a rubber," Carmela blurted out, addressing Angela at first but then also glancing over at Elizabeth to indicate that warning applied to her as well.

"You don't wanna have him go away maybe for a coupl'a years and leave you behind with a little bundle of joy. It don't matter that both of your husbands are my brothers, neither. I'm sure that my ma would love to have grandchildren right away, but she ain't gonna be the one raising them alone while your husbands are off to war, just like mine. I told my Tony he had to wear a rubber and he started with the whole 'I can't because I'm Catholic' routine. But I told him that there was no way I was gonna wind up pregnant, so if he wanted any at all before he left, that's what he had to do."

Once more, Elizabeth was struck by Carmela's bluntness that so very much contrasted with the proper demeanor her mother had established for the Buchanan household. If other Italian girls were anything at all like Carmela, once you became family to them, this all would take some getting used to!

Then again, Elizabeth thought, so far none of the DeLucas had conveyed the icy disapproval that her own mother had, unrelentingly, from the moment of Elizabeth's and Carlo's engagement, through the wedding and continuing through this very morning.

Perhaps then, Elizabeth contemplated, these brusque Italian girls and their families weren't so bad after all.

*   *   *

The three women each finished another Pall Mall and then headed back inside Saint Michael's. Taking note of his newest daughter-in-law's reappearance, Giuseppe DeLuca waited until Angela finished easing her way through the crowd and had rejoined her new husband a short distance from where Giuseppe stood. At that point, the older man mustered all the strength he could into his voice, hoping that would be enough to be heard above the clamor that had yet to diminish since festivities began hours earlier.

"Everyone! Everyone! Everyone!"

The room quieted a bit…but just a bit.

"Everyone!" Giuseppe DeLuca repeated. Finally, after another thirty seconds of repeated attempts, Giuseppe decided that he could proceed and that his words would be heard.

"We're getting close to the finish of our celebration here," he said in his heavily accented tones, "and then we're gonna move the festivities to our house."

A mild chorus of approval came forth from some of the more jovial – and inebriated – celebrants. One less-than-approving person, though, was Angela's father. Bruno Antolini was hosting this affair. The disdain on his face clearly indicated to anyone looking at him rather than Giuseppe DeLuca that Bruno Antolini was not pleased with the other man abruptly seizing center stage.

Giuseppe DeLuca either didn't notice Antolini's scorn, or he didn't care.

"I know that there were many toasts earlier," Giuseppe continued, "but I wanna add one more toast while we are all still here."

He paused for a moment, first looking at his newest daughter-in-law and then searching the room until he saw Elizabeth.

"Elizabeth!" Giuseppe called out. "Elizabeth!"

Elizabeth DeLuca was surprised to be singled out. After all, this was Tony's and Angela's day; hers and Carlo's had been last Saturday.

"Elizabeth!" her father-in-law called out again. "Come up here with Angela!"

Suddenly feeling apprehensive, though she couldn't quite put her finger on why, Elizabeth complied with Mr. DeLuca's request. In the meantime, Angela had eased herself away from her new husband and shuffled over to join the older man. When Elizabeth reached the spot where Giuseppe and Angela stood, the older man began speaking again.

"In only four days, two more of my boys will be boarding the train at Pennsylvania Station to go off to war."

Technically, both Carlo and Tony DeLuca were directly headed to the next phases of their respective military training, but what their father had just bluntly declared – going off to war – was immutably on the horizon for both of them, sooner or later. The cold directness of the man's words instantaneously spread a somber mood throughout the room.

"My son Vinnie is already away, and before too long," Giuseppe paused for a brief moment to glance over at his youngest son, who was standing next to his mother about ten yards away, "my son Michael will go away also after he graduates from high school."

More than a few of the people gathered this Saturday afternoon in the basement of Saint Michael's wondered just where Giuseppe DeLuca was going with this speech. In less than thirty seconds, he had cast a gloomy black cloud over this joyous wedding celebration. For his part, Bruno Antolini glared at the man who was now all but ruining his daughter's wedding day!

"But these girls…" Giuseppe continued, motioning to both Elizabeth and Angela with his right hand. Suddenly Giuseppe seemed to choke up, but he persevered.

"These girls," he repeated, "are gonna help my boys' mother get through having her sons away at war."

The unspoken corollary sentiment: these girls would also help Giuseppe DeLuca cope with the ever-present anxiety and fear of having *his* sons away at war.

"I know that Tony and Angela, and Carlo and Elizabeth, got married fast once the war started. Just like my Carmela and Tony DeMarco did back in January. And that some other people think that young boys and girls getting married so fast with a war going on isn't such a good idea."

Elizabeth immediately thought, Was that a veiled reference to my mother? Who else could her father-in-law mean? Despite the occasional mother who felt that the time hadn't quite arrived to surrender her daughter to a new husband, instant wedding fever had swept the entire city of Pittsburgh, just as it had the entire nation. Elizabeth knew for a fact that Angela's mother had been 100 percent in favor of her daughter's marriage to Tony DeLuca, just as Giuseppe and Rosalia DeLuca had favored their daughter Carmela's marriage only weeks after her sudden engagement. Giuseppe DeLuca just didn't seem like the type of man who would speak in the abstract; to philosophize about whether anonymous other parents did or did not favor this sudden rash of furlough weddings in the face of sudden global warfare. So who else was left, other than Katherine Buchanan?

But if Giuseppe had intended a shot across the bow to let Elizabeth know that he was well aware of Katherine Buchanan's distaste for not only the DeLuca family but Italians as a whole, he held his cards close to his vest. He didn't lock eyes with Elizabeth following his words, nor even slip a pregnant pause into his words. He just kept on speaking.

"Our house is gonna feel empty, other than Carmela still being at home while her Tony is off to war. So that's why my wife is so grateful that Angela will come to live with us, to help make our house feel a little less empty."

Elizabeth cast a sideways glance at Bruno Antolini, and as expected, Angela's father was icily glaring again at Giuseppe…and making no attempt to hide his own distaste at the DeLuca father's words.

Elizabeth noticed that Giuseppe was *now* looking at her, and she quickly redirected her vision from Angela's father to her new father-in-law.

"And maybe before too long, Carlo's wife Elizabeth will come to live with us also, and make the house feel even less empty."

A very short pause, and then Giuseppe raised his glass of Chianti.

"So I say *cin cin!*"

The words were echoed by one and all who were present in the Saint Michael's basement, and anyone with a glass in his or her hand at that moment joined Giuseppe DeLuca in drinking a toast.

With the conclusion of the man's words, dozens of conversations instantly sprung to life all around the room. As their father-in-law turned to accept congratulations for his words from several of the celebrants, Angela and Elizabeth both slipped away from Giuseppe, out of earshot.

"Wow!" Angela exclaimed, though in a low-enough voice that hopefully what she was about to say wouldn't be heard by anybody other than Elizabeth.

"I can't believe he said that about your mother, even though he didn't specifically mention her!" she continued.

So Angela had picked up on that also! For a moment, Elizabeth was unsure how to respond. She could simply nod in agreement or squeak out an "uh-huh," or perhaps she might offer her own analysis about what Giuseppe DeLuca had just said…not only the not-so-veiled reference to Elizabeth's parents but also the brazen nature in which he flaunted that Angela would henceforth be living in the DeLuca household rather than that of Bruno Antolini.

But could she trust Angela? Elizabeth didn't know her new sister-in-law that well. Would confidences she shared with Angela, whether semi-innocent or provocative or even potentially incendiary, remain under wraps?

The truth was, though, that Giuseppe DeLuca hadn't said anything about the apparently unnamed Katherine Buchanan that Elizabeth herself wouldn't utter in an unguarded moment. As unpleasant as Katherine Buchanan had been in the months leading up to last Saturday's wedding, the nastiness had resumed and even heightened all day yesterday after Elizabeth and Carlo returned from their short honeymoon to Niagara Falls. Carlo had spent the entire day with his brother and family, preparing for his older brother's wedding, while Elizabeth had endured the nonstop biting wrath of her mother back at the Buchanan home. Catty remarks about Rosalia DeLuca's plain appearance and heavily accented speech; offensive statements about the DeLuca family's lack of wealth; affronts to Carlo's education and appearance and even his decision to enlist in the Marine Corps…the only thing that Katherine Buchanan hadn't done was to come right out and call Elizabeth's new husband an Italian greaseball!

Elizabeth processed all of this information in a split second and then replied blandly to Angela, "Well, he has the right to think what he wants, especially since my parents didn't come today, even though Carlo's father went out of his way to make sure that your father invited them."

There. A tepid response; one in which Elizabeth didn't overtly disparage her own mother. Angela could read into Elizabeth's words what she wanted to, but Elizabeth felt safe that she hadn't spoken anything that could come back to haunt her if her new sister-in-law turned out to have a malevolent nature.

Angela's initial response was a simple, knowing smirk. The look clearly conveyed to Elizabeth not only that Angela could quite well guess what had gone on in the Buchanan household yesterday, but also that she was fully aware what Elizabeth had done with her guarded reply. Angela apparently then felt compelled to make the first real overture of confidence to her brand-new sister-in-law, because she said to Elizabeth in hushed tones,

"Well, I know for certain that my father is furious with what Tony's father said! Not that any of it was wrong, or any sort of surprise. My parents know of course that I'm going to be living with Tony's parents now that we're married; it just seems right. But the fact that Tony's father came right out and said so, as part of that toast…well, it was like he was trying to rub my father's face in the fact that I would be living under his roof now, not my own father's."

Elizabeth relaxed a little, and looked over at Giuseppe DeLuca and then back at Angela. She contemplated the reputation that Carlo's father had: a nice enough gentleman, but perhaps too nice; even a bit of a pushover. The Depression had buffeted Giuseppe around from one menial job to another as he did his best to keep his family in their house and to put meager amounts of food on the table. Elizabeth was well aware of what her own father had done in the earliest years of the Depression while Prohibition was still the law of the land. The truth was that there was a slight touch of pride in the knowledge that, faced with financial ruin, Spencer Buchanan had no compunction about stepping over the line and engaging in bootlegging activities with the aim of restoring his family's wealth and maintaining their social standing.

Even Angela's father was somewhat of a shady character. Bruno Antolini was known to run numbers out of his corner bar in the Morningside neighborhood of the city where so many Italian families lived; the same neighborhood where the DeLuca home was. He was also known to sometimes put a bit of money on the streets to people in need, and later to show no compunction about calling in fearsome men to collect any unpaid debts along with the very generous interest payments due on those loans.

But Giuseppe DeLuca? He had been a brakeman on the Pennsylvania & Lake Erie Railroad in his younger years, and later moved from that always-dangerous job to become a maintenance laborer in the P&LE rail yards until the Depression deepened. Finding himself unemployed in early 1934, Giuseppe did whatever he could to earn a few dollars here and there until the country started coming out of the Depression with the start of the European war...but he always stayed on the proper side of the law.

Thinking about what he had said during his toast, though, Elizabeth and Angela were both struck with the same thought: perhaps Giuseppe DeLuca wasn't quite as passively mild-mannered as most everyone perceived him to be.

*   *   *

"Wow, I'm exhausted!" Carlo DeLuca proclaimed as he slipped into his side of the tiny bed in his childhood bedroom that he was now occupying – albeit only for a few days longer – with his new wife. The single bed was barely wide enough for both Carlo and Elizabeth, but neither one minded. After all, Elizabeth would very soon be slumbering in that bed by herself...perhaps for years to come, even! So a bit of discomfort and tight quarters was nothing either of them was in the mood to complain about, that was for certain.

"But I'm not too exhausted for this," Carlo continued as he draped his left arm around Elizabeth to pull her towards him, his tones now smoothly suggestive. He began kissing Elizabeth, who eagerly kissed him back as she draped her left leg over his body, pulling his waist and everything below into her. The sense of urgency was overpowering for both of them, and after barely a minute of kissing and roaming hands Carlo released Elizabeth as he turned back towards his nightstand. He opened the drawer, and even in the darkness he quickly found what he was looking for.

As Carlo opened the package and then put on the condom, Elizabeth's mind flashed back to Carmela's words while standing on the sidewalk outside of Saint Michael's:

"You don't wanna have him go away maybe for a coupl'a years and leave you behind with a little bundle of joy."

For a brief moment Elizabeth was torn. They would have had less than two weeks together as man and wife before he went off to war. Maybe a "little bundle of joy" to mother and care for was what she should be trying to achieve, to help her cope with the emptiness of a husband fighting for his life across one ocean or another.

It didn't matter, Elizabeth realized as Carlo slid on top of her. He wasn't leaving her any say in the matter.

Chapter 2

Wednesday, May 6, 1942

Elizabeth DeLuca leaned down to retrieve this morning's *Pittsburgh Post-Gazette* from just outside the DeLuca's front door. She unfolded the paper and was overjoyed at the oversized bold-typed headline:

THE WAR IS OVER!

Carlo would be coming home now. Their married life could finally begin, and they could now start a family. She couldn't wait to relay the news to everyone else in the family. First she would inform Angela, who was walking down the stairs at this very moment…

Elizabeth awoke with a start. She was no longer standing at the front door, drinking in the splendid early spring morning along with the glorious news of her dream. She was upstairs in the tiny bedroom, pressed tightly against her husband as a few glints from the morning's first light filtered through the blackout curtains. Elizabeth's heart sank. Carlo would not soon be on his way home from the war, because he hadn't even gone away yet! The gloomy reality was that this very morning, he would be departing Pittsburgh's Pennsylvania Station, and only the good Lord above knew when – if – Elizabeth would see him again.

Elizabeth tried desperately to swim back down into the dream where her husband wouldn't be taken away from her a few short hours from now, but it was no use. She knew that she was awake for good. For a brief moment Elizabeth felt compelled to wake Carlo and tell him about her dream, but she decided against it. She knew by now that Carlo would invariably awaken at 6:15 a.m. almost to the second, so she decided to let him sleep another twenty minutes or so until he woke on his own.

Elizabeth slipped out of bed, fished for her slippers, and then tiptoed down the stairs. She carefully eased open the DeLuca's front door to hopefully prevent the usual squeaks and groans that emanated from the aging hinges...something she hadn't done in her dream, she just realized. Exactly as she had done in the dream, though, Elizabeth knelt down to retrieve the morning's *Post-Gazette*. Then she stopped dead in her tracks as she took in the ominous headline that was so very much unlike the wonderful one in her dream:

Japanese Make Landing Attack Against Fortress on Corregidor

Everyone knew it was coming: the end of the line in the Philippines. Bataan had fallen a month earlier, and there was little hope for the remaining Americans valiantly holding out there against the fearsome Japanese army. Elizabeth's thoughts instantly flew to her husband sleeping upstairs. Was that where Carlo would be sent when it was his time to fight? To try to free the Philippines from the Japanese after they had plenty of time to entrench and fortify their positions there?

With a shudder Elizabeth forced her eyes away from the terrible headline as she shut the door and walked back inside the close quarters of the DeLuca living room. Sinking into one of the two armchairs, she once again gazed at the morning paper but forced her eyes away from the horrifying news that she had already absorbed, trying to find some other story to focus on. Unfortunately, the majority of this morning's *Post-Gazette's* front page contained some sort of war-related news, on the battlefield or the home front. But that was to be expected, was it not?

Elizabeth's eyes finally lit onto a story on the bottom left side of the front page. More than 2,000 volunteers from all over Pittsburgh were assisting more than 3,000 teachers in distributing sugar ration books at schools around the city. At this very moment, Elizabeth craved a cup of coffee just as much as she did a cigarette. They all knew that sugar rationing would soon be underway, but the newspaper story drove the point home. Would the simple pleasure of a sweetened cup of coffee soon become a scarcity?

The squeaking of the stairs jerked Elizabeth's head in that direction, and a few seconds later she saw Angela descending, doing her best to tiptoe downstairs. Once she reached the bottom of the stairs, Angela looked out into the living room and noticed that Elizabeth was seated there.

"I thought I heard somebody else get up," Angela whispered as she headed in Elizabeth's direction, just loud enough for her sister-in-law to hear.

"Uh-huh," Elizabeth said gloomily. "I wanted Carlo to sleep a little bit longer, but I was so wide awake that I swear I was ready to scream if I had to lay in bed any longer, just staring at the ceiling. I had this dream…"

Elizabeth began to describe her vivid dream to Angela, but she only was able to get about ten seconds into her description before her sister-in-law interrupted.

"I had almost the exact same dream, too!" Angela proclaimed, the excitement in her voice unmistakable even though she was talking in barely above a whisper. "I think it was around two or three this morning. Except in my dream Tony's father came bursting in through the door to tell everyone – we were all sitting in the living room, and I think you were there also – that the war was over and that everyone would soon be coming home!"

Angela continued to excitedly describe her dream, her narration becoming more and more jumbled as she went on. Elizabeth half-listened because her own mind taunted her by replaying the imaginary scenes of her own dream once again.

"That's strange that we had such similar dreams," Angela continued.

Elizabeth shrugged.

"Probably not," she countered. "After all, we're both in exactly the same situation, with Carlo and Tony both getting on the same train and neither of us knowing when we'll see our husbands again."

Angela let out a deep sigh.

"I guess so," she replied as she lit a Pall Mall and then offered the pack to Elizabeth.

"I just...I don't know," Angela continued gloomily, "we've known all along that they were leaving soon, but even yesterday it seemed like it was still a little ways off, not right around the corner. Do you know what I mean?"

Elizabeth nodded as she lit the cigarette she had just been given.

"Me too," she despondently agreed. "Almost like this morning would come and we would find out it was all a bad dream, or maybe them leaving had been called off. I don't mean us having those dreams; I mean for real. I guess we both have to face it that today's the day."

She handed the *Post-Gazette* to Angela.

"Look at the headline," Elizabeth muttered. Misery loves company, so why should Elizabeth wallow in sorrow and fear by herself, right?

Angela let out a deep breath as she read the short, menacing headline. Then she placed the newspaper on the small end table next to the armchair where she had sat.

"I don't wanna read it now," she said. "All I want is a cup of coffee to go with my cigarette."

As Angela was rising from the chair, Elizabeth briefly thought about telling her sister-in-law what she had just read about the sugar rationing. But then she decided not to. Angela would learn soon enough along with everyone else what, if any, impact rationing of sugar – not to mention gasoline and butter and God knows what else – would have on their daily existence as they feared for the lives of those away at war.

*   *   *

One by one the rest of the DeLucas began filtering down the stairs, beginning with Tony and Carlo and then soon followed by their sister Carmela. Next came Giuseppe and Rosalia; the father trying to put on a brave face, but the mother making no attempt at all to hide her anguish.

Still, despite her grief, Rosalia did what any good Italian mother and wife would do: she immediately began preparing a special breakfast for her departing sons. The women all helped Rosalia as Giuseppe remained with his sons in the living room.

"You see this?" Carlo handed the *Post-Gazette* to Tony. "I wonder if that's where they'll send me."

Tony quickly absorbed the ominous headline that spelled the imminent end for the brave holdouts on Corregidor, and then he scanned the first couple of paragraphs in the article.

"I dunno; maybe," Tony replied as he began to read. "Maybe me, too, given that it's also a lot of Army guys, not just Marines, getting clobbered there."

Giuseppe studied his oldest son's face as he read the newspaper story, and then looked over at Carlo. If either of them was frightened or worried about what was almost certainly ahead for them in this war, neither was betraying that fear. To their father, each seemed to have a grim determination that whatever his future might be. It was already written and would be revealed sooner or later, so why worry now?

Michael was the last one down the staircase, seemingly timed perfectly for when his mother and sister and new sisters-in-law began scooping eggs and potatoes and sausage patties onto the plates that had already been placed on the kitchen table. Michael didn't even break stride as he muttered " 'mornin' " to his father and two brothers and kept walking into the kitchen. Giuseppe was puzzled by his youngest son's demeanor, considering that in a few short hours both of his brothers would be leaving. Perhaps, though, Michael's seemingly detached manner as he breezed through the living room was a way for him to cope with the fact that by this afternoon, he would be the only one of his four brothers still at home in Pittsburgh…and almost certainly not for too much longer.

Giuseppe, Tony, and Carlo all rose to follow Michael into the kitchen, and they all headed towards their customary chairs. Michael's filled plate was already on the table and he began digging in, but his sixth sense must have told him to glance up at Giuseppe. When his eyes caught those of his father's, Giuseppe gave a few rapid shakes of his head that clearly signaled to Michael to stop eating.

When Rosalia and the other women had finished serving the breakfast and took their own seats, Giuseppe quickly spoke up.

"We don't normally say nothin' before eating breakfast at this table," he began. "But just like when Vinnie went away to the Air Corps, I wanna say a few words about Tony and Carlo."

All eyes were on Giuseppe DeLuca as he continued.

"Both you boys are goin' off to war," he continued, still using the same phrasing from his toast at Tony and Angela's wedding this past Saturday. Had it only been four days? In many ways those few brief days had mercilessly whizzed by for every family member. Paradoxically, though, in other ways it already seemed to be such a long time ago that they had all gathered at Saint Michael's for the wedding. For Angela, it felt as if she and Tony had squeezed months or even years of time into those four days. As her father-in-law continued, she said a silent prayer to herself that those four days – and nights – would not turn out to be the sum total of her married life; that Tony would come back from the war, and they would be able to pick up their life together from that point.

"...I know you have to be brave," Giuseppe was saying as Angela's attention once again was on Mr. DeLuca's words, "but I also want both of you boys to be smart. I never had to go to war myself, so I can't tell you what to do and what to think. But pay attention in this training you both got comin' up and learn as much as you can so you can be okay no matter what happens, and then come back home after the war is over. Until then, we'll all say prayers every single day for your safety; and for Vinnie's, too, and" – he looked over at Michael – "for Michael's, too, when he goes."

Rosalia DeLuca had dissolved into sobs long before her husband finished speaking. Taking note of his wife's tears, Giuseppe briefly wondered if he should have said anything at all this morning. But if he hadn't said anything, and then one or even both of these boys didn't make it back from the war, he would forever regret having missed the opportunity to let his sons know that they would constantly be in his thoughts and prayers.

The morning's breakfast became a silent, subdued, and somewhat uncomfortable affair. Elizabeth's mind raced, trying to come up with something – anything! – to say to break the silent tension. But she was so afraid of saying the wrong thing that she fought the urge to bring up the weather, rationing, movies, or anything else.

When the final bites of breakfast had been consumed, Giuseppe rose wordlessly from the table and headed back into the living room, followed by his sons. As soon as they were all out of the kitchen, Rosalia DeLuca rose – also without saying anything – and began clearing the dishes from the table. Angela and Elizabeth were used to this routine by now after living in the DeLuca house for the past four days, and they quickly joined Rosalia and Carmela as the women worked quickly to make the kitchen as spotless as it had been only an hour or so earlier.

As she cleared the table Elizabeth looked over at Angela, who was beginning to wash the plates that were already resting in the sink. By tonight, Elizabeth would be back home at her parent's house, where she would remain until Carlo eventually came home for good from the war. Angela, however, would remain right here in the DeLuca home. How strange that would probably be for Angela, Elizabeth mused, living under the roof of Giuseppe and Rosalia DeLuca almost as if she were one of their own daughters. A sister of Carmela's, rather than a sister-in-law. Angela's life would be so very different than it had been only a week earlier. If Tony were still home and the married couple would simply be living at his childhood home to save money for a place of their own eventually…well, that would be one thing. But would Angela be able to adapt to this unfamiliar new life without her husband by her side?

For Elizabeth, though, returning to Spencer and Katherine Buchanan's house would be as if she were returning to her pre-married life; to the days when she was dating Carlo, or maybe even before she had begun going out with him.

She might as well be turning back clock and calendar to the days when she was little more than Katherine Buchanan's precious little debutante, submissively taking step after step along the life's journey that the older woman had constructed for her daughter.

Elizabeth dreaded that thought almost as much as she dreaded the thought of her new husband going off to war.

*   *   *

"Pennsylvania Railroad now boarding for Harrisburg! Now boarding for Harrisburg, the Pennsylvania Railroad…"

The announcement from the Pennsylvania Station loudspeaker was a signal for tears to again flow freely. Elizabeth began sobbing loudly as she clutched Carlo tightly. Perhaps if I refuse to let go of him, her mind irrationally insisted, he won't be able to get on that train and he'll have to stay here at home!

Angela's mind seemed to have settled on the same illogical argument as Elizabeth's, because she fiercely hugged Tony as she wept every bit as loudly as her sister-in-law. The two DeLuca brides were hardly the only ones on the Penn Station platform who loudly sobbed as they handed their husbands over to the Army or Navy or Marine Corps, with the Pennsylvania Railroad serving as the intermediary. So nobody else seemed to take notice of Angela or Elizabeth, since almost all the others present at the train station this Wednesday morning were consumed by their own anguish and fear.

"Final boarding call, Pennsylvania Railroad for Harrisburg! All aboard!"

Carlo had to ease Elizabeth away because he knew his mother and sister, and even his father and brother, wanted to say their goodbyes. A few seconds later, Tony did the same to Angela. The brothers quickly made their rounds of their family members, and by the time both had finished, even their eyes were glistening. Neither one audibly wept; after all, they were seconds away from jumping on a train with hundreds of other soldiers and sailors and Marines and airmen, every one of them leaving Pittsburgh for some military post or base. Neither Carlo nor Tony wanted to travel hundreds of miles with other military men who might think of the DeLuca brothers as sniveling babies.

The goodbyes completed, Tony first and then Carlo boarded one of the passenger cars near the middle of the train, and in an instant they were both gone.

* * *

The rest of the day felt like a surreal dream to both Elizabeth and Angela. Elizabeth followed Angela back to the DeLuca house where she remained through the lunchtime meal; but when Angela and Carmela left to accompany Rosalia on her rounds to the market and the butcher shop and the bakery, Elizabeth quietly headed home.

Katherine Buchanan was in a glorious mood all afternoon, and Elizabeth struggled mightily not to explode at her mother's exuberance. Katherine hummed along with nearly every song playing on the Philco, and even sang a verse or two of some of the songs. She flitted about the spacious living room, cheerily dusting many of the knickknacks and mementos scattered about the room. Elizabeth had never in her entire life seen her mother so ebullient, and the sights and sounds infuriated her!

Of course her mother was gleeful, because as every moment of that afternoon clocked by, the distance between Elizabeth and her husband became a little bit farther. By nightfall Carlo will have already transferred trains in Harrisburg and be southbound, on his way back to Parris Island and the Marines.

Even worse than this horrid gleefulness, though, were the wordless signals that Katherine Buchanan unmistakably sent to her daughter with a deliberate, well-timed glance. When Bob Eberly and Helen O'Connell began singing "Tangerine," Katherine slowly turned her head towards her daughter, a cold smile of victory playing on her lips. That popular song had been played four times – four! – during the hours of dancing following Elizabeth's and Carlo's wedding. The first time was simply because of the song's popularity, but the other three were in response to explicit requests by Carlo for the band leader to play the Marine's favorite song.

There's your Italian husband's favorite song, Katherine's look conveyed; but where is he *now* while you're here listening to the song being played?

* * *

"Doesn't it feel good to be back home?"

Spencer Buchanan's question, posed to his daughter just as they began supper, wasn't intended to perpetuate the same malevolence that his wife had imparted throughout the afternoon. He was only innocently inquiring if, after living in a strange house for the past four days, returning to the only home she had ever known was somewhat of a comfort for Elizabeth…particularly in these trying hours immediately following her brand-new husband's departure for the Marines.

Still, the question provoked the same reaction in Elizabeth that her mother's looks and glances during the past several hours had done; especially because in Elizabeth's peripheral vision she could see her mother smirking in response to Spencer's question. Elizabeth fought back the explosive response that was threatening to erupt and instead replied to her father's question with a deliberately serene:

"Yes, it does feel good to be home; but it also feels very strange also, now that I'm a married woman."

"Yeah, but doesn't it feel strange being married and not knowing when you'll see your husband again?"

Elizabeth looked to her left. The question had been offered by her older brother William. At twenty years of age, William had graduated from Peabody High a year ahead of Elizabeth in the spring of '40 and had headed to college at the University of Pittsburgh that fall. However, by the time the calendar had rolled over to 1941, he had already been expelled after being caught cheating on a freshman mathematics exam.

In Katherine Buchanan's mind her husband was among Pittsburgh's elite, and she had urged Spencer to speak to the University of Pittsburgh authorities and convince them to give their son another chance. The truth was, though, that Spencer Buchanan was far from influential enough to interdict his son's expulsion. Such sway might possibly be available to those with last names such as Carnegie or Mellon, should such drastic measures be called for on behalf of some black sheep distant relative; but the Buchanans of Highland Park were nowhere close to being in the same league as those distinguished families.

Since his dismissal from Pitt, William Buchanan had done very little other than lounge around most days. Like his father, William Buchanan belonged to the Witherspoon Club in the Oakland neighborhood of the city, not far from the University of Pittsburgh where his matriculation was no longer welcome. But whereas Spencer Buchanan's limited influence couldn't keep his son enrolled at Pitt, it was enough to maintain William's "old boys' club" membership, despite the young man's dishonor.

"I don't want to think about that," Elizabeth replied to her brother's question about Carlo's departure. She cast a quick glance at her mother before looking back at her brother and continuing.

"I just want to keep thinking that every day that passes is one day closer to when I'll see him again."

William's reaction: a snort, followed by an exchange of looks with his mother.

"How romantic," he said dismissively, sarcasm dripping from his words. "But I guess soon enough he'll be slogging through some steaming hot jungle somewhere in the Pacific, and he'll be thinking about you back here waiting for him. I guess that's what love is these days, with the war going on and all that."

Elizabeth's eyes shot fire at her brother.

"Well, maybe you'll be right beside him in that same steaming hot jungle in the Pacific, so you can tell him in person how much I miss him!"

William's nonchalant shrug just infuriated his sister even more.

"You're going to get called up sooner or later!" Elizabeth angrily continued. "You just sit around doing nothing all day, not even working at a war plant or anything! Maybe it won't be the Marines like Carlo, but you'll at least wind up in the Army!"

Another shrug from William.

"Maybe," William replied indifferently.

"Or maybe not," he continued in suspiciously unconcerned tones as he shared a knowing glance with his father across the table.

Chapter 3

Thursday, May 7, 1942

"I don't think I can take another day of this!"

Elizabeth and Angela sat at the lunch counter at Jack Canter's the next afternoon, a popular lunch destination in the city's Oakland neighborhood. Angela had called her sister-in-law right around 10:00 this morning and asked if Elizabeth wanted to meet her for lunch. Elizabeth had all but screamed "Yes!" into the telephone in reply. An hour later Elizabeth boarded the Negley-Highland streetcar a few blocks from her parents' house while Angela grabbed another streetcar in Morningside, just around the corner from the DeLucas' home. Both lines converged in Oakland a few short blocks from the luncheonette, and since Elizabeth arrived first she went inside to grab a couple of seats at the counter before the place filled up for the lunchtime hour.

Elizabeth waited to see if Angela had any reaction to her exasperated words, but since her sister-in-law didn't immediately respond, she continued.

"I swear my mother is over-the-moon happy that I'm more or less a prisoner in her house while Carlo is…is…"

Elizabeth choked back a sob at the thought of Carlo on a southbound train at this very moment, by now closing in on his return to Parris Island where he would soon be belly-crawling through the mud underneath barbed wire with live bullets firing over his head.

"Well I can already tell," Angela interjected, "that living at Tony's house ain't gonna be no picnic, neither."

She proceeded to regale Elizabeth with a narrative of Rosalia DeLuca frequently bursting into an unprovoked staccato of sobbing as she brooded around the DeLuca house all day yesterday after returning from Pennsylvania Station, and resuming the weeping this morning until Angela left to meet Elizabeth.

"I know she's terribly sad because Tony and Carlo – Vinnie, too – are all gone, but it's…"

Angela struggled for the right words.

"I dunno," she continued. "It's like this constant reminder that I might not see my brand-new husband for years, even! I mean, I know that's exactly what the situation is, but to have Tony's mother reminding me of it almost every single second of the day…"

Angela's voice trailed off, and the two young DeLuca wives sat silently for a minute or so, each smoking a Pall Mall while staring sullenly at the luncheonette's countertop.

"And this is only the second day of them being gone," Elizabeth finally spoke.

"Yeah, and yesterday wasn't even a full day," Angela added, looking over at her sister-in-law. "Maybe it will be better tomorrow, or the next day; but maybe not. Who knows, right?"

Elizabeth let out a deep sigh, along with an oversized puff of cigarette smoke.

"I don't think I can take another day of this," she repeated her earlier proclamation. But whereas when she had spoken those same words only moments earlier they had been all but screeched in frustration, this latest utterance was more of a despairing whisper.

The appearance of the waitress pulled both girls' thoughts away from their agony, and they quickly scanned the menu. Each decided on The Secretary's Special: a canned peach half-filled with cottage cheese and accompanied by a couple of Melba toast pieces. The waitress quickly refilled each one's coffee and then moved on to the next group of customers.

After nearly another full minute of silence, Angela offered:

"Maybe we should go see a movie after lunch. This way I won't have to go back to Tony's house until close to supper, and the same for you at your house."

Elizabeth shrugged.

"That sounds like a good idea," she answered, though her response wasn't as enthusiastic as Angela might have hoped. "I wonder what's playing?"

Angela looked to her right and saw a copy of this morning's *Post-Gazette* sitting in the just-vacated space. The newspaper had been meticulously folded back to its original state by the businessman who had been reading it, so Angela was able to take in the headline with a quick glance. Nothing about the fall of Corregidor, she noticed. Instead she saw a top-line headline that read "French Surrender Madagascar to British," which reminded Angela what a strange war this was. Whereas the British and Free French were, of course, allied with the United States in their fight against Germany, across the world off the coast of Africa the British were attacking and had now seized that island nation from the control of the Vichy French, who were in league with the Nazis. How bizarre the world had become!

Farther down the front page, however, Angela did locate a story about the fall of Corregidor: "Drive on Philippines Is Pushed by Japs," the blandly stated headline read. To Angela it seemed that the newspaper editors felt obligated to continue to report the terrible news coming out of the Philippines, but at the same time they overtly demoted that bulletin to the status of "just one more story from the war front," perhaps in an attempt to keep from damaging the home front morale any further.

Angela didn't bother reading any of either story: Madagascar or Corregidor. After all, what more was there to say that she hadn't already heard on last night's or this morning's Mutual Network news programs? She flipped through the paper until she found the movie section, and then laid the paper between Elizabeth and herself.

"What about this one? *King's Row?* Ronald Reagan and Ann Sheridan?" Angela pointed to the bottom of the page.

Elizabeth quickly shook her head.

"Carlo and I saw it last week," she replied. "Not only that, it was pretty depressing." Elizabeth proceeded to quickly relate a synopsis of the film's dark plot, including the vengeful and unnecessary amputation of Ronald Reagan's character's leg by his girlfriend's physician father.

"*That* kind of a movie certainly won't cheer us up," Angela agreed as her eyes shifted to the right.

"How about *Call Out the Marines?* It's a comedy."

Too late Angela realized that just because of the title alone, this film wouldn't be the best for Elizabeth right now, given Carlo's departure.

Elizabeth didn't comment on the title, though. Instead, it was her turn as she pointed to the movie listing directly below Angela's last suggestion.

Her finger resting on the listing for *The Fleet's In*, Elizabeth offered, "Let's go see this one. I like William Holden and Dorothy Lamour."

Angela nodded.

"The Jimmy Dorsey orchestra, too," she noted what the listing stated. "Sure, sounds good to me."

"It's playing at the Ritz downtown," Elizabeth said. "We can finish lunch and then catch a streetcar down there."

"Sure," Angela agreed, just as their lunches arrived. The waitress then topped off their coffee cups and dropped a check for $1.64 between the two girls before moving on.

"Want part of the paper?" Angela asked Elizabeth as they began to eat.

"Sure," Elizabeth replied. "My father only gets the afternoon *Pittsburgh Press* at home, so I didn't get a chance to read any newspaper this morning."

"Tony's father took the *Post-Gazette* with him to work this morning, so I didn't get a chance to see any news, either," Angela replied as she handed the first section to Elizabeth and kept the second section for herself. Let Elizabeth read the war news, Angela thought to herself. She would distract herself with the gossip and fashion columns and the movie news; even the sports section that her Tony would have been reading if he were here with her right now. The girls ate slowly as they each scanned their respective sections for the next couple of minutes.

Out of the corner of her eye Angela saw a pained look come to Elizabeth's face.

"What is it?" Angela asked.

After a few more seconds, Elizabeth looked away from the paper and over at Angela as she replied.

"It says that the prisoners from Corregidor probably include a group of Army nurses," Elizabeth said.

"Wow," Angela replied, contemplating the thought. "Can you imagine that? If it was me and you, let's say, and we had been captured by the Japs and were being sent to a prisoner camp?"

Angela shuddered as she added, "Or worse?"

Elizabeth quickly shook her head back and forth a few times to force away the images.

"I don't want to think about that," she gloomily responded. "This whole thing…this whole war…"

She left the sentence unfinished, but Angela knew what her sister-in-law meant.

"I know, it's all so topsy-turvy. Girls get taken prisoner. We have no idea when we'll see our husbands again. Everything is just so strange…"

Angela's voice trailed off, but what she had just said served only to bring Elizabeth's thoughts full circle. How could she stand one more day like this?

*   *   *

Both Elizabeth's and Angela's moods improved a little bit while watching *The Fleet's In.* That was, though, until the song "Tangerine" appeared in the film. Elizabeth had forgotten that the song was featured in this movie, and the very first notes immediately transported Elizabeth back to dancing with Carlo during their wedding reception, and the four times that the song had played.

And of course the song also immediately carried Elizabeth back to only yesterday and her mother's cold contemptuous smile when this very same song began playing on the Philco.

Throughout the rest of the movie, Elizabeth half-watched the film while her mind refused to let go of that one tortured question: how could she stand one more day like this one?

The film ended shortly after 4:00, and the girls decided to walk around downtown for a little bit before turning to their respective households for the rest of the evening. The morning's rain had ended in the early afternoon, and the temperature had dropped almost ten degrees in the past hour as the winds picked up slightly, giving the late afternoon hours the classic slightly chilled feel of a mid-spring Pittsburgh day.

"Angela! Angela!"

An instant later:

"Angela! Elizabeth!"

Both girls turned and saw their sister-in-law Carmela approaching.

"Hi!" Carmela exclaimed when she came within earshot of her new in-laws. "What are you doing downtown?

"We went to lunch and then to see a movie," Angela replied. She quickly related the day's details to Carmela.

"I'm just getting off work," was Carmela's response. "I thought I would walk around a little bit before catching the streetcar back home."

"That's what we're doing," Elizabeth chimed in. "Killing time, I guess."

"How was work today?" Angela asked Carmela.

The question reminded Elizabeth that Carmela had taken a job only days after Tony DeMarco's early February departure for basic training at Fort Dix. She worked at a small factory that made military shoes and boots for the Army. The factory was located up on Mount Washington, just on the other side of the Monongahela River from downtown Pittsburgh. Unlike Elizabeth and Angela, who both wore springtime-weight, knee-length print dresses, Carmela was dressed in slacks and a utilitarian-looking blouse…a style that was rapidly becoming a uniform of sorts for the many female war plant workers throughout Pittsburgh and elsewhere. A young woman dressed so casually yet strolling around the heart of Pittsburgh might have been a relatively rare sight before the war, but these days the downtown streets were filled with women dressed just like Carmela…with nary a disapproving look from the businessmen or matrons with whom they shared the sidewalks and lunch counters and streetcars.

"Nothing special," Carmela shrugged. She worked as a stitcher, sewing together individual pieces of shoes and boots as they made their way along the assembly line. The work was generally tedious, but it came with two main advantages, Carmela would always tell anyone who asked. First, the results of her labor were going directly to soldiers and sailors and airmen and Marines as they went through training and later as they fought the country's hated enemies. As a result, Carmela took exceptional pride in her work. Anytime she might be tempted because of fatigue or boredom to cut corners, she would remind herself who the recipients of her shoes and boots would be, and then steel herself to avoid any slipshod handiwork.

And, of course, the second advantage was that for much of the day, five or six or even sometimes seven days each week, she had hours of distraction to help her half-forget the heartbreaking fact that her newlywed husband wasn't by her side, nor would he be for many months or even years to come.

The three of them strolled around downtown for another forty-five minutes, but Elizabeth's mind only half-absorbed the Italian girls' chit-chat, and she contributed little other than an occasional "uh-huh" or "I know" to the conversation. Scattered thoughts – previously unconnected fragments – were starting to fuse together. Carmela's job at the war plant; those women who had decided to become Army nurses but who were now tragically prisoners of the fearsome Japanese enemy; and even the name of the lunchtime meal that she had ordered: The Secretary's Special.

* * *

That night, during dinner and afterwards, Elizabeth absorbed her mother's barbs with surprising indifference; almost as if she were engaged in a card game with her mother and had just the right cards hidden up her sleeve, waiting for the right moment to play them.

Just around 9:30 p.m., as Elizabeth began to climb the staircase at the stately home to go to her bedroom for the remainder of the evening, Elizabeth paused to look back at her mother who was seated on the sofa, reading the latest issue of *Look* magazine.

"I'm going to look for a job tomorrow," Elizabeth pronounced before proceeding upstairs. No doubt her declaration had caught Katherine Buchanan by surprise, because not a word of protest followed her up the staircase. She walked to her room and closed the bedroom door behind her, fully expecting her mother to come barging in at any second with a protest along the lines of "What is this nonsense about a job?"

Nothing.

For the next hour and a half Elizabeth remained sleepless as she contemplated her mother's lack of reaction, and her own disposition shifted from initial relief to eventual seething. Just before finally drifting off to a troubled night's sleep, Elizabeth settled on what she supposed was the most likely reason her mother hadn't thus far barged into the girl's room.

Katherine Buchanan obviously thought her daughter's declared intention to find a job was just an impulsive whim, not to be taken seriously because it would soon pass.

55

Chapter 4

More than two weeks passed until Elizabeth DeLuca found what she was looking for, and the prize came as a result of one of the many relatively new government agencies that came into existence as a result of World War II. American life had been inundated years earlier by the alphabet-soup agencies of the Great Depression and the New Deal: WPA, CCC, PWA, and dozens of others. Many of those federal agencies still existed but had now evolved to modified missions dedicated to the war effort. They had also been joined by more recent governmental creations, such as the Office of Civilian Defense, the War Production Board, and the Bureau of Economic Warfare.

And the Office of Price Administration, or the OPA.

During these spring months of 1942, life on the American home front was dominated by two major worries. At the top of the list, of course, was the fate of millions of young Americans who were already off to war or who would soon be. Not too far behind, though, were daily concerns about prices and rationing. The OPA in its current incarnation came into existence a few months back in January of '42. Then, as with so many governmental agencies, regional administration offices quickly sprung up all over the nation. And with those many offices came thousands of new jobs that needed to be filled.

America was already facing a jobs crisis, but one that was the polar opposite of what had dominated the entire decade of the 1930s. Instead of too few jobs for those who wanted – who needed – to work, World War II America already had far too many jobs that couldn't be filled because of one simple fact: millions of American men of prime working age now had new "jobs" as soldiers or sailors, or Marines or airmen.

American companies and governmental agencies were just beginning to turn their attention to a previously untapped source of workers for jobs that heretofore would have been filled by those able-bodied men who were now property of the U.S. military. Tens of thousands of American women, just like Carmela DeMarco, joined the workforce of a nation newly at war. And many, many more would follow.

*   *   *

"*Why* are you looking for a job, Mrs. DeLuca?"

The question was asked with obvious cynicism. This Mr. Talbot obviously had not warmed to the idea of women in his office, even as secretaries, Elizabeth could easily tell; that was for certain!

Elizabeth was dressed as professionally as a young woman might be: her best mid-calf cream print dress along with a precious pair of silk stockings and heels, her hair carefully styled and lightly curled. Yet the personnel manager was treating her as if she had disrespectfully barged into his office to demand a job while wearing Carmela's standard war plant uniform, or perhaps even the coveralls and red polka dot bandana that women in heavier war manufacturing jobs were now wearing. Elizabeth was very conscious that she was in an office setting, not a war plant, and was certain that she had dressed appropriately…despite the derision clearly radiated by this narrow-eyed Mr. Talbot.

Elizabeth did her best to ignore the personnel man's disdain and responded with the same well-rehearsed narrative that she had offered nearly a dozen times over the past two weeks.

"My husband is in the Marine Corps, Mr. Talbot, and after he finishes his infantry training he will be off to war. I desperately want to do my part here at home to help the war effort, especially with so many jobs needing girls because our boys are off to war."

Elizabeth hated the thought of denigrating not only her own energies and abilities, but essentially those of an entire gender as she all but groveled before this self-important little man. But during the past two weeks she had learned that so many of these pedantic personnel managers wanted to be certain that any woman they hired had it in her pretty little head that if it weren't for the war, she would be nowhere near their factory or war plant or office.

"Have you any secretarial experience at all?" The personnel manager sighed and all but rolled his eyes as he asked that question, Elizabeth noticed.

"No I don't, Mr. Talbot, but I do know how to type. I'm a very fast learner and I'm certain I can learn the job very quickly, and not be a burden to the office."

Outwardly Elizabeth's manner while responding to the personnel manager's questions was professional and cool, yet inside she silently seethed.

Mr. Talbot leaned back in his chair and folded his fingers together across his chest. He appeared to be in deep deliberation as he looked down at Elizabeth's application and then across his desk at Elizabeth; and then back down at her application.

Finally, after nearly a full minute of this deep contemplation (which Elizabeth suspected was really an act rather than genuine deliberation), Mr. Talbot sighed again.

"I think we can give you a try, Mrs. DeLuca, though I do wish to emphasize once again that these are very unusual times. I cannot promise you a particular length of employment, and I can definitely state that should the war come to an end in the next few months and our boys come home, that your employment will come to an end."

Elizabeth was struck by the man's blunt manner of speaking that bordered on rudeness; but at the same time, she had no qualms at all with what he said. Should the war somehow miraculously come to an end in the next few months, and should Carlo be on his way home, she would gleefully leave this job behind so their married life could belatedly get underway.

"I understand perfectly, Mr. Talbot," Elizabeth replied in a manner that was both cheerful and professional at the same time. "Thank you very much for your faith in me; I promise I won't let you down."

Mr. Talbot's response was a disinterested grunt as he moved Elizabeth's application to the "HIRED" box on his desk.

*   *   *

Elizabeth's first workday wasn't particularly memorable, other than being introduced to many of the OPA workers here at the Oakland neighborhood office. The secretarial supervisor, Mrs. Watkins, shepherded Elizabeth and two other girls who were also newly hired around the offices. Elizabeth wondered if she should furiously scribble notes onto her yellow pad as Mrs. Watkins explained the many responsibilities of the office. Neither of the other girls made a move to write anything down, though, so Elizabeth didn't want to rub anybody the wrong way by appearing to be overeager.

Aboard the streetcar on her way home that afternoon, Elizabeth felt herself shudder several times. Each time she asked herself the same question: what did I just get myself into? Was this only about sending a message of defiance to her mother? Elizabeth had never before held even a part-time job, as many of the less-well-off girls at Peabody High did during the latter years of the Depression. Was she really up for making a thirty-minute streetcar ride early each weekday morning from her father's comfortable Highland Park home to this new job, working a full day, and then traveling back home in the very late afternoon hours?

Maybe she should just accede to her mother's latest plan for Elizabeth's life and enroll at the University of Pittsburgh this coming fall. Elizabeth had been an adequate student at Peabody High and might well have enrolled at Pitt last fall, especially since her mother saw college as a means to drive a wedge between Elizabeth and Carlo. Largely because of her mother's insistence, though, Elizabeth had balked at the idea. Elizabeth had an inkling that she and Carlo would eventually become engaged (though of course she had no foresight of Pearl Harbor and the war hastening the time frame), and didn't want to buckle down in college only to quit as soon as she got married. Now, though, with Carlo gone for so long…

Confused and apprehensive, Elizabeth picked up the afternoon *Pittsburgh Press* that had just been abandoned on the seat to her left when the man sitting there left the streetcar at Penn Avenue. She took in the bold-typed, all-caps headline:

AMERICAN BLOW AT AXIS NEAR AS AIR CHIEFS GO TO LONDON

Elizabeth's thoughts immediately went to Carlo's brother Vinnie: her own brother-in-law whom she barely knew. She skimmed the United Press story that accompanied the headline and another related UP story to the immediate right. Both stories told the same tale: American air attacks flying out of Britain against German strongholds across the continent were just around the corner as the Army Air Forces continued to build up its contingent of planes and airmen based in Britain.

No matter where Vinnie was right now, whether still stateside somewhere or perhaps part of the earliest contingent already setting up operations in Britain, Carlo's brother would soon be facing mortal combat against this feared enemy. Vinnie had written a letter home that arrived a few days earlier, and the censor had carelessly failed to excise several lines in which Vinnie fretted about a particularly troublesome aspect of his training as a B-17 tail gunner.

So now they all knew. The Air Corps hadn't assigned Vinnie as an airplane mechanic or a field hospital orderly or a cook, or some other type of ground crew position. He would be up in the air as the USAAF bombers faced tremendous odds trying to strike blows against Hitler's so-called Fortress Europe.

Elizabeth sighed. She wasn't even thinking of her own husband and what he would soon be facing, most likely somewhere in the Pacific. Nor was she thinking about Angela's husband Tony and wherever the Army sent him to fight. Here was Vinnie DeLuca, a boy she barely knew, front and center in her thoughts for the moment.

Elizabeth placed the *Press* back on the empty seat to her left with forceful determination. If her husband and his brothers could face their fears and put their lives on the line, then Elizabeth Buchanan DeLuca was certainly capable of enduring long workdays to do the teensiest, tiniest part to help the war effort. After all, she wouldn't be working on a war plant assembly line as Carmela did in the shoe and boot factory. Elizabeth wasn't quite sure that she was cut out for that type of work, war effort or not. But an office job? And only until the war ended?

That was the least she could do.

*   *   *

"Want to meet for pie and coffee?"

Elizabeth had called Angela shortly after a tense dinner. Katherine Buchanan apparently hadn't believed that her daughter would ever be offered a job, or that

Elizabeth would actually accept one that was offered. When Elizabeth regaled her parents and her brother William with a somewhat glamorized version of her first day at the OPA office, they all seemed stunned that Elizabeth had actually begun working in this new war administration position.

Curiously, though, once the shock seemed to wear off, William began asking a series of questions about the OPA's role in the loathsome but necessary war rationing effort. He was particularly interested in what might be in store for new types of ration coupons and stamps, and seemed disappointed that Elizabeth knew almost nothing about such plans.

Elizabeth didn't give her brother's questions much consideration, and soon the suppertime discussion shifted to the day's war news. Still, more than a few icy glares from Katherine across the table directed at her daughter made Elizabeth not want to remain in the Buchanan house after supper. And because she yearned to tell Angela about her first day, she telephoned the DeLuca house and asked for Angela when their father-in-law answered.

"Sure," was Angela's reply to Elizabeth's overture to get together shortly. Then in lowered tones, "Is everything all right?"

"Yes," Elizabeth answered. "I just want to tell you about my first day working at the OPA."

"You got it!" Angela squealed in excitement. "That's fantastic!"

"I'll tell you all about it tonight if you can meet me," Elizabeth offered again.

A very short pause from the other end of the line and then in a near-whisper:

"Definitely; I need the break, I've been here all day."

Angela didn't say anything further, but she didn't need to. Elizabeth knew that little had changed at the DeLuca household over the past two weeks, especially when it came to Rosalia's gloomy disposition.

They arranged to rendezvous at a coffee shop in the city's East Liberty neighborhood that was just about the same distance from both of their houses. The evening sunshine was still out, and the air felt stickier than almost any other day so far this spring. Summer would be here soon, Elizabeth thought. What a strange, sad summer it would be, though. Only a year ago, during the summer of '41, she and Carlo had spent nearly every day together. Following their graduation from Peabody High in early June, Carlo took a job down in the Strip District at an Italian-owned produce wholesaler. He had to be at work by 3:30 a.m. every single morning, and sometimes the work hours were crushing; but Carlo wound up with plenty of spending money to lavish on Elizabeth. They went to the movies several times each week and enjoyed picnics and sometimes just went for long drives in the rusted '37 Packard Six he was able to buy before the summer was out.

The streetcar's arrival at the stop closest to the coffee shop shook Elizabeth's thoughts back to the present. Somehow, she needed to stop wallowing in these despondent recollections of past days, better days. Yet at the same time, Elizabeth felt compelled to hold onto those memories as some of the only threads left between her and Carlo.

Angela had already arrived and had ordered coffee for both of them. Elizabeth slipped into the booth opposite from Angela, who barely waited for her sister-in-law to be seated before exclaiming: "Tell me all about it!"

Elizabeth related an abridged tale of her terse interview with Mr. Talbot, the personnel manager; but she made sure to tell Angela that she had felt on edge the entire time until he unenthusiastically told Elizabeth that the job was hers. Since Elizabeth hadn't done much today, there wasn't much more to tell Angela.

"Do you think I can get a job there?" was Angela's question when Elizabeth had finished her narrative.

The question caught Elizabeth off guard, though it really shouldn't have. Ever since Elizabeth had told Angela about her idea to find a job after the two of them had met up with Carmela that afternoon in downtown, Angela had frequently declared that she was seriously thinking about doing the exact same thing. Yet during the past two weeks, while Elizabeth filled out application after application, Angela had taken no actions of her own in that direction. After a week or so, Elizabeth dismissed Angela's occasional remarks as little more than frustrated musings in the face of whatever the latest angst was inside the DeLuca household.

"I don't know for certain, but I suppose so," Elizabeth finally replied. "I don't think I can do anything to especially help you since today was only my first day, but when Mrs. Watkins was showing the other new girls and me around, I saw a lot of empty desks. So I'm sure they have positions open."

Angela replied as she nodded:

"I think I'll go down tomorrow morning and put in an application."

Elizabeth couldn't help asking the question.

"Did something happen today? I mean, you've mentioned finding a job off and on ever since I started looking for one, but you haven't filled out any applications yet, right?"

Angela was about to respond but the waitress came over to the table with coffee refills. Each girl ordered a slice of apple pie and after the waitress departed Angela answered Elizabeth's question.

"It wasn't anything in particular today; just…I dunno…"

Angela struggled for the right words and eventually continued.

"I feel like I'm in stuck inside of this very weird dream, day after day. It's not just living at Tony's house; it's every minute of every day! I got married, but *that's* like a dream now! I swear, sometimes I feel like I'm caught between two worlds but I don't exist in either one."

Angela's sigh of exasperation was one that Elizabeth herself might have let forth.

"I know exactly what you mean," Elizabeth said quietly as she sipped her coffee.

Chapter 5

"This is unusual," Mr. Talbot said as he scanned Angela's employment application for a secretarial position at the OPA. "Just yesterday I hired a young woman also named Mrs. DeLuca."

"That's my sister-in-law," Angela quickly explained. "She married my husband's brother…"

"Ah," Mr. Talbot interrupted as he leaned back in his chair. He threaded his fingers together across his chest just as he had when appearing to contemplate Elizabeth's fate a day earlier.

"I'm afraid that I can't hire you then," he said to Angela. A shocked look immediately came to Angela's face, but Mr. Talbot appeared not to take notice as he continued.

"It's our office policy not to have girls from the same family working together here at the Office of Price Administration," he explained as he placed Angela's application in the NOT HIRED box on his desk. "We have a great deal of important work to accomplish, and if we have secretaries who are sisters, or as in your case sisters-in-law, I'm afraid that too much socializing and family gossip will take place on the premises during business hours and interfere with our work."

Angela was livid, but she was able to keep her anger in check. Exploding at this pompous blowhard would accomplish nothing, and might even cost Elizabeth her job if this Mr. Talbot decided to punish Elizabeth for her sister-in-law's outburst.

She rose in her chair, turned towards the door behind her, and was about to leave Mr. Talbot's office without any remarks whatsoever, when she heard him say:

"You might try the War Production Board."

Angela halted and turned back to Mr. Talbot.

"The War Production Board," he repeated. "I believe they are looking for secretaries. Do you have any other girls in your family working there as secretaries?"

She wordlessly shook her head.

"They are around the corner on Craig Street," Mr. Talbot pointed in the general direction even though they were in his windowless office inside the OPA building.

Angela was able to muster a semi-enthusiastic "Thank you, Mr. Talbot." She was still steamed at this man and his presumption that "girls from the same family will just socialize and gossip all day," but at least she came out of this frustrating interview with a solid job lead.

*   *   *

Angela's interview with the personnel manager at the War Production Board mirrored Elizabeth's irksome one a day earlier at the OPA, but also concluded with the successful outcome of being hired as a secretary. Both Angela and Elizabeth would be earning exactly the same amount: thirty cents per hour, which had been the federal minimum wage for the past two and a half years.

Fortunately neither girl needed to pay for food and shelter out of that meager amount, given their respective living situations. While twelve dollars a week wasn't much money, each girl also received her husband's $50.00 monthly pay as a private. All together, Elizabeth and Angela each wound up with about $100 each month. Even after deductions for income taxes and war bonds, they would end up with a fair amount of walking-around money each month for lunches, pie and coffee, movies, and new clothes to wear to their jobs.

That Sunday after church services, Giuseppe DeLuca hosted the belated first Sunday family cookout of 1942. Elizabeth attended and noted the vast difference from those of the previous year, with three of the four DeLuca boys sadly not there. However, Giuseppe invited several of the neighboring families, so the tiny backyard didn't feel quite so empty in the absence of Tony, Vinnie, and Carlo.

Much of the discussion throughout the afternoon was about the surprising and wondrous news coming out of the Pacific. The headline in that morning's Sunday *Pittsburgh Press* said it all:

JAP PLANE CARRIERS DESTROYED; 11 ENEMY WARSHIPS DAMAGED

The news about the major clash between the naval forces of Japan and the United States at Midway Island had been trickling out over the past few days. Today's United Press story boldly stated that during several days of fighting at Midway and on the surrounding seas, two and perhaps even three Japanese aircraft carriers had been destroyed by the Navy's planes. One or two other enemy aircraft carriers had been badly damaged, the story also reported, along with a number of battleships, destroyers, and cruisers. As with most wartime news, people were coming to realize, details were fuzzy and often subject to change. Further, if one were to pick up an old newspaper and reconsider blaring headlines from the first couple months of war about spectacularly successful allied counterattacks and crippling blows already struck against the enemy, the level of exaggeration and even outright falsehoods would now be painfully apparent. Still, this news seemed genuine and was spectacularly welcome. Admiral Nimitz himself was quoted in the story as declaring "Pearl Harbor has now been partially avenged."

The elation at this splendid war news, however, was tempered somewhat for those present this afternoon. Plenty of fighting lay ahead, so the DeLuca boys would all still be putting their lives on the line. Still, the news was so very welcome by one and all, especially after the terrible reports from Corregidor a month earlier and Bataan a month before that, and from all across the Pacific in the months that had followed the attack at Pearl Harbor.

Michael DeLuca wandered over to where Angela and Elizabeth were sitting, each slowly eating a hot dog. The youngest brother of the girls' husbands had just graduated from Peabody High the previous Thursday.

Michael sat down on a folding lawn chair next to where Elizabeth and Angela were seated and took a long pull from his bottle of Fort Pitt beer. He sighed and then said, in a quiet voice, "Don't tell Ma and Pop yet, but I've decided to enlist in the Army like Tony. I was thinking about the Marines like Carlo or maybe the Air Corps like Vinnie did, but I finally decided it's gonna be the Army."

Both girls were quiet for a moment, and then Angela spoke.

"Why don't you just wait for your draft notice? You'll get it sooner or later, but until then you won't have to go."

Michael shook his head.

"Nah," he answered before taking a smaller sip from his beer. "Not with Tony and Carlo and Vinnie already in the service. I don't wanna just sit around. It's gonna happen eventually, might as well get it over with."

"You haven't said anything to your parents yet?" Elizabeth asked.

Another shake of Michael's head.

"Not yet. I didn't want to say anything today and ruin the cookout with Ma crying and all that. I'll talk to them tomorrow, and then go down to the recruiting station later in the week. My buddy Paul Ricci is probably gonna enlist with me, and maybe they'll send us to basic training together."

Michael finished the last of his beer, and then addressed both of his sisters-in-law.

"Hey, so when you both write Tony and Carlo, go ahead and tell 'em that I'm enlisting."

He directed his attention to Angela.

"Tell Tony that maybe I'll wind up seeing him somewhere out there."

* * *

That night after dinner, upstairs in Tony DeLuca's old bedroom that she now occupied, Angela sprawled out on the lonely bed and began writing.

June 7, 1942

My dearest Tony,

I miss you as much as ever. I received your latest letter and am thankful that you are well. I know you are training hard and not getting much sleep.

Today your Pop had a cookout. It was so strange without you there. Carlo and Vinnie also. Michael was there of course and he asked me when I wrote you to tell you that he decided to enlist in the Army. He's going down to the recruiting station this week. I'm sure that he will write you after that to let you know if he passed his physical.

We listened to the Pirates game on the radio. They won, and I know you wish you were there to listen to it.

Now for the big news. I have a job now! I just started last week, working at the War Production Board in Oakland. I'm a secretary, as I'm sure you guessed. I tried to get a job at the OPA where Elizabeth works, but believe it or not they wouldn't hire me there. They said they can't have two girls from the same family working together. But fortunately I went right over to the WPB and was hired right away.

The job is okay. The girls I work with are nice. Mostly I get to help out with the war, even though it's only a little bit.

I guess that's it for this letter. I'll write you again in a couple days to let you know how the job is going. I'm sure that your Ma and Carmela and everyone else write you all the time, but they all say hello to you.

Please be safe and come home to me soon.

All my love,

Angela

Chapter 6

One sticky mid-July day, Elizabeth came back from lunch with Angela at the Sun Drugs counter. The first sound Elizabeth heard upon coming up the stairs to the second floor of the OPA offices was sobbing.

Elizabeth's heart felt as if it had leaped into her throat. She instantly knew what had happened. Not the specifics – those would become known in another ten or fifteen seconds – but she knew.

She slowly entered the work area from the stairwell and came face to face with Joan Vernon. Joan's husband Mike was an Air Corps pilot, going through flight training at Thunderbird Field out in Arizona. Joan's eyes glistened, but Elizabeth could still hear the sobbing coming from somewhere behind Joan.

"It's Vicki," Joan whispered to Elizabeth.

Elizabeth looked past Joan and saw Vicki Mendelsohn half-bent over, crying uncontrollably. Audrey Williams and Doris Marx were on either side of Vicki, holding her tightly. Elizabeth was certain that if Audrey and Doris weren't supporting Vicki, the anguished woman would have collapsed to the ground in anguish.

"Her husband was killed in a training accident at Camp Elliott out in San Diego," Joan continued whispering. "They just delivered the telegram to her house right before lunch, and Vicki's mother came right over to tell her."

Elizabeth continued staring hard at Vicki even as Joan continued her explanation. The poor woman! Vicki was a little bit older than Elizabeth and Joan and a lot of the other girls in the office; twenty-five or twenty-six, Elizabeth figured, though she didn't know for certain. Vicki's husband – Bart, Elizabeth recalled his name – had enlisted in the Marines, just like Carlo, and they had been married just over five years. He and Vicki had two children, and Vicki's mother watched the toddlers each day while the girl worked at the OPA.

Elizabeth didn't know Vicki Mendelsohn all that well. They had gone to lunch a couple times as part of a larger group of girls, but their desks were a bit apart from each other's. Aside from a few occasions of chit-chat in the coffee area, they hadn't interacted much since they both came to work at the OPA back in June.

Still, this tragic news hit Elizabeth like a thunderbolt. In Carlo's last letter that she received only yesterday, he wrote that he would soon be "on his way west." No doubt the censors would have excised a specific reference to "Camp Elliott" or "San Diego," but anyone with a loved one in the Marines knew that Camp Elliott was one of the Marines' major training bases. Even without specifically declaring as such, parents and wives of Marines already knew that the standard trek awaiting their sons and husbands was from Parris Island to Camp Elliott...and then eventually to the Pacific.

That could have been Carlo. Or it could be Carlo. Bart Mendelsohn was a casualty of war even before making it overseas and facing the enemy. So far in this war, other than at Pearl Harbor, far too many American fighting men had met a tragic end as a result of training accidents; almost as many as at the hands of either the Japanese or Nazis. War was deadly business, Americans were coming to realize, even when the enemy was nowhere in sight.

Elizabeth waited until a couple of other girls hugged Vicki and cried along with her, and then did the same.

"I'm so sorry," Elizabeth sobbed as she held tightly to the poor woman. She struggled for something else to say, but words escaped her. After a few more seconds, Elizabeth stepped aside to let the next OPA secretary in line comfort the grieving brand-new widow.

The rest of the afternoon and that entire evening, Elizabeth was deeply troubled. She could barely concentrate on work, and after going home she said very little at dinner. She kept thinking about poor Vicki Mendelsohn, her husband suddenly gone for all eternity; their marriage interrupted and then cruelly ended by the war.

At least Vicki had her children. Bart Mendelsohn was gone now, and perhaps after mourning her loss for a long while Vicki might fall in love and get married again. But the two children that Bart had given Vicki would be her eternal reminders of the five years together that they had been given. The sorrow would – hopefully – slowly dissipate over time, and Vicki would be left with the bittersweet memories of a love cut short.

Suppose, though, that a telegram would be delivered tomorrow, or next week or next month, bearing words that coldly informed Elizabeth that Carlo DeLuca had met the same fate as Bart Mendelsohn. Unlike Vicki, Elizabeth would be unable to take comfort in the many memories from five years of marriage. Nor would she have any children as a timeless memorial to her husband.

Should such a telegram be delivered to Elizabeth, she would be left with almost nothing.

Chapter 7

Michael DeLuca had enlisted in the United States Army back in early June, just as he said he would. Curiously, though, two months later he was still at his parents' home in Morningside, restlessly awaiting his orders to report for basic training. Some thought this delay was peculiar, given the nation's urgent and growing need for trained soldiers all across the globe. But as it was explained to Michael when he visited the Army recruiting station in Oakland to find out what the delay was, the Army itself was still frantically ramping up its training facilities in the summer of 1942. So many new soldiers had enlisted in the months following Pearl Harbor that there simply weren't enough Army posts and available training slots to get all of these new soldiers into boot camp as quickly as the Army desired. Complicating the situation was the Army's policy of sending draftees off to basic training as quickly as possible once draft notices were delivered, pushing many volunteer enlistees back even further for their own reporting dates.

As a result, delays of a month or two – sometimes three – between when somebody like Michael DeLuca enlisted and when he stepped off the bus to face his fearsome drill sergeant for the first time were increasingly common. For this reason, Michael was still at home when his brother Tony came back to Pittsburgh for a quick four-day furlough in early August of '42.

Angela had first gotten word of her husband's return in a letter he had written back in early July but which arrived only three days before Tony himself did. "I can't say where they're sending me after my furlough, but I'm so glad I get to come home to see you" were the words that Angela read over and over for days until she peered out the window one Saturday morning and saw Tony walking up the stairs to the DeLuca house. In his letter he had stated that he couldn't be certain of exactly when he would be arriving in Pittsburgh, so for anyone to go down to the train station to wait for him was foolish. Whenever he did arrive at Pennsylvania Station, he would immediately grab a taxi or hitch a ride home.

Angela raced to the open doorway and nearly ran through the screen door as she rushed to the porch to throw herself into Tony's arms.

"Oh my God I'm so glad to see you!" Angela burst out in rapid fire as the tears of joy streamed down her face. For months, she had steeled herself for the unpleasant likelihood that she might not see Tony again until the war was somehow, someday concluded. But here was this blessed gift of his return, even if only for a few short days.

Angela maintained her tearful grip around Tony even as Rosalia, Giuseppe, Carmela, and Michael rushed out the door to crowd around Tony and Angela on the front porch. Eventually Angela reluctantly gave way to Tony's family members, allowing each one to greet their returning soldier.

The rest of that Saturday afternoon and early evening was a blur for Angela. She never left Tony's side; yet after he departed the following Wednesday, Angela could recall very little that actually happened or was discussed during those initial hours following the moment of her fierce welcome-home hug. She was so grateful for this unexpected gift of being together with her husband that she simply basked in the pure joy of the two of them being together, and her mind apparently couldn't be bothered absorbing any details.

Angela's clarity of memory would begin somewhere around 7:00 that evening, when Tony rose from his mother's table after supper, snuffed out his Chesterfield, and announced that he was going out. The sudden look of shock on Angela's face was only a second or two ahead of the rebuttal from Giuseppe DeLuca.

"Whaddya mean, you're goin' out?" Tony's father asked, though the question was clearly more of a demand for an explanation.

"Some of the guys are getting together over at the Fairlane," Tony responded, referring to the East Liberty bowling alley that was a frequent hangout for the guys from surrounding neighborhoods. "Rocky Santucci is also home on furlough, and he heard that Vic Folino might also be…"

"You'll stay here with your wife." Giuseppe DeLuca's words were spoken in even tones, but there was no mistaking that he was giving his son an order that was to be unquestioningly obeyed, just as if that direction had come from Tony's commanding officer.

Angela surreptitiously looked over at Tony's mother, hoping to catch her eye, but Rosalia DeLuca was looking down at the kitchen table. Angela then cast a look towards Carmela, who curiously was mimicking her mother's exact mannerisms. This was between Tony and his father, mother and daughter were clearly signaling Angela, even though Tony's wife was clearly at the center of this brewing controversy.

There would be no disagreement, however. Tony seemed to want to offer a rebuttal to his father's command, but Angela noticed that just as he was about to speak he abruptly clamped his lips together. Tony looked over at Angela, offered a tight smile, and then plopped right back down in his chair.

Angela so very much wanted to quiz Tony why, on his first night back in Pittsburgh in three months, he had even entertained the thought of leaving her to hang out with his buddies. Old habits, perhaps? Angela wasn't sure, but since Tony had now dismissed the idea, Angela decided it was best to drop the whole matter rather than start a tussle with the clock already ticking away the minutes of her husband's furlough.

After dinner, Angela and Carmela began helping Rosalia clean up, as usual. Tony and his younger brother followed their father into the living room, where Michael immediately headed over to the Admiral and flicked the dial to warm up the radio. After about fifteen seconds the warming-up static gave way to Harry James and "Sleepy Lagoon." The DeLuca women could easily hear the song from the kitchen as Michael raised the volume.

"Go be with your husband," Rosalia suddenly said to Angela. "Carmela and I will finish the pots and pans here."

Angela gratefully looked over at Rosalia, who nodded towards the living room to emphasize that Angela should go there right now. She walked into the living room and as soon as Tony noticed her, she said, "Your Ma told me to come out and be with you."

Tony shrugged in response as Angela settled onto the left side of the worn sofa that faced the radio. As soon as

Tony had lit two Chesterfields, he sank down next to his wife. He handed one of the cigarettes to Angela, who inhaled deeply. She once again became perturbed by the strange exchange that had happened in the kitchen moments earlier, but she was still determined not to let her pique ruin this special gift of scrunching next to her husband in the middle of a war, listening to the smooth tones of Harry James.

"You wanna listen to *Noah Webster Says?*" Michael asked Tony, ready to twirl the Admiral's dial with the expertise of an Army radioman and tune into the popular quiz show.

"Leave the music on," Giuseppe DeLuca told his youngest son even before Tony could respond. Giuseppe looked around his house, wishing it were larger so he and Michael – as well as Rosalia and Carmela, when they finished in the kitchen – could go into some other room and give Tony and Angela some privacy. Alas, his Morningside home was a modest one, and he didn't relish the idea of going back into the cramped kitchen. Shortly after seven o'clock was way too early to go to bed, of course, so that left out the upstairs.

Suddenly a thought occurred to him.

"Come on," he said to Michael. "Let's take a walk down to Del's," he said as he rose from his chair, referring to Angela's father's bar. "We can listen to the Saturday night fights from Madison Square Garden."

Before Tony could utter a word, Giuseppe pointed a thick finger at his oldest son.

"You stay here with your wife."

Giuseppe then walked into the kitchen where he remained for about ten seconds, then returned to the living room and headed straight for the door. Michael finally caught the significance of what his father's intentions were, and he looked back at his older brother and sister-in-law and said with a smirk:

"Enjoy smooching, you two."

"Come on, you," Giuseppe growled as he gave Michael a medium-strength but still friendly slap on the back of his head before the two headed out the door.

When neither Rosalia nor Carmela appeared in the living room in the next ten minutes – which was plenty of time for the two of them to have finished the couple remaining pots and pans – Angela figured that her father-in-law must have told his wife and his daughter to remain in the kitchen for a while to give Tony and Angela some privacy. Sure enough, Angela could hear the two of them talking when "Who Wouldn't Love You?" ended and the radio was silent for a few seconds before yet another Kay Kyser song – this one "Jingle, Jangle, Jingle" – began.

What a wonderful evening this would be! Not only was her husband here with her, but his family had conspired to give Tony and Angela at least a little privacy. Upstairs, later tonight, she and Tony could share the intimacy of becoming reacquainted with each other. For now, Angela felt as if she was in heaven, snuggled next to Tony on the couch as the radio played one hit song after another. These were the exact same songs she had listened to night after night for weeks or even longer on this very same radio, but the simple fact of Tony's presence tonight had the effect of bestowing each with special new meaning. He would be gone soon enough; and Angela hoped that the sensations of this evening would somehow magically carry through afterwards whenever she heard these same songs in the months ahead.

"I wish we could go dancing," Angela mused as the Glenn Miller version of "Kalamazoo" began playing.

"We could, if you want," Tony said hesitatingly. Sensing that Angela noticed his hesitation, he added, "Pop seemed to want us to stay here, though."

"It is Saturday night, though," Angela countered.

Tony pondered the idea for a moment.

"I wonder if Pop would be mad if we went out."

"I don't think so," Angela quickly replied. "I think he just wants to make sure that we're together and having a good night. If we go out together and go dancing, I'm sure he'll be okay with that."

Angela suddenly had an idea.

"In fact," she said, peering at Tony, "why don't you call your friend Rocky and anybody else, and see if they want to go with us. You wanted to hang out with your buddies, and this way you can do that and we'll still be out together."

"Yeah, okay," Tony nodded and rose from the sofa, then walked over to the telephone on the table near the kitchen door. While Tony began making calls, Angela headed back into the kitchen, where Rosalia and Carmela were sitting at the kitchen table.

"Tony and I are going out dancing," Angela said and then briefly explained the idea. She then looked directly at Carmela.

"You want to go with us?" Angela asked.

"Sure I would," Carmela immediately answered. "I ain't been out dancing since my Tony left."

"I'll call Elizabeth also," the thought occurred to Angela, "after Tony is done using the phone."

By the time phone calls had been made and plans arranged, a group of eleven would rendezvous at the popular Crawford Grill nightclub around 9:00 that evening. Angela and Tony headed upstairs to get ready, and the second they walked into the tiny bedroom it dawned on Angela that she was entirely alone with her husband behind closed doors for the first time since he arrived home earlier that day.

Apparently the same thought occurred to Tony, because he reached to pull Angela towards him and the two proceeded to kiss with the urgency of a young married couple that hadn't seen each other for three months. Finally Angela pulled away, gave her husband a lust-filled grin, and reluctantly said "later, after we get home."

Tony only sighed as he pulled Angela towards him for a final couple of kisses. As they resumed kissing, Angela cursed herself for making that remark about wanting to go dancing. Otherwise they could fall onto the bed and continue being reacquainted with each other. A few seconds later, though, hearing Carmela's footsteps out in the hallway, Angela realized that her sister-in-law and especially her mother-in-law were also in the house, which would have made for quite an awkward situation had Tony and Angela been inclined towards any early evening intimacies.

Why, though? That question nagged at Angela as she changed into more appropriate clothes for a nightclub. She and Tony were married; this wasn't like before when fooling around had to be done surreptitiously, wherever they could somehow find a place to be alone. Why did she feel if they were to have fallen together onto the bed, that at any second Rosalia DeLuca would burst through the door, shouting her objections in a furious combination of Italian and heavily accented English? And if that were to happen, Angela would somehow wind up being in the wrong, even though she would have been in her own bed, with her own husband, and it was mother-in-law who technically would be the unwelcome intruder.

Even with Tony home, Angela realized as she fished for a set of earrings that might be elegant enough for a nightclub, being a newlywed was so very strange as a result of the war.

* * *

What a glorious night! Angela glanced at her wristwatch and saw that the clock had ticked past midnight. The final notes of Benny Goodman's "Jersey Bounce" wound up the house orchestra's most recent set that had begun with "Tangerine," the third time that song had been played that evening. Angela glanced over at Elizabeth each time "Tangerine" played, and her sister-in-law certainly looked melancholy, obviously lost in memories of her own absent husband. At least Elizabeth didn't seem resentful that Angela's husband was here this evening while Carlo wasn't. Other than "Tangerine" being unfortunately played so frequently, Elizabeth seemed to be having an enjoyable evening. She didn't dance at all, whereas Angela barely left the dance floor from the moment they arrived. Even Carmela danced a fair bit throughout the evening, though only with the fellows she knew from high school or the neighborhood...but not with any of the dozen or so other men who intermittently wandered over to the group to ask Carmela for a dance.

As the orchestra began its break, Angela was torn about what to do next. She was having such a marvelous time, and felt that she could remain here dancing until the Sunday morning sunrise, if the nightclub were somehow to be able to remain open. Yet as the evening passed, her urge to be alone with Tony, in bed, heightened almost by the minute. Angela didn't want to be a party-pooper, as the saying went; but since time together with Tony was unhappily such a limited commodity, she decided that she had now had her fill of dancing and nightclubs for the evening.

"Let's go home now," she whispered to Tony as they walked off of the dance floor back to the crowded table where their group had gathered. She deliberately offered this suggestion in a breathy whisper, barely an inch away from Tony's ear, knowing exactly what reaction that intimate act would provoke. She could actually feel the huge grin immediately come to Tony's face even as her lips were still so close to his ear.

"Sure, doll," Tony said. They continued back to the table to say their goodbyes, which were held up slightly because of a new arrival who had wandered into the nightclub while Angela and Tony were out on the dance floor. Mickey Rossi had been one of Tony's best friends all the way through high school, and in the years since they both graduated from Peabody High, the two had remained the closest of friends. Mickey had enlisted in the Army at the same time Tony did, and the two had hoped they would head to basic training together and maybe even wind up in the same outfit. The United States Army had a different idea, though; and as with Tony's brother Michael, Mickey Rossi wound up facing several months of one delay after another until he finally received his orders. Mickey had still been in Pittsburgh when Tony and Angela got married, and had even been a member of Tony's wedding party. But whereas Tony headed off to infantry training that Wednesday morning, Mickey Rossi finally left for boot camp two days later, with his own infantry training still months ahead of him.

"Tonnnnny!" Mickey shouted as Tony and Angela approached. Angela could already tell from Mickey's eyes and speech and mannerisms that he was well inebriated.

"Mickey!" Tony shouted back. "You made it through boot camp! Howya dooooin'?"

The two friends gave each other soldierly slaps on the back and immediately launched into a rapid-fire exchange of tales from their respective Army lives. Angela initially was perturbed, given where she had Tony had been headed before he encountered his friend; but after a few minutes of irritation Angela figured that another half hour or so before they lustfully fell into bed wouldn't be the end of the world.

"So when ya headed over to North Africa?" Mickey slurred. At the mention of "North Africa," Angela quickly pivoted her head toward her husband and his friend, and she immediately caught the shocked, wide-eyed look on Tony's face.

Angela watched as Tony shook his head back and forth several times, quickly and tightly; that "No! Shut up now!" gesture that is intended to be a clandestine signal, but in reality is so easily recognizable by anyone gazing directly upon someone doing it.

"Whaaat?" Mickey slurred again, apparently not catching his friend's implication. "You know; North Africa, the invas…"

Mickey never got a chance to finish his sentence because Tony quickly stepped forward and brusquely threw an arm around Mickey's shoulders. In almost the same motion Tony began pulling Mickey away from Angela, Rocky Santucci, and the others, out of earshot. Mickey stumbled, but Tony had such a tight grip on his friend that Mickey didn't come close to falling. Mickey Rossi staggered away, powerless to avoid going wherever Tony was taking him.

Angela watched Tony stop about ten feet away, Mickey still tightly secured. She intently watched Tony angrily say something to his friend, Tony's right hand now clasping the back of Mickey's neck. Several times during Tony's angry monologue he harshly shook Mickey's neck and head, apparently feeling that doing so was necessary to ensure Mickey's attention. Finally Angela saw Mickey nod his head a few times and shrug his shoulders. Tony released the grip on his friend's neck, and Angela saw him give Mickey a few friendly light smacks on the drunk man's left cheek before they walked back over to the group.

"Sorry 'bout that," Mickey sheepishly offered to Angela and Rocky and everyone else who had gazed upon the angry exchange. His voice was still heavily slurred, but Tony's brusque physical reaction seemed to have sobered Mickey up a bit…at least for the moment.

"It's okay," Rocky Santucci responded. "We're all a little soused, that's for sure." As he spoke, Rocky seemed to exaggerate a slur into his own speech to hopefully lessen their friend's discomfort.

The unsettling encounter between Tony and Mickey was soon forgotten. Tony and Angela wound up staying at the Crawford Grill until after 1:00, when the group left en masse. The joint was still jumping, though, Angela took note. Mickey Rossi stayed behind because he had been a late-comer. Besides, he had just met a woman who quickly seemed to only have eyes for him, and the two of them were dancing to Harry James' "One Dozen Roses."

They all boarded the same streetcar a couple of blocks away from the nightclub that would take them to Oakland, and from that point they would split up and take various trolley lines back to where each one lived. Rocky Santucci and his wife Tina were headed back to Rocky's parents' house that was only around the corner from the DeLuca home, so they went the entire distance alongside Tony and Angela.

Tony and Rocky were deep in quiet discussion about something that they obviously wanted neither of their wives to overhear. Tina had fallen asleep – or passed out, more likely – which left Angela alone with her thoughts.

The night had been a splendid one: an inarguable fact, Angela told herself. Yet two things bothered her. First, of course, was that strange, tense exchange between Mickey Rossi and Tony. The tension had fortunately evaporated as quickly as it had appeared, but Mickey's slip let Angela know that sooner than later, her husband would be fighting in North Africa. She knew Tony wouldn't confirm this fact even if she asked him directly, and she wouldn't dare; but Tony's reaction to Mickey's indiscretion told Angela everything she needed to know. She, of course, didn't know when an invasion might take place, or specifically where, or through what means. Before too much longer, though, she knew she would see headlines in the *Pittsburgh Press* or hear the news bulletins on the Blue Network or Mutual about American boys joining the fight alongside the British in North Africa, and she would know that Tony was there.

Angela was also paradoxically troubled by what a wonderful night it had been. *This* is what married life is supposed to be like: a Saturday evening family supper and then dancing the night away at the Crawford Grill or some other nightclub. They would then journey home on the streetcar so very late at night, and finally she would climb into bed to make love with her husband.

The war had cheated her. The war teased her with this tiniest tidbit of normalcy but also taunted her that after this coming Wednesday, this one magnificent night and perhaps one or two others in the days directly ahead, were the *only* ones that Angela and Tony DeLuca would be granted for a very long time.

* * *

Early Sunday afternoon, Angela and Tony were scouring the entertainment pages of the *Pittsburgh Press*, trying to decide what movie to go see this afternoon. Angela suspected that Tony would actually rather go see the Pirates play a doubleheader against the Cardinals at Forbes Field this afternoon. To his credit, Tony didn't even raise the subject, even though his brother Michael kept dropping hints all morning about the baseball games.

Selecting a movie was actually turning out to be more difficult than either could have imagined. Tony bluntly informed Angela that he wasn't interested in seeing some propaganda-style war film. That ruled out *Eagle Squadron*, *Flight Lieutenant*, and *Sergeant York*, all of which were playing at nearby theaters. They settled on *Men of Texas* with Robert Stack and Jackie Cooper at the Harris Theater downtown. The film wasn't quite the lighthearted comedy that Angela would have preferred, but she was wholly in agreement that watching a glamorized Hollywood version of either this world war or the previous one (in the case of *Sergeant York*) wasn't quite what this weekend called for.

Neither Angela nor Tony saw much of the movie, because as soon as the newsreel and cartoons had given way to the feature film, their necking commenced. They had deliberately selected seats in the otherwise empty back row, and even as the opening credits were rolling, Angela realized that she had far less interest in the film than in reliving so many earlier, more carefree, more lustful movie dates with the man who was now her husband.

If they didn't have Tony's room back at the DeLuca house where they would be together again tonight, Angela was sure that Tony would have attempted to go well past his roving hands in the back row of the Harris. The pent-up frustrations of so many months apart hadn't come close to being satiated when they were finally alone in the sticky dark hours so very early this morning after returning home from the Crawford Grill. Still, Angela reluctantly put a halt to Tony's attempts to entice her into doing anything that, if caught, would likely result in them being arrested on a morals charge. A pimply-faced usher with a flashlight telling them to knock off the necking: that was one thing. Angela had no desire to ruin the rest of Tony's furlough by having him spend it in a jail cell.

That evening, Elizabeth joined her in-laws for Sunday evening supper. Elizabeth, of course, assisted Carmela and Angela in helping Rosalia in the kitchen while Tony relaxed in the living room alongside his brother and father, each of them enjoying a bottle of Fort Pitt.

"Good thing we didn't go see the Pirates today," Michael offered as the 6:00 Mutual Network news came on. "They lost both games; that woulda been a waste to go see."

"Yeah, I guess so," Tony offered, thinking how his brother kept coming back to the two of them going to see the Pirates play, even though Tony had made no overtures to do so. It finally dawned on Tony that Michael probably felt cheated, having spent so little time with his oldest brother during this brief, unexpected furlough. Michael himself would be leaving soon enough, Tony realized, and for months had been all alone here after Tony and Carlo had left back in May.

With Michael being the youngest and Tony the oldest, the two hadn't been the closest of brothers while growing up. Tony and Vinnie had usually paired up, just as Carlo and Michael did. But with Vinnie and Carlo away, right now – and only for a couple more days – it was just Tony and Michael here.

"How 'bout you and I go see 'em tomorrow afternoon?" Tony suddenly offered. "The Pirates and Cardinals, last game of the series. Angela's gonna be at work, so you and I can go see the game."

"Yeah?" Michael quickly responded, unable to keep the grateful excitement from that single word.

"Yeah," Tony nodded as he took another pull from his beer. "Maybe since they lost both today they'll have gotten that outta their system, and they'll win one for us tomorrow."

"Maybe," Michael nodded, grinning.

A few moments later Carmela stuck her head out of the kitchen to let her father and brothers know that Sunday supper was ready. As soon as everyone was seated, Giuseppe said a quick grace. Even though he felt as if he should make mention of Tony being home on furlough, he refrained from any mention of his oldest son's brief visit, because he knew tears would instantly flow from his wife's eyes. They were all well enough aware that Tony's presence was fleeting; why make mention of it and upset his wife? Not to mention bringing up Carlo…

The radio news headlines throughout the day, along with several special bulletins, had been all about the United States invading Guadalcanal a few days earlier in an attempt to seize the offensive against the Japanese. The battle was raging not only on land, but in the air and at sea. Even the earlier clashes at Midway and Coral Sea paled in comparison to the scale of this battle that was only just beginning.

The American troops were accompanied by soldiers from England, Australia, and New Zealand; but it was already abundantly clear that among all of the ground forces in this campaign, the starring role had been granted to the United States Marines. Everyone gathered around the DeLuca table this Sunday evening was just as aware as Elizabeth was that Carlo was almost certainly among those Marines attacking the Japanese at Guadalcanal. They had hung on every word from the radio newscasts and bulletins all day, and every single one of them dared not imagine the terrible specter of a Western Union man knocking on the door, bearing his message of injury or death.

"Why isn't your brother in the Army yet? Or another service?" Giuseppe DeLuca suddenly asked Elizabeth. He desperately wanted to draw his own thoughts away from worrying about Carlo or regretting the brevity of Tony's furlough. Besides, he was curious – as were many – why the able-bodied William Buchanan seemed immune to the draft thus far, even if he apparently didn't possess the patriotic fervor to enlist in one of the armed services. Elizabeth's brother wasn't enrolled in college, nor did he hold down a job at a war plant or any other enterprise essential to the war effort. Just what was going on here?

Elizabeth was unprepared for the question, and stammered a reply that she concocted on the spot.

"I don't know. I mean, I guess he hasn't gotten drafted yet, and maybe is waiting to hear from his draft board first before he enlists. Maybe he's waiting to see about getting back in college so he can become an officer…"

Elizabeth continued for a bit longer, and then her voice trailed off. Giuseppe DeLuca simply nodded, though everyone present could see that he didn't believe a word of Elizabeth's half-hearted explanation.

That night, after returning home, Elizabeth confronted her mother. Spencer and William were "out somewhere," Elizabeth was informed when she asked her mother about their whereabouts, which made this the perfect time for this long-overdue conversation.

"Why isn't William in the Army?" Elizabeth came right out and demanded.

Katherine Buchanan was ready with her answer.

"He's 4-F," was her short reply.

"What do you mean, he's 4-F?" Elizabeth countered. "He didn't even get a draft notice, and I know for a fact that he never tried to enlist."

"He's 4-F," Katherine repeated.

"You already said that," Elizabeth responded, trying to keep her irritation in check.

When no further explanation was forthcoming from her mother, Elizabeth continued.

"How could he be 4-F if he never took a physical?"

Katherine Buchanan's reply surprised her daughter.

"He did take a physical."

"When was this?" Elizabeth demanded.

"Back in early May," Katherine responded, and then couldn't resist adding, "during those couple of days when you were staying at Carlo's instead of living here at your home."

Elizabeth ignored the dig.

"How come nobody ever said anything to me?" she demanded.

"It wasn't your affair," was her mother's dismissive reply.

"So he got a draft notice?" Elizabeth pressed.

Katherine appeared to ponder the question before replying.

"No, he didn't."

"He tried to enlist?" Elizabeth asked, the doubt in her voice unmistakable.

Katherine Buchanan could have easily nodded, or offered a simple "uh-huh" in response in hopes of putting this matter to rest. But she knew that her daughter wouldn't let this matter go without a satisfactory explanation. Elizabeth would later press William himself for details of his unsuccessful attempt to enlist, which of course had never actually happened.

"No, he didn't try to enlist," Katherine finally said, knowing that at this point she had locked herself into confiding in her daughter.

"I don't get it!" Elizabeth was just about yelling now. "If he didn't receive a draft notice and didn't try to enlist, then how could he have taken a physical and gotten a 4-F?"

Katherine sighed. She was tiring of this inquisition from her daughter. Still, she couldn't bring herself to spill the complete ugly truth...yet.

"Your father met with some men from the draft board, and they gave William a special physical. They found a ruptured eardrum, so they classified him as 4-F."

The explanation made absolutely no sense to Elizabeth.

"Why would the draft board give William some kind of special physical just because Father met with…"

The lightning bolt of instant, insightful clarity struck Elizabeth.

"He paid them off," she interrupted herself, her words slow and pained. "Father paid the draft board men to give him a 4-F…" Elizabeth was speaking as much to herself as she was to her mother as her mind put the pieces together.

"How much?" she demanded, staring directly at her mother.

Katherine Buchanan's mind was whirling, trying to devise yet another cover story, but finally she decided enough was enough. Elizabeth was a grown woman; she was capable of hearing the truth.

"Three thousand dollars," she confided. "Fifteen hundred each for two draft board men. They took William in the back, gave him a physical, and wrote him up for a punctured eardrum and classified him as 4-F. That's all there is to the story."

Elizabeth felt herself sink down onto the plush sofa, which fortunately was right behind her. Otherwise, thinking back later on this terrible encounter, she might well enough have collapsed onto the floor and smacked her head on some hard surface.

Her mind churned with images of her brother flitting about the city, unconcerned with the war – other than devising ways to profit from it, as Elizabeth well knew – and apparently immune from being drafted into the Army. These images were then succeeded by others…of Carlo…

"Right this very minute," she said through clenched teeth, "my husband is almost certainly fighting for his life on Guadalcanal. And pretty soon Tony will…"

Elizabeth caught herself before she blurted out what they had all inadvertently learned the previous night about North Africa. She was furious, but she had just enough restraint to keep herself from unintentionally creating a "loose lips sink ships" moment, as Mickey Rossi had done.

"Tony will be fighting somewhere," Elizabeth changed the trajectory of her angry rebuttal. "And everyone who Carlo and Tony know will also be fighting. In fact, everyone that *William* knows will be fighting…"

"Not everybody," Katherine Buchanan interrupted. Elizabeth waited for her to continue, but no further elaboration was forthcoming. Still, Elizabeth picked up on her mother's meaning. Spencer Buchanan apparently wasn't the only well-to-do man spreading around a couple thousand dollars to keep his son safely immune from being sent off to war.

Elizabeth sank back onto the sofa. Her mind insisted on continuing with the imagined but likely genuine moving images of Carlo jumping off of a Marine landing craft under fire and digging into a beach on this distant island that none of them had ever heard of before. Then there was Carlo was rushing forward on the beach, still under intense enemy fire. Marines on both sides of him were swiftly cut down by the Japanese guns. She could almost feel Carlo's fear in the midst of terrible combat against the fearsome entrenched enemy. It might only be a matter of time until Carlo himself...

"Maybe if you hadn't insisted on marrying that boy against my wishes," her mother's voice interrupted those horrific images in Elizabeth's mind, "you would now instead be engaged or even already married to some wonderful man whose family had enough influence to keep him home safely from the war instead of leaving his wife behind, probably for years."

Katherine Buchanan had apparently had enough of this discussion. She turned to leave the dignified living room, but couldn't resist a parting word of "advice" for her daughter.

"Wealth has its privileges, Elizabeth. I thought you had learned that growing up. But privilege is something that can easily be squandered, as you've done...against my advice, I might add. Maybe this will be an important lesson for you."

*   *   *

The next two days passed like a blur for both Angela and Elizabeth. Angela frustratingly worked each day, her regular hours, frantically wishing that she could somehow take both days off to enjoy every single remaining, yet fleeting, hour of Tony's furlough by his side.

Elizabeth, for her part, tried her best to forget about her mother's horrid revelations – not to mention Katherine

Buchanan's elitist and vindictive parting shot about "wealth has its privilege" – and concentrate on her work at the OPA. But every time Elizabeth was somehow able to drag her thoughts away from that nauseating encounter, she immediately and intensely feared for Carlo's safety; for his very life.

For both of the DeLuca wives, these mid-August days were particularly trying for reasons far beyond the sticky Pittsburgh summer weather and the overpowering presence of the war. Angela wasn't much of a baseball fan, but she would have joyfully accompanied Tony and Michael to see the Pirates play that afternoon, only blocks from where she worked. Every so often she could hear a faint roar from the direction of Forbes Field, and her thoughts immediately flew away from the work on which she was so desperately trying to concentrate to her own conjured images of her husband and her brother-in-law enjoying each other's company as they rooted for their hometown team. That evening at supper, Michael and Tony excitedly related highlights of the Pirates' victory that partly avenged their doubleheader loss the day before, as well as their day together.

The minutes mercilessly ticked by, and on Wednesday morning the dreaded moment arrived. Unlike Monday and Tuesday, Angela decided to plead for the morning off from work so she could accompany Tony to Pennsylvania Station, and was successful in her efforts. As with his departure back in early May, tears flowed freely amidst the sounds of sobbing all across the train platform. Angela fiercely clutched her husband and then finally yielded him so he could say his farewells to his parents and his brother. She hugged him once again, unable to hold back a fresh set of tears and sobs, until Tony finally had to gently pull himself away so he could board the departing train.

Then he was gone.

Chapter 8

The mid-December Christmas party at the Witherspoon Club was a deeply entrenched annual tradition dating back to 1911. If neither the Great War nor the worst years of the Depression could bring about a hiatus, then neither could this new war against Germany and Japan that had just entered its second year.

Even last year, only six days after the sudden attack on Pearl Harbor, the Christmas party had proceeded as scheduled. That occasion had certainly been a subdued one; but curiously, once the party had gotten underway, the war was all but forgotten, at least for several hours. Last year, it seemed as if people were desperate for a few hours of merciful respite from the daily barrage of terrible news coming out of Pearl Harbor, Wake Island, Guam, the Philippines, and elsewhere across the Pacific.

Last year's party had been an uncomfortable one for Katherine Buchanan – her husband and son also – not particularly because of the newly declared war, but because Elizabeth had insisted on being accompanied by her Italian boyfriend from Morningside. Those in attendance who came in contact with Elizabeth and Carlo were properly cordial, but stares and whispers followed the couple throughout the evening, much to Katherine Buchanan's mortification.

The mood this chilly mid-December night inside the stately club would certainly be more reflective of an entire world at war than a year earlier when the shock of Pearl Harbor was temporarily brushed aside out of desperate necessity. How could those in attendance avoid discussing the war throughout the evening when every aspect of their lives was now impacted by the global conflagration? In fact, this year's atmosphere at the club in the weeks leading up to the annual party reflected the cautious optimism in the face of the latest news from the war theaters. The Americans had successfully invaded North Africa to join the British there. Together, the Allies seemed to have the Nazis and Italians on the run after more than a month of fierce fighting, at least according to the daily newspaper headlines and the radio reports. In the Pacific the terrible combat on Guadalcanal had been underway since August, and after frenzied back and forth assaults throughout November a costly yet resounding American victory was now in sight.

Elizabeth's husband was likely still fighting on Guadalcanal; and because of Mickey Rossi's slip that night at the Crawford Grill back in early August, she knew as well as Angela did that Tony DeLuca was somewhere in North Africa as part of Operation Torch. For these reasons Elizabeth didn't feel much like attending any Christmas party, let alone one at the stuffy club that she so much identified with her mother's snobbery.

Still, when Saturday afternoon arrived and Katherine Buchanan insisted that Elizabeth be dressed and ready to leave by 5:30, Elizabeth could only muster token resistance. The truth was that the thought of a Saturday night alone, with Christmas now less than two weeks away, was more than Elizabeth could bear. Earlier in the day she had called Angela and was dismayed to hear that Angela was accompanying Carmela to a family gathering at her in-laws that evening. Elizabeth expected that Angela would extend an invitation for Elizabeth to accompany her and Carmela to the DeMarco home, but surprisingly none was forthcoming. Her feelings hurt, Elizabeth decided not to put up much of a fight at her mother's insistence about the Witherspoon Club party.

When 5:30 came, Elizabeth followed her parents and her brother William out the door and into Spencer Buchanan's elegant 1939 Packard Twelve. Every time Elizabeth set foot in her father's car, she was struck by the difference between this magnificent vehicle and Carlo's rusted '37 Packard Six. Both automobiles may have come from the same manufacturer, but Elizabeth could clearly distinguish a world of difference between the two.

During the twenty-minute drive to Oakland, Elizabeth pondered one of the curiosities of the war. Last year at this time, night had already fallen and the identical drive to the Witherspoon Club had been through the snowy blackness of a frigid mid-December evening. Tonight, though, the sun was still twenty minutes or so from setting, thanks to Pittsburgh's clocks being on Eastern War Time since February. The effect was the same as the daylight savings time change that many municipalities chose to adopt during the summer; but the extra hour of daylight had never been in place during winter since an earlier brief experiment by President Wilson during 1918, at the end of the Great War.

Something about making this drive in the daylight made Carlo seem even farther away to Elizabeth. He had picked her up in his Packard Six for plenty of wintertime dates last year right around this time of day, before and then after the war began. On every single one of those dates they had driven away in the intimate blackness of night, Elizabeth nestled next to Carlo in the Packard's front seat, even though the six o'clock hour hadn't even arrived yet. This evening, the last vestiges of sunlight stubbornly hanging onto life were unsettling. *Everything* is different now, and don't forget it; this disquieting reminder seemed to mock Elizabeth.

Another unsettling aspect of the short drive for Elizabeth was being in such close proximity to her brother. Ever since learning about her father's surreptitious payments to ensure that William received 4-F status, Elizabeth's dislike for her brother had grown to the point where she couldn't stand even looking at his usually smug face, or to be anywhere near him. She had hoped that William would have already spent this Saturday afternoon at the Witherspoon Club as he usually did, sitting and drinking, and not come back home only to have to return to the Club just a short time later.

No such luck, though. Wherever William had been this Saturday he had made it home by 4:30, and there was no question he would be driving with his parents and Elizabeth this evening.

"Hey Pop," William asked as soon as the Packard Twelve glided away from their King Avenue home. "Did you see the *Press* this afternoon? About the liquor shortage?"

Elizabeth immediately shot a look to her left and glared at her brother. She knew exactly where William was headed with this conversation, even before he said anything further.

"No, I didn't," Spencer Buchanan replied, still looking ahead and concentrating on the road.

"It says that the state stores are almost out, and by next week it might be impossible for anyone to find any whiskey or anything else."

This time Spencer Buchanan half-turned around as he replied.

"Really?"

"Yeah," William continued. "It says that the state told the stores that their warehouses are empty, but that up in New York and over in Ohio and West Virginia, there's plenty in their warehouses."

"Is that so?" Williams's father answered slowly...thoughtfully.

Elizabeth's angry glare shifted from her brother to her father, and then she glanced over at her mother. Katherine Buchanan seemed uninterested in this conversation between her husband and her son. Apparently if there were money to be made by a Buchanan, regardless of the means, she was all for it and needn't concern herself with the details.

"I'm thinking that maybe I make some trips to Ohio and West Virginia next week," William mused. "I figure that going and coming back over the state line in a nice big Packard Twelve should be pretty easy without getting stopped and frisked..."

Elizabeth couldn't help her loud sigh of agitation. William paused for a brief second, looked over at his sister in his usual unconcerned manner, and then continued his narrative of how he could probably clear a cool two thousand dollars next week alone by bringing back liquor and quietly selling it to desperate companies and people, even restaurants and lounges, who needed Scotch and rye and gin and bourbon – anything – for the holidays. Elizabeth did her best to tune out her brother's gleeful recitation and instead focused on looking out the window, counting the seconds until she could be out of this car and away from her scheming family.

*   *   *

Once inside the Witherspoon Club, Elizabeth began to relax a little bit. Two quick whiskey sours certainly helped, along with one short conversation after another with girls she hadn't seen very much since last year's party. Several of these girls had also become furlough brides earlier this year, and Elizabeth exchanged tales of what they knew about their respective husbands' wartime service. Carol Higgenboth – now Carol McCullen – had received a V-mail letter only yesterday from her new husband, an Air Corps pilot likely flying B-24s over Africa during the current fighting. He hadn't said much in his letter, but the censors still had a field day excising almost an entire third of what he had written. Still, Carol had been thrilled to receive the first letter from her husband in nearly two months.

Maude Ringgold strolled over to the group. Elizabeth had seen Maude only a month earlier, during lunchtime in Oakland. But so much had happened since mid-November, including Maude's husband Oliver receiving a stateside assignment to Camp Kilmer in New Jersey. Oliver was scheduled to arrive there shortly after New Year's Day, and would temporarily be assigned there for at least two or three months until moving on to a follow-on posting.

"I can't wait!" Maude exclaimed.

At first, Elizabeth was puzzled by her girlfriend's excitement. True, her husband would be stateside rather than at one of the war fronts. But Edison, New Jersey, was still hundreds of miles away from Pittsburgh.

Suddenly Elizabeth had an idea why Maude was so ecstatic.

"You're going with him?" she asked Maude.

"Of course I am!" Maude exclaimed, as if her intentions should have been obvious. "Oliver wrote me that there are billets on the post for married sergeants, and he's already pulled some strings to make sure that we'll have one."

Maude paused to finish the last of her gin and tonic.

"I know he'll have long hours because of the war and everything, but at least we'll have most nights together."

Suddenly Maude's exuberance nosedived and instantly transformed into bittersweet resignation.

"Until the Army sends him away again, that is."

After the group dispersed, Elizabeth found herself standing alone for a few minutes, contemplating what Maude Ringgold had just shared. What a wonderful gift in the middle of a war: to be able to spend a few precious months with her new husband while he was stateside. But that joy was immutably destined to be short-lived; it came along with a brief, finite life span, just like a bottle of milk or a box of tomatoes. Elizabeth wondered how she would react if she were in Maude's place, accompanying Carlo to some stateside posting at a Marine camp…but only for a couple of months. Would she cherish each and every day with him? Or would she be morosely focused on every passing day taking them a touch closer to his inevitable departure, just as when he had left so soon after their wedding?

"Your drink is empty."

Elizabeth's musings evaporated instantly. She immediately and involuntarily looked down at her glass – which indeed was empty, except for the remnants of two ice cubes – and then over at the man who had addressed her. As soon as Elizabeth locked eyes with him, he continued.

"May I get you a refill?"

Elizabeth's first impulse was to offer a polite "no, thank you" to this man, but instead she replied:

"Thank you; please."

"Whiskey sour?"

"Uh-huh," Elizabeth nodded.

The man reached out his right hand towards Elizabeth, and for a brief instant she thought he was initiating a handshake. Then she realized that he was offering to take her empty glass, which she then handed to him.

He was gone for about two minutes, and the entire time Elizabeth fretted over what she had just done. No doubt when this man came back he would want to engage her in conversation rather than just hand her a fresh drink and then simply slip away.

But what was the harm? After all, this was a Christmas party. Elizabeth had already talked with almost every girl she knew who was there, and God knows that she didn't want to be anywhere near her mother or brother. And after the car ride over here, her father fell into that category, at least for today.

Elizabeth was still deliberating with herself when the man arrived, smiling, bearing a fresh whiskey sour. He handed the drink to Elizabeth and his smile broadened even further. Elizabeth was powerless to avoid returning the smile, and for a brief surprisingly comfortable moment the two stood silently, just smiling at each other.

Finally the man broke the silence.

"I'm Calvin McKinnon," he offered.

"Elizabeth Buchan… I mean Elizabeth DeLuca," was the response.

"Aha!" Calvin McKinnon's smile broadened even more. "I detect a newlywed!"

Elizabeth chuckled.

"That's exactly it, Mr. …"

"Uh-uh!" the man interrupted Elizabeth with a good-natured wagging of his index finger. "Calvin, or better yet, Cal."

"Okay Calvin," Elizabeth agreed. "Anyway, you're correct. I'm still getting used to my married name, even though it's been nearly eight months."

"DeLuca?" Calvin cocked his eyebrows. "You don't look Italian to me," he teased.

"Not by birth," Elizabeth retorted good-naturedly, "but definitely by marriage."

The two bantered back and forth for a minute or so as Elizabeth took in this man's appearance. He was at least four or five inches taller than Carlo; close to six feet, or maybe even right at that mark. Even underneath his impeccably tailored tuxedo Elizabeth could see that he had the lean-muscled body of someone who spent many hours each week enjoying the typical exercises of those who belonged to the Witherspoon Club: squash, tennis, and swimming. His sandy-blond hair was much closer to Elizabeth's hue than Carlo's typical Italian jet-black hair was, and his blue eyes contrasted with Carlo's brown eyes.

Anybody walking past the two of them who didn't know that Elizabeth was married to a totally different man might easily presume that Elizabeth and Calvin McKinnon made a handsome couple.

"You're not in the military, Calvin?" Elizabeth felt as if she had to say something to ease herself back from this meeting-somebody-very-intriguing atmosphere that had quickly settled over the two of them.

"I'm afraid not," was McKinnon's reply. "I'm 4-B…"

"What's that again?" Elizabeth interrupted, unable to recall the meaning of that particular military service classification from among the many number-and-letter combinations.

"It means that I'm a government official who is deferred by law from being able to serve in the military because of some critically important job," he explained.

His words could easily have been taken by Elizabeth as conveying a distasteful air of self-importance, but the manner in which Calvin McKinnon spoke was pleasantly matter-of-fact rather than offensive.

"I was just transferred here from Washington to be the Deputy Director for Steel Production for the local WPB district," he continued.

"My sister-in-law works at the WPB!" Elizabeth exclaimed. "She's a secretary in the Oakland office."

"That's wonderful," Calvin said. "I'll be working at the downtown office, since that's the district's headquarters. They want us very close to all the steel companies that are so critical to the war effort, and since United States Steel is headquartered downtown, that's where I'll be most of the time."

"And you're the Deputy Director?" Elizabeth peered quizzically at him. He looked so young! Not much older than she was, in fact.

Calvin nodded and, apparently, he also read Elizabeth's thoughts.

"You're probably thinking that I'm too young for a job like that," he grinned. "I'm twenty-four, in case you were wondering…"

"No I wasn't!" Elizabeth interrupted defensively.

Calvin brushed off her objection and proceeded with his explanation.

"I majored in industrial management at Georgetown," he continued, "and then spent the next two years after I graduated working on Lend-Lease. My specialty is something called Rapid Wartime Metals Production and

Provisioning...RWMPP, you know how the government loves acronyms. Anyway, I just seem to have a very keen insight into the whole business of wartime metals production, and then getting all that steel and aluminum and copper quickly shipped to the war plants. After Roosevelt began the WPB back in January, I shifted over there from Lend-Lease, and I was assigned to the steel desk."

Elizabeth looked at him, slightly puzzled.

"That's what they call the group in the WPB and RWMPP that specializes in all of the steel companies across the country. Our mission is to help them continue shifting their production from peacetime to wartime. I spent all of this year up until Thanksgiving working in Washington, and now they want me to be assigned here as the Deputy Director to work directly with the companies that have headquarters or major operations in the Pittsburgh area."

Their conversation continued through the next hour, and two more whiskey sours for each of them. After the first ten minutes they found two seats at an otherwise abandoned table, and they remained there for the duration of their discussion. Elizabeth found herself leaning towards Cal, smiling frequently, the way a woman does when she meets someone particularly enthralling.

They talked about the similarities of and differences between growing up in Pittsburgh and the Virginia suburbs of the nation's capital. Cal told Elizabeth what college life at Georgetown had been like. He talked about the difficulties of a wartime move from Washington to Pittsburgh which was thankfully made less problematic by having few possessions to bring along. They commiserated about the trials of wartime rationing. Elizabeth described how she and Carlo decided to get married before he went away to war, and how she had been filling her days since his departure. They discussed everything!

Much later, Elizabeth would wonder what might have happened if that conversation had proceeded into a second hour, and perhaps even a third. They might have risen from the table to share a dance or two...this handsome young college graduate with the important war job clutching Elizabeth Buchanan DeLuca, loosely at first and then tightly, intimately as song after song played and they both became lost in the music and the moment.

As it was, though, Elizabeth put an abrupt end to the discussion when she glanced away from Cal for a second and looked across the room to catch her mother staring at them with that same icy smile of victory that Katherine Buchanan had worn the afternoon of Carlo's departure, just as "Tangerine" came on the radio.

* * *

That night Elizabeth had a dream that in retrospect was hardly unexpected. She was reliving her wedding right down to the last detail, except instead of Carlo DeLuca she was marrying, it was, of course, Calvin McKinnon. Emotions in the midst of a dream are a curious matter, Elizabeth knew. Some dreams are matter-of-fact, emotionless scripts clocking through the theater of one's mind, while other dreams carry with them the most lifelike sentiments: joy, fear, contentment, anger, and all the rest. These latter dreams, such as this one that Elizabeth experienced, are every bit as richly textured as reality in the dreamer's mind.

In this particular dream, Elizabeth recalled after she awoke in a cold sweat, what she felt for the dreamworld incarnation of Calvin McKinnon could only be described as overwhelming love. The sensations were very disturbing to Elizabeth, given that in real life she, of course, was married to a totally different man.

Yet real life was also able to grab a toehold in this dream. Several times in the dream Elizabeth looked towards the first row and saw her mother's face bearing the warmest, most loving and genuine smile Elizabeth had ever seen on the woman. Even while still ensconced in the dream and definitely after she awoke, Elizabeth was disgusted by her mother's smiling approval because of how very different it was than when Katherine Buchanan had donned her faux smile as she absorbed the real-life sight of her daughter marrying Carlo DeLuca.

The dream, and especially how Elizabeth's mind had conjured her mother's approving reaction to the imagined wedding, bothered Elizabeth so much that she barely slept the rest of the evening. Fortunately the next day was a Sunday, so when 6:00 a.m. came and she finally was able to drift back into sleep for more than a few troubled minutes, Elizabeth slept straight through until after 10:00 that morning.

She so very much needed to talk to someone about this dream, yet her only real confidante these days was Angela. Perhaps a dozen times, Elizabeth mentally rehearsed a discussion with Angela in which she confided the tale of her long conversation with Calvin McKinnon at the Christmas party and then her troubled dream that followed that very night. Each time, Elizabeth's imaginary dialogue was halted by the same disturbing thought: if word made it back to the DeLuca family that Elizabeth had chatted up a desirable young bachelor at a Witherspoon Club Christmas Party while Carlo was most likely fighting for his life on Guadalcanal, tensions with her in-laws would immediately spring to life. Even worse: those strains would almost certainly carry over to her life with Carlo after he came back home, perhaps for years to come.

Since the world in which families such as the DeLucas and DeMarcos and Antolinis inhabited was so very different than that of the Buchanans – and McKinnons, for that matter – Elizabeth doubted that word of her intimate conversation with Calvin McKinnon would ever come to the attention of Carlo's family…that was, unless Elizabeth herself would be the one to introduce the subject.

True, there was always the chance that Calvin McKinnon might be at the Oakland WPB offices one day and, upon finding out that Angela DeLuca and Elizabeth DeLuca were sisters-in-law, mention that Christmas party conversation to Angela. But the chances of such an encounter with a mere WPB secretary in a different office seemed slight; nor did he seem the type to make the rounds of the WPB secretarial ranks inquiring if anybody happened to be related to Elizabeth DeLuca…a World War II home front version of the Cinderella tale, in a way.

Even if that unlikely connection were to come about weeks or months later, plenty of time would have passed with Elizabeth having no further contact with Calvin McKinnon. Therefore she was confident that she could brush the whole matter aside with Angela if it ever did come up, and the tale of the 1942 Witherspoon Club Christmas Party would harmlessly fade away.

Consequently, Elizabeth decided to keep the matter to herself and not bring it up at all to Angela. Just to be on the safe side, Elizabeth avoided Angela during the first two days of the work week, telling Angela each day that she wasn't able to meet for lunch. When a variation of her dream unexpectedly recurred Tuesday night (this time Carlo was disturbingly serving as Calvin McKinnon's best man), Elizabeth extended the moratorium for another two days. Finally, worried that Angela would become suspicious that something was amiss merely because an entire week had passed without the two girls seeing each other, Elizabeth did meet Angela for lunch on Friday afternoon. The occasion was uneventful, and by the time Elizabeth left work at 5:00 that afternoon, she was confident that the entire matter had already slipped away into nothingness.

Elizabeth's thoughts during the streetcar ride home amidst snow flurries that blustery Friday afternoon were focused on the lead story in the *Pittsburgh Press* she picked up from a newsstand just before boarding the trolley. "SALES OF GASOLINE HALTED" the headline screamed. The story went on to bluntly state that because of the overwhelming military needs for gasoline, particularly in North Africa, anyone holding A, B, and C ration coupons along the Atlantic Seaboard was out of luck when it came to trying to gas up their vehicles. Even farm equipment and construction vehicle operators with their own special coupons were covered by the ban, though the article speculated that most likely those operators had fuel stockpiles they could tap into until the sale ban was lifted. Only commercial vehicle operators – those who qualified for T ration coupons – could still purchase gasoline, with no timeline given for when these new restrictions would be lifted for all the others.

The new harsh measures would, of course, be administered by the OPA. Elizabeth had known for several days that the ban would be announced anytime. Sure enough, during the Mutual Network's noon news that had been blaring above the lunchtime noise at Jack Canter's, President Roosevelt himself made the announcement.

For days Elizabeth had been entertaining the vindictive satisfaction that her father and his precious Packard Twelve would be impacted by the ban. But as the restrictions became official, she realized that rationing had taken almost no toll at all on the Buchanan family since measures began going into effect earlier this year. Whether sugar and coffee for their breakfast table, or tires and gasoline for the Packard, thus far the Buchanans had lacked for nothing at all. Her father was somewhat circumspect about how they had come to be unaffected by all of these wartime rationing measures, but Elizabeth's brother showed far less discretion. William never came right out and declared that he was involved in black market dealings for ration coupons and even the rationed goods themselves. Yet Elizabeth had no doubt at all that her brother's maneuverings, and her father's as well, were every bit as much on the other side of the law as Spencer Buchanan's bootlegging had been.

Elizabeth's thoughts were still fixated on the latest rationing news as she exited the streetcar and bundled up for the short but frigid walk home. Her musings shifted to tomorrow's forecast for even colder temperatures, and then the two threads of thought fused into one as she hoped her father's or brother's "connections" would keep them from running short on fuel oil this winter, rationing and the OPA notwithstanding. Elizabeth immediately felt guilty for harboring these selfish thoughts, but human nature was still human nature, after all...

Elizabeth opened the front door and rushed in as quickly as she could to get out of the frigid weather, but within seconds she felt as if she had not only entered the stately, toasty warm house, but also a new reprise of her troubled dreams from the past week. Sitting in one of the wingback chairs in the living room, talking to Elizabeth's father, was Calvin McKinnon!

Elizabeth's eyes narrowed at first and then immediately widened as she took in this scene. The two appeared to have been engaged in conversation that halted when the front door opened. Calvin's left hand held a crystal tumbler of Scotch whisky that appeared to have just been filled...or perhaps refilled, because Elizabeth had the feeling the young man had been there for a little while already.

Cal was the one who broke the silence.

"Your mother was kind enough to invite me to dinner this evening," he offered to Elizabeth. His words came along with a smile, but it struck Elizabeth that this smile wasn't nearly as warm and inviting – or harmless – as the many he had offered one week earlier during the Christmas party.

Elizabeth didn't immediately respond, though her eyes traveled from Calvin McKinnon to her father for a brief instant, and then for a longer time to her mother who had just entered the living room from the kitchen. Katherine Buchanan was also smiling, and unlike in Elizabeth's dream about the imaginary wedding, this smile was that cold, all-too-familiar one of self-bestowed triumph.

To Elizabeth's credit, as she congratulated herself many times throughout that night while stirring sleeplessly in bed, she didn't rise to the bait. Instead she fell back on one of the lessons from her debutante days: the importance of maintaining outward grace in all situations, even when one might be so very uncomfortable in one's own mind. Elizabeth chatted amicably with Calvin about their respective work weeks. They all discussed the latest rationing news at length, as well as – of course – the latest war news from North Africa and Guadalcanal in particular, but also the Soviet Union and Burma. Calvin brought up a news story that wouldn't be in the newspapers until the following day: the tale of famed World War I flying ace Eddie Rickenbacker being found alive more than three weeks after a crash landing at sea, having miraculously survived the entire time with several others in the Pacific aboard a life raft.

Elizabeth concentrated her efforts on maintaining that all-important outward grace, yet she did allow herself a few moments of private amusement at her brother William's discomfort throughout dinner. She could almost read his thoughts. This man McKinnon might be with the WPB rather than the OPA and its rationing powers, but a government man was still a government man; and because of his "business dealings," William Buchanan wanted no part of any government men. His sister might work at the OPA, but William was apparently confident that blood was thicker than water, as the saying went, and that Elizabeth wouldn't dare betray either William or their father.

The pre-dinner Scotch whisky gave way to Châteauneuf-du-Pape with the rich dinner of roast beef and potatoes, and then after-dinner brandy served in Spencer Buchanan's finest snifters. Elizabeth and her mother drank along with Spencer and William and Calvin McKinnon, though, of course, proportionately less for each woman than the men. Finally the eleven o'clock hour arrived, and after listening to the Blue Network news, Calvin McKinnon departed. Elizabeth waited for whatever overture that she expected to be forthcoming: a suggested lunch together during the week, or perhaps drinks after work one evening. But to his credit, Calvin McKinnon made no such propositions. Elizabeth was certain that they were eventually coming, but apparently not this evening before Spencer Buchanan gave young Mr. McKinnon a ride back to his downtown hotel room at the William Penn, where the WPB was housing him for the foreseeable future.

As soon as Elizabeth's father left with Calvin, William muttered "I'm going out" and staggered out the door. Fortunately with the Packard in his father's possession, the well-inebriated William Buchanan would be unable to get behind the wheel of an automobile, and was forced to take the streetcar, just as any lesser person might do.

William's parting left Elizabeth alone with her mother, and at that point Elizabeth's hours-long exercise in maintaining outward grace concluded for the evening.

"What was *that* all about?" she angrily asked her mother.

At least her mother didn't play games by responding with "What's *what* all about?" or "I simply don't know what you mean." Still, Katherine Buchanan apparently decided to maintain a touch of façade with her initial response.

"I thought it would be nice for him to have a Friday night dinner with someone from the Club rather than have to eat alone at the William Penn."

"I don't believe you for a second!" was Elizabeth's fuming reply through clenched teeth. "And besides, how do *you* know *anything* about him at all?"

Katherine was ready for that particular question.

"Well, of course I spoke with him during the Christmas party, as did your father. We thought…"

Elizabeth interrupted: "Well of course you spoke with him after you saw me talking to him, to try and find out as much as you could so you could try to push me towards him. *That's* what you mean to say!"

Elizabeth was shocked by her mother's reply as Katherine Buchanan shook her head.

"I talked with him *before* you ever did, I'll have you know."

For a brief moment Elizabeth was thrown off her angry track of questioning, but then she digested the unspoken significance of her mother's words.

"So *that's* why he came over in the first place to refill my drink and to talk with me," she responded slowly, her mind churning even as she was speaking. "*You* sent him over to me; he didn't just happen to wander up…"

"So what if I did?" Katherine interrupted, something she rarely did. "He happened to strike up a conversation with your father while I was standing there, and he seemed like such a nice young man, with such an important job…"

"I'm a married woman!" Elizabeth all but screamed at her mother. "You had *no right* to do that!"

Elizabeth's mother was ready with her response, as if the words and tone had been rehearsed and precisely shaped numerous times in her mind.

"*What* marriage? To some boy you dated in high school? Whom you married on a whim because the war started and you wanted to hook him before he went off to the service, just like your two Italian sisters-in-law did?"

Katherine's eyes narrowed as she continued.

"To a *husband*" – that one word carried mocking tones – "whom you haven't seen in seven months and won't see for who knows how many more months or even years? What kind of marriage is *that?*"

Elizabeth's eyes went towards one of the brandy snifters resting on the end table next to the wingback chair where Calvin had sat. She came so very, very close to grabbing that snifter and hurling it with all her strength against the wall, but in that last instant before she actually did so, she caught herself. She was just about say the most horrid things imaginable to her own mother when Katherine spoke again. This time, though, tears instantly came to Elizabeth's mother's eyes and her voice quivered as she continued.

"I only want the best for my daughter, and what you have now is *not* the best. You're married to some Italian boy you hardly know and barely were with before he went away. And even if he comes back, is he going to be the kind of husband you really want? Look at last year, when you insisted on bringing him to the Christmas party. I was watching you all night. You were so uncomfortable because you *knew* he didn't fit in with anyone else there. If it hadn't been for Pearl Harbor and him telling everyone that he was going to enlist in the Marines, nobody would have given him two seconds of their time."

Katherine paused to wipe away a streak of tears from her left cheek first, and then another from her right one.

"I watched you with Calvin last Saturday, and *that's* the kind of man you need to be with. Someone with an important job, who went to a good college and who has a bright future ahead of him. This war won't last forever, and even if Carlo comes back, he'll be behind a soda fountain or stocking shelves at some grocery market, or maybe working at some corner bar. Maybe he'll go out to Homestead and work in the steel mills. You won't have all of the finer things that you should have; that you grew up with. You'll just be one more Morningside or Bloomfield Italian wife, even though you're not even Italian!"

Elizabeth's mother let out an audible sob.

"My own daughter…" Her voice trailed off but after a brief pause she continued, her voice suddenly bearing the persuasive tones of a practiced lawyer delivering a closing argument.

"You can get your marriage annulled, and I promise you that no one will think you did anything wrong. You got engaged and then married in the heat of the moment, so soon after the war began, when girls all over were doing such crazy things without thinking them through."

Elizabeth's voice was surprisingly calm as she finally replied to this bombshell from her mother.

"I'm going to ask you to forget what you just said to me," she said evenly, "and not only that, I don't ever want you to say anything like that again to me."

Her eyes narrowed as she forcefully stared at her mother and added a single word.

"Ever."

Katherine Buchanan sniffed and quickly shook her head.

"I can't do that," she responded. "Your happiness and your future mean too much to me to let you ruin your entire life. Now is the perfect time for you to come to your senses and get out of that ridiculous marriage. An annulment will be so easy to get because you were really only with him for less than two weeks before he left, and…"

Katherine continued pleading with her daughter, but in Elizabeth's head her mother's voice became something like the static on the radio that overpowers any words being spoken underneath the high-pitched humming and crackling. Thinking back on this encounter, Elizabeth could never be quite sure when she slowly walked away from her still-pleading mother. She could recall only brief disjointed fragments from her mostly sleepless night, and nothing at all from any dreams she may have had. Even the details of the next morning were disturbingly vague.

Clarity came back to Elizabeth DeLuca's memory sometime around 2:00 on the afternoon of Saturday, December 19th, 1942 when she arrived at the DeLuca home. Just as Elizabeth's father-in-law had mused during his toast on that early May afternoon when his son Tony married Angela, an occasion that now felt as if it had taken place many years earlier, Elizabeth DeLuca would now be living in the home of Giuseppe and Rosalia DeLuca, along with her sister-in-law Angela.

Chapter 9

Elizabeth's New Year's Eve letter to Carlo crossed with the telegram that she would soon receive.

December 31, 1942

My darling Carlo,

I can't put into words how much I miss you on this New Year's Eve, as I do every single day. I can't help but think back to one year ago, when you and I ushered out that troubled year of 1941 that began this terrible war. We both wished that 1942 would be a much better year but deep in our hearts we knew that this year now concluding would be a very trying one for both of us.

Still, as this year gives way to 1943 only a couple of hours from now, I am trying to think about the good things that did happen during 1942; and of course, the best thing of all is that I am now your wife. The fates have kept us apart for so much of this year, but I can only hope that before too much longer passes we will be together.

Of course I'm not going out anywhere this evening to celebrate. I'm spending the evening with your mother and father, and Angela and Carmela, quietly at home. And that brings me to another reason for this letter. I hadn't yet mentioned this in any of my letters that I wrote in the past couple of weeks but it's time to tell you that I am now living at your parents' house, just as Angela has been. I would rather not go into all of the depressing details, but let's just say that I had a severe falling out with my mother and I think it's best that I no longer live in the same house with her. Even this latest conflict is really the continuation of a long string of tensions that go back to our wedding. I'm very sad about this, but at the same time your parents have made me feel welcome there, and together we can share our thoughts and prayers for your safety.

I don't know exactly where you are right now, and I know that you can't tell me. Just know that every second of every day, you are in my thoughts and in my heart, and I can't wait until we are together again.

By the time you receive this letter wherever you are, it will likely be well into January and this new year of 1943 will be underway. I pray that this will somehow be the concluding year of this war and that we will be reunited soon.

All my love to you,
Elizabeth

When Elizabeth wrote, "I don't know exactly where you are right now," she was exactly right. She had no way of knowing that by New Year's Eve, Carlo was no longer in the midst of combat on Guadalcanal. Instead, he was now convalescing in a Navy hospital in Pearl Harbor. More than three months would pass before Elizabeth's letter would finally catch up to her husband.

1943

Chapter 10

The Navy Department telegram that was delivered to the DeLuca home on the fifth day of this new year read:

REGRET TO INFORM YOU YOUR HUSBAND CORPORAL CARLO DELUCA WAS ON 24 NOVEMBER 1942 WOUNDED IN ACTION IN THE PACIFIC YOU WILL BE ADVISED AS REPORTS OF CONDITION ARE RECEIVED TO PREVENT POSSIBLE AID TO OUR ENEMIES DO NOT DIVULGE THE NAME OF HIS SHIP OR STATION=

Even after marrying Elizabeth during his furlough following boot camp, Carlo DeLuca had kept his parents' house as his official home of record. For this reason, the Western Union man delivered the telegram directly to the DeLuca home in Morningside, even though it was addressed to Elizabeth...who otherwise would have been living at her own parents' house if it hadn't been for that terrible falling-out with her mother several weeks earlier. Elizabeth was at work that Tuesday morning, as were Angela and Carmela and Giuseppe, so the miserable duty of receiving the horrific telegram fell to Rosalia DeLuca.

After Carlo's mother finished wailing and had composed herself enough to think clearly, she frantically telephoned the Dravo Shipyard where her husband had been working since the previous autumn. Almost fifteen minutes passed until Giuseppe's voice came on the other end, instantly causing Rosalia's anguished sobbing to resume. For close to a minute Giuseppe was convinced that one of his sons had been killed in action because his wife was unable to coherently form even two or three syllables. Finally, he was able to piece together the words "Carlo" and "wounded"; and even as Giuseppe began to worry about how badly his son had been wounded, he said a silent prayer that – as far as anyone knew – Carlo was still alive.

Giuseppe received permission to leave work early. The shipyard was located on Neville Island in the middle of the Ohio River, about ten miles downriver from downtown Pittsburgh. He waited impatiently for the next ferry to take him ashore on the north side of the Ohio, where the shipyard employees were required to park. Then he raced Carlo's '37 Packard Six that he was now driving through the twisting and turning roads, then back across the Allegheny River until he reached the Oakland neighborhood. He parked and then hurried inside the OPA offices.

At the first glimpse of her father-in-law, even before she noticed his ashen face, Elizabeth felt all of her strength and will instantly drained out of her. If she hadn't been sitting at her secretarial desk, she certainly would have collapsed to the ground. Tears instantly sprung to her eyes as Giuseppe approached.

Suddenly realizing the terrifying effect his unexpected appearance was having on his daughter-in-law, Giuseppe blurted out as quickly as he could:

"Carlo was wounded, not killed. We got the telegram." To make sure the words got through to Elizabeth, he repeated, "He was wounded, not killed. Back in November. That's all we know right now."

Giuseppe DeLuca then added, fighting back his own tears as his worry – and frustration – finally bubbled over, "I don't know why they took so long to let us know."

*   *   *

Elizabeth both wished and prayed that there was some way in which she could communicate directly with Carlo, but of course that was impossible. She took only slight comfort in the second telegram that arrived three days later informing her that Carlo had been evacuated to Hawaii after a short stay in a field hospital, and that his condition was reported as "stable and improving."

Later – much later – Elizabeth would look back on the initial dreadful telegram and find a touch of humor in the final sentence that strongly advised her not to disclose "the name of his ship or station" to prevent possible aid to the enemy. Even if Elizabeth had been overheard by an enemy spy in Oakland or Morningside or downtown Pittsburgh stating that her husband had been wounded on Guadalcanal, as she surmised, of course the Japanese knew for a fact that the Marines were fighting all over Guadalcanal and had been for months! She realized that the verbiage was standard and probably was automatically inserted into every single telegram informing a family back home that a loved one had been wounded or killed, but Elizabeth could still find some very dark humor in that passage when she so desperately needed to disrupt the horrid tension.

For now, all she could do was hold vigil during every waking moment she was at the DeLuca home. But even as Elizabeth was praying for Carlo's well-being and recovery, the questions, one after another, haunted her. Had he lost a limb? Had he been burned all over his body? And worst of all: had he suffered some sort of serious brain trauma and no longer would even know who Elizabeth was? Elizabeth realized that "wounded in action" was inclusive of the widest possible spectrum of possibilities, all the way from a minor nick by a Japanese bullet to miraculously still being alive despite the most severe and debilitating of wounds. Until she received further information, Elizabeth could only pray for the best but also prepare herself for the worst.

∗   ∗   ∗

Witnessing her sister-in-law's anguish created a maelstrom of her own trepidation for Angela. The back-and-forth tussle in North Africa showed no signs of ending as January of 1943 gave way to February. That meant, of course, that Tony was probably smack in the middle of the fight against the Axis, every single day. Several nights each week Angela's sleep was violently interrupted by at least one nightmare of Tony either killed or seriously wounded. Angela would wake up shaking and weeping, and on one occasion, also shrieking in agony. Elizabeth had rushed into Angela's bedroom that night and had stayed with her until daylight, neither one of them able to fall back to sleep.

Angela's fears for her own husband's safety turned out to be wrong. The DeLucas wound up receiving word from

Tony before they were given any further news about
Carlo's wounds or his recovery. His unit had been pulled
from the North African battlefields just after New Year's
Day and was then sent "somewhere else," as he had
phrased it in the letter that Angela received the second
week of February. Angela considered this surprise
appearance of the first letter from her husband in more
than three months the best Valentine's Day gift she could
possibly have received, given the circumstances of the war.

One week later, Elizabeth received an even happier
Valentine's Day gift herself, even though the lovers'
holiday had already occurred a few days earlier. The gift
came courtesy of another telegram, but this time the
missive read:

AM COMING HOME SOON CANNOT
PROVIDE DETAILS YET WILL WRITE OR
CALL WHEN I CAN CARLO=

Chapter 11

March 6, 1943

Each day, Elizabeth anxiously awaited further word from Carlo. She fretted every single minute she spent at work, knowing that if Carlo were able to place a long distance call to the DeLuca house anytime during normal working hours, she would miss that one opportunity to hear his voice.

She would race inside every single day after returning from work and immediately grab the stack of mail that Rosalia habitually placed on the end table next to Giuseppe's chair. Every single day she would look for that long-awaited V-mail letter from Carlo, but day after day no such letter appeared.

Finally the first Saturday of March arrived: a snow flurry-filled morning that saw the temperature dive from above freezing at midnight into the teens by daylight. Elizabeth, Angela, and Carmela all planned to brave the frigid weather and go see a movie that afternoon. *Star Spangled Rhythm* was now playing at the Loews Penn downtown. An afternoon spent with Bob Hope, Bing Crosby, Veronica Lake, Betty Hutton, and dozens of other stars in this extravagant production might just do the trick to get the girls' minds off of Carlo and Tony, and also Tony DeMarco – Carmela's Tony – who was believed to be over in England.

The morning mail delivery arrived just after 9:00 that morning, and the mailman had so many letters to deliver that he knocked loudly on the screen door rather than try a futile attempt to squeeze all of the mail into the tiny receptacle to the left of the front door. Carmela had been the one to answer the frantic knock, her heart leaping into her throat. When she saw that the person on the other side was the mailman and – thank God – not a Western Union man, she grabbed the stack of mail as quickly as she could to prevent too much of the late winter chill from invading the DeLuca house.

"There's a V-mail from Carlo!" Carmela joyously squealed, bringing Elizabeth sprinting down the stairs. Elizabeth had barely reached the bottom of the staircase when Carmela shouted, "There's another one!"

By the time Elizabeth reached the front door, Carmela had shouted "and another one!" two more times. In all, this Saturday morning bounty contained a total of six letters from Carlo to his wife, along with two he had written to his mother, one to his father, and another to Carmela.

Elizabeth wasn't alone when it came to the morning jackpot delivered by the mailman. Angela received three V-mail letters from Tony, and Carmela received four letters from Tony DeMarco. Michael had contributed three letters to the bounty, to each of his parents and the other to his sister. Two letters from Vinnie awaited anxious reading by his mother and one by his father. Giuseppe DeLuca also had a letter awaiting him from his son Tony, so all four of his boys had thought enough to write their pop.

All four women settled onto sofas and into chairs and began quickly reading their letters. Every ten or fifteen seconds, one of them would shout out some piece of news from the letter currently being read. When fifteen minutes or so had passed, they had all pieced together the tales of Carlo, Tony, Vinnie, and Michael DeLuca, as well as Tony DeMarco.

Carlo had been wounded two days before he and his fellow Marines would attempt to somehow celebrate Thanksgiving Day in the midst of the brutal battle against the Japanese, following a month of back-and-forth attacks by both sides. He left out any details of a specific operation or campaign, knowing that the censors would not only excise those sentences but probably take away a sizable surrounding portion just to be safe. He did state in the first letter, though, that he had been hit in his left shoulder by one Japanese bullet and barely a couple seconds later had been shot in his right shoulder as well.

Carlo was quickly taken to a field hospital on Guadalcanal, where he remained for three more weeks. He then was evacuated to a Navy hospital ship, and after another two weeks that ship began its perilous journey across the Pacific to the gigantic new Marine Corps hospital that had just opened at Pearl Harbor.

All along his journey, his wounds had continued to slowly heal; and by the time he reached Pearl Harbor, he was almost ready to go right back on the line, or to train for whatever island invasion would be next. The Marine Corps had different plans for Carlo, however, and he received orders to report to Camp Lejeune, North Carolina, where he would spend several months serving as a drill sergeant. He had been promoted from private first class to corporal just before the Guadalcanal campaign began, and had received word just before departing for

Pearl Harbor that he had been promoted again, this time to sergeant.

The first leg of Carlo's journey back would take him from Hawaii to somewhere along the mainland Pacific Coast. Elizabeth could tell that he was deliberately not divulging where he would land, nor by what means he was traveling. But the best news of all was what Elizabeth already knew from the telegram she received several weeks ago: Carlo would get a short furlough home in Pittsburgh before it was time to head south.

As with Carlo, Tony and Michael DeLuca were being careful not to disclose too much information in their letters. However, Angela picked up enough hints that Tony was now somewhere in England...perhaps even alongside Tony DeMarco, since Carmela's letters from her Tony contained some of the same details that her brother had related. Michael's letters contained fewer specifics than any of the others, but he seemed to be in England as well.

Elizabeth tried to piece together a timeline for when she might see Carlo hurrying up the front steps of the DeLuca house, the same as Tony had done back in August. For all she knew, today could even be the day! After a moment of entertaining such a delicious possibility, Elizabeth realized that more likely it would still be another couple weeks; perhaps a month or even longer. After all, she didn't know how Carlo would be crossing the Pacific back from Hawaii. Hopefully he would be doing so on some sort of transport plane, but they could always put him on a Navy or Merchant Marine ship instead, which would, of course, take much longer as the vessel zig-zagged its way eastward.

Then, once he arrived in Los Angeles or San Francisco or San Diego or wherever his destination was, Elizabeth also didn't know if he would be making his way to Pittsburgh via a transport plane or if he would be forced to travel by railroad. He might even be sent cross-country via some sort of military vehicle transport caravan. So while it was possible that Carlo could be showing up at any moment, if he had to endure traveling by ship followed by land, then his arrival was likely still a ways off.

How can I possibly stand all this anticipation? Elizabeth asked herself this question. The past two months have been bad enough with the gyrations of first hearing about Carlo being wounded and then anxiously awaiting any further word. Then it was the nearly unbearable several weeks of waiting after receiving Carlo's telegram until the treasure trove of V-mail letters arrived just today. How could she possibly bear yet another prolonged waiting period?

As it was, Elizabeth's attentions were soon diverted – at least in part – to unexpected drama in her own family.

Chapter 12

March 8, 1943

The following Monday Elizabeth was the first one awake in the DeLuca household. She tiptoed downstairs and opened the front door to retrieve the morning *Post-Gazette*. Elizabeth had already lit a Pall Mall and she settled into one of the chairs, figuring that she would wait until at least one more person in the household was awake before she began grinding any beans for the morning coffee.

A short article on the front page directly below the main headline caught her eye. "Admiral Hits War Job 'Slackers' " was the headline of this particular story, and the first few lines related some admiral's concern over an increase in absenteeism in the many war industries.

The word "slacker" immediately caused Elizabeth to think about her brother. Suddenly an eerie feeling came over her. Elizabeth would never fully understand what happened next, nor would anybody fully believe this part of her tale whenever she found herself discussing the events of the next few days.

She felt some sort of force actually draw her eyes away from the story she was reading, and she could actually feel her hands anxiously wanting to turn to another page inside the paper. All the while Elizabeth was wondering just what it was that she was feeling, she was aware almost in an otherworldly manner that she indeed was turning to another page of the morning newspaper.

She watched her hands fold the paper back as her eyes landed on another headline. Even before she read a single word of the story, she knew.

Sugar Ration Violations Charged

Bench warrants for the arrest of four alleged violators of the Second War Powers Act yesterday were authorized by Federal Judge J. W. Green because they were charged by OPA officials with unlawful handling of sugar in business transactions. The accused men are Stanley Croft, a retail grocer at 4483 Cole Street; William Buchanan, of 3311 King Avenue;...

In the months and years that followed, Elizabeth would often chastise herself when she would recall the flash of vindictive jubilation the very second she read her brother's name. Her mind's eye then instantly took flight and negotiated both time and space to be able to witness the very first horrified reaction of Katherine Buchanan when she received word of her precious son's impending arrest.

Later on, reliving these feelings of elation in the face of her own family's trials usually left Elizabeth feeling incredibly guilty. This was, after all, still her brother. No matter what horrible things Elizabeth's mother had said to her back in December, William himself had said or done little to intentionally and directly injure his sister. His callous selfishness and greediness disgusted Elizabeth, especially when so many others had answered the call of duty by enlisting or complying with their draft notice, or working in a war plant, or attending college, knowing that upon graduation they would almost certainly serve as an officer in one of the armed services. But directly injuring Elizabeth? William barely gave his sister the time of day or even a fleeting thought.

Elizabeth's guilty feelings about her spiteful reaction would usually evaporate when her mind insisted on continuing with the tale of this Monday morning and she would then be forced to painfully relive what happened as soon as she arrived at work.

"Mr. Talbot wants to see you," Mrs. Watkins, the secretarial supervisor, tersely stated even before Elizabeth could get settled at her desk. Suddenly filled with trepidation, Elizabeth meekly complied. She could feel clammy perspiration all over her body as she followed Mrs. Watkins down the hallway to the personnel manager's office.

Mr. Talbot wasted no time.

"I'm afraid that we must terminate your position here, effectively immediately," the personnel manager declared in tones that curiously sounded both menacing and disinterested at the same time.

"Did I do something wrong?" Elizabeth blurted out.

"Your brother did," came the sharp rebuttal, sounding as if Elizabeth had no right to even ask for elaboration on her dismissal.

Elizabeth's right hand flew to her mouth. Until Mr. Talbot mentioned her brother, she hadn't even entertained the thought that her brother's impending arrest would have any direct impact on her, let alone her job. But now it was all so clear. The article had mentioned that William and his partners in crime had been charged by OPA officials. And where did she work? The OPA, of course!

"Mr. Talbot, I had nothing to do with it!" Elizabeth protested. "I don't even live in the same house with my brother anymore! I didn't know anything about this at all..."

Elizabeth's voice trailed off, her last sentence spoken with far less conviction than her first two. The truth was that Elizabeth *did* know about her brother's black market dealings. She may not have known the details, but all the while Elizabeth lived at her mother's house William had taken no pains at all to disguise the big picture of his activities from his sister.

Mr. Talbot doesn't need to know any of that, she quickly told herself. This was all so unfair!

"That may be the case," Mr. Talbot declared tersely, "but the facts are that the brother of an OPA secretary has engaged in very serious black market activity. We simply cannot afford the appearances of impropriety within this office."

"But the article I read said that he sold sugar to some grocery market without getting ration coupons back in return! I don't even see how I *could* have had any part in that, even if I did do something wrong. It's not like I stole ration books and gave them to him!"

The frustration boiled over as tears formed in Elizabeth's eyes. She *hated* this little man, especially for so unjustly bringing her to tears!

"I didn't do anything wrong!" Elizabeth was close to yelling now.

"Mrs. DeLuca," Mr. Talbot responded, emphasizing Elizabeth's last name in a manner that made it abundantly clear that he expected nothing less than black market dealings from an Italian…never mind that neither Elizabeth nor even her brother were Italian.

"You may argue all you want," the personnel manager continued, "but the fact remains that you are being dismissed effective immediately. You will follow Mrs. Watkins back to your desk where you will collect your things, and then you will be shown out of the building."

With that final statement, Mr. Talbot looked away from Elizabeth back to some piece of paper on his desk and kept his eyes glued on that sheet until he heard the door to his office close following Elizabeth's departure.

* * *

"That is so unfair!" Angela commiserated with Elizabeth that evening.

"I know," Elizabeth said dejectedly. "It's" – she struggled for the right words – "it's almost like my mother somehow got revenge on me. William gets arrested, or is about to get arrested, I don't even know. And *I* wind up losing my job!"

"Haven't you called to find out if your brother has been arrested yet?" Angela interrupted.

Elizabeth shook her head.

"I don't want to talk to my mother, or William, or anybody. Even my father; he's involved in black market dealings and is as guilty as my brother is. I'd be surprised if they weren't in cahoots on this whole thing with the black market sugar, but somehow my father wasn't implicated."

"Maybe they were," Angela mused. She and Elizabeth were alone in the kitchen, each enjoying a cigarette and slowly sipping an after-dinner cup of coffee. The coffee supply in the DeLuca household was dwindling, and Giuseppe had no coffee ration coupons remaining until his next allotment. One pound of coffee every five weeks didn't go very far, that was for sure. Angela allowed herself a private thought that perhaps a bit of black market coffee would be welcome if that could be arranged; but given what had just happened to her sister-in-law over illegal dealings, she didn't dare put voice to those wishful musings.

"I wonder what will happen to him?" Angela contemplated. "Do you think they'll put him in jail?"

Elizabeth shrugged.

"I don't know," she replied. She had a fleeting image of her hoity-toity brother locked up in a jail cell like a common thief, but quickly forced that vision from her head. In the aftermath of losing her OPA job because of William's illicit dealings, Elizabeth could only entertain the worst possible desires for her brother's fate. Elizabeth believed in fate, however, and was convinced that too much hatred and ill wishes for her brother – no matter how well-deserved – could easily backfire on her.

Or Carlo. She shuddered at the thought of wishing only the worst possible outcome for her brother, only to soon learn that Carlo's ship homeward from Pearl Harbor had been torpedoed, or his plane shot down, or any one of a thousand other terrible outcomes.

"Did you find out yet what your brother actually did?" Angela loved juicy gossip and pressed for some sordid revelations.

"You know how we have ration coupons we have to take to the market for sugar and coffee and all that?" Elizabeth began.

"Uh-huh."

"Well apparently those markets, when they get sugar themselves to sell to us, they have to turn over some sort of commercial Sugar Purchase Certificate to the place where they bought the sugar from. I guess they're rationed sugar and everything else just like we are, but of course they get a lot more so they can sell all those goods to regular people."

Angela cocked her head, not quite following yet.

"Anyway," Elizabeth continued, "William knew some guy who worked at a soda pop bottling plant over on the North Side. They use lots of sugar, right? So William goes to where this guy works late one night and he and this guy load 4,000 pounds of sugar…"

"Into your father's Packard?" Angela interrupted.

"No," Elizabeth responded, "into a truck. I guess he borrowed it; I'm not really sure."

Elizabeth was slightly piqued at the interruption. Angela did that a lot – Carmela also – and Elizabeth wasn't fond of being interrupted mid-sentence, courtesy of her own proper upbringing.

"Anyway," she began again, "William takes the truck to some grocery market and unloads all the sugar. What's *supposed* to happen if this were all on the up-and-up is that the grocery man hands over his Sugar Purchase Certificate along with paying for the sugar, just like we do with ration coupons when we go to the market. But he doesn't; plus, the sugar was stolen from the soda pop plant, anyway. This means the grocery man can sell all of this extra sugar on the black market if he wants, or just have a lot of extra stock when all the other markets run out until the next rationing period starts. Plus, he still can use his Sugar Purchase Certificate to buy even more sugar the legal way."

"Wow," Angela said, now fully understanding the story. "I wonder how your brother cooked up that scheme?"

Elizabeth shook her head.

"I'm not sure."

Suddenly Elizabeth was very, very tired of discussing her brother, black market sugar, or pretty much anything else related to this despicable situation.

"I wonder where Carmela is?" Elizabeth asked, desperate to change the subject.

"I dunno," Angela shrugged. "She's been coming home late a lot lately."

"Is she working double shifts?" Elizabeth wondered aloud, knowing that Angela didn't actually know the answer to that question.

"I dunno," Angela repeated.

*   *   *

"I need you to be there with me," Katherine Buchanan pleaded over the telephone. The mother had been the one to break the months-long silence since Elizabeth had moved out to place a call to her daughter. The haughty sense of entitlement was gone, at least for now.

Barely a month had passed since William's arrest, but when it came to black market dealings, the wheels of justice apparently moved swiftly. Three weeks after his arrest, he and his cronies were tried and convicted in less than two hours. His sentencing was quickly set for one week later: tomorrow.

"Please," Katherine Buchanan added.

Elizabeth should have felt an overwhelming sense of redemption in light of her mother's begging. Yet as her mother continued pleading for her daughter to be by her side when William was sentenced, the dominant emotion that enveloped Elizabeth was pity. Not so much pity for her mother, or her brother, or the situation he was – they were – in. Elizabeth's pity was for what had been lost; what should have been. The Buchanan family possessed modest inherited wealth and lived a life of relative ease. Yet her brother always wanted an edge; he had to be the most deviously shrewd one around who would somehow wind up with an outsized share that exceeded the normal rewards of any actual work on his part. That insolence had gotten him expelled from college, and now might land him in jail.

Their father might have steered William in a different direction. He, too, had danced on the edge of dangerous endeavors during the beginning of the Depression that coincided with the latter years of Prohibition, but he came through unscathed. Instead of breathing a huge sigh of relief and remaining on the respectable side of the law, however, the black market opportunities that surfaced soon after the beginning of the war were too much for Spencer Buchanan to resist. Now, however, he had his son to do his dirty work while he contented himself with pulling the strings from backstage. Elizabeth didn't yet know if her father had been directly involved in this particular black market sugar scheme. Even if he hadn't, however, Elizabeth thought back to the conversation in the Packard on the way to last December's Christmas party at the Witherspoon Club. William might have been the one to cook up the scheme to bring back illicit liquor from West Virginia and Ohio, and was the one who actually did the dirty work. But Spencer Buchanan had absolutely given the blessing for his son to engage in not only those illegal activities, but countless others.

Even Katherine Buchanan shared the blame for William's fate; at least that's how Elizabeth saw it. To Elizabeth's mother, the pursuit of wealth and status trumped all else. William had been expelled from college, and Katherine Buchanan wouldn't hear of a future for her son where he would simply do an honest day's work in return for modest wages. He was a *Buchanan*, and in her mind that name was interchangeable around Pittsburgh with "Carnegie" or "Mellon." Elizabeth could clearly see how delusional her mother was, but while living under her mother's roof, Elizabeth had been powerless to influence her mother otherwise.

"Fine," Elizabeth finally responded to her mother's pleas, as much out of weariness as for any other reason.

She could no longer daydream about her brother being sentenced to a huge fine, or jail, or whatever the judge had in store for him. She just wanted this brief, sorry chapter of her life over so she could get back to the joyous anticipation of Carlo's homecoming.

Quickly, though, Elizabeth regretted agreeing to her mother's appeal. For the rest of this unseasonably warm Tuesday evening, Elizabeth couldn't help but envision a nightmare scenario that began with her brother William somehow getting off with a mere slap on his hand. In these terrible visions, Elizabeth turned to her mother inside the courtroom only to be greeted by that same soulless, frigid smile that Katherine Buchanan had offered her daughter so many times before. The message behind the horrid smile was a reprise of that hateful rejoinder to Elizabeth last August, this time declaring victory for her son despite him having been caught red-handed and then convicted.

Wealth has its privileges, Elizabeth. I thought you had learned that growing up. But privilege is something that can easily be squandered, as you've done…against my advice, I might add. Maybe this will be an important lesson for you.

* * *

Reality was very different than Elizabeth's worried vision. Moments after the judge gaveled court into session, he began pronouncing his sentence on each of the guilty defendants. Elizabeth watched the blood drain from her brother's face when the judge began with the grocer, Stanley Croft.

"Mr. Croft: after pleading guilty to the charges, you have cooperated fully with the authorities. This court hereby fines you fifty dollars, and that represents the total sum of your penalty."

Elizabeth could see her brother now glaring at Stanley Croft, and the grocer doing everything he could to avoid eye contact with William.

"Mr. Buchanan," the judge proclaimed. William hesitated for a moment and then rose to his feet.

"Mr. Buchanan: in addition to your conviction of crimes under the Second War Powers Act, this court has received information from Mr. Croft that you, sir, have illegally and immorally paid to obtain unwarranted 4-F status. This court sentences you to a fine of five thousand dollars. Additionally, your service classification will be immediately changed to 1-A, and since you are now available for unrestricted military service, you will be consigned to the custody of the United States Army for immediate enlistment processing."

Elizabeth watched her brother sink back into his seat, but a split-second later her attention was diverted to her mother, sitting to Elizabeth's immediate left. Katherine Buchanan began such tortured wailing that the bailiff was ordered to remove her from the courtroom so the judge could continue sentencing the remaining two defendants. Elizabeth remained in the courtroom with her ashen-faced father, but her mother's anguished yowling out in the hallway could easily be heard inside.

Elizabeth could only think that if Katherine Buchanan's son-in-law had been killed in action on Guadalcanal instead of being wounded, leaving her daughter a widow, this grief-stricken sobbing reaction would be nowhere in sight.

Chapter 13

April 21, 1943

The blaring headline of the afternoon's *Pittsburgh Press* confirmed the horrifying news that had broken earlier in the day on all of the radio news programs:

FLIERS WHO BOMBED TOKYO PUT TO DEATH BY JAPANESE

"BARBAROUS EXECUTIONS ANNOUNCED" read the secondary headline, leading into the United Press story that related President Roosevelt's official announcement of the executions. As with so much of the war's news, many of the details were frustratingly lacking. The War Department believed that out of the eighty total Doolittle Raid flyers, eight of them had fallen into the hands of the Japanese. United Press was reporting that all eight had been sentenced to death but also that the Japanese had commuted the death sentences for some of them. The War Department, however, did not have the details on who or how many may have been spared.

Elizabeth DeLuca couldn't help but put herself in the place of some poor flyer's wife or mother, probably secretly knowing for some time that her loved one had been captured by the Japanese but now not knowing if he had been executed or might still be alive as a prisoner.

How many more weeks or months, or even years, would pass until his fate was finally revealed? Elizabeth shuddered at that thought.

Elizabeth was reading the front section of the *Press* that contained this horrifying story as well as a companion one that finally related some of the details of the raid that had occurred just over one year earlier. All the while she was reading, Elizabeth's mind was partially in the past, recalling that the daring Doolittle Raid had occurred only one week prior to her wedding…which of course reminded Elizabeth that her wedding anniversary was coming up in only four more days, and still no word from or appearance by Carlo. Every day that passed without further news made Carlo's "AM COMING HOME SOON…" telegram and his V-mail letters seem more of a mirage than reality. Elizabeth could only hope – could only pray – that he had been diverted to some other mission and hadn't been shot down or torpedoed on his way back to the States.

To try and take her mind off of the war – and Carlo's fate – Elizabeth's eyes shifted to another front page article that told of the upcoming rationing points reduction for frozen foods; especially larger, commercial-sized containers. Even though, the article stated, this points reduction was intended to aid hotels, restaurants, and other commercial users of frozen foods, the story also noted that "housewives as well as institutional users" were also permitted to purchase the larger sizes.

Reading about anything to do with wartime rationing, however, unfailingly took Elizabeth's thoughts to her own family. She had deliberately avoided any contact with her mother since William's sentencing two weeks earlier, so Elizabeth had no idea if her brother had been forcibly sent off to Army basic training yet. For that matter, Elizabeth had no idea how her mother was coping with this seismic disruption to the order of her own personal universe; the cold slap in the face that wealth apparently isn't immutably paired with privileges, especially ill-begotten ones.

Elizabeth was still pondering what might be occurring at the Buchanan household in Highland Park even as her eyes still scanned the *Press* for other stories to take her mind off of her constant worries, when she heard a series of rapid knocks on the front door. Her head jerked up a split second before Angela's did. Elizabeth caught Angela's eye for a fraction of a moment, and then she bolted from the sofa and raced to the front door to open it. For the first time in almost a year, Elizabeth DeLuca was face-to-face with her husband.

Watching Elizabeth fling herself into Carlo's arms as she stammered, "Oh my God I'm so glad to see you!" instantly took Angela back to her Tony's brief homecoming six months earlier. For a fleeting second jealousy flared in Angela, wishing that it were her own husband who had miraculously appeared on the other side of the door rather than Elizabeth's. The jealousy passed quickly, though. This was her own husband's younger brother, alive and apparently well after being wounded on Guadalcanal. How could she not be happy for him, and for Elizabeth?

Elizabeth was still fiercely hugging Carlo as Rosalia DeLuca hurried out of the kitchen into and then across the living room. Rosalia didn't wait for Elizabeth to release Carlo; instead, she threw herself into the hug from the side. For close to another full minute Carlo, his wife, and his mother all clutched one another on this Wednesday springtime afternoon.

More than a minute passed until the cluster of hugging DeLucas finally let go and shuffled a few feet into the house. Upon entering the house, Carlo spied his sister-in-law, and greeted her with a weary, somewhat subdued:

"Howya doooin' Angela?"

As Angela replied with, "I'm good; I'm so glad that you're back home!" she took in the sight of her brother-in-law. For someone who had been wounded in combat, Carlo looked good; at least Angela thought so. He was wearing his green winter service uniform, which no doubt was keeping him warm enough in that afternoon's drizzly fifty-degree weather. He didn't seem too skinny, so despite the tribulations of his time on Guadalcanal, the Navy and Marines had apparently been feeding him well since his evacuation.

Still, Angela thought after only that first glimpse, there was something a bit "off" about her husband's younger brother. She didn't know him all that well, but Angela had spent enough time with the DeLuca family that she had developed a pretty good sense for what was normal with each of her husband's brothers. Maybe it was that far-away stare in his eyes as he gazed about the living room that he hadn't seen in almost an entire year...

"I will make you a meal right away," Rosalia's voice interrupted Angela's thoughts. Angela watched her mother-in-law hurry into the kitchen. Dinner would be about two hours from now, as soon as Giuseppe DeLuca returned home from work right around 6:00. But a good Italian mother would no more tell her returning Marine son that food wouldn't be forthcoming for several more hours than she would invite Hitler or Tojo to join them for supper this very evening.

Elizabeth's sobbing had finally slowed, but as soon as Carlo turned to give his wife yet another hug, a fresh bout of tears and weeping overtook Elizabeth. She could do little more than throw herself into his arms again, weeping uncontrollably. Carlo held his wife tight, but Angela – staring at the two of them from about five feet away – detected a pained look on Carlo's face, as if he were suddenly uncomfortable with the very close proximity of his own wife.

Finally, Elizabeth's crying slowed to an occasional blubber. She released her tight hold on Carlo, replacing the hug with her left hand gripping her husband's right arm as the two of them sank onto the sofa. Elizabeth finally noticed what Angela had already detected: Carlo's distant, quizzical stare as he continued to gaze around the living room of the house where he had lived all his life, as if seeing it for the very first time.

Carlo's gaze shifted to Elizabeth, and he locked eyes with her as he spoke.

"I can't believe...I don't think it's sunk in yet...I mean, I can't believe that..."

He left the jumbled string of half-sentences unfinished, yet Elizabeth instantly knew what her husband was trying to say.

He couldn't believe that he was finally home, safe and sound...for now, anyway.

*   *   *

"Nah, I wasn't too worried," Carlo said, though his words were somewhat muffled since his mouth was half-filled with mashed potatoes as he spoke. He was about five minutes into the narrative of his evacuation from Guadalcanal to the Navy hospital in Hawaii, at Pearl Harbor. Angela had asked Carlo if he had been scared zig-zagging across more than 3,000 miles of ocean aboard a Navy hospital ship that would have made a nice, juicy target for a Japanese sub, or perhaps a Jap dive-bomber flying off of an aircraft carrier roaming out there in the Pacific.

The truth was that the journey had been a particularly worry-filled one for Carlo and the hundreds of other wounded Marines, soldiers, and sailors who were being ferried away from the island. They were all in uncharted waters, so to speak. Guadalcanal was the first significant offensive in the Pacific made by U.S. forces against their fearsome enemy, which meant that this was the first time large numbers of wounded Americans needed to be continually evacuated from the battlefield all the way back to the distant hospitals being set up for their further care. Until the Navy hospital ship docked in Hawaii, many of the wounded men aboard the ship – including Carlo – expected a General Quarters announcement at any moment, warning of an impending Japanese attack. For weeks afterwards, Carlo's sleep was interrupted two or three times each night as he abruptly awoke from one nightmare scenario or another in which he was back on the hospital ship as it was bombed or torpedoed.

Carlo's family didn't need to know any of this, though. Resigned fears aside, he had made it safely back to Hawaii from Guadalcanal and then once again across the Pacific aboard a returning troop ship. He was here; he was home. That was all that mattered.

That night, after gathering with the rest of the family around the Admiral radio and listening to Tommy Dorsey's program and then Eddie Cantor on NBC Red, Carlo and Elizabeth excused themselves to head upstairs shortly after 9:30 p.m. Elizabeth was powerless against the embarrassment that she knew had turned her face crimson as they said their good nights. *Everyone* in the DeLuca living room, including Carlo's parents, knew what was about to transpire. To their credit, no one asked an embarrassing question such as "Where are you two going so early?" Angela caught Elizabeth's eye, but she didn't say anything either, nor did she even yield a knowing smirk. Carmela had departed shortly after dinner, fortunately for Elizabeth, who was certain that Carlo's brassy sister would have been the one to offer some sort of pointed, off-color remark.

Upstairs, in Carlo's tiny room, he began casually undressing with the lamps and overhead light still on. Elizabeth walked over to the light switch to shut off the overhead light and then moved towards the side of the bed closest to the door to shut off that lamp.

"Nah, leave it," Carlo said.

She looked over towards her husband.

"The lamp; leave it on, and the other one too," he added, just in case his wife didn't comprehend his first utterance.

Elizabeth was taken aback by his request...or demand, or whatever it was. Not that they had been able to spend much time in bed as man and wife, thanks to this horrid war, but each time had been in a pitch-black room: nighttime outside, and no lights on inside.

"I just wanna look at you," Carlo added, apparently feeling that some sort of explanation was necessary to assuage his wife's puzzlement.

"C'mere," he added, but Elizabeth didn't immediately move towards him.

"C'mere," he repeated, though this second request had an edge to his words; a demand much more than a request.

This time Elizabeth complied, taking a half-dozen steps across the tiny room to where Carlo stood by the chair where he had dropped his uniform jacket and shirt. He was still wearing his khaki undershirt and his uniform trousers, along with his socks and spit-shined shoes.

Elizabeth reached her husband. He slipped his left arm behind her and gruffly pulled her towards him. Their lips met and to Elizabeth's surprise, his kisses were more fervent than they had ever been before. She could sense an urgency in her husband, as if many months of pent-up desire for his wife combined with the sheer relief of making it home alive were suddenly overflowing.

Carlo roughly ground his face into Elizabeth's as they kissed. At first the sensation was not only unfamiliar, but also extremely unsettling. Elizabeth felt as if she was kissing a stranger for the very first time.

Soon, though, the strangeness itself became arousing, and urgency began to overtake Elizabeth as she felt waves of lusty desire percolate and then wash over her. She began to pull Carlo into her but she was shocked when he immediately reached behind her and lifted her slightly off the ground, and then took four or five steps towards the bed. He all but threw her onto the bed as he hastily opened his brass Marine Corps-issue belt buckle. He quickly thrust his trousers and khaki underwear downwards – though he didn't remove them, he left them bunched around his ankles – and then brusquely forced both of his hands underneath Elizabeth's skirt. Finding the top side edges of her panties, he pulled them down and off of her legs in a swift motion only a split-second before he leaned forward and abruptly entered her.

Elizabeth might have been frightened by a Carlo DeLuca she had never before seen. Instead she found herself exhilarated as he rapidly thrust into her, still standing besides the bed instead of being on top of Elizabeth as he had done every time before. The lights were on in the room, but Elizabeth's eyes were tightly shut as she surrendered to a sense of erotic ecstasy that she had never before experienced.

It wasn't until after they had finished this first time (a much more sedate encore followed twenty minutes later) that Elizabeth realized that Carlo had neglected to use a condom.

Chapter 14

The next day Carlo and Elizabeth remained at the house until lunchtime. Rosalia DeLuca fussed over her son from the moment he appeared at breakfast throughout the entire morning. Angela called in sick from the WPB, feeling guilty all the while that she had just done so for her brother-in-law but hadn't even tried last August for her own husband, other than the day of his departure. But she had still been a relatively new employee at the WPB back in August during Tony's furlough, and had been afraid to endanger that precious job. Now, months later, she was well aware that almost every other WPB secretary called in sick whenever her husband or brother or some other close relative was home on furlough, with no repercussions. So Angela felt no compunction whatsoever in doing the same.

No such luck for Giuseppe DeLuca, however. Following his usual early breakfast, he retrieved his lunch pail that Rosalia had packed and drove off to the Dravo Shipyards, just as he did every weekday and also on Saturdays. Elizabeth watched her father-in-law hesitate as he donned his overcoat to ward off the morning chill that was so unwelcome by this late April date. He seemed to want to offer an explanation for why he couldn't call in sick just as Angela had just done, and spend precious time with his son while Carlo was home on furlough. Elizabeth noticed Giuseppe actually shake his head rapidly a few times as if trying to eject the impulse to spill whatever it was that was on his mind.

By now, they all knew that Giuseppe was working on something very important for the war effort down at the

Dravo Shipyards. Rumors circulated that the workers were building some revolutionary type of landing vehicle that would be used when the time came to invade Europe, as well as during future island invasions in the Pacific. Giuseppe was, of course, close-mouthed about such details, and every person in the DeLuca household knew better than to press him about what were apparently highly sensitive war secrets.

After a rich lunch of stew that Rosalia DeLuca had begun making the previous night, Carlo and Elizabeth went for a walk around the neighborhood. The temperature had climbed only a little bit further from the morning's chill, but the clear skies and sunshine made the forty-five degree afternoon pleasantly comfortable as they walked.

"I saw Maude Ringgold at the Christmas party," Elizabeth offered. "You know, Maude Wilson from Peabody?" she added, referring to her friend's maiden name.

"Oh yeah," Carlo added. "She married that guy who went to Allderdice who she was going with during high school, right? Oliver? Played football and baseball?"

"Uh-huh," Elizabeth nodded. "He's being assigned to Camp Kilmer in New Jersey for a couple of months, and she's going with him."

"Oh yeah?" Carlo replied. After pondering the news for a moment, he added:

"She must be happy, huh?"

"Definitely," Elizabeth agreed. She almost added what she had immediately thought at the time Maude shared the news: that the joy of being together despite the war would be cut short when the Army eventually ordered him elsewhere. But there was no sense in offering that sentiment, even though it had been Maude Ringgold herself who had spoken words to that effect.

"Who else have you seen?" Carlo asked as they turned the corner from Morningside Avenue, the neighborhood's main street, onto Hampton Street. Elizabeth gave Carlo a rundown of the Peabody girls she had encountered during the past eleven months and what she knew of their sweethearts, husbands, and brothers who were off at war.

"You should have been here back in August when Tony was here," she mused, then quickly realized what she had said. She nervously looked over at her husband. Fortunately, he accepted Elizabeth's words with a good-sized helping of dark, bitter humor.

"Yeah, well…I sure woulda liked to have been here, but I was up to my eyeballs in Japs at the time."

"Oh my God, I'm so sorry…" Elizabeth blurted out.

Carlo shook his head and scrunched his lips in that "don't worry about it" manner.

"Nah, that's okay. Seriously, I really woulda wanted to be here while Tony was back; it's a shame I wasn't."

Elizabeth looked at the ground in front of her.

"I know," she said quietly, before adding once again, "Sorry…"

"So how was he? Tony?" Carlo asked as he crushed the remnants of a just-finished Chesterfield into the sidewalk.

Elizabeth looked back towards her husband.

"Pretty good. We all went out that first night to the Crawford Grill; ten or eleven of us, including Carmela."

"Yeah? How was it?"

Elizabeth struggled with how to respond to that question. She instinctively wanted to answer "it was fun," but for one thing, she herself hadn't had a particularly enjoyable time that evening. She had been grateful to get away from her mother's house for a few hours and be in the company of people other than the OPA secretaries at work. But with Carlo away at war, and not having anybody to dance with, the evening had been…just okay.

Besides, if she used words and phrases such as "fun" or "the place was jumping" or "we all had a great time," how would Carlo take such a sentiment? As he had reminded her only a moment ago, Tony's visit had coincided with the first days of the Guadalcanal invasion. The Marines had miraculously met little initial resistance due to the luck of landing under the cover of bad weather, but the vicious clashes with the Japanese defenders of the island quickly followed as they moved inland. How would Carlo truly feel about news of his wife, his sister-in-law – even his own brother and sister – laughing and boozing and dancing the night away as he was encountering the feared enemy for the first time on some tiny island thousands of miles from home?

"It was good," she finally quietly replied.

Both Carlo and Elizabeth felt the need to change the subject. Noticing that they would shortly be approaching King Avenue as they crossed from Morningside into the tonier Highland Park neighborhood, Carlo slowed his pace as he lit another cigarette and then halted. As soon as Elizabeth noticed that Carlo had stopped, she did likewise.

"You never told me in that letter you wrote on New Year's Eve exactly why you moved out of your parents' house," Carlo said quietly. "You said that you had a big falling-out, or something like that, with your mother, but that was all. So what happened?"

Elizabeth hesitated. The full story – the true story – starred Katherine Buchanan as a horrible, almost evil human being. Ever since her brother's arrest and conviction, though, Elizabeth saw her mother more as a pathetic creature caught up in a never-ending cycle of dishonesty and selfishness driven by her unquenchable desires.

Even more: to bare her soul to her husband about the schism with her mother, Elizabeth would have to confess her lengthy, intimate Christmas party conversation with Calvin McKinnon and then the aftermath of her mother's dinner invitation to him. And, of course, the full story also included Katherine Buchanan's disgusting plea to Elizabeth to have her marriage to Carlo annulled so she could land a "more worthy" suitor such as the Georgetown man. As the months passed, Elizabeth felt more and more confident that she had done nothing at all wrong the evening of the Christmas party. The machinations had been entirely concocted by Katherine Buchanan, both at the party itself when Katherine steered the young man towards her daughter, and then certainly with that surprise dinner invitation the following week.

Yet during both the Christmas party and six days later at the Buchanan home, even though unknown at the time to Elizabeth, Carlo DeLuca was recuperating from not one but two bullet wounds suffered during the terrible fighting on Guadalcanal. How would he react to Elizabeth confessing that she had spent an entire hour deep in discussion with a handsome young government man – a stateside government man – and that the conversation had emboldened Elizabeth's mother to lay her attempted dinner invitation trap the following Friday evening?

Carlo would almost certainly blow up at Elizabeth upon hearing her story...and to Elizabeth's way of thinking, he would be fully justified in doing so, even though nothing had even come close to happening between Calvin and her. She simply couldn't risk sharing the full story with Carlo, even though she had done nothing wrong.

"It was all about my brother," she finally replied after a short hesitation. "When I found out that my father had paid off the draft board men to make William 4-F..."

Elizabeth paused as she struggled for the right words.

"Even though I didn't know yet that you had already been wounded by then," she finally continued, "we all knew for months that you were almost certainly over there on Guadalcanal. You were risking your life every single day, and he was just sitting at home doing all of his dirty black market business..."

She swallowed, pausing for a brief second before continuing.

"...and then my mother said something to me about wealth having its privilege, and that's why William deserved to stay out of the Army, and that I had squandered all of my privileges when I married you...or something like that..."

Elizabeth went on for a little while, trying to put into words the terrible bitterness and disenchantment she had immediately felt as her mother's haughty words. This part was all true, and was easily told to Carlo without venturing into the role that Calvin McKinnon and the Witherspoon Club Christmas Party had played leading up to the terrible climactic encounter.

"I just decided then and there, right on the spot, that I couldn't live under the same roof with her anymore. I remembered what your father had said at Angela's and Tony's wedding about me maybe also living at your house one of these days while you were still gone."

She looked sadly over at her husband.

"And that's what I did."

That last part of Elizabeth's explanation, however, was untrue. Her decision to move to the DeLuca home, in fact, hadn't come until after her mother's appeal to Elizabeth to have her marriage to Carlo annulled, effectively declaring it a terrible mistake that desperately needed to be undone. She might have shared that final straw with Carlo while still leaving the Calvin McKinnon angle out of the story. Perhaps some day in the future, however, there would be a reconciliation between mother and daughter. In that event, Carlo's knowledge of Katherine Buchanan's appalling words would, of course, poison any semblance of a normal relationship between Carlo and his mother-in-law. Thus, Elizabeth decided on the spot that she would take those inexcusable, vicious words to her grave without her husband ever knowing of them.

Carlo couldn't shake the feeling that his wife was leaving something out of the story…something important, in fact. Yet he decided not to press the issue.

"I guess I don't blame you," he replied as he offered Elizabeth a Chesterfield, which she accepted. "Especially how things turned out with your brother getting arrested and then sent off to the Army, anyway."

"Let's turn back," he continued as he absentmindedly executed a drill-perfect about-face movement, turning away from King Avenue as though by venturing a few more steps across the neighborhood boundary between Morningside and Highland Park, he would be delivering Elizabeth back into the poisonous dominion of Katherine Buchanan from which she had escaped.

"While I was still living there," Elizabeth quietly mused as she followed Carlo's lead and turned back down Hampton Street, "if I didn't have my job at the OPA to go to every day, I think I would have gone crazy. At least when they fired me because of William, I was already living at your house. I can't even imagine being trapped in my mother's house after losing my job…"

Elizabeth's voice trailed off before continuing.

"Believe me, now it's nothing like it was with my mother right after you left, before I got the job, but…"

Seeing the confused look on Carlo's face, she backtracked to clarify what she was referring to.

"I mean now, living at *your* house. It's not that long since I lost my job, and ever since then there's always been the chance every single day that this would be the day you finally came home. So that kept me occupied. But…"

She paused again, seeming to struggle for the right words.

"I know this might sound bad, and I don't mean it that way, but I don't want to just sit around your mother's house day after day, even though it's nothing like having to put up with my mother before I went to work at the OPA. So I guess I'll go find another job…"

She choked out the additional few words.

"…after you leave again."

"You know what?" A thought had suddenly come to Carlo.

"Huh?"

"You know how you said that Maude Wilson was gonna go with her husband to Camp Kilmer for a coupl'a months?"

Elizabeth immediately knew what Carlo was going to say next.

"I hear that Camp Lejeune has married sergeants' billets, so why don't you come down there with me? There's gonna be some times that I'll be out bivouacking or doin' night maneuvers. But at least some of the time I figure I'll be off in the evenings, and maybe even on Sundays. So we can spend at least a little bit of time together. Just like Maude Wilson – I mean Maude Ringgold, I guess – said about goin' to Camp Kilmer with Oliver."

Elizabeth was stunned into silence. After no response was forthcoming from her, Carlo halted just before turning onto Morningside Avenue and turned towards his wife, who also stopped in her tracks.

"So whaddya think?" he asked.

Still silence.

"About coming with me?" he added.

After close to half a minute more of silence, at the point when Carlo DeLuca was ready to think that for some unknown or inexplicable reason his own wife was dismayed at the thought of being at his side for however brief a time it might be, Elizabeth finally responded.

"Do you really think it's possible?"

* * *

For the remainder of Carlo's furlough, both Carlo and Elizabeth worked feverishly on one task or another related to her accompanying him to Camp Lejeune. As soon as they returned home from their walk, Carlo immediately hopped onto a streetcar over to the Marine Corps recruiting station in the Oakland neighborhood. A few words to the recruiting sergeant during which Carlo, of course, mentioned that he was now both a Guadalcanal veteran as well as a Purple Heart recipient, resulted in Carlo's unrestricted access to a coveted military phone line. He placed a call to the Adjutant's Office at Camp Lejeune, and by the time an hour had passed, he had been granted permission to be accompanied by his wife for the duration of his assignment there. Additionally, he had also secured a married sergeant's billet that would – at least based on what the duty corporal told Carlo – be comfortable enough for Elizabeth to spend her days while Carlo was on duty.

"It ain't the Taj Mahal, Sarge, that's for sure," the corporal on the other end of the line told Carlo, "but it'll be okay for your wife."

Elizabeth purchased additional train tickets that matched the ones Carlo had been issued. She scurried about the DeLuca home for several days, packing not only lightweight clothing that she figured would be appropriate for the sticky North Carolina summer, but also household items and even a few knickknacks that might make the dreary military post housing she anticipated more hospitable for her and Carlo.

A few nights later, Carlo and Elizabeth quietly celebrated their first wedding anniversary. Carlo's mother cooked an extra-special Sunday dinner of pot roast, potatoes, and canned carrots, with a genuine cake for dessert. Rosalia splurged and spent more than the usual allotment of ration coupons and stamps, especially for the butter, milk, and eggs needed for something other than the usual makeshift "war cake" they had all become accustomed to.

Ordinarily, Elizabeth and Carlo might have gone out on the town following dinner to continue celebrating their anniversary. Being a Sunday night, though, lounges and nightclubs were closed, and neither Elizabeth nor Carlo felt much like taking in a movie. Instead, they settled onto the sofa with Carlo's parents, Angela, and Carmela to listen to the radio for the rest of the evening. They caught the second half of the Jack Benny program and then stayed with the NBC Red network for Abe Lyman's *Band Wagon* and then the amusements of Edgar Bergen and his dummy Charlie McCarthy. Following the comedy act came

Elizabeth's favorite radio soap opera, *One Man's Family*, a program she had listened to since she was a young girl.

Finally the nine o'clock hour came, and Giuseppe rose to twirl the dial to Walter Winchell's program. Elizabeth and Carlo shared a knowing glance, and after another minute or so Carlo rose from the sofa.

"I think we're going to turn in," he offered. Unlike his first night home, however, Carmela was present in the living room as Elizabeth followed Carlo up the stairs.

"Just keep the racket down, you two," Carmela proclaimed loudly. Elizabeth looked back at Carmela and caught her sister-in-law's smirk. She thought about offering some sort of pointed rejoinder, but decided not to in front of Carlo's parents.

Besides, Elizabeth's mind was preoccupied with another thought that had haunted her for days now: the absence of a condom the night of Carlo's homecoming, and what that might mean.

*   *   *

For days, even though Elizabeth was grateful for this unexpected opportunity to accompany her husband to a strange new place for at least a few months – in the midst of a war, no less – she found herself almost panicky with apprehension. Two evenings before her planned departure, while Carlo accompanied his father to Bruno Antolini's corner bar for some one-on-one father-son time, Elizabeth slipped away with both Angela and Carmela for pie and coffee at the coffee shop in East Liberty.

As soon as the sisters-in-law were seated, Carmela – who for a change hadn't disappeared after dinner for reasons unknown – asked Elizabeth, "Are you alright? I swear you look like you're gonna have a stroke or somethin'."

Elizabeth stared hard back at Carmela.

"Do I really look like that?"

Before Carmela could respond with some smart-aleck remark or another, Angela chimed in.

"You look just like someone who decided to do something and now you're not so sure that it's the right thing to do."

Elizabeth let out a deep sigh, just as the waitress brought three cups of coffee to the table. She waited until the waitress departed to retrieve the three slices of pie before responding.

"I'm just so nervous about going with Carlo all the way to North Carolina! I've never been anywhere other than Ohio before. It's so far away; and it's a Marine camp, too! He'll be training Marines all day and I'll be all there by myself…"

"Maybe you'll make friends with other Marine wives," Angela interrupted.

Elizabeth shook her head slightly. She was about to reply but caught herself. For one thing, the waitress had returned with the three slices of apple pie, and Elizabeth didn't want to say anything personal or intimate in front of this stranger. But even after the waitress was out of earshot, Elizabeth didn't respond to Angela's suggestion.

She was incredibly uncomfortable at the thought of consorting with the wives of other Marine instructors at some godforsaken training base hundreds of miles away, down in the south. Elizabeth was ashamed of the reason, and couldn't bear to verbalize those sentiments to either of her sisters-in-law, let alone have a coffee shop waitress overhear her.

Estrangement aside, Elizabeth DeLuca was still Katherine Buchanan's daughter. Try as she might, that Buchanan haughtiness was still pulsing at least a little bit through Elizabeth's very essence. She might have married a down-to-earth Italian boy whom fate turned into a battle-hardened Marine. But all those years of living as Katherine Buchanan's precious, entitled daughter were a hard thing to shake.

And to Elizabeth's shame, she was helpless to think of these other Marine wives whom she would soon encounter in North Carolina as anything other than lesser women than Elizabeth Buchanan DeLuca was. Would she ever truly break free from her mother's molding?

*   *   *

Still another quandary facing Elizabeth was whether to tell her parents that she would be soon departing Pittsburgh for several months...and if so, how she should break the news? Angela was all for Elizabeth telling her parents in person.

"At least this way you'll see how things are there...you know, after..."

Angela didn't finish her sentence, but both Elizabeth and Carmela knew that Angela was referring to William Buchanan's conviction and consignment to the Army.

"I don't think I can," Elizabeth morosely answered. "The thought of being face-to-face with my mother just..."

Elizabeth likewise couldn't finish her sentence, but there was no need.

"How about just your father, since he would then tell your mother?" was Carmela's suggestion. For a few moments, that idea appealed to Elizabeth. But eventually she realized that even if she wanted to approach only her father, locating him – particularly without Katherine's presence – would be a near-impossibility. Spencer Buchanan held no steady job, and his "business dealings" took him all around the city in an entirely unpredictable manner, every single day. Elizabeth thought that perhaps she could find him alone at the Witherspoon Club, but unlike her brother – whose daily presence at the Club until his arrest was a virtual certainty – Spencer Buchanan frequented the club far less often. Even if she devoted the next day to haunting the Witherspoon Club in search of her father, Elizabeth had no guarantee that he would make an appearance.

In the end, the three women agreed that it would be perfectly acceptable for Elizabeth to write a letter to her parents, telling them of her departure. She could make the letter succinct enough to include only the most essential details: the date of her departure; when she would arrive at Camp Lejeune; how to reach her in case of a family illness or other emergency; and when she would likely return to Pittsburgh. A mailed letter would bring no immediate backlash or recriminations, nor even any bitterly snide remarks about following her Italian Marine husband down to some backwater military post. Elizabeth wouldn't be tempted to defend her decision, nor would she be at risk for blurting out some horrid retort to a biting remark from her mother.

Still, Elizabeth felt very much like a coward for deciding upon this course of action; but with everything else on her mind, the last thing she needed was any unwanted and unnecessary controversy with her mother.

*   *   *

The morning of their departure had finally arrived, and following another grim breakfast around the DeLuca table, Carlo and Elizabeth would soon head toward Pittsburgh's Pennsylvania Station and the late morning train that would begin their journey southward. Carlo's father was able – miracle of miracles – to swap work schedules for the day with another man who regularly worked the second shift. Giuseppe thus would be able to accompany Rosalia and Angela (who again called in sick) to the train station. Carmela said her goodbyes to her brother after breakfast before she departed for work, and seemed especially despondent. In fact, Elizabeth thought as she watched the tearful goodbye scene, Carmela had been uncharacteristically subdued the entire time Carlo had been home. Her regular post-supper departures had caught the attention of everyone in the household, and despite Carmela's standard explanation of "meeting some of the girls from work," both Elizabeth and Angela had the feeling there was more to the story. Some nights, Carmela didn't even make it home for supper, returning to the house close to – or even after – midnight. Elizabeth, though, was so caught up in the frenzy of preparing to head south with Carlo that any intrigue on the part of Carmela DeMarco was at the back of her mind.

Dawdling for about an hour before their departure to Penn Station, Carlo settled onto the sofa for his final look at the *Post-Gazette* for what he figured would be a long while. For a change, the big bold headlines didn't blare war news. Instead, the top story was about the crippling strike by more than 20,000 Western Pennsylvania coal miners that had now shuttered forty-seven mines, in defiance of a War Labor Board order several days earlier. The industrial effort on behalf of the war was, of course, closely linked with the availability of coal, and so the WLB had directed a three-man panel to intervene in the wage dispute between the union and the coal mining operators. Nobody in the DeLuca family, even the larger extended *famiglia*, worked as a coal miner; yet the possible consequences of this labor action were not lost upon Giuseppe or Carlo, nor any of the women.

"Hey, the Pirates won yesterday," Carlo said out loud as he read the news story of their victory in the season's first home game. Even though the comment was directed at his father, who was enough of a baseball fan himself, Carlo was immediately awash in sorrow that his father was the only other man in the house to hear the news. In years past, Carlo and all three of his brothers would have immediately begun tussling over possession of the sports pages to read the story of the game and check the box score. Now, though...and it was only happenstance that Carlo was in Pittsburgh himself to read the game story firsthand in the morning paper. He hoped that wherever Vinnie, Tony, and Michael were at the moment, they were out of immediate danger, rather than locked in deadly combat with the enemy.

Carlo turned his attention back to the box score, taking note of the names listed as Pirates' players. Some were familiar: Vince DiMaggio for one, who, unlike his more famous brother Joe or his other brother Dominic, was still in a baseball uniform rather than a military one. A few others were names that Carlo recognized from seasons past, but several of the players were new wartime fill-ins for those major leaguers who had either enlisted or been drafted for military duty. The war was taking an even greater toll on the ranks of Major League Baseball and other sports in 1943 than the previous year had. This year would even see a girls' baseball league out in the Midwest, giving rise to rumors that Major League Baseball might soon be shuttered for the duration of the war due to an insufficient number of skilled players.

"We should get going," Giuseppe DeLuca's voice interrupted Carlo's musings. Carlo looked up at his father, who in turn was half-looking at his wristwatch but also gazing at his son. Carlo could swear that his father looked as if he were about to cry…something he had never before seen.

"Yeah, okay Pop," Carlo sighed as he rose from the sofa, setting the morning's *Post-Gazette* back onto the couch.

"Take it with you," Giuseppe nodded towards the paper. "You can read it on the train."

"Nah, that's okay," Carlo retorted. "I've seen enough."

He looked over at Elizabeth, who was standing by the stairs.

"Besides, Elizabeth will be with me, and I'm sure we'll take in the scenery going by, and talk, and all that stuff."

The two suitcases that Elizabeth was taking, along with Carlo's Marine Corps seabag, had already been loaded into the trunk of the Packard Six. The DeLuca family slowly filed out of the house, with Carlo bringing up the rear. As if scripted for a Hollywood tearjerker war picture, he paused at the front door stoop to turn and gaze intently back inside the house. Carlo stood there for close to half a minute, not noticing that his wife, his parents, and his sister-in-law had all likewise halted in place on the front porch and were staring morosely back at him. No one dared put into words what each one thought, and what they were all certain Carlo was thinking before he finally sighed and pulled the front door closed behind him.

Would his luck hold out enough the next time he was in combat, and then the next time, and God only knew how many more times, for him to return home to see this house once again?

*   *   *

The scene at the train station was both familiar and foreign to Elizabeth. Familiar, because just as when Carlo and Tony departed a year ago, and when Tony left after his brief summertime furlough, the sorrowful departure brought tears and sobbing to Rosalia DeLuca and also Angela. Foreign, because this time Elizabeth wasn't being left behind on the platform as the Pennsylvania Railroad train came to life and chugged away. This time, instead of weeping as she saw her husband or his brother off to war, she instead received tearful farewell hugs herself from Giuseppe and Rosalia and Angela. Elizabeth would be back soon enough; but for now, she was the recipient of a heartfelt, sad goodbye that – she couldn't help thinking – she would give anything to receive from her own mother.

*   *   *

Carlo and Elizabeth watched the springtime scenery roll by for the first hour of their trip. The mid-Pennsylvania countryside was alive with farmers plowing and planting. Neither Carlo nor Elizabeth had spent much time over the years outside of the innards of Pittsburgh, and both were captivated by mile upon mile of fields and pastures, offset in the distance by now-green rounded-top mountain ranges.

"It was just like this last year when Tony and I went through," Carlo mused. "We both stared out the window all the way to Harrisburg, just like me and you are doing."

"It's just so different than the city," Elizabeth proclaimed while still staring out the window, powerless to divert her eyes from the wondrous farmland panorama.

She finally forced her eyes away from the view and looked at Carlo.

"I wonder what it would be like to live out here? You and me?"

Carlo was helpless against the snort he let forth.

"You mean be farmers? Us?"

Elizabeth shook her head.

"No, I wasn't thinking about it that way. I just meant living out here, away from the city, where everything looks like it's so peaceful and fresh and…"

"Yeah, but what about a job?" Carlo interrupted. "I think out here that unless you're a farmer…well, there probably isn't anything else."

"I don't know," Elizabeth countered. "There's probably still grocery stores where people buy food and such, and machine shops where the farmers get parts for their tractors and equipment. Small diners and coffee shops, too. Probably not everybody out here is a farmer; people have to work at those other places."

"I guess," Carlo shrugged.

"I'm just saying," Elizabeth continued, "that after the war…"

Elizabeth continued speaking, but to Carlo her words immediately faded into an unintelligible droning following "after the war." By now, courtesy of nearly four months of vicious combat on Guadalcanal that culminated in him being shot twice, Carlo was convinced that "after the war" was a concept he didn't dare entertain.

After another hour, Carlo asked Elizabeth if she minded if he caught a little shut-eye. Elizabeth was perfectly fine with the idea, and in less than thirty seconds Carlo was fast asleep. Elizabeth stared at her husband for a couple of minutes, lost in thought. Finally, she figured that this would be the perfect time to pen that letter that she dreaded writing.

April 28, 1943

Dear Father and Mother,

I am writing to let you know that I am going with Carlo to Camp Lejeune, North Carolina, for a couple of months. I left Pittsburgh this morning of April 28th and will arrive there late Thursday night.

Carlo finally made it home for furlough last week, just as he had said in his telegram back in February. He doesn't know yet exactly how long he will be at Camp Lejeune, or where he will be going next. But married Marine instructors are permitted to have their wives accompany them, just like Maude Ringgold did earlier this year to Oliver's Army post.

If you need to reach me by mail or telegram you can contact the Camp Lejeune Adjutant's Office and they will forward the letter or telegram to me.

I will write you again to let you know when I am back in Pittsburgh, probably later this summer.

Your daughter,

Elizabeth

Elizabeth read over the letter three times. Its brevity and impersonal nature (she couldn't bring herself to sign the letter "Love, Elizabeth") saddened her, but such were the terms of her relationship with her own parents. If she were married to Calvin McKinnon and were accompanying him on some important WPB assignment to Birmingham, Alabama, or Gary, Indiana, or some other steelmaking city for several months, Elizabeth was certain that her mother would be down at the Witherspoon Club almost every day, bragging to anyone within earshot about her big-shot son-in-law's posting and how lucky Katherine's daughter was to have landed such a catch. In real life, though, accompanying a wounded Marine who had survived nearly four months on Guadalcanal...well, that was truly beneath a Buchanan, was it not?

Elizabeth shook away the gloomy thoughts as she folded the letter into an envelope. She licked and then attached the three-cent "Win the War" stamp she had brought with her, and then carefully wrote her parents' names and address on the envelope before sealing it. She would mail the letter from the platform in Harrisburg when they arrived in a few hours to change trains. And once the letter had been mailed...well, she hardly expected to hear anything from either of her parents, especially in the absence of some emergency. However, she had done her duty, and that would have to be enough.

Chapter 15

June 7, 1943

"Are you ready for lunch?"

Angela looked up from her typewriter and saw that both Francine Donner and Abby Sobol were standing by her desk. Ever since Elizabeth's departure five weeks earlier, Angela had been joining these two girls for lunch almost every workday.

"Sure," Angela replied. "Give me one more minute to finish this letter that Mr. Jakowski needs to send out."

"Okay," Angela's friend Francine agreed. "We'll wait downstairs, out in front of the building. It's beautiful today, so we might as well get as much sunshine as we can before being cooped up again all afternoon."

Angela nodded absentmindedly as she turned her attention back to Mr. Jakowski's chicken-scratch on the yellow tablet. Of all the WPB managers in the Oakland office, his handwriting was the absolute worst! Given the important nature of letters sent by the WPB, complete accuracy in both words and figures was paramount. Whichever secretary happened to receive one of Jakowski's memos to type, that poor girl often needed to make a trip or two to the man's office to ask for clarification of some nearly illegible handwriting. And, as fate would have it, Stan Jakowski was easily the most ill-tempered WPB manager in the Oakland office. Every request to interpret his handwriting was invariably met with a scowl at the very least, and often an undeserved scolding. Most of the WPB managers dictated their letters and memos to a secretary, yet for some reason Stan Jakowski eschewed dictation and insisted on writing his own documents in longhand before handing them over for typing...much to the chagrin of every WPB secretary in the building.

Angela sighed as she concentrated on the final paragraph...fortunately a short one, and miraculously one that was actually readable. She typed the final few sentences and then did a quick inspection of her handiwork after pulling the sheet of paper from the typewriter. Everything looked fine, so Angela quickly took the letter over to the corner of the office and slid it into the large wooden box marked OUTBOUND.

Satisfied that she could forget about work for the next hour, Angela bounded down the stairs and out into the glorious sunshine. Francine and Abby were each smoking a Chesterfield while they waited, so Angela reached into her pocketbook for her pack of Pall Malls and quickly lit one. They were only headed right around the corner, to the ever-popular Jack Canter's, so they could afford to take a few minutes to loiter in place and enjoy their first lunchtime smokes. Inside the WPB building the managers and other male workers smoked freely throughout the day, in their offices and also when walking about the open portions of the building. The secretaries, however, were afforded no such freedoms since their hands were expected to be busy almost every second, typing or filing or taking dictation. One very short smoking break in the morning, and another mid-afternoon; that was it for the WPB secretaries, other than during their lunch hours.

"I got a letter from Joseph," Abby Sobol told Angela. "I already told Francine about it."

"Is he okay?" Angela asked. Abby's boyfriend was a newly minted Army Air Forces flyer who should have just arrived in England, according to Abby's reading between the lines of his letters. Joseph Coleman was his name, and he had gone to high school at Schenley, only a few blocks from where they were standing this very minute.

Francine Donner's fiancé was also an Air Corps pilot…Joseph Coleman's older brother Jonathan, in fact, who also was about to begin flying out of England. Each brother now held the rank of first lieutenant. Because their sweethearts were brothers, Francine and Abby had become exceptionally close. Their desks were next to each other on the second floor of the WPB office, and the two of them were just about inseparable.

Even though Abby Sobol had gone to Peabody, the same as Angela, the two didn't know each other well at all during high school. Abby had graduated only a year ago in '42, a full year after Angela did, and hadn't hung around with the group of mostly Italian girls that Angela belonged to. Abby knew Elizabeth back in high school a little better than she did Angela…but only slightly.

Angela had become friendly with Francine first, back in the summer of '42 not long after they each began working at the WPB. At the time, though, Francine and Jonathan Coleman were on the outs. Francine had told Angela a fair amount about her then-former boyfriend, but didn't offer an explanation for why they had broken up the previous Christmas, not long after Pearl Harbor. One time when they were having lunch together, though, Angela was talking about her own lightning-fast wedding, as well as

Elizabeth and Carlo's. She then asked Francine if she and Jonathan had discussed getting married during the early days of the war before they had broken up. Francine's eyes immediately began to tear up, and it was all the poor girl could do to keep from dissolving into a blubbering mess right there at the Sun Drugs lunch counter.

So on the Monday after last Thanksgiving when they all came back to work, Angela was shocked to find Francine showing off her engagement ring. However it had happened, Francine Donner and her flyboy fellow had reconciled over the holiday when he was home on furlough, and were now engaged after eleven months apart. They had decided that their wedding, however, would wait until the end of the war.

It was during that same Thanksgiving holiday that Abby Sobol met Francine's fiancé's younger brother, also home on furlough, and had quickly fallen for him. Both of the brothers departed right after Thanksgiving to go back to their flight training base way out in Arizona, though. For the past six months these two girls and the two brothers shared letters but nothing more...just like Angela and Tony ever since his own brief furlough last summer.

"He's fine," Abby answered Angela's question. "The censor had a field day with his letter, which made me furious! I could tell from what was left – and trust me, there wasn't a lot! – that what was cut out probably didn't need to be."

Angela sighed. Many of Tony's letters came through with only one or two portions censored...sometimes nothing at all. Other letters were all but unreadable because so much had been cut out. Angela was certain that some censors went way overboard, and it was the poor wives and mothers and sweethearts back home who paid the price. Angela wondered if the censorship was the same for letters from home that were bound for soldiers and Marines who were stateside, or in the V-mail letters headed overseas. She guessed that was the case, and made a mental note to ask Tony that question the next time she wrote him.

Francine and Abby waited for Angela to finish her cigarette and then the three of them walked over to the luncheon diner. Three adjoining seats opened up at the counter just as they walked in, and Abby hurried over to grab them before anybody else made an attempt.

"Did you see this?" Francine was gazing at the headline of the morning's *Post-Gazette* that the previous occupant of her space had left behind. The headline read:

ALLIED INVASION PLAN COMPLETED

Francine placed the newspaper where all three girls could read it, and they each scanned the story. The story was actually about a massive B-17 raid on Italy – "the largest formations of Flying Fortresses ever sent from Africa," the article read – and at least on the first page of the paper didn't mention anything specific about some sort of "invasion plan."

Still, Angela felt her stomach tighten. She had picked up clues from Tony's last few letters that his next destination would likely be Italy. Talk of invading France and taking on the Germans there had faded for now; the next logical new battlefront to open was Italy. Word from Tony back in February that his unit had been pulled from

North Africa, even while the fighting was still raging, gave rise to speculation that another invasion was brewing. Sure enough, when Francine flipped the paper to Page 3 and the continuation of the story, the interior headline read "U.S. Armada Blasts Invasion Stepping Stones."

Last November, courtesy of Mickey Rossi's slip that night months earlier at the Crawford Grill, the breaking news of the North Africa invasion had come with the knowledge that her husband was among the American liberators. Angela didn't have the same absoluteness resulting from a friend's loose lips this time around, but she was all but certain that the first word of an invasion of Italy would mean Tony was back in combat again.

* * *

Several weeks later, on a rainy Monday, Angela had plans to again have lunch with Francine and Abby. When noon approached and neither Francine nor Abby had appeared at her desk, Angela headed to the far side of the second floor where the other girls' desks were located. She spotted Francine, who was in the process of retrieving her purse from the drawer of her gray, government-issue steel desk.

"I was just about to come get you," Francine said. "I swear this morning's workload has been the worst!"

"I know," Angela agreed. The frenzy of activity this Monday morning had been so fast-paced that Angela hadn't even been able to get away for a five-minute cigarette break.

"Where's Abby?" Angela asked, noting the absence of Francine's friend.

A tight-lipped frown immediately came to Francine's face.

"She's not going to have lunch with us today," Francine said in subdued tones that hinted of irritation.

"Why not?" Angela asked, puzzled not so much by the news of Abby's absence but more by Francine's reaction.

Francine took Angela by the arm and steered her towards the stairwell door.

"I'll tell you on the way," was all she said.

The two women headed down the stairwell and then outside, each popping her umbrella as soon as possible to ward off the rain; cigarettes could wait until they were out of the rain again. A rumble of thunder could be heard in the distance.

"So what's going on with Abby?" Angela asked as they began quickly walking, doing their best to dodge puddles without bumping into other umbrella-carrying lunchtime pedestrians. The lunch counter at Grant's Five and Dime, a couple blocks away, was today's destination.

Francine sighed.

"She's having lunch with Jeffrey Belkin."

Angela made the connection after several seconds.

"You mean Mr. Belkin? From the office?"

"Uh-huh," Francine nodded. She stepped to her right to avoid a sizable puddle, and Angela eased around that same puddle on the left side.

"They went out on a date Saturday night," Francine added.

"What about Joseph?" Angela blurted out.

"I know," Francine said, her voice clearly betraying her exasperation at her friend Abby's decision. "Mr. Belkin asked her out last Wednesday, and she immediately told me and asked what I thought she should do."

"What did you tell her?"

"I told her to say no!" Francine bluntly replied. "Especially with Joseph just getting to England, and probably flying against the Nazis any day now."

The girls arrived at the front door of the Five and Dime. They lowered their umbrellas almost in unison, shook off the rain, and then headed inside.

"It just didn't seem right," Francine added as they maneuvered towards the lunch counter toward the back of the store.

*   *   *

For the rest of that afternoon and throughout the evening, Angela was surprisingly bothered by Francine's revelation. Angela still didn't know Abby Sobol all that well, and whatever that girl did had absolutely no bearing on Angela's life.

Still, Angela was troubled. Despite Abby's persistent relaying of news about "my fellow" or "my boyfriend" that she learned from his frequent letters, the girl and the Air Corps flyer had actually spent only a couple of days together this past Thanksgiving holiday. Unlike Francine and Joseph's brother, who had been high school sweethearts and were now engaged, Abby's romance with Joseph Coleman was a short-lived one. True, they had faithfully written each other for many months now, but that was the extent of it. Who knew how many more months or even years it would be until Abby saw Joseph again? They had made no promises to each other as Francine and Jonathan had, so technically Abby was free to go out with Jeffrey Belkin or anybody else who asked her on a date.

Still…something wasn't quite right about the circumstances of Joseph Coleman flying off to drop his bombs on the Nazis, thinking that his girl was waiting for him back home, yet in fact she was keeping company with another man. And in this case, Angela knew that Jeffrey Belkin was 4-F, which is why he was working at the WPB rather than being in uniform. The whole thing just didn't sit right with Angela, but she took comfort in the fact that Abby Sobol's situation was not hers.

Oh well, Angela finally decided before turning in for the night. Abby Sobol's predicament was one for a single girl, not a married or even an engaged one.

Angela would soon learn differently.

Chapter 16

July 1, 1943

"Mrs. DeLuca?"

The melodious southern accent of the nurse's voice immediately shook Elizabeth away from the jumble of worries that had enveloped her brain. Curiously, the first new thought that came to Elizabeth was surprise that this girl's voice wasn't harsh, commanding, perhaps even mannish. After all, the woman was a stern-looking Navy nurse, her hospital whites donned with a silver bar on one collar. Still, if Elizabeth had shut her eyes, she would have hardly been surprised if she had been addressed by some hoop-skirted Southern belle, straight out of *Gone With the Wind*.

Elizabeth forced away those random musings. She had been waiting in the Camp Lejeune hospital's open seating area for nearly four hours following the quick visit with the disinterested Navy doctor and then the corpsman who painfully drew her blood for what had seemed like an eternity. Elizabeth had expected that she would be waiting around the hospital for a little while following the lab work until she was seen again; but close to four hours seemed excessive.

Still, it wasn't as if Elizabeth needed to be somewhere else at the moment. Carlo wouldn't be home from training his recruits for at least another three hours. Or this could be yet another night where the phone rang in the tiny sergeant's billet house, bearing the expected ten- or fifteen-second call from Carlo to tell his wife that their training day was far from over, and he might not be home now until after midnight. And at that point Elizabeth would wrap up Carlo's dinner and put it into the Frigidaire, and proceed to eat her evening meal by herself.

"Yes?"

"Would you follow me, please?"

Elizabeth stiffly rose from the wooden bench. She followed the nurse back to a small examining area, where the lieutenant handed Elizabeth a glass jar. In lowered tones, the nurse explained that she needed a urine specimen and then directed Elizabeth to a nearby washroom where she could take care of the task in private. As Elizabeth complied with the request, she fought off the irritation that she had been forced to wait for hours when she just as easily could have taken care of this specimen immediately after her blood had been drawn. Even having Navy medical personnel running the show at the Marine Corps Camp hospital didn't seem to make matters any more reasonable. No wonder military men complained non-stop about the seemingly nonsensical manner so many things were done in the Marine Corps...or any of the other uniformed services, for that matter.

Upon exiting the washroom, Elizabeth found the Navy nurse waiting for her.

"We have to wait 72 hours for the results, but since it's already Thursday, you'll have to come back on Monday and we can let you know. But that's only one extra day you'll have to wait."

Elizabeth involuntarily exhaled a loud sigh.

"It'll be all right, honey," the Navy nurse smiled and reassured Elizabeth, also patting her hand in a gesture of comfort. Then the nurse added:

"You probably shouldn't say anything to your husband until you know for sure. You don't want to get his hopes up, and then if it turns out that you're not..." the nurse's voice immediately lowered, but only for the next word "...pregnant, he'll be all disappointed. Try to enjoy the Fourth of July on Sunday and put all of this out of your mind, if you can."

Elizabeth sighed. She wanted to rebut the nurse's suggestion – how could she *possibly* put "all of this" out of her mind? – but she could tell the lieutenant needed to get moving to the next patient. Besides, what good would come from unloading her fears and anxiety onto this total stranger, anyway? The one Elizabeth needed to talk to was Carlo. Even as she was walking down the corridor to the hospital's front doors, Elizabeth contemplated whether she should follow the nurse's advice and hold off saying anything to Carlo until she knew for certain that she was carrying his child. Finally, as she exited the building and was immediately blasted with the later summer afternoon blazing sunshine, Elizabeth decided to adhere to the advice she had just been given. After all, she had kept this little secret for more than two months now, through two missed periods and more than a half-dozen occurrences of morning sickness. Waiting four more days until she had lab test confirmation wouldn't make a bit of difference.

During the twenty-five-minute walk from the camp's hospital back to the cramped, stuffy house that she and Carlo had been assigned, Elizabeth was helpless to keep her mind from wandering back to the previous night's dream. In the dream she had been back in the Pittsburgh OPA office where she had worked until her brother's black market dealings led to her being fired. The dream began with her walking up the stairwell, returning from lunch, and hearing sobbing coming from the second floor. Just as had happened in real life a little under a year ago, Elizabeth came face-to-face with Joan Vernon.

"It's Elizabeth," Joan said in this dream.

That's strange, dreamworld Elizabeth DeLuca thought; *I'm* Elizabeth. How could that be?

Still, just as she had done in real life, Elizabeth looked past Joan and saw a cluster of her coworkers huddled around a sobbing, half-bent-over woman. Elizabeth walked slowly towards the group of women, and when she was a few feet away, they all stepped away and she was face-to-face with herself. Just before Elizabeth bolted awake, she noticed that her wailing dreamworld counterpart was accompanied by a four- or five-year-old son who was tightly clutching his mourning mother's leg.

While she fought to prevent being pulled back down into this terrible dream, Elizabeth looked over at her sleeping husband. Carlo had finally made it home around 9:30 that night, and following a quick supper had collapsed right into bed. Elizabeth's eyes were now focused enough to see that the luminescent radium hands of the nightstand clock read 12:55, and she knew that Carlo would be awake in less than four hours. She slipped out of bed, fished for her slippers that were necessary to prevent splinters from the unvarnished wood plank floors, and headed to the kitchen, where she quickly lit a Pall Mall. She desperately needed a smoke…and to think.

Actually, the more Elizabeth contemplated the dream, the more unsettled and despondent she became. She clearly recalled that last year, in the immediate aftermath of learning about the sudden death of Marine Private Bart Mendelsohn, Elizabeth had thought that at least a little piece of him would still be alive in the two children he had given Vickie.

As Elizabeth lit her second Pall Mall off of the fading remains of the first, she was powerless against the unnerving thought that not only was she *definitely* pregnant, but also that this yet-unborn son or daughter had been given to her because Carlo's fate had been sealed. The tragic dream had been a premonition. Carlo had survived two enemy rifle wounds on Guadalcanal, only to be able to return stateside and then to forego using a rubber that first time with his wife in almost a year. From just that one time without any protection, Elizabeth had become pregnant. She would give birth to this child months from now, long after Carlo had departed Camp Lejeune and probably while he was fighting for his life on some other Pacific island. He would never even see his son or daughter before meeting his end on that island, or maybe the next one, or the one after that.

*   *   *

The 4:45 a.m. alarm woke Elizabeth, as it did most mornings. Some mornings she obeyed Carlo's half-mumbled "go back to sleep" directive that came a split second after he shut off the alarm, but most other days she pulled herself out of bed to be able to spend fifteen or twenty minutes with her husband while he quickly shaved and dressed.

Before Carlo could even offer his routine "go back to sleep," Elizabeth was out of bed and on her way to the kitchen. She plugged in the electric coffee maker that she had wisely brought with them from home, and lit her first Pall Mall of the day while she waited for the coffee to brew. Carlo, like all Marine drill instructors here at Camp Lejeune, would eat breakfast with his infantry trainees sometime around 6:15 after morning calisthenics and their first four-mile run of the long training day. The first few days down here Elizabeth had popped a couple of slices of bread into the toaster for Carlo, but finally one morning he had grumbled to his wife that coffee – *just* coffee – was all he wanted and had time for.

Just as the coffee was ready, Carlo appeared in the walkway leading from the tiny living room to the kitchen. Every morning that she was awake with him, Elizabeth's most immediate thought was that he looked like he belonged on a Marine Corps recruiting poster with his crisply starched uniform, badges and campaign ribbons, and sergeant's stripes. Most mornings, though, he also wore a scowl that she wished he would save for his infantry trainees rather than display it for his wife.

"Coffee'll be ready in about a minute," Elizabeth offered, receiving only a nod and a grunt in return. Elizabeth knew that Carlo's perpetual bad mood had nothing to do with her, yet she was powerless against feeling so terribly offended whenever she came face-to-face with the gloom that perpetuated their depressingly few moments of home life here at Camp Lejeune.

Carlo lit a Chesterfield and plopped onto one of the creaky wooden kitchen chairs for a couple of minutes. At precisely 5:15 a.m. he would barge into the barracks where his trainees slept, screaming at the top of his lungs while banging a metal garbage pail with his wooden baton. Carlo hated this morning ritual from his boot camp days and later his own infantry training, and being on the other side as an infantry training instructor was surprisingly almost as disturbing to him.

"Is something wrong?"

Carlo's voice snapped Elizabeth's thoughts back to the moment. The stirring nausea, no doubt a warning that another bout of morning sickness was looming, had drawn Elizabeth's thoughts away to the quandary of her probably pregnancy.

"I think I'm pregnant," Elizabeth blurted out. She hadn't planned on uttering those words. All last evening and night, and upon waking this morning, she had intended to follow the Marine nurse's advice and wait for Monday and the test results. But for whatever reason, Carlo's question instantly pulled those words from her like a powerful magnet.

Elizabeth watched her husband's eyes widen. She was all but certain that the look on his face was one of overwhelming worry and fear, but then Carlo seemed to will away that expression.

"Are you serious?"

Elizabeth nodded.

"I won't know for certain until Monday," she replied before launching into an abbreviated tale of yesterday's visit to the camp hospital.

Carlo exhaled; a painful sigh.

"Well," he finally said, "I guess we'll see what they say on Monday."

His rose from the chair and walked slowly to the stove, taking the cup of coffee that Elizabeth held out to him. His eyes caught the time on the dusty kitchen wall clock – 5:08 now – meaning that he had barely enough time to hop into the D.I. jeep he had been issued and drive the mile and a half distance to the trainee barracks. Carlo took two quick gulps of the coffee and set the cup on the counter. Taking note of his wife's obvious worry, he took a step in her direction, placed his arms on either side of her, and pulled her into what Elizabeth immediately realized was their first real hug in weeks.

"It'll be all right," Carlo said soothingly as he kissed Elizabeth on her forehead first, followed by a quick peck on the lips.

Elizabeth nodded, tears immediately coming to her eyes. She fought the urge to tell Carlo about her dream from the night before going to the camp hospital; the one that she was convinced foretold Carlo's death in combat somewhere far away in the Pacific. Not only did she realize there was no time to relate the details of that dream, but Elizabeth also was convinced that sharing the miserable details with her husband would somehow seal his fate. There was always the chance that the dream was just that – simply a dream, rather than an actual premonition – so

Elizabeth would just keep the wretched specifics from Carlo.

"We'll talk about it tonight," Carlo said as he stepped away from Elizabeth and headed to the door.

Elizabeth's reaction that she dared not verbalize: maybe we will if you don't drag yourself home so very late, miss dinner again, and fall exhausted into bed only to wake up tomorrow morning to do this all over again.

*   *   *

Back in May, the morning of the fourth day after arriving at Camp Lejeune and getting settled into the depressingly tiny, dirty sergeant's billet house ("It ain't the Taj Mahal, Sarge, that's for sure" had turned out to be an understatement, even Carlo realized), Carlo had told Elizabeth that he would be home sometime between 6:30 and 7:00 for dinner. When he finally came home a little after 9:00 that evening, Elizabeth told Carlo that she had put his supper back in the refrigerator, but she would warm it up for him if he was still hungry.

"Damn it to hell!" Carlo exploded. "Don't you dare try to make me feel guilty for missing dinner!"

Carlo continued yelling and swearing for about thirty more seconds, stopping only when he took note of Elizabeth's hand clasped over her open mouth, her eyes wide with shock...and fear.

Carlo blew out a deep breath.

"Sorry," he muttered. "It's just...I don't know..."

He launched into a jumbled, rambling explanation of what Elizabeth could tell was a horrible day. Even though Carlo was no longer a lowly Marine recruit or trainee, and even though he wasn't in the midst of life-or-death combat at the moment, life as a wartime Marine was obviously anything but a picnic.

That night had been the only time Carlo had openly vented his frustrations at his wife, yet the constant strain and stress took a toll not only on Carlo, but on Elizabeth as well. Elizabeth tried to tell herself that at least they were together, in the midst of a worldwide war, no less! They had spent such a brief time together after their wedding, and it was almost a year from their tearful train station goodbye until she even saw him again. Carlo would be leaving soon enough. Elizabeth should be grateful for every single moment they had together, no matter how times he didn't make it home for dinner, or was forced to stay away for days at a time because of field combat maneuvers with his trainees.

Even on nights when Carlo did make it home for supper, the remainder of his evening was often filled with hours of reports to painstakingly complete for marksmanship and physical fitness testing and other training scores, and even the occasional disciplinary measure for trainees who got drunk and became disorderly on the post or in town. Also, Carlo's commanding officer often called extra meetings for his drill instructors, making the long hours even longer.

But at least we're together some of the time, Elizabeth would tell herself over and over.

Elizabeth was desperate to talk this all over with Angela, but six hundred miles of distance lay between the two sisters-in-law for the moment. Elizabeth didn't dare put anything on paper that smacked of a complaint about her husband. She knew that Rosalia DeLuca might very well decide to open a letter herself from Elizabeth despite the envelope being addressed to Angela, and not take kindly at all to any negative sentiments about one of her sons, even ancillary ones. Talking with Angela would have to wait until Elizabeth returned to Pittsburgh.

Being in the midst of a military post, Elizabeth also couldn't help but think of her brother. What had become of him? He should be finishing Army basic training right about now. Was he headed next for Army infantry training, the same as Tony DeLuca had done? Or had he been assigned to a different specialty: armor perhaps, or maybe artillery? Or possibly some sort of supply or other non-combat role? Elizabeth's animosity towards William was almost gone now, and she wished that she would hear something from her brother. Maybe their mother had written him that Elizabeth was temporarily at Camp Lejeune with Carlo, but Elizabeth doubted that very much. He of course could write her at the DeLuca home in Morningside and Rosalia could forward that letter, but so far nothing at all. Not that Elizabeth expected to hear from him, but still…

*   *   *

Despite her initial trepidations, Elizabeth had actually made friends with a few of the wives of other drill instructors. The transitory nature of wartime D.I.

assignments meant that wives came and went from Camp Lejeune along with their husbands, so the cliques and power hierarchies among the sergeants' wives that might have formed with longer-term peacetime assignments never really took hold. Elizabeth found that most of the other wives, no matter what part of the country they came from or what their respective backgrounds might be, were mostly like she was: grateful for whatever brief time with their husbands they had been granted, and fearful of what was almost certainly coming after this drill instructor assignment was concluded and he found himself invading some island far away in the Pacific.

Most weekday and Saturday afternoons right around 1:00, Elizabeth would join Rosemary Lucchese and Maria Esposito, the neighbors on either side of her house who both happened to be Italian housewives from New Jersey, for the fifteen-minute stroll to the central mail center for those living in the camp's housing area. The oppressive North Carolina summertime heat and humidity made the daily walk a trying one, but at least the women were able to get away from their respective houses and outside for a little bit. Elizabeth would be dripping with perspiration by the time she made it to the mail center, and by the time she made it home, she would invariably be lightheaded from the brutal summer weather. Yet the time spent most days with these women who were the closest thing she had to friends down here was something that she wouldn't have missed.

Now that she had told Carlo that she might be pregnant, Elizabeth felt no compunction about swearing these other two Marine wives to secrecy and sharing the news of her likely pregnancy with them. Surprisingly,

Elizabeth was no more than a minute into her story before Rosemary Lucchese interrupted her.

"Oh my God! You too? I'm pregnant also! I just didn't want to say anything because…I don't know…"

Elizabeth took some small comfort in hearing that Rosemary feared the same thing she did: that her baby, whenever he or she was born, was some sort of "exchange" for the life of her husband that would soon be over.

"I think we all feel this way," Rosemary Lucchese said when Elizabeth shared her own fears. "There was this one girl who left just before you got here, Dorothy Kaminsky – I think she was from Pittsburgh, too, like you. She found out that she was pregnant and she kept saying that she hoped she'd lose the baby, because then maybe her husband would come back from the war safe because she wouldn't have any children yet, and then he would be around to give her some."

"That's awful!" a shocked Elizabeth exclaimed. "Did she really say that?"

"Swear to God!" Rosemary Lucchese insisted.

The women reached the mail center that adjoined the adjutant's office, and the fans inside brought instant relief from the heat and humidity. Elizabeth knew that the inside of the building was actually as hot, maybe even hotter, than the outdoors. But the moving air from the fans always brought relief, at least for a few minutes.

The corporal at the counter knew these women by now, so he didn't need to ask their names before retrieving the waiting mail. Nothing awaited Rosemary Lucchese today, to her disappointment. Maria Esposito had two letters waiting for her: one from her mother in Hoboken, and another from her brother who was an Army sergeant currently somewhere in Europe. Maria announced who each of her letters was from. At the mention of the words "my mother," Elizabeth had a fleeting thought that under normal circumstances, she would so very much welcome a letter from her own mother.

Fate – or God – sometimes answers a thought as if it were the most impassioned prayer. Sure enough, the corporal handed Elizabeth a single letter and Elizabeth took in the return address:

Mrs. Katherine Buchanan
3311 King Avenue
Pittsburgh 6, Pennsylvania

"Who's yours from?" Rosemary asked, noticing Elizabeth staring at the piece of mail as if it might be poisonous.

Elizabeth hesitated, started to answer; but somehow couldn't bring herself to say the words "my mother."

"You okay?" Maria now noticed Elizabeth was just staring at the letter.

Finally, Elizabeth came back to the present moment.

"Yes; sorry. It's from my mother," she answered, looking first at Rosemary and then at Maria.

Noticing Elizabeth just standing there with the envelope unopened, Maria asked, "Aren't you going to read it?"

Elizabeth sighed, and then finally opened the envelope.

June 21, 1943

Dear Elizabeth,

I suppose it's about time that I reply to your letter in which you informed me that you were spending your summer at a Marine Corps post. I imagine that you're very lonely there without your family, in strange surroundings. However, you'll be back in Pittsburgh soon enough, though I imagine that you will continue living at your in-laws in Morningside instead of at your home.

I wanted to write you to let you know that your father and I were at the Witherspoon Club for supper this past Saturday night, and we saw Calvin McKinnon. He was dining by himself so we invited him to join us at our table. He talked fondly of the time you spent together during last year's Christmas Party at the Club, along with supper at our house that following week. He told me to send his best regards to you, and that he most sincerely looks forward to seeing you at this year's Christmas Party, if not before.

I trust that you will inform me when you return to Pittsburgh.

Your Mother.

*   *   *

The first thing Elizabeth did when she walked into her house, even before grabbing a towel to wipe away the perspiration from her head and her face, was to locate a kitchen match and then burn her mother's letter. How dare she! For many months now, Elizabeth had presumed that the Calvin McKinnon "business" – if that's what it even was – was locked away for all eternity. Even her brief recollection and contemplation of the matter back in April, as she did her best to explain the schism with her mother to Carlo, had ended without having to mention her encounter with the young government man, left her convinced that the entire matter was in the past forever.

But now…this letter from her mother…

Elizabeth could clearly detect a viciousness in her mother's written words; a not-so-veiled threat that Katherine Buchanan's meddling in her daughter's marriage was far from concluded. Elizabeth's mother most likely had no idea of the mail delivery system here at Camp Lejeune, or that Carlo was rarely in his house during daylight hours. She might well have presumed that a mailman delivered letters and parcels directly to a recipient's front door twice each day, just like at home, and that perhaps Carlo himself would be the one to take receipt of this letter rather than Elizabeth. Perhaps Carlo would open the letter himself, out of curiosity, and read the passages about Calvin McKinnon. At the very least, hungry for news from home, he would want to know what Elizabeth's mother had written. He would confront Elizabeth; the two of them would have a terrible fight; and maybe, just maybe, that would be the catalyst to an irreparable breach in their marriage as Carlo headed off again to war, convinced that his wife was at least contemplating unfaithfulness in his absence.

Elizabeth's mind insisted on replaying her thought processes from when she had told Carlo why she had moved out of her mother's home. She was as convinced as ever that she had done nothing wrong, but Elizabeth knew very well that Carlo might easily envision a "yeah, but what if..." scenario in which that harmless Christmas party conversation with Calvin McKinnon did, in fact, go further than just talking.

Elizabeth had a sudden thought: the baby! Maybe with her being pregnant, or after she gave birth...maybe even if Carlo were to somehow find out about his wife's Christmas party discussion with the young government man, he would be far less concerned that something might happen in the future with Elizabeth carrying or later caring for his child. Katherine Buchanan could try her hardest to disrupt her daughter's marriage, but to no avail, thanks to the baby.

Still, Elizabeth was infuriated at her mother, and worried about what might come next from that horrid woman.

Chapter 17

July 12, 1943

Angela flicked the Admiral radio to life the moment she walked in the door of the DeLuca home, shortly before 6:00 this Monday evening. For a fleeting moment she was surprised that the radio wasn't already on, given the big news of the Allied invasion of Sicily over the weekend. Apparently, though, Angela's mother-in-law couldn't bear the thought of listening to war bulletins knowing that her son Tony was likely smack in the middle of the fighting; maybe even her youngest son Michael, as well.

After warming up for about ten seconds the radio came to life just in time for Bill Cullen's fifteen-minute local news program. British forces under the famed General Montgomery, along with American troops, were reported to be capturing major Sicilian towns one by one as they forged ahead. General Patton was leading the American Seventh Army, and General Eisenhower was reported to be visiting the Sicilian battlefront.

Amidst all of the news about battles and towns and famed battlefield commanders, however, Angela's thoughts were preoccupied with her husband's likely role in this latest invasion. The Allied forces were reported to be facing off against both the Italian Army and the Germans. There was something especially unsettling about Tony being part of an invasion force making its way through the Sicilian countryside and towns where his ancestors had come from; perhaps even engaging distant cousins on the battlefield.

"Angela?"

At the sound of her name Angela turned and saw her mother-in-law, who had just come into the living room from the kitchen. Rosalia was stirring a mixing bowl filled with dough for biscuits that she would place into the oven the moment Giuseppe arrived home, any minute now.

"Can you go see what's wrong with Carmela? She came home early from work today and has been upstairs in her room crying, and won't come out."

Angela gasped as her hand flew to her mouth.

"Oh my God…Tony?" Angela blurted out, referring to Carmela's husband Tony DeMarco.

Rosalia shook her head.

"No. That was the first thing I asked her, that maybe Tony's mother got a telegram. But that's not it. As far as anyone knows, he's still fine."

Thank God, Angela thought, thinking also of her own Tony.

"Did she say what was wrong then?" Angela asked.

Rosalia DeLuca shook her head and then shrugged.

"She no wanna tell me."

Angela blew out a breath as she turned towards the stairs.

"Okay, I'll go talk to her."

Even before Angela reached the top of the stairs she could hear sobbing coming from Carmela's room. She walked the couple of steps across the narrow hallway to Carmela's door, directly across from the top of the stairwell, and knocked.

"Carmela?"

No immediate response other than the sobbing from the other side of the door becoming louder.

One more time: "Carmela?"

"Can I come in?" Angela added.

Angela expected to hear a fervent "no!" or perhaps a muffled "go away" from inside the room. Instead she heard footsteps and then the door opened.

Carmela looked terrible. Her eyes were red and puffy from what likely had been non-stop crying for several hours now. Her eye and face makeup had dissolved into blotchy patches.

"What's wrong?" Angela asked as she followed Carmela back into the room, closing the bedroom door behind her. Carmela was still facing away from Angela, walking slowly back towards her bed. Angela watched the back of Carmela's head shake slowly from side to side.

"I can't tell you," Carmela finally muttered.

Angela paused for a few seconds as she absorbed those words.

"What do you mean, you can't tell me?"

Carmela turned and plopped back down onto her bed.

"I can't tell you," she repeated.

"Carmela? Something is wrong if you're this upset. Tell me and maybe I can help you," Angela pressed.

Carmela just sat slumped on her bed, her head lowered into her body, sadly shaking her head back and forth.

"I just can't tell you," Carmela repeated yet again, but this time after a few seconds she added:

"I'm so ashamed."

Angela suddenly felt her own stomach churn. Whatever was going on with her sister-in-law must be *really* bad. She crossed over to the bed and sat down to Carmela's left. After a few seconds she reached over to grasp her sister-in-law's hand.

"I'll just sit here with you," Angela said as soothingly as she could, "and if you feel like talking, I'm right here."

The two women sat side-by-side for several minutes. Carmela's frantic weeping had slowed to an occasional sob. All the while, Angela's mind churned through numerous reasons that had caused this breakdown, but none seemed plausible.

Finally, Angela heard Carmela mutter:

"He left without even telling me."

Angela's grip on Carmela's hand involuntarily tightened at these words. She didn't know the details – yet – but coupled with Carmela's earlier utterance of "I'm so ashamed," Angela suddenly had an idea about what had happened.

* * *

Over the next hour, Angela dragged the full story, or pretty close to the full story, out of Carmela.

"I didn't mean for nothin' to happen at first," Carmela had said. "We ate lunch in the cafeteria with the same group a lot, and he was always sorta funny."

Later in her narrative:

"One night after work right before last Thanksgiving, we both took the incline together down from Mount Washington. I was getting ready to get on the streetcar to come home and he said to me, 'Why don't we get a quick drink.' Nothin' happened that night, even though I musta had about five whiskey sours. But I started thinkin'…"

Still later:

"This one Thursday night about a week before Christmas, we walked around downtown after work, looking at the Christmas windows in all of the stores. I was kinda nervous, figuring that I might run into you or Elizabeth, or someone else I knew; especially since he kept holding my hand or putting his arm around me. So I told him that, and he said, 'Let's go get a hotel room then,' which we did, over at the William Penn since it was so close."

And more:

"I hated getting letters from Tony, because he was always sayin' how much he missed me and couldn't wait to get back home. And here I was messing around with this other guy the whole time. And even worse than getting letters from Tony was writing ones back to him. I hadda do my best to pretend that nothin' was happening; that I was home waiting for him, just like you were for your Tony, and Elizabeth was for Carlo."

Finally:

"I started thinking that I was gonna get my marriage annulled because I was really in love with Patrick."

*   *   *

What had triggered Carmela's near-breakdown began with arriving at work this morning and learning that this man – Patrick Doyle, his full name turned out to be; an older man, about twenty-seven or twenty-eight – had abruptly quit. Carmela heard the news from one of the women on her assembly line who had picked up enough clues to suspect that something was going on between Carmela and Doyle. This other woman was a bit too gleeful when she relayed the news that she herself had only just heard; but since that news hit Carmela like the proverbial ton of bricks, she didn't even notice the other woman's perverted joy in being the one to inform Carmela that she had been callously abandoned.

Carmela hurried off to find their supervisor, Mr. Coleman. The shift supervisor was not in the best of moods, considering he now was down one worker for the day – at least – without any prior notice. And, given the wartime labor shortage, hiring a replacement – man or woman – would likely not occur before the end of this week, at least.

"He left a note on my desk, probably last Friday night after I left, saying that he was taking a job at the big Ford plant out in Michigan, at Willow Run; the one that makes all those B-24s," Gerald Coleman complained to Carmela. "The note said that he was quitting immediately, and wouldn't be in today because he was taking a train there over the weekend."

As he was explaining the situation to Carmela DeMarco, Mr. Coleman was wondering why the girl had sought him out specifically to inquire about the absence of Patrick Doyle from this morning's shift. Gerald Coleman suddenly realized that there might have been some hanky-panky going on between these two; but he immediately told himself that was none of his concern.

"He made sure to tell me to send his final paycheck to the Ford plant, so I suppose that's the only reason he even left a note to give his notice," the supervisor grumbled. "He shoulda just told me last Friday before I left the plant, rather than leave a note that he knew I wouldn't find until I came in this morning."

That snake! Carmela had been with him last Friday night after work...an evening that both Patrick and Carmela worked an extra four hours after their regular day shift ended, Carmela now recalled. In fact, the extra working time to help meet a big War Department order for boots had been at Patrick's suggestion! He must have sneaked over to Mr. Coleman's empty office to leave that note at some point before he and Carmela left the factory, knowing that it wouldn't be until Monday that it was discovered.

Patrick had seemed evasive when she left him somewhere around 11:30 Friday night after doing her best to plan when they would next be together that weekend. He hadn't answered the phone in his Oakland apartment at all when Carmela called dozens of times over the weekend, even in the wee hours of Sunday morning. Carmela had been terribly worried that something had happened to him, even though her mind insisted on offering the possibility that he might be running around on her. Carmela was worried about what she might learn when she came to work this morning, but she had never expected this!

Carmela could do nothing other than hurry out of Mr. Coleman's office, down the hallway, and out of the building, sobbing the entire way. She did her best to keep her crying under control while she was still in the building, but as soon as she reached the outdoors, she let out a horrendous wail of despair. Passersby quickly looked away, figuring that this poor girl must have gotten word that her husband or sweetheart had been killed in the war.

"He just left? Just like that?" Angela was incredulous by the end of Carmela's sorrowful narrative. From the way Carmela told the story, Angela had supposed that this Patrick Doyle had fallen in love with Carmela just as she had with him. According to Carmela, he had hinted that this...*thing* with Carmela was far more than some casual wartime dalliance between an unmarried man and a lonely war wife.

Apparently, though, he had just been toying with Carmela.

* * *

Angela had dodged her mother-in-law's questioning when she finally came back downstairs close to 7:30, long after dinner had been finished. Rosalia DeLuca realized that Angela knew much more than she was letting on about Carmela's predicament, and wasn't buying Angela's "she's upset about something that happened at work" evasive explanation. Rosalia figured that she would get to the bottom of this whole business sooner or later, so she just let the matter drop while Angela warmed up some of the *pasta e figioli* that had been the evening's meal. Angela ate alone in the kitchen before reluctantly coming out to the living room to listen to the radio for the evening. Carmela had finally stopped crying but had apparently passed out for the night from exhaustion, so it was just Angela and her in-laws listening to their regular Monday night selection of *Cavalcade of America, The Gay Nineties*, and then the *Lux Radio Theater* over on the Columbia Network. The *Lady Esther Screen Guild Players* was next, but Angela was entirely unable to concentrate on the story line, so she said her good nights and headed upstairs to her room.

Angela barely slept that night. She also felt incredibly guilty that every time she began thinking and worrying about her own husband being back in the midst of combat in Sicily, her mind insisted on overwriting those worries with contemplation about this shocking revelation of Carmela's infidelity.

A month earlier, Angela had been surprisingly bothered by the news of Abby Sobol deciding to date Mr. Belkin at work while her sweetheart was flying dangerous bombing missions against the Nazis. After a short period of fretting, Angela had finally suppressed her dismay with the realization that Abby was a single girl, and in fact had only been granted a few days with Joseph Coleman anyway, many months earlier.

But now, her very own sister-in-law…and a married woman! How could Carmela have done such a terrible thing?

Angela's very own words from more than a year earlier, that cavalier response on the day of her own wedding when Carmela brazenly asked if she and Tony were already sleeping together, kept popping into her head:

There's a war on, ya know.

This awful war! Not only was it forcing millions of young men into the mortal danger of combat, but the cruelty of war also invaded the marriages and romances of those same men. Joseph Coleman was off flying bombing missions, probably with his girl's picture propped up on the instrument panel in his bomber's cockpit, while that same girl was off gallivanting with another man. Tony DeMarco might be in Sicily alongside Angela's Tony, or maybe training day and night for the eventual invasion of France, overjoyed at the appearance of each V-mail letter that came from his wife; and all the while Carmela had been flirting with and then sleeping with some 4-F schlub. And then that same lowlife schlub had callously discarded Carmela and slithered out of town over the weekend, probably never to be heard from again.

Why had Carmela done such a thing? At several points during her rambling, tear-filled narrative, Carmela had begun to venture into an explanation for her deplorable behavior, but never completely explained herself before either veering off into another topic or dissolving into a fit of sobbing that rendered her unable to speak. However,

Angela had pieced together enough from her sister-in-law's ramblings to realize that Carmela's explanation – her justification – was something along the lines of "I just didn't feel like we were *really* married, because Tony and I have spent almost no time at all together as a married couple."

Carmela's mind apparently insisted on rationalizing everything that had happened, from the first attraction to Patrick Doyle to flirting with him to falling into bed with the man, as little more than a high school girl with a boyfriend still finding some new boy interesting and attractive…and then moving on from one boyfriend to the next. And all because the war had prevented any sort of normalcy from taking hold in Carmela's marriage to Tony DeMarco.

Angela was especially bothered this night because she was powerless against acknowledging that, morals and wedding vows before God aside, she felt much the same way about Tony DeLuca as Carmela did about her Tony. Other than those few short days back in August of '42 when her Tony was home on furlough, Angela didn't feel as if she and her Tony had much of an actual marriage either, all thanks to the dreaded war.

Angela felt so guilty for these thoughts. She hadn't even come close to doing anything like Carmela, but then again she had never been tempted. Suppose, though, that one day later this week at Jack Canter's or the Sun Drugs lunch counter she found herself sitting next to a handsome young man, and the two of them happened to strike up a conversation? Angela hadn't seen her husband now for nearly a year, and perhaps another year – or more – would pass until she saw him again. Would she be strong enough to resist the natural urges for companionship and even intimacy that might begin percolating? Angela had always thought so; but with this new knowledge of what Carmela had done, Angela was no longer certain.

And then: what about her husband? And his brother Carlo? And Tony DeMarco? And millions of other American military men? If many of their wives and sweethearts back home seemed to be all but powerless to resist temptations of the flesh with their men gone to war, was it not very likely that those same men were giving in to – or even seeking out – diversions among foreign women and girls?

Perhaps Tony DeMarco had kept company on more than one occasion with some English girl who lived near his post in England: some flirty young lass, or maybe even a lonely British war bride, whom he met and danced with at a local pub. Or if Carmela's husband was now rolling through Sicily as part of the Allied invasion force, was he consorting with a string of Italian girls along the way? Angela had not a shred of proof that any such dalliances had actually occurred. Yet in light of Carmela's shocking revelation, Angela could envision any one of these scenarios as clearly as if it were playing out right in front of her eyes at this very moment.

For weeks, ever since learning about Abby Sobol's nascent relationship with Jeffrey Belkin, Angela had been saddened by the conjured image of Abby's Air Corps sweetheart flying off to face the Nazis with a photo of Abby propped up in his cockpit, unaware that his girl had found another fellow. Perhaps though, Lieutenant Joseph Coleman filled his off hours in the company of young English girls or maybe even British prostitutes who set up shop near the flyer's Air Corps field. If that were the case – even beyond the mere handful of days the two of them had spent together last Thanksgiving – should Abby entertain a single guilty thought about dating that 4-F man at work?

She desperately needed to talk to someone about all of these thoughts! However, the only natural confidante for such a discussion was her sister-in-law Elizabeth; and until Elizabeth returned to Pittsburgh from Camp Lejeune, such a conversation was an impossibility. She supposed she could write Elizabeth about what she had learned about Carmela and also share her own worried contemplations, but there was always a chance Carlo would see that letter. Angela had sworn to Carmela that she wouldn't tell Tony – Angela's Tony – anything about the sorrowful, sordid tale that Carmela had confessed. Carlo's name hadn't come up in Carmela's request or Angela's promise, but certainly that assurance of girl-to-girl confidentiality also excluded Tony's brothers.

Angela would simply have to wait until Elizabeth returned home to confide in her. In the meantime, Angela was on her own as she confronted her own late-blooming doubts about the wisdom of a hurried wartime marriage.

Chapter 18

July 21, 1943

The first cramp felt much like an upset stomach encroaching on her digestive system, but the second one was more like being kicked in the gut by a horse. Elizabeth rushed into the bathroom with barely enough time to throw up into the toilet instead of on the floor, but even as she was doing so she knew this wasn't just another normal bout of morning sickness.

She hesitatingly reached down with her right hand, under her dress, and felt for any wetness or stickiness. Nothing, at least so far. To be certain, she examined her hand for any signs of blood, but there was nothing to see.

When she felt that she could stand without either doubling over in pain or falling over from dizziness, Elizabeth pulled herself up and staggered to the front door, and then lurched outside. The late morning stifling humidity immediately launched another wave of nausea, and Elizabeth fought off the overpowering urge to throw up right onto the patchy weeds in the tiny front yard. She stumbled next door to Rosemary Lucchese's house, and weakly pounded on the door.

Rosemary only needed a fraction of a second's glance at her neighbor to know something was terribly wrong.

"We have to get you to the hospital!" Rosemary proclaimed even before Elizabeth could say anything.

Elizabeth nodded weakly, but then muttered:

"I don't think I can walk there."

Rosemary pulled Elizabeth inside the house.

"I'll call them and get them to send an ambulance," she said. After getting Elizabeth settled onto the worn sofa, she rushed into the kitchen, grabbed the phone, and quickly dialed "0" for the camp operator. Nearly thirty seconds passed before the corporal on duty answered.

"I need the hospital right away!" Rosemary yelled. "We need an ambulance over in the sergeant's housing area!"

"Okay, ma'am," came the staticky reply. Another minute passed before an orderly answered. Rosemary quickly began to explain the situation, but was interrupted with:

"Ma'am, there's been an accident out on the artillery range. All of our ambulances are out there right now."

"She can't walk! She's sick!" Rosemary shouted into the phone. "We need somebody to take her to the hospital!"

"Ma'am, we can try to get someone to come over in a Jeep and pick her up to bring her to the hospital. I'll try to find someone; give me your address and hold tight."

Rosemary Lucchese quickly recited her camp housing address, and then hung up. She hurried back into the living room. Elizabeth's eyes were closed, and for a moment Rosemary thought her neighbor had passed out...or maybe worse.

Elizabeth's eyes opened.

"I feel a little better now," she said weakly. "It doesn't hurt anymore..." Her voice trailed off.

"We still have to get you to the hospital," Rosemary said. "There aren't any ambulances, though, there was some sort of accident at the artillery range and they're all there. But they are going to find someone to drive a Jeep over here to bring you to the hospital."

"What sort of accident?" Elizabeth mumbled.

"What?"

"The artillery range; you said there was some kind of accident and all the ambulances were over there. What happened?"

"I don't know," Rosemary answered nervously. "But let's not worry about that right now, I'm sure Carlo is fine."

"Marco too," she added, referring to her own husband.

"Uh-huh," Elizabeth nodded as her eyes closed again. She was so tired! Maybe if she rested for a little while, she would feel better...

Nearly a half-hour passed before the Jeep appeared at Rosemary Lucchese's house. Two corpsmen hurried inside and helped load Elizabeth DeLuca into the vehicle, but Elizabeth was blissfully unaware of their efforts. She had passed out awhile back, and didn't regain consciousness until she had been inside the camp hospital for close to an hour.

"Mrs. DeLuca?" a voice called to her. Elizabeth finally opened her eyes and recognized the same Navy nurse, the lieutenant who sounded like a Southern belle, who had tried to assuage Elizabeth's worries several weeks back.

"Mrs. DeLuca?" came the voice again. "Mrs. DeLuca?"

Elizabeth tried to speak but was only able to clear her throat. She did open her eyes a touch, so the nurse was able to tell that she was awake.

"Doctor?" Elizabeth croaked. Receiving no response, she tried again.

"Where's the doctor?" she weakly asked the nurse.

The nurse's face took on a pained look as she sighed, but she quickly resumed her professional decorum.

"All of the doctors are either out at the artillery range or in surgery right now," the nurse replied.

"Where's the doctor?" Elizabeth repeated.

The nurse tried again.

"There aren't any doctors available right now, Mrs. DeLuca," sadness creeping into her syrupy voice.

"Am I going to be all right?" Elizabeth asked, cognizant enough to be concerned that not one single doctor was available to attend to her.

"You should be just fine," the nurse replied.

Elizabeth hesitated before asking the inevitable follow-up question.

"How about the baby?"

This time, no reply from the nurse, as the lieutenant was powerless to avoid looking away from this poor woman.

*   *   *

For the next month and a half, until she boarded the train back to Pittsburgh, Elizabeth's thoughts were consumed with her miscarriage and the events leading up to that heartbreaking occurrence. Even though she would never know for certain, Elizabeth still obsessively tried to discern what had caused her to lose her baby. Maybe it was those daily walks for the mail, outside in the oppressive summertime heat and humidity. However, Rosemary Lucchese was still carrying her child with no complications, at least by the time Elizabeth left Camp Lejeune, and nearly every day Rosemary had walked the same route alongside Elizabeth.

Perhaps weeks of constant stressful dread that began with her mother's letter had been the cause, at least in part. Elizabeth's mind was consumed with one conjured scenario after another in which her mother's malicious meddling led to irreparable strain between Elizabeth and Carlo. Surely such relentless worry couldn't be good for a pregnant woman, Elizabeth thought.

Then: after her symptoms began, the baby might still have been saved if she had been home in Pittsburgh, close to excellent medical care, rather than on a Marine Corps post without any sort of transportation. And even after finally arriving at the hospital, if she had been treated right away by a doctor, rather than having all of the Navy physicians otherwise engaged with the aftermath of a tragic artillery accident that had killed seven and wounded twenty more Marines, might that have made a difference?

Just maybe, though, miscarrying could have simply been "one of those things" – the words of the Camp Lejeune doctor who finally saw her, an exhausted Navy lieutenant commander who came by to check on Elizabeth in the hospital late that night. The doctor surely didn't mean to come across as callous and unfeeling. Elizabeth sensed that he was simply trying to be matter-of-fact with her, since he followed his remark by telling Elizabeth not to worry: she most likely could get pregnant again without any difficulty, and that one miscarriage didn't necessarily have to be a precursor to another.

Carlo did his best to comfort his wife; as much as he could, anyway, given that his training schedule for his Marines didn't let up one iota, even after Elizabeth's miscarriage. But during the moments they were together, from a stolen ten or fifteen minutes most mornings to the infrequent but glorious Sundays on which duty did not call, Carlo went out of his way to be as affectionate as possible to Elizabeth. He thought that perhaps he should try to make her pregnant again right away, but the Navy doctor had taken him aside and cautioned him against any "direct relations" with his wife for at least one month; maybe even longer, depending on how her recovery went.

Occasionally Elizabeth contemplated what Rosemary Lucchese had told her about that one woman, Dorothy Kaminsky, who perversely thought that losing her baby might be some sort of omen to bring her husband back safely from the war so he could *then* fulfill his destiny to make her pregnant. Not that she wanted to or even tried to, but Elizabeth couldn't bring herself to see her own miscarriage as equivalent to some sort of convoluted talisman that would somehow lead to Carlo's safe return.

Elizabeth could only think back to the aftermath of that terrible afternoon, almost one year ago exactly to the day, when Vicki Mendelsohn learned her husband had been killed. Elizabeth could clearly recall, when thinking about the blessing of Vicki's two children in the aftermath of losing her husband, that she herself would not have any children as a timeless memorial to her husband, should he perish in combat. She forlornly acknowledged that upon receiving word of Carlo's death, she would be left with almost nothing.

Chapter 19

September 5, 1943

"It looks a lot like the middle of Pennsylvania," Elizabeth remarked quietly as she gazed out the window of the *Tamiami Champion*, the train she and Carlo had boarded in Fayetteville. The train had just passed through Richmond, and was about three hours outside of Washington. When they arrived at Union Station in the nation's capital, Elizabeth would transfer to the Pennsylvania Railroad's *Liberty Limited* for the remainder of her journey home to Pittsburgh.

Carlo, however, would not be accompanying his wife from that point. His recently issued orders called for a week's stay in the nation's capital, where he would participate in a top secret joint War Department-Navy Department conference on Japanese battle tactics. Marine Corps and Army veterans of the major invasions and land campaigns in the Pacific thus far in the war – Guadalcanal, New Guinea, and New Georgia – were being called upon to help adapt U.S. battle doctrine to how the Japanese had responded to American amphibious assaults, as well was what the Marines and Army troops had encountered from the enemy as they moved inland.

Carlo knew that a number of new island assaults against the enemy were just around the corner, though he was well aware that the specifics were a closely held secret by the military brass. In fact, following his week in Washington he would backtrack forty-five miles or so down the Potomac to the big Marine Corps base at Quantico, where he would report for several weeks of amphibious assault tactics training for Marine sergeants. And then, he would be off to the West Coast and very soon afterward, onward to the Pacific…

"A lot of farms," Elizabeth continued, doing her best to keep her thoughts away from their impending separation, not to mention what she knew was inevitably in her husband's future. "Not as green, though…"

"That's 'cause it's already September," Carlo interjected, as eager to divert his thoughts from his own future as Elizabeth was. "A lot of stuff has already been harvested, even down South here, and what's left is already turning brown."

Elizabeth sighed. The summer of 1943 had begun with a different train ride, through the first traces of springtime rebirth: young grass that had only recently greened, newly plowed fields awaiting planting, trees bearing newly budded leaves…everything was new and fresh and promising. Now, a short four months later, the signs of the inevitable fast-approaching conclusion to this summer were all around her as she morosely stared out the train window. The chilly winds of autumn were just around the corner, and would be followed too soon by the leafless trees, spent farmers' fields, and the cold, gray skies of yet another winter.

How could *this* summer, of all the summers of her life, have flown by so quickly? Time could be a merciless tyrant. Elizabeth had been granted the unexpected luxury of four entire months alone with her husband, in the midst of an all-consuming war. Yet when Elizabeth thought back on this summer of 1943 that wasn't even concluded, as hard as she tried, she could only remember scattered fragments, almost every one enveloped in disappointment and despondency. She knew that Carlo wasn't to blame for having so little time to be with her, the entire spell she was with him at Camp Lejeune. And it certainly wasn't his fault that she had lost her baby through a miscarriage. Yet shouldn't those trials and tribulations have been counterbalanced at least somewhat by the remembrance of joyous moments…at least a few? Elizabeth tried her hardest, but happy memories of this summer of 1943 were all but nonexistent.

However, Elizabeth realized, time could also be a healer. Frustration and despair could well soften and even fade as days and weeks and months passed. Maybe a nostalgic tinge, newly overlaid onto sporadic moments from the summer, might eventually bestow those brief occasions with outsized significance. The Fourth of July picnic, for one: Carlo off duty for the day, now knowing that Elizabeth was carrying his child, spending an entire day with his wife in the small community park in town, mercifully away from Camp Lejeune. Elizabeth had enjoyed far too few moments like that one over the past four months; but they had been there.

She would give anything to have a do-over for this just-concluded summer!

But even as that thought came to Elizabeth, it evaporated just as quickly. Even if she could have somehow mastered the powers of the universe and turned back the calendar four months, Carlo would still have had exceptionally long duty days, far in excess of what he had anticipated when he suggested that Elizabeth accompany him. She most likely still would have lost her baby. They had done the best they could under the circumstances, and it was up to Elizabeth – and Carlo – to be grateful for a handful of stolen moments they might otherwise not have been granted.

At least thinking about the past – the actual past, or even some conjured Pollyanna-ish alternative – kept Elizabeth's thoughts away from the future. Not hers, particularly, but rather Carlo's. He hadn't shared everything he knew or had been told, but Carlo had told her enough that Elizabeth knew this gathering in Washington and the short assignment to Quantico were only brief interludes before Carlo's destiny as a combat Marine resumed. He wasn't to be stationed stateside, in D.C., or Virginia or anywhere else. He wouldn't be assigned to a neighborhood recruiting station somewhere, or sent to Parris Island or back to Camp Lejeune for another stint as a drill instructor. Very soon, he would be back in the Pacific, and Elizabeth shuddered at the thought.

* * *

The *Tamiami Champion* arrived at Union Station at 11:40 that morning, which meant that Elizabeth and Carlo had nearly six hours until her train to Pittsburgh departed at 5:25. Carlo was required to report to the adjutant at the newly built Pentagon by the end of the day, but no precise time had been specified on his orders. With a final afternoon to spend together, Carlo and Elizabeth hailed a cab and headed to the historic Georgetown neighborhood for lunch. The excursion had been Carlo's idea; another drill instructor from Camp Lejeune had suggested he treat his wife to a nice lunch there when the two of them hit D.C., if Carlo were able to find the time. When he broached the idea to Elizabeth with the mention of "Georgetown," a remembrance of Calvin McKinnon disagreeably forced its way into her thoughts. The young man had regaled Elizabeth with his tales of attending Georgetown University, which must be close by; at least that's what Elizabeth presumed from the common names.

She forced those thoughts away as quickly as they had appeared. Thanks to her mother, Elizabeth would likely still need to cope with the aftermath of an innocent Christmas party conversation that might perversely be used against her. Today was not the day for such worries; today was a day for Elizabeth and the one man that she knew she loved, before war took him away from her again.

A leisurely lunch at a charming restaurant was followed by an hour or so of unhurried strolling through the ancient streets. But as Elizabeth had gloomily philosophized aboard the train on the way to Washington, time could truly be a merciless tyrant; and too soon it was time to hail a cab back to Union Station.

*   *   *

"Please be careful," Elizabeth sobbed, hugging Carlo so very tightly. Unlike Carlo's departure from Pittsburgh's Penn Station nearly a year and a half ago, here at Union Station in the nation's capital it would be Elizabeth boarding a train with Carlo remaining behind. Yet the tearful farewell and the all-encompassing fear for her husband's safety were hardly distinguishable from how Elizabeth had felt back in May of '42.

"I will; I promise," Carlo replied with the slightest catch in his voice. He did his best to maintain his own composure – for his wife's sake – and to be strong for her. Carlo had a hunch that later on this evening, when he checked into whatever accommodations he would be assigned for the week, he might well break down himself if he found himself alone. Until then, he told himself, he had to be the strong one of the two of them; he owed that to Elizabeth.

"*Liberty Limited* final boarding for Baltimore; York, Pennsylvania; Harrisburg; Altoona; Pittsburgh; Crestline, Ohio…"

Carlo hesitated a moment before gently releasing Elizabeth and softly saying:

"That's you; you have to go now."

His words brought forth a fresh burst of sobbing from Elizabeth. In years to come, when thinking back to the Second World War and all that happened, among her most vivid remembrances would be their tearful partings while standing along railroad station platforms.

"I know," she murmured. Elizabeth tilted her face upward just as Carlo kissed her: gently at first, and then passionately.

"*Liberty Limited* final boarding…" the announcement came once again.

"Please write me when you can," Elizabeth said, her voice cracking.

"I will; I promise."

The porter had already loaded Elizabeth's luggage onto the train, so all Elizabeth had to do was pivot and walk a dozen steps through the open door of the nearest platform. Yet her legs were lead weights; every single painful stride would be one step farther away from Carlo, almost certainly for a very long time.

Still, she forced herself to take one laborious step, then another, and then another. Then she was quickly aboard, looking back over her shoulder as the train began to groan and squeal, almost as if in protest to being called upon for yet another long journey that would separate so many loved ones from each other. The train began to move, and Elizabeth hurried to an open seat by a window where she could stare back at Carlo until he was out of sight.

Back on the platform, Sergeant Carlo DeLuca stared somberly as the *Liberty Limited* began rolling down the tracks. In less than a minute, Elizabeth was gone.

Chapter 20

The *Liberty Limited* chugged into Pittsburgh at 1:19 in the morning, yet Angela was waiting at Penn Station for her sister-in-law. Elizabeth had sent a telegram to the DeLuca home when she knew her train schedule, asking if anyone could possibly meet her even at that late hour. She had been nervous about sending a telegram, given how the appearance of a Western Union man at someone's front door these days invariably caused instant terror. Yet by the time Elizabeth knew what date and time she would be arriving back in Pittsburgh, she wasn't certain that a U.S. mail letter would make it in time; and she didn't relish the idea of making her way home from Penn Station to Morningside by herself in the middle of the night.

Angela had recently obtained her own driver's license, so she volunteered to be the one to pick up Elizabeth. Midnight had come and gone and it was now Labor Day, which meant that the WPB offices were closed today and Angela was off of work for the day. She hadn't seen her sister-in-law for four long months, which actually felt more like four long years because she had so much to tell Elizabeth!

After a tearful greeting, Angela suggested that instead of going straight home, the two of them head to one of the all-night coffee shops that had been springing up in and around downtown over the past year, largely to accommodate war plant workers who toiled any hour of the day or night. They could chat for hours if they wished, and then tiptoe into the DeLuca house and both sleep late without the need to wake at any certain hour.

Despite the late hour, Pittsburgh's Penn Station bustled with the energy of the war's home front. The platforms and corridors and waiting areas were packed, and nearly every concession stand was operating as if it were the middle of the afternoon. Fifteen minutes passed before a porter was available for the girls. The man carried Elizabeth's baggage out to the parking lot, where Angela pointed out Carlo's Packard Six that had become the DeLuca family automobile with Carlo away. When she saw Carlo's ever-more-rusted vehicle that was so familiar to her, Elizabeth let out a small gasp at the fresh, painful memories of leaving Carlo only hours earlier that came flooding into her mind. Mistaking her sister-in-law's gasp for dismay at the state of the vehicle Angela was using to pick up Elizabeth, Angela offered sarcastically:

"What? You were expecting that I'd bring the Duesenberg instead?"

Angela's catty remark referred to the luxury automobile of the Depression years that so few could afford in those days; a sentiment she just blurted out because, for some strange reason, Elizabeth's gasp made Angela instantly think about her sister-in-law's hoity-toity Highland Park upbringing and her black market-dealing family.

However, Angela quickly noticed even in the darkness of the Penn Station parking log that Elizabeth's eyes were glistening, and suddenly the reason for Elizabeth's gasp – and tears – was glaringly obvious. The sudden sight of her husband's car had instantly saddened the poor girl, given that she had just left her husband only hours earlier after four months together! How could Angela have been so callously obtuse?

Fortunately, Elizabeth didn't react at all to Angela's acerbic remark; but Angela still felt compelled to offer an apology while the porter finished loading Elizabeth's suitcases into the trunk.

"I'm sorry, I didn't mean…"

A "don't worry about it" wave of Elizabeth's hand halted the apology, and Angela wisely decided to let the matter fade away.

"I have so much to tell you!" Angela proclaimed as she climbed behind the wheel and brought the sputtering Packard to life.

Elizabeth glanced over at her sister-in-law through the darkness as Angela carefully backed out of the parking space, and offered:

"Me, too."

*　*　*

Angela couldn't help herself. After a little bit more small talk during the three-minute drive to the coffee shop, as much as she wanted to hear about Elizabeth's glorious four months with her husband (or so she presumed), as soon as they were seated in the coffee shop, Angela finally blurted out what she had been bursting to share with her sister-in-law from the moment Elizabeth appeared at the train station:

"Carmela had an affair!"

Elizabeth's eyes widened and her mouth dropped open in shock. She was about to respond when the waitress came to take their orders. The *Liberty Limited* had a dining car, but between the immense desolation at having to leave Carlo and also having enjoyed such a splendidly elegant lunchtime meal, Elizabeth hadn't touched a bite during the train ride home. She was famished now, so this late-night coffee shop visit called for more than just pie and coffee. She ordered a turkey and gravy sandwich, and Angela – despite having gorged herself on two helpings of Rosalia DeLuca's lasagna earlier that evening – decided on the same.

As soon as the waitress departed, Angela launched into a detailed, even slightly embellished, recitation of Carmela's sorrowful, months-long tale that began with not-so-innocent flirtation and ended with the shock of being spurned. Elizabeth listened patiently as Angela spilled one sordid detail after another. When Angela had concluded her account, and after the waitress had finished delivering their turkey sandwiches and refilling their coffee before departing, Elizabeth began her own commentary that had been percolating as she listened to the story.

"I guess we shouldn't...I don't know, shouldn't be surprised..."

Elizabeth paused to gather her thoughts, taking a small bite from her sandwich as she did. After she had finished chewing and swallowing, she continued.

"Remember how, for months, she kept coming and going at strange hours? She wouldn't be home for dinner and come in really late; or she would be at supper, and then tell us that she was leaving to go meet friends from work. I don't know, I guess it always seemed like something was up with her. Maybe we should have figured it out ourselves, just from how she was acting."

"Maybe," Angela countered, "but remember, this was while you were waiting to hear about how Carlo was doing after being wounded, and then after you found out he was coming home, waiting every day for more information or for him to just show up. And then rushing around to go to Camp Lejeune with him."

Angela paused for a sip of her now-lukewarm coffee.

"And don't forget," she continued, "I was all worried about Tony in North Africa, until I found out that he wasn't there anymore. We both had plenty of things to worry about ourselves. So even thinking back and realizing that she was giving us...I don't know, clues or whatever...we both had our own problems."

Both girls were silent for a few moments while they took a few bites each from their sandwiches, before Angela picked up where she had left off.

"What do you think about what she said? The reason or excuse or whatever it was for why she had the affair in the first place?"

Just to make certain that Elizabeth knew what she was referring to, Angela added, "That she didn't feel like she was really married to her Tony because of the war and never really spending any time with him at all after they got married?"

"I don't know," Elizabeth muttered, shaking her head as she spoke. "War or not, they still took their wedding vows..."

Angela surprisingly blazed with irritation as she interrupted her sister-in-law's musings.

"That's easy for you to say! You just spent four months with *your* husband in the middle of a war! So how would *you* know if being that lonely would be enough to drive Carmela do something stupid without really thinking it all through?"

Elizabeth's own anger in her response to Angela's accusation far surpassed that displayed by her sister-in-law.

"Oh really? I'll have you know that for four months I barely saw Carlo! He would wake up at a quarter to five, every day but Sunday, and half the time he wouldn't even make it home for dinner! Maybe even more than that! So don't think that we were on some long vacation to get away from the war and everything!"

Elizabeth became even angrier.

"And don't forget that until he came home, I didn't see Carlo for every bit as long as Carmela didn't see Tony DeMarco! And the same with you and your Tony! In fact, you had your Tony home for four or five days last year, however long it was, so for me it was even longer that I hadn't seen Carlo! So don't you *dare* tell me that I don't have an idea what being lonely for my husband, month after month, is like!"

Elizabeth was just about shouting at this point, but fortunately this particular coffee shop was all but deserted by this late hour. A hefty steelworker was sitting at the counter, wearily drinking coffee and smoking a cigarette after a twelve-hour shift, catching up on the war news from the previous afternoon's *Pittsburgh Press*. The man briefly swiveled around to look at these two women in response to Elizabeth's angry rebuttal. But after a few seconds he turned back to his newspaper, not particularly interested in whatever the disagreement was between these two gals.

Both Elizabeth and Angela noticed that the man had looked in their direction, and that was enough to immediately tamp down Elizabeth's anger...as well as prevent an equally heated reaction from Angela in response to being yelled at.

"Sorry," Elizabeth murmured. "I guess you hit a nerve or something..."

"Yeah, I'm sorry also," Angela interrupted. "I had no idea..."

Angela paused for a couple of seconds to gather her thoughts.

"I guess I was just jealous that you got to spend four whole months with Carlo, while I haven't seen Tony in more than a year now. Plus I'm almost certain that he's part of the Sicily invasion..."

"Why didn't you write me about all of this? About Carmela?"

Angela sighed.

"Carmela swore me to secrecy; not to even tell my Tony. I was worried that if I wrote you and told you, and if Carlo saw the letter, then if he said anything to his brothers or his father and Ma DeLuca somehow found out, there would be hell to pay."

Elizabeth nodded.

"I guess I can see that," she agreed. "But what about you being worried about your Tony over there in Sicily? I barely heard from you the whole time I was there!"

"Same for you!" Angela countered, irritation flashing again. "I only got three letters from you the whole time!"

"I know, I'm sorry," Elizabeth murmured as she cast her eyes downward. "Kind of the same thing with me, I guess. I was worried that if I wrote you about…about Carlo having to spend so much time doing his training and him never at home, it would sound like I was complaining. And if Ma DeLuca saw that…"

"Oh yeah," Angela interrupted, nodding, immediately in tune with Elizabeth's thoughts. "It would sound like you were complaining to me about Carlo, and just like I said about Carlo knowing about Carmela, there would be hell to pay."

Angela paused as the waitress came to clear their plates and refill their coffee.

"I guess," she continued when the waitress was again out of earshot, "a lot of this business is just you and me, confiding in each other. I kept wishing you were around when I found out about Carmela so I could talk to you about it…"

"Same with me about Carlo," Elizabeth interrupted. "I figured that I could talk to you about it just like I am now, and that I would feel better. I just couldn't put all of that into a letter."

"That's the other thing with that whole business about Carmela," Angela offered. "I kept thinking over and over about what she said: about not feeling really married to her Tony. Every time I kept thinking about what a terrible thing she did, I would also wonder what I would do in her place if it were me instead of her. I mean, suppose I was sitting next to some guy at the Sun Drugs or Grant's lunch counter one day and we happened to strike up a conversation, and then I happened to see him there again a few days later and sit next to him again; and then before too long…well, you know…"

Angela sighed and then continued.

"Haven't you ever felt like that? Like one day you'll wind up talking to a strange man and before you know it you…I don't know, almost forget that you're married and something happens there? Because of the war? It's been in the back of my mind for a while now, I guess, and especially after finding out about Carmela's affair, I don't know why, but I keep thinking about it."

Angela took a gulp of her cooling coffee before adding:

"I missed talking to you all summer; we can talk about anything. I'm not even sure why I'm telling you all this; maybe it was building up all summer with finding out about Carmela and everything, I don't know…"

In a split second, Elizabeth's mind churned through a number of thoughts. First: was this some sort of confession on Angela's part, or just worried musing that the war-caused separation from her husband had finally taken her to the brink? Second: Angela was right; the two of them had become extremely close in the year that followed their marriages, and during the past four months Elizabeth had missed talking with and confiding in Angela every bit as much as her sister-in-law had just stated.

But third: what was behind several unprovoked, irritated outbursts by Angela (that in turn triggered Elizabeth's own angry rebuttal), especially after not seeing Elizabeth for months? The two of them had never even exchanged a cross word dating back almost a year and a half now, to when they had become furlough brides and sisters-in-law in rapid succession. This just didn't seem like the same girl with whom Elizabeth had become so close, and in whom Elizabeth had confided so many of her own hopes and fears.

Elizabeth sipped her own lukewarm coffee and, taking all of these jumbled thoughts into consideration, answered Angela's question.

"No, I haven't felt like that," Elizabeth answered quietly, slowly shaking her head…and avoiding looking directly at Angela as she replied.

Angela seemed to accept Elizabeth's answer at face value. She sighed once again before asking:

"So tell me more about being with Carlo at Camp Lejeune. Did anything else happen this summer down there?"

Elizabeth engaged in another burst of rapid-fire contemplation before shaking her head. This time she steeled herself to stare, poker-faced, directly at Angela as she answered.

"No; nothing really."

Chapter 21

September 27, 1943

Ordinarily, Elizabeth DeLuca would have been nervous to be seated in her supervisor's cramped office with the door closed. Instead, she was fuming; and she didn't care what Gerald Coleman thought about her anger.

"Mr. Coleman, I've told him probably a dozen times that I'm a married woman and don't want anything to do with him!"

The supervisor sat behind his desk and patiently listened to Elizabeth's complaint about one of her war plant coworkers not only repeatedly coming on to her for a while now, but also doing so in an increasingly abusive manner. Elizabeth had begun working in the military shoe plant a week after returning to Pittsburgh from Camp Lejeune, more or less taking Carmela's old job; though with the continued rapid growth of the war plant's work force, Elizabeth could never quite be sure if it was Carmela's exact position that she now held. But the stitching work was exactly the same as Carmela had done, in the same position on the same assembly line. So Elizabeth was quite comfortable thinking of herself as Carmela's successor.

Whereas Carmela had eventually been receptive to the overtures from one of her co-workers and then began her affair with Patrick Doyle, Elizabeth had no interest in any hanky-panky with any of the war plant men. Within the first three days Elizabeth worked there, though, four men had brazenly propositioned her despite being fully aware that Elizabeth was married to a combat Marine sergeant who would soon be on his way back to the Pacific. Three of these men had taken Elizabeth's rejections in stride, but one of them – a burly leather cutter named Janusz Nowak – persisted in his overtures. Elizabeth had the overpowering feeling that Nowak had been aware of Carmela DeMarco's clandestine affair with Patrick Doyle, and likely figured that Carmela's sister-in-law would be equally receptive to the same proclivities and merely required the proper amount of encouragement. Time and again, the man propositioned Elizabeth, and didn't seem fazed at all by annoyed rejection.

The final straw had been this morning, when Nowak stealthily came up behind Elizabeth about a half-hour after their shift began and brusquely grabbed her left arm. Elizabeth had whirled around to come face-to-face with the man, who sneered:

"Whaddya say, doll, about cuttin' out the playin' hard to get, already? Let's you and me…"

Nowak never finished his sentence. Elizabeth yanked her arm out of the man's grasp and instinctively kicked him in his right shin as hard as she could. Nowak let out a yelp of pain as a hateful look instantly came to his face, but Elizabeth was already hurrying on her way to the supervisor's office. Even if she found herself fired for kicking the man, enough was enough, already!

Gerald Coleman gazed back at this angry young woman. He disliked controversy, yet he knew that as a shift supervisor he had the responsibility to deal with situations such as this one. Until very early in 1942, Coleman had never found himself with such weighty workplace concerns. He was a cobbler by trade, for many years running his own little shoemaking and shoe repair shop not far from his Polish Hill home. With the outbreak of the war and the enlistment of his two oldest sons in the Army Air Forces, however, Gerald Coleman had felt obligated to do his own part for this all-consuming home front war effort. He landed this position as a shift supervisor in a large war plant that was charged with producing and then delivering to the boys in the military something Gerald knew very well: well-constructed, durable shoes and boots. He kept his own cobbler shop going in the evenings and on weekends, so between solemn responsibilities such as dealing with Elizabeth DeLuca's angry complaint and being dead on his feet most of the time, this war was taking quite a toll on Gerald Coleman, even though his own soldiering days had ended long ago in 1918.

Coleman was just about to respond to Elizabeth DeLuca when the telephone in his office rang. He held up his left index finger – that universal "hold on a moment" signal – to Elizabeth as he answered the phone. Elizabeth watched as, barely two seconds into the call, Gerald Coleman's eyes widened and the color instantly drain from his face as his mouth fell. He dropped the phone, and with the receiver away from the man's ear, Elizabeth could hear a woman's loud, anguished shrieking coming from the phone's handset.

He tried to pick up the telephone handset but fumbled it back onto his desk, not once but twice. Finally he was able to grasp the phone again.

"Irene…"

"What did it say?"

"Irene…"

"When?"

Several additional short bursts, and then a somber:

"I'm on my way. I'll go tell Tommy."

He hung up the phone and sank back into his chair, but only for a couple of seconds before popping back up to a standing position. All this time Elizabeth was watching her supervisor, feeling her heart sink for the man because of what obviously was terrible news he had just been given.

"My son," Gerald said, looking at Elizabeth. "He's an Air Corps pilot and they just sent a telegram saying that he was shot down."

"Oh my God, that's awful!" Elizabeth blurted out. The natural question in response to his news was one that Elizabeth didn't dare ask, but Gerald Coleman gave Elizabeth the answer to her unspoken question.

"He was reported as missing in action," Gerald Coleman said.

"I'm so sorry, Mr. Coleman!" Elizabeth offered, her own eyes filling with tears.

The supervisor was already headed towards the door when he stopped.

"You take the rest of the day off," he told Elizabeth, "and tomorrow when you come in, Nowak will be gone from the plant and won't bother you again."

Elizabeth was dumbfounded. It hadn't occurred to her that her supervisor would fire the bullying man, if that's what Gerald Coleman was telling Elizabeth what would happen. At best, she hoped that the supervisor would take pity on her and move her to another assembly line, in a different part of the plant; perhaps even in a different role. Elizabeth had heard enough stories about men in war plants persistently and sometimes viciously bothering girls who were viewed as unwelcome intruders into the male work world. Elizabeth had yet to hear of a story where one of these men was fired and the woman allowed to continue without any changes to her position or employment status.

Time would tell. Obviously, Gerald Coleman was focused on a far more ominous matter than Elizabeth DeLuca's workplace peace of mind. But when Carmela had suggested that Elizabeth apply for a job at the place where she had worked until recently, she had also told Elizabeth that Mr. Coleman had seemed like a straight-up guy. So maybe the world was changing: at least here in this particular war plant, and at least a little bit.

* * *

That evening while helping the other DeLuca women prepare dinner and set the table, Elizabeth told Angela in hushed tones about being in her supervisor's office at the moment he received the horrifying news of his son being shot down. Neither Elizabeth nor Angela wanted their mother-in-law to overhear them talking about someone receiving horrendous news from the war front. Less than a year had passed since that terrible morning that Rosalia DeLuca had been delivered the telegram informing them all about Carlo being wounded in the Pacific, and the old-country Italian woman was prone to so many superstitions. Perhaps even the simple act of hearing firsthand about another family's wartime sorrow inside her own home would be enough to convince Rosalia that more bad news was coming to the DeLuca household. Neither Elizabeth nor Angela wanted that on their heads, so the conversation about Gerald Coleman's son was one to keep from their mother-in-law.

Carmela, however, was a different story. Noticing her two sisters-in-law clandestinely conversing in hushed tones outside of the kitchen, she naturally wanted to know what the big secret was. Elizabeth quickly filled Carmela in.

"That's awful!" Carmela exclaimed in tones slightly above a whisper. "Mr. Coleman is such a nice man, too!"

Angela didn't know anybody who worked at the shoe and boot war plant other than Elizabeth – and earlier, Carmela – and for whatever reason, neither Elizabeth nor Carmela had thought to use any reference other than "my supervisor" when mentioning Mr. Coleman in their respective tales. Elizabeth had been about to tell Angela about this latest harassment at the hands of Janusz Nowak as the reason for being in her supervisor's office in the first place when the poor man received the ominous phone call from his wife.

"Did you say Coleman?" Angela blurted out.

"Uh-huh," Elizabeth nodded, and then added, "Why?"

Angela swallowed.

"Is he from Polish Hill?"

"I think so," Elizabeth replied slowly, and then repeated, "Why?"

"Do you know what his son's name is? The one who was shot down?"

This time, Elizabeth shook her head.

"I don't think Mr. Coleman mentioned his name. At least I don't remember."

And then, for a third time:

"Why?"

Angela sighed. Just before she began to answer she heard noises from the kitchen, where Rosalia was bustling among the cooking pots, probably wondering why all three of the younger women had slipped out of the kitchen.

Angela looked back towards the kitchen for a few seconds until she was convinced that her mother-in-law intended to remain there.

"There's two girls at work who have boyfriends that are brothers named Coleman, and both of them are Air Corps pilots. Actually, one of the girls, Francine, is engaged to one of them – Jonathan – and the other is sort of the girlfriend of the other brother – Joseph – even though she's seeing some other man at work now."

Elizabeth thought hard, but couldn't recall either of those names being mentioned by Gerald Coleman.

"Is their father named Gerald? That's Mr. Coleman's first name," Carmela interjected.

Angela shrugged.

"I don't know," Angela replied.

*   *   *

Angela's night was a difficult one. She endured several jumbled dreams in which Tony DeLuca was somehow the son of this Mr. Coleman, whom she of course had never met, but in one dream looked just like Giuseppe DeLuca, while in another nightmare looked just like President Roosevelt. In one of the dreams, Elizabeth was the one who shared the tragic news with the entire family that Tony DeLuca – an Army Air Forces pilot rather than an infantryman – had been shot down on a bombing run over Germany. In another dream, Tony was also an Air Corps pilot, but the bad news delivered to Angela was that he had abruptly left the Army Air Forces to take a job at the Willow Run B-24 plant near Detroit, where he would remain forever.

Angela was dead tired the next morning, and she dreaded what the workday might bring if her suspicions were correct. Sure enough, she was in the process of grinding the remnants of a just-finished Pall Mall into the sidewalk before heading inside when a grim-faced Francine Donner approached.

"I got terrible news last night," Francine immediately declared without any sort of prelude.

A horrified look immediately came to Angela's face, but before she could say anything in response, Francine continued.

"Jonathan's brother was shot down. A couple weeks ago; they got the telegram yesterday. He wasn't killed; or at least the War Department didn't report him as killed, he's listed as Missing in Action."

"I know!" Angela finally blurted out.

"What?" Francine responded immediately. How in the world could this other girl possibly have known about Joseph Coleman?

Angela quickly explained the connection with her sister-in-law's supervisor. Francine noted the small-world connection, but she was far more concerned about the terrifying task that awaited her.

The two women entered the WPB building and headed up the stairs to the second floor. Francine's eyes scanned the floor until she found Abby Sobol. She and Angela walked slowly in the direction of Abby's desk. When they were about fifteen feet away, Abby looked up and saw her grim-faced friends headed directly toward her. Abby didn't know what the girls were about to tell her, but she knew with all the certainty in the world that it wasn't good news.

"Joseph was shot down," Francine said despondently, able to look directly at Abby for only a second or two before gazing downwards.

"He was reported as missing, not killed, so he might..."

"Oh no! God no!" Abby shrieked, her right hand covering her mouth that was wide open with horrific disbelief. She instantly dissolved into a fit of uncontrollable sobbing. Secretaries from all around the second floor immediately looked in Abby's direction. Most knew that she had been seeing Jeffrey Belkin for several months now, so they presumed that it must be a brother or other close relative about whom Abby had obviously received terrible war-related news.

Hearing the racket from out on the main part of the WPB's second floor, Jeffrey Belkin stuck his head out of his office door and looked in the direction of the wailing that was growing even louder. His eyes widened when he saw that it was Abby Sobol doing the crying. Belkin knew that Abby had no brothers or close cousins fighting the war; but even without that knowledge, he still would have known for a fact whose wartime misfortune had caused his own girlfriend to react this way.

* * *

"She was going to write Joseph a Dear John letter," Francine somberly told Angela as the girls sat at the Sun Drugs lunch counter. Abby had gone home for the day. All morning both Francine and Angela had found it very difficult to concentrate on their work; their lunch hour couldn't have come soon enough.

"Back in August," Francine continued.

"But she didn't?" Angela asked as she toyed with her cottage cheese. Even the meager amount of food in the Secretary's Special wasn't appetizing today.

Francine shook her head.

"I ran into his younger brother Tommy, down at *Weisberg's* when I was produce shopping. He works there, just like Jonathan used to. He kept asking over and over about Abby, and saying things like Joseph had written him to say that he would think about Abby when he was flying a mission so he could make it through to come home to her; those sorts of things. I don't know why, but I couldn't take hearing that anymore; the idea that Joseph thought Abby was still waiting for him the way I was waiting for

Jonathan. So I told him that Abby was seeing someone else and that she was about to write him to tell him."

Francine paused but the forkful of salad she speared came nowhere near her mouth; her appetite was as absent as Angela's was.

"Tommy asked me to tell Abby not to write the letter. I kept asking him why, and he kept saying that he didn't know, but it would be better if she didn't write him…at least not just yet. So I told him that I'd tell her, but I couldn't promise that she would listen or that she hadn't already just written and mailed the letter."

"That's strange," Angela mused. "I wonder why his brother thought that way. It's almost like he had a premonition that Joseph would get shot down."

Francine shrugged.

"I don't know. Maybe he did, and he figured that if he was taken prisoner, then at least he would have the idea that Abby was home waiting for him, and that could get him through being in one of those German prison camps."

Francine let out a sigh of despair.

"Or if, God forbid, Joseph got killed when he got shot down, then his last thought wouldn't be about Abby having jilted him for someone else."

Chapter 22

November 25, 1943

Elizabeth only half-listened to "Paper Doll" as she set the DeLuca family's Thanksgiving table. For one thing, the Mills Brothers song had been at the top of the charts for an entire month now with plenty of radio play on programs such as *Tune Factory*, which Elizabeth was listening to at the moment. She liked the song but it was wearing on her by now, having heard it dozens of times in recent weeks.

Beyond the over-familiarity of the song, though, Elizabeth's thoughts were partly a mile or so away, at her parents' home in Highland Park, and also in part thousands of miles to the west out in the Pacific. Her parents' home: last year at this time for the Thanksgiving holiday, she had still been living there. The fallout from the Witherspoon Club Christmas Party was still several weeks away. Thanksgiving 1942 in the Buchanan home hadn't been particularly memorable to Elizabeth, other than her heart aching for and worrying about Carlo. Her husband had been fighting on Guadalcanal this time last year, and Elizabeth wouldn't know until after New Year's that two days earlier Carlo had been wounded.

Once again this year, Carlo was almost certainly spending his Thanksgiving somewhere far away in the Pacific. Fighting had been raging on two islands in the Gilberts – Tarawa and Makin – since Saturday. The U.S. Marine Second Division was reported to be bearing the load on Tarawa, and Elizabeth picked up hints from

Carlo's most recent letter that he had been sent back to his old Guadalcanal unit. Makin, the other island in the Gilberts that was targeted, was invaded the same day as Tarawa but miraculously had already fallen to the American attackers. In fact, FDR's oldest son, Marine Corps Lieutenant Colonel James Roosevelt, was reported to have been among the American military leaders who took Makin in only about seventy-two hours.

Even more soldiers and Marines had been fighting on another island called Bougainville, out in the Solomons, since the beginning of the month. So one way or another, Carlo was almost certainly engaged in combat somewhere out there at the moment...if he hadn't again been wounded as he had been on Guadalcanal last year, that was. Maybe he had been with Colonel Roosevelt and the other Marines on Makin, which would mean he was already finished with combat, at least for the moment, due to the American victory.

"From the Mutual Newsroom in New York," the solemn-sounding announcer interrupted as "Paper Doll" was abruptly halted with thirty seconds or so still remaining in the song. Elizabeth froze in place. War bulletins often contained ominous news but sometimes they offered promising reports, and people all across the United States halted everything when one came on whatever radio station they might be listening to.

"United Press is reporting that the island of Tarawa, a key Japanese stronghold in the Gilbert Islands, has fallen to the United States Marine Corps. No formal Japanese surrender has yet occurred, but war correspondents from United Press and elsewhere report that the Marines now have control of the entire island and have begun mop-up operations. To repeat: the Marine Corps has taken the island of Tarawa. Stand by for further bulletins. We now return you to your regular local radio programming."

As much of a relief as it was to hear of an American victory – particularly the second lightning-fast one in rapid succession, unlike the many months the Guadalcanal Campaign had lasted – the aftermath of a victory brought with it an accounting of American casualties. Dead and wounded would be counted; telegrams to loved ones would be sent and received; and so many American families would mourn their lost loved ones or worry about those who had been wounded.

Catching sight of Angela entering the kitchen from the living room, Elizabeth asked, "Did you hear? About Tarawa?"

Angela shook her head.

"The Marines took the island from the Japs," Elizabeth continued. "In only a couple of days, just like that other island."

Angela let out a relieved sigh.

"That's a relief," she replied, just in case the meaning of her thankful exhalation was lost on Elizabeth. "If Carlo was there, then he should be done fighting."

Elizabeth's eyes locked with Angela's, and Angela knew exactly what Elizabeth's natural follow-on was. Their glance said it all, though, so Elizabeth didn't put voice to her natural worries. She simply nodded and quietly replied:

"I hope so."

"Any news about Italy?" Angela asked.

Elizabeth shook her head.

"No, Mutual had a special UP bulletin about Tarawa. I missed the regular news earlier, but it will be on in…"

Elizabeth glanced at the wall clock in the kitchen that showed the hour of 5:00 p.m. quickly approaching.

"…about 10 minutes," she continued.

Angela shrugged. Right now just she and Elizabeth were in the kitchen. Rosalia had gone upstairs for a moment, as had Carmela. Giuseppe DeLuca was tinkering with a woodworking project in the basement while the women finished cooking and setting the table. They would call him when it was suppertime: about forty minutes from now, Elizabeth figured.

"It doesn't matter," Angela said despondently. "It's the same news all the time, anyway. I mean from Italy. It's probably going to be a long one there, just like North Africa was."

Angela now knew for a fact from one of Tony's V-mail letters that he had, in fact, been part of the Allied invasion of Sicily back in the summer, and she was all but certain that he was now in the follow-on offensive on the Italian mainland. The American forces had landed near Salerno back in early September while their British allies chose Calabria, not far from Sicily, as their landing point. Both allies fought their way inland from their invasion points through the autumn of '43, and now all of southern Italy was in Allied hands. The approaching winter presented new challenges as the Allies began to press northward to Rome, however, and those on the home front with loved ones fighting there – like Angela – fretted about what might come next.

All of a sudden, Angela let out an anguished sigh and sank into one of the kitchen chairs. Her sister-in-law looked at her sharply.

"What's wrong?" Elizabeth asked, alarmed.

Another sigh, as Angela slowly, sadly shook her head back and forth a couple of times.

"It's all the same," came Angela's cryptic response.

Elizabeth cocked her head.

"What do you mean?"

"It's all the same," Angela repeated. "This year and last year."

She let out another weighty sigh and looked up at Elizabeth.

"Last Thanksgiving Tony was fighting against the Germans in North Africa, and so were the British. This Thanksgiving he's fighting against the Germans in Italy, and so are the British. Last Thanksgiving, Carlo was fighting the Japs on Guadalcanal way out in the Pacific. Now he's fighting the Japs on Tarawa or one of those other islands way out in the Pacific."

Tears glistened in Angela's eyes.

Angela glanced towards the door leading from the kitchen to the basement.

"We'll all be sitting around the table for Thanksgiving supper soon, and Pa DeLuca will talk about Tony and Carlo, and also Vinnie and Michael, and how we all pray that they're safe and that they'll be home by next Thanksgiving. Just like he did last year; probably even the exact same words, just like a recording."

A tiny sob escaped from Angela before she continued.

"It's just the same thing; last year and this year. They say that we're starting to win, but how much longer? What about next Thanksgiving? The same thing all over again, just in different countries and different islands? And then the Thanksgiving after that?"

Angela's tears began to slowly slide down her cheeks. Then she put voice to the sentiment that had been so vivid for both Elizabeth and her in the days and weeks following their husbands going off to war; a sentiment that until now, both women had been able to keep at bay, at least a little bit.

"I don't think I can take another day of this," Angela DeLuca said, her voice cracking.

Elizabeth struggled for something to say, but since Angela had been the one to tearfully declare exactly how Elizabeth herself felt, she was powerless to do anything other than let her own tears spill slowly from her mournful eyes.

Chapter 23

December 11-12, 1943

Elizabeth's three distressing dreams (or had there been four of them?) the night of the 1943 Witherspoon Club Christmas Party were hardly unexpected. She hadn't attended the party, of course, but Elizabeth was well aware that this Saturday night had been the date of the occasion.

In the first – and most vividly recalled – dream, Calvin McKinnon had merrily strolled up to Elizabeth while she was standing with her mother, in line at the club's elegant bar to order drinks. He wordlessly handed her a telegram, every single word of which Elizabeth could recall with perfect clarity after she woke:

REGRET TO INFORM YOU YOUR HUSBAND SERGEANT CARLO DELUCA WAS ON 1 DECEMBER 1943 KILLED IN ACTION IN THE PACIFIC YOU ARE ADVISED BY THE DEPARTMENT OF THE NAVY AND YOUR MOTHER KATHERINE BUCHANAN TO MARRY MISTER CALVIN MCKINNON AS SOON AS POSSIBLE =

Just before Elizabeth forced herself awake, her dreamworld mother snatched the telegram from her daughter's hand, narrowed her eyes, and sneered:

"See? I told you this was what would happen! You should have listened to me! You already would have a child by now, not a miscarriage from that greaseball!"

The other two – or three, or who knew how many – dreams were variations on the same theme. In each of them, Elizabeth had been powerless to keep away from the Witherspoon Club and all that it came to represent to her, and she found herself in the midst of hundreds of gaily celebrating men and women, seemingly oblivious to the war fronts in Europe and the Pacific. In one of the other dreams Elizabeth and Calvin reprised their hour-long discussion from the previous year, and it wasn't until the end of that enjoyable conversation that he lazily reached into the inner pocket of his tuxedo to pull out the telegram of death and hand it to Elizabeth.

Shortly after 5:00 a.m. Elizabeth had enough with trying to sleep and fished for her slippers and quietly headed downstairs. Enough with the terrible dreams! She eased the front door open to retrieve the Sunday *Pittsburgh Press* that was waiting in the chilly morning blackness. Elizabeth absorbed the headline on her way to the sofa:

U.S. Fliers Down 138 Nazi Planes, Lose 20 in Heavy Raid on Emden

She scanned the accompanying front-page story as she lit a Pall Mall. The Eighth Air Force had again gone after the German port city of Emden, this time with an unusually large air armada. In the resulting air battles that surrounded the bombing raid, the Luftwaffe lost 138 of their planes: a fairly heavy toll, the United Press story related, though less than half the record number of German planes shot down by the Air Corps in an enormous air encounter back in August.

The Army Air Forces hadn't escaped unscathed, though, losing seventeen bombers and three fighters, according to the *Press* story.

Elizabeth set the paper down on the sofa as she slipped over to the kitchen to quietly make coffee. The story noted that this raid was the sixth one on this German port city. How many more missions needed to follow for whatever the Air Corps was trying to accomplish? Heavy Luftwaffe losses aside, how many more American air crews would be shot out of the sky along with their planes, either to their death or ending up in Nazi prison camps?

Elizabeth suddenly had a curious thought. Today was now December 12th. Would the ominous "killed in action" or "missing in action" telegrams for – what would that be, more than 170 American airmen? – be transmitted in time for their families to know by Christmastime that their loved ones were either dead or missing? Or would those families sit around their Christmas Eve or Christmas Day tables and say prayers for the continued safety in combat of those men, oblivious to the fact that those prayers were now for naught?

And where were those 170 or so families? Were any of them here in Pittsburgh? Far away in Los Angeles or San Francisco? In some small farming village in central Pennsylvania or southern Virginia that Elizabeth and Carlo had passed on their train journeys this past summer?

In a strange way, Elizabeth's intense contemplation of the fate of these airmen helped push aside the distressing dreams she had endured this previous night. The headline she had read reported a somber truth: twenty American planes had been lost in this raid on some distant German town she had never heard of before. In fact, given the wartime reporting that often downplayed American losses and exaggerated those of the enemy, the toll could even be higher than twenty aircraft and their crews.

In contrast, her troubling dreams of Carlo's death and her fate now in the hands of Calvin McKinnon – and her mother! – were playing only in the theater of her mind. They were just that: dreams, not reality. In no way was Elizabeth being complacent about her husband's fate far away in the Pacific. For all she knew, the first week of January, 1944, could well reprise the first week of this year that was almost concluded, and a telegram bearing news of Carlo being wounded – or worse – could be awaiting her.

I just have to force those fears out of my mind, Elizabeth told herself, the same as I've been doing ever since Carlo went away to war.

The coffee was ready; and as Elizabeth lit another Pall Mall and poured herself a cup, she said a silent prayer for all of those Army Air Forces flyers – and their families – whose misfortune only weeks before Christmas of 1943 had been so unfeelingly wrapped up into a single, cold statistic in the morning's headline.

Chapter 24

December 31, 1943

My darling Carlo,

I'll begin with the same exact words (at least I think so) that I wrote to you last New Year's Eve: I can't put into words how much I miss you on this New Year's Eve, as I do every single day. In some ways, this New Year's Eve is almost the same as last year. I don't know exactly where you are, and I hope and pray that you're alright. If you're still fighting somewhere, please stay safe. If you're finished for a while, then I hope it's a long, long time until you have to fight again.

This has been such a strange year. In some ways it's been terrible, since it began with finding out that you had been wounded in action. But then we found out that you were okay and I had the wonderful surprise that you were coming home.

Even better was something I never would have expected, to spend the entire summer with you. The summer flew by so quickly, though, and I know you were so busy. And we had the tragedy of losing the baby. It all went by in a blur, and seemed to be a summer filled with problems for both of us. Yet when I think back, I wouldn't trade being able to spend four months with you for all the money in the world!

I haven't told anybody - Angela, Carmela, your mother, and certainly not my mother - about losing the baby, or even being pregnant. I don't know exactly why I didn't say anything to anybody, but I didn't. And at this point, I'd like that to be just between us. I can't really explain why. I know you haven't mentioned anything about the baby in your letters to your mother or to anybody else at home, because they would have immediately asked me. And I really hadn't thought much about it over the past few months. But I guess as this year ends and 1944 begins, I'd like us to have a fresh start with EVERYTHING bad behind us.

I don't know if you received any letters recently from Vinnie, but in case you didn't he was home in Pittsburgh for two days at the beginning of December. He made it home safely after all of his missions and now is going through Air Corps officer training, and then will train to be a pilot. (I'm hoping the censors don't cut this out - I didn't write anything that is sensitive like where he's training or anything else. So PLEASE Mister or Miss Censor, don't cut out this paragraph!)

I miss you terribly, and I pray that by next New Year's Eve this awful war is over and that you're home for good. Please write me soon.

All my love to you,

Elizabeth

1944

Chapter 25

March 17, 1944

Through the beginning months of 1944, a kind of fatigue settled over the American home front. For every capital-lettered, bold-typed headline that screamed "1,600 U.S. PLANES HIT BERLIN" – as last Tuesday's *Post-Gazette* had reported on Page 1 – many other newspaper stories and the radio reports from Mutual and NBC Red and the other networks wearily and matter-of-factly reported news of stubborn counterattacks still forthcoming from the enemy on one war front or another. Just last week the Japanese had launched an offensive on Bougainville, the island battle that began early last November, shortly before the invasions of Tarawa and Makin. Unlike those other two islands that each saw American victories in a matter of days, vicious fighting on Bougainville was still ongoing more than four months later, with no end in sight. The darkest days from the earliest months of the war, when the enemy Axis powers appeared to be all but invincible, might be far in the past now. Yet every gain, in every battle and on every front, was not only hard-fought but also susceptible to challenge and even reversal, due to the back-and-forth offensives between both sides that still hallmarked this war.

Elizabeth had received several V-mail letters from Carlo. Piecing together tidbits from his communiqués, she knew that he wasn't fighting on Bougainville, and she was almost certain that he had been part of the ferocious fighting on Tarawa. Reports of how heavy the Marines' casualties had been on that blood-soaked island had leaked out, but Carlo had survived; and he had apparently been among the fortunate Marines who hadn't been wounded, either. Now, he was "somewhere out in the Pacific, I can't tell you where," no doubt training for yet another island invasion before too long.

Angela sadly knew that, unlike Carlo, her husband was still locked in battle as the Americans and British struggled to push into Northern Italy, months after taking the southern part of the country. Word from Tony had been sparse, but two precious V-mail letters since New Year's had given Angela enough information to be almost certain where he was; and the newspaper headlines and radio bulletins told her what he was facing. The fighting in Italy was especially vicious, with the Germans extracting a heavy toll on the American and British forces. If the Nazis were proving this difficult as the Italian campaign shifted to the northern part of the country, what would the eventual invasion of France bring in the way of brutal resistance by the mighty German army?

Angela and Elizabeth – and Carmela, and most everyone else they knew – were all in agreement: they were all sick of the war, not only for the obvious reasons, but also because happy news of any kind was almost non-existent.

But occasionally, someone else on the home front did receive happy news.

* * *

Today being Saint Patrick's Day, Gerald Coleman arranged for a wee bit of Irish hospitality for his workers near the end of the day shift. All production quotas for the week had been met by 2:30 that afternoon, so at 3:00 more than 150 workers gathered in the cafeteria area at the Mount Washington war plant.

The firing of Janusz Nowak last September had been a wake-up call to those workers still reluctant to work on an assembly line alongside women or who saw these female workers as little more than potential playthings, and for the most part tranquility hallmarked the workdays at the plant. Dalliances still occurred – even illicit ones with one or both parties married to someone else, as had been the case with Carmela when she worked there – but they were conducted quietly, with no disruption to shoe and boot production, nor harm to morale among the plant workers.

Gerald Coleman circulated among the tables in the cafeteria, making small talk with each group of workers for a few minutes. He had just reached the table where Elizabeth DeLuca and five of her coworkers had gathered, all of them sipping beer in honor of the Irish holiday.

"Mr. Coleman? Mr. Coleman?" came the breathless voice of Betty Harkness, who served as Gerald Coleman's all-around assistant for scheduling, typing reports, and other administrative functions. Betty was all but running across the cafeteria floor toward Gerald once she spotted him. She had stayed behind at her desk to finish up today's production report before eventually joining the festivities.

Elizabeth looked over at Gerald Coleman just as his face took on that same look of sudden shock as when she had been in his office that day last fall when he received word about his son being shot down. Oh no, Elizabeth immediately thought; it must be his other son! Or maybe his son Joseph hadn't survived after all and had now been reported as killed in action. Oh, the poor man!

"Mr. Coleman! Your son is alive!" Betty Harkness shouted when she neared the cafeteria table. "Your wife just called and said they sent a telegram; the Red Cross did! He's been officially reported as a prisoner of war, and he's alive!"

Elizabeth saw the tears of relief immediately slide from Gerald Coleman's eyes. For close to half a minute he said nothing, nor did he move a muscle. Everyone else around the table, Elizabeth included, offered their congratulations and prayers for the wonderful news. Finally, Mr. Coleman seemed to make a great effort to muster enough strength to stand.

"I need to go home," he muttered. "I need to see this telegram with my own two eyes."

Elizabeth and everyone else at the table nodded responded with "of course" or "I know" or some other similar short acknowledgment. Mr. Coleman headed away from the table towards the cafeteria doorway, slowly at first but then picking up speed as if the energy that had drained from his body was now returning.

Suddenly the thought occurred to Elizabeth: I should call Angela! She can let those two girls she works with know the good news, because most likely they haven't heard yet! Elizabeth looked at the cafeteria wall clock that showed the time as 3:55, which meant Angela would still be at work, unless the WPB was stopping work early today as well. She quickly explained to the others at her table what she was going to do and then hurried out of the cafeteria to the closest hallway telephone. Fortunately no one else was using the phone. She removed the handset, dialed "0," and when the operator came onto the line, Elizabeth quickly said,

"Could you please connect me to the War Production Board in Oakland?"

"Hold please," came the near-mechanical response. A couple of seconds passed and then the operator added,

"Which War Production Board? Oakland or downtown?"

"The one in Oakland," Elizabeth replied quickly and evenly. She fought to keep the irritation from her voice. For all she knew, every second counted trying to reach Angela as the clock ticked towards the end of the workday, and Elizabeth had already told the operator she wanted the office in Oakland!

"Hold please," the operator repeated. This time, after a couple of seconds, Elizabeth heard the ringing coming from the other end of the line.

None of the secretaries had her own telephone at her desk, and by the time the main WPB switchboard operator had contacted the second floor operator, who then had to locate someone to go find Angela DeLuca, nearly ten full minutes had passed. All the while, Elizabeth kept saying short prayers that Angela didn't leave work early, with today being both Friday and St. Patrick's Day. Fortunately, today was business as usual at the WPB, Saint Patrick's Day notwithstanding.

"Hello?" Angela's choked, anxious, almost tearful voice came on the line, and Elizabeth realized that she hadn't told any of the operators with whom she had spoken who was calling Angela, or why. Angela almost certainly thought that something terrible had happened, maybe even to her Tony.

"Angela, it's me, Elizabeth," came the rapid-fire reply. "Nothing's wrong, I swear! Nothing's wrong!"

"Oh my God," Angela replied, "you scared me!"

"I'm sorry, I didn't even think about that. I'm calling because there's fantastic news! Mr. Coleman from work...his son who was shot down last year? He's alive! His son, I mean! He's in a German prisoner of war camp. The Red Cross sent a telegram, and he just got a call from home to let him know."

For a second or two Angela wondered why in the world Elizabeth was calling to share this news, but the realization hit her just as Elizabeth continued.

"You can let those girls at work know; both of them, the one who's engaged to his brother and the other one who was his girl for a little bit. I'm sure she wants to know that he's alive, too."

"Uh-huh," Angela responded as she looked back to the center of the room from where she had taken the call. She could see both Francine and Abby at their desks.

"I'll go tell them right now," Angela excitedly continued, and then added:

"You know what? We might go out and have a drink or two to celebrate the good news, especially with it being St. Patrick's Day. So I might not be home for supper. I'll call Ma DeLuca to let her know if I do go out."

Angela's words were met with a long pause on the line before Elizabeth said:

"Oh, okay."

Another few seconds of pause, and then:

"Well, I just wanted to call you so you could tell those girls the good news. Goodbye."

Click.

As Angela hung up the phone, she was puzzled by Elizabeth's sudden coolness at the end of the call. Maybe Elizabeth had wanted Angela to invite her to go out with these other girls after work, even though she didn't know them; that's probably it, Angela realized. For a brief instant she considered calling Elizabeth back to retroactively invite her to tag along, but just as quickly Angela realized that she didn't have a phone number for the plant where Elizabeth worked. She could probably call the operator and get connected that way, and she contemplated doing just that.

In the end, though, Angela decided to let the matter lie. She saw her sister-in-law plenty. Why, just last weekend the two of them had seen three movies together. They had headed downtown to the Loew's Penn for a Saturday matinee showing of *Song of Russia* with Robert Taylor and Susan Peters, and then stayed downtown for another movie that night after eating dinner out; this time *Passage to Marseille* with Humphrey Bogart at the Stanley. As if that wasn't enough, Carmela joined them Sunday afternoon for a double feature at the Senator consisting of two favorite oldies from the latter part of the previous decade: *A Star is Born* with Frederic March and also *Made for Each Other* with Carol Lombard and Jimmy Stewart.

The girls had specifically chosen the Sunday matinee of older movies to escape from the war, but the second feature wound up doing the exact opposite. As they watched the drama, they couldn't help but think about the war. Jimmy Stewart was now an Army Air Forces Major, known to be flying B-24 missions over Germany and occupied Europe; and of course poor Carole Lombard had died more than two years ago now, in an airplane crash returning from a War Bond Tour.

Angela forced her thoughts back to the present. She spent *plenty* of time with her sister-in-law – both of her sisters-in-law, in fact – so if she wanted to have a drink or two or three with Francine Donner and Abby Sobol to celebrate the sudden good news that Abby's former beau was alive, Elizabeth didn't need to be there for *that* occasion.

Angela hurried over to Francine's and Abby's adjoining desks. Wanting to avoid startling them or catalyzing unnecessary fear when those girls would notice her speedy steps, Angela deliberately disregarded the rules of governmental office decorum and all but shouted:

"Joseph is alive! Joseph Coleman! He's alive!"

At these words both Abby and Francine looked up at the rapidly approaching Angela DeLuca.

"My sister-in-law just called me," Angela continued, "Joseph's father got a call at their war plant! The Red Cross sent a telegram that he's alive in a German prisoner camp. That's all they know now, but he wasn't killed when he was shot down! He's alive!"

Abby's right hand flew to the center of her chest as her head tilted back slightly.

"Oh my God!" she blurted.

A split second later, Francine's head quickly pivoted in the direction of her friend.

"Abby! That's wonderful news!"

Abby's tears had already begun by this point, and she was unable to respond to Francine's utterance with anything other than a sobbing, choked "I know..."

In all this time working at the WPB, Angela hadn't become particularly close with Abby, especially after the other girl began dating Jeffrey Belkin. Still, Angela couldn't help but scurry around Abby's desk when she arrived there to be able to give her a hug of relief.

"We need to go out and celebrate!" Francine proclaimed before Angela could even make that suggestion.

"It's Saint Patrick's Day," Francine added, "so it's absolutely perfect!"

Both Francine and Angela looked over at the still-sobbing Abby, who hesitated and then slowly, wearily nodded. Phone calls were made to the appropriate households to let Francine's mother, Angela's mother-in-law, and also Abby's mother know that their respective Friday night dinner tables would each be short one person. Francine then needed to use the women's room and Angela went with her – but not Abby – and when they returned Abby wasn't at her desk.

"She must have already gone downstairs," Angela suggested, so she and Francine hurried down the stairs and then outside the WPB building. Initially, they saw no sign of Abby. They were just about to reenter the building to look for her when Abby finally appeared.

The girls each lit a cigarette and decided to head toward one of the closer Irish pubs, a place called Dugan's over on Forbes Avenue, about a half mile from the WPB office. The pub was already packed when they arrived, but as luck would have it, three men in business suits had apparently been drinking the afternoon away and had just now decided to call it a day. Angela was the first to notice the men getting ready to leave, and she hurried over to claim the table and the seats for her small party. She endured a touch of mostly harmless flirting from the men, who were so plastered that none of them could muster enough energy – or even string together two or three coherent sentences – to really put the moves on these women who wanted their table.

The WPB secretaries settled into their chairs, and then Angela volunteered to make the first beer run over to the polished dark mahogany bar across the room from where they had been able to find seats. Angela alternately eased and elbowed her way through the crowd, and after no more than a two-minute wait at the bar, she was able to secure three Duquesnes that she ever-so-carefully maneuvered back to the table with only a few small spills along the way.

With each of the girls now in possession of a beer, Francine Donner offered:

"To Captain Joseph Coleman, for successfully bailing out of his plane and still being alive. It's a shame we had to wait all these many months to find this out, but at least he's alive, and now we know it!"

Glasses clinked and healthy gulps of the pilsner that was among the local favorites followed.

"Are you going to write to him?" Angela asked Abby before adding, "I hear you can write to German prisoners through the Red Cross."

Angela's question and follow-on suggestion were surprisingly awarded with a glare from her coworker.

"What would I say to him?" Abby sharply responded. "That I'm seeing somebody else now? He'll think that as soon as I found out he was shot down I forgot all about him and latched onto another man, just like that."

"Well, you could tell him that's not the case..." Angela replied but was interrupted by another tart response from Abby.

"Oh sure," the sarcasm in Abby's voice was evident. "I'll tell him that I started seeing someone even *before* I found out he was shot down! I'm sure he'll like that a whole lot better!"

"Don't bite *my* head off!" Angela snapped back in return. She was about to continue with her fiery retort when Francine interjected.

"Okay, okay, it's a touchy situation; we all know that. But we shouldn't get angry at each other. This is fantastic news, remember! Joseph is alive!"

Both Angela and Abby let out deep sighs simultaneously.

"I know," Abby nodded. She looked over at Angela.

"I'm sorry," Abby continued. "I know you were only trying to help."

Abby took another sizable gulp from her beer and then continued. "I've been thinking about this for the past hour since your sister-in-law called, and in some ways it was…I don't know, easier when I thought that Joseph was dead. I know that sounds horrible, but…okay, maybe not easier…"

Both Angela and Francine remained silent as Abby searched for the right word or phrase.

"Less complicated," Abby final continued. "I guess that's the best way to describe it. Joseph was probably dead, even though there was no official word, and I was now dating Jeffrey. Before I found out he was shot down, I used to worry about what I would do when Joseph came back from the war, if I was still with Jeffrey…or maybe even married to him! But since Joseph was probably dead – and I know this sounds horrible – it all was less complicated."

Abby paused for another chug of her Duquesne that was now almost gone.

"I went and told Jeffrey," Abby pivoted somberly, "about Joseph being alive and a war prisoner."

Suddenly both Angela and Francine realized why they hadn't been able to find Abby when they returned from the women's room, thinking incorrectly that Abby had already headed down the stairs and down the building. She must have been in Jeffrey Belkin's office, sharing what she had just learned.

"Oh my God," Francine muttered. "That must have been rough."

Abby sighed again as she shrugged.

"I had to tell him," she quietly replied.

Angela asked hesitatingly:

"What…um…does this mean for you two?"

Just to make sure Abby knew which "you two" she was asking about, Angela added:

"I mean, you and Jeffrey?"

Another shrug; another sigh.

"Nothing, I guess," Abby replied somberly. "I suppose if you think about it, things are just back to the way they were before we found out Joseph was shot down. He'll come home from the war…"

All three girls simultaneously knocked their knuckles onto the wooden table for good luck, as Abby proceeded.

"…and if Jeffrey and I are still together, or if we've gotten married, he'll find out then."

*   *   *

"Was your friend Alice happy to hear that Mr. Coleman's son was still alive?"

Angela had arrived back at the DeLuca home shortly after the others finished supper, and she was sitting in the kitchen with Elizabeth and Carmela. Giuseppe and Rosalia were in the living room listening to *Gang Busters* on the Blue Network.

"Her name is Abby," Angela corrected Elizabeth, and then continued. "But yes, she was happy…well, sort of."

Carmela and Elizabeth both shot puzzled looks in response to Angela's words.

"I don't really know how to describe it," Angela continued. "I mean, she's definitely happy that he's alive, but since she's with someone else now, she said that finding this out makes things more complicated for her."

Angela paused to chain-light a new Pall Mall from the dying embers of her current one, and then added:

"At least that's the way she put it."

"It's just all so strange," Carmela shook her head and then echoed Angela's actions, lighting her own new cigarette. Carmela instinctively pivoted her head towards the kitchen door, even though she was absolutely certain her parents couldn't hear her. Still, she lowered her voice to barely above a whisper.

"When I was seeing Patrick, I used to have dreams all the time that I got one of those telegrams telling me that Tony had been killed."

She looked over at Angela and clarified, even though both of her sisters-in-law knew exactly whom she was referring to.

"I mean my Tony. Anyway, I know what your friend is saying. If two guys are in the picture it *is* complicated, and as horrible as it sounds, you can't help thinking what if one of them was…"

She lowered her voice even more to the point where both Angela and Elizabeth could barely hear her.

"…dead. Things would be so much less complicated then. And you feel so guilty even though you can't help it, and you really don't want that to happen."

Elizabeth shook her head and stared morosely at the cooling half-filled cup of coffee sitting in front of her.

"It's all because of the war," she muttered. "I know I've said that maybe a hundred times in the past two years or however long it's been, and I've heard both of you say the same thing as much as me. Everything is so topsy-turvy, with husbands and fiancés and boyfriends off to war, and everything that we've always thought about...I don't know, being with them just went right out the window."

Elizabeth noticed Carmela's head drop to the point where her chin was just about tucked into her chest.

"I'm sorry," Elizabeth said. She had never directly talked about Carmela's affair with her sister-in-law, but Carmela knew that Angela had shared the sorry tale when Elizabeth returned from Camp Lejeune last September.

Carmela shrugged as she took a deep puff from her cigarette.

"It's okay," she nodded. "You know what, though? I've thought about the whole thing for eight months now, ever since he left me. Girls have been having affairs for years, and they didn't need no husband off to war to do it, neither. It was just a lot easier to do when Tony wasn't around, but also it's because he wasn't around that I probably had the affair in the first place."

Carmela paused before continuing.

"But I couldn't swear on a stack of Bibles that if Tony hadn't been off to war I wouldn't have had an affair. Chances are I wouldn't, because I wouldn't have been working at no war plant. But just the way Tony and I got married, so fast, right after Pearl Harbor..."

Carmela looked back again at the kitchen door, and then returned her gaze to her sisters-in-law.

"Could I tell both of you something that you'll keep secret?"

Angela replied with a quick "uh-uh" that overlapped Elizabeth's "of course."

"Now maybe it's because of the affair," Carmela said somberly, "but if I could somehow turn the clock back to January of '42, I wouldn'ta married Tony. I'm not sure I even woulda gotten engaged if I had really thought about how long he was gonna be gone. I mighta said something like 'after you come home we'll see about pickin' up where we left off' – somethin' like that – but knowing what I know now, I wouldn'ta gotten engaged, and I definitely wouldn'ta gotten married."

When she finished speaking, Carmela let out a lengthy sigh, as if by sharing this deeply personal and closely held secret with her sisters-in-law she had suddenly unburdened herself of a tremendous weight. She stared expectantly at Angela first, and then at Elizabeth, and each of Carmela's sisters-in-law knew exactly what she expected in response: ideally an acknowledgement that they both felt the same way about their hasty marriages to Carmela's brothers, or if not, then a proclamation to the contrary.

Neither Angela nor Elizabeth wanted to be the first to respond to Carmela's statement: to her challenge. Finally, Carmela's eyes narrowed and she demanded of Angela,

"What about you? And my brother?"

Angela hesitated, and then stammered her response.

"I think…I mean, I guess I still…I still would have gotten married to Tony when…when I did."

Carmela then wordlessly demanded Elizabeth's response, which was much the same as Angela's had been a moment earlier.

Carmela contemplated the responses from her sisters-in-law, but didn't say anything further.

* * *

That night, Carmela dreamed that she was back working at the shoe and boot war plant. In her dream, she had never married Tony DeMarco before he went off to war, nor had she become engaged to him. He was still a part of the dream, in absentia; but he was little more than "some boy from the past" who had departed for some faraway battlefield following Carmela's declaration that when (unspoken: if) he returned, she *might* consider picking things up again with him. She was now seeing Patrick Doyle, and the dream ended as she departed with him late one Friday night for the long drive to Michigan where that coming Monday they would both start new jobs at the Willow Run B-24 plant…and also a new life together.

In Angela's dream, she likewise had not married nor had become engaged to Tony DeLuca. Her dream was a short one, in which she was primping herself and fussing over getting her hairdo to be just absolutely perfect for when the man she had recently met at the Sun Drugs lunch counter came to pick her up for their first date.

Elizabeth's dream more or less mirrored those of her sisters-in-law. Carlo left for the Marines neither married nor engaged to Elizabeth, and was now just a distant memory of the prewar past. In her dream Elizabeth was waiting at Washington's Union Station for the *Liberty Limited* that would soon be arriving, carrying Calvin McKinnon and several other important WPB steel men. As she waited so very patiently, Elizabeth was humming "Tangerine," dreamworld Calvin's favorite song.

Chapter 26

June 16, 1944

War front news had been forcing its way into American homes for a long while now, even before Pearl Harbor, as fighting raged in both Europe and Asia for several years even before America was dragged into the war. For the past week and a half, however, so much was happening on all the war fronts that both Angela and Elizabeth felt as if their heads were spinning every time they picked up a newspaper or clicked on the radio news. The Allies had taken control of Rome on the fourth of June after the Germans declared it an open city and withdrew. Two days later the world held its breath as the massive invasion of France got underway. Not to be outdone far away in the Pacific, yesterday the Americans continued their relentless campaign against Japanese strongholds by invading an island called Saipan in the Northern Mariana Islands.

Elizabeth was absolutely certain that Carlo was among the Marines who, according to the morning *Post-Gazette*, had quickly secured the beachhead on Saipan and were now moving inland against the dug-in Japanese defenders. But then there was the other story about Saipan on the morning paper's first page, the one with the headline "Yanks Face Dangers of Battle On Saipan Confident and Cocky," written by a United Press war correspondent who was with the invading Marines and soldiers. Near the beginning of the article, Elizabeth read these ominous words:

> It is likely that Saipan will combine the worst features of the two most famous battles of the Pacific – Tarawa and Guadalcanal.

Elizabeth shuddered as she read that single sentence over and over. Carlo had been party to *both* of those "famous battles" – Guadalcanal in '42 and Tarawa last November – and had been wounded during the first. Why was he apparently destined to be a firsthand witness to military history in the making across the Pacific, year after year?

Elizabeth was, of course, powerless to do anything except finish her morning coffee, shower for work, catch the streetcar for downtown and then take the incline up to the war plant on Mount Washington, and do her best to make it through yet another morning and afternoon and evening of constant fear.

*　　*　　*

Angela's day began much the same as her sister-in-law's had. However, she had awakened a half hour earlier than Elizabeth and had skipped coffee and breakfast this morning, rushing out the door the moment she was dressed. Everyone in the Oakland WPB office had been told on Wednesday that a bigwig from downtown was going to be visiting the Oakland office early that morning, and every single employee was required to be in the building a half-hour earlier than normal. Angela had no idea what this was all about, nor did anyone else that she asked. To make matters worse, coming in early didn't mean being able to leave early, nor even any extra pay – however miniscule – for the additional thirty minutes. So Angela had already left by the time Elizabeth appeared in the DeLuca kitchen for coffee, a couple of cigarettes, and to read the worrisome news, one story after another, in the morning *Post-Gazette*.

Angela arrived at the WPB building with about two minutes to spare and rushed inside, not taking time for a final morning cigarette before the morning secretarial frenzy began. All of the WPB workers were already gathered together on the second floor, crushed together as tightly as they could be in front of, behind, and besides all the secretarial desks in the middle of the large open bay floor. Angela could see Mr. Jenkins, the Oakland branch's manager, talking to someone at the far side of the room, and figured that must be the big shot from downtown.

Angela looked to see if she could find Francine Donner or Abby Sobol, but Mr. Jenkins began speaking before she located either of the other two women. Chances were, though, that even if Angela had noticed Francine and Abby, she would have been unable to weave her way through the packed crowd of WPB workers to reach them.

"All right everybody," Mr. Jenkins' voice at first could barely be heard over the din from the crowd of workers, but the racket quickly subsided.

"As we all know, the gigantic invasion of Northern France ten days ago, the one that we've all been waiting for, was the largest amphibious assault in the history of the world. Many thousands of ships took part in the invasion, and every single one of those ships was made of plenty of steel, much of which came from right here in Pittsburgh. Many of the landing craft for the invasion were also built over on Neville Island using good old Pittsburgh-made steel."

Mr. Jenkins paused for a second to look over at his guest, and then glanced forward as he resumed speaking.

"The man standing next to me is Mr. Calvin McKinnon, who is in charge of the steel desk for the WPB downtown. Mr. McKinnon is the man who has, for the past two years, coordinated the efforts of the United States government and our steel companies right here in Pittsburgh. It's not an exaggeration for me to say that without Mr. McKinnon's leadership, it's doubtful that as many ships — and also airplanes and tanks and artillery pieces — would have been built, because we would not have had enough steel manufactured, or have been able to get all of that steel to the right war plants all across the country as quickly as needed."

Mr. Jenkins paused again for a quick moment and then continued.

"Now that the invasion of France has occurred, and appears to be successful with our men moving inland towards Cherbourg according to this morning's paper and the radio news bulletins, Mr. McKinnon asked if he could say a few words to all of you here in the Oakland office."

Mr. Jenkins took a small step to his right as Calvin McKinnon stepped forward. A few of the secretaries in the audience applauded him for a couple of seconds, but when widespread applause didn't break out, their muted clapping ceased. Most of the gathered WPB workers gazed at this seemingly too-young man whom they had just been told had played such an important part in the war production effort. A few of the secretaries also hungrily eyed the handsome young government man.

"Thank you," Calvin McKinnon began. "I asked Mr. Jenkins here if I might share a few thoughts with all of you this morning, and he graciously agreed to my request. It does appear that the invasion of northern France has been successful. Our brave soldiers are not only moving inland to take the fight to the Nazis, but the beaches appear to have been secured. Every day, more and more artificial harbor facilities are being built to keep supplies flowing to our advancing soldiers, along with new units of Army men making their way to the battlefront, from our many thousands of Navy ships into France."

Calvin McKinnon went on for another ten minutes or so to describe the important role of steel in the war effort that led up to the recent invasion, and to laud every one of the Oakland office WPB workers – the secretaries as well as the managers and administrators – for doing their part to link up steel production with the war plants. He concluded his combination thank-you and morale-boosting speech with:

"Our brave men still have a great deal of tough fighting ahead of them in the months ahead, both in Europe and over in the Pacific, and we can't afford to let up now. Our war plants still need to produce many more ships, and tanks, and airplanes, and artillery pieces, and all the other weapons that we need to win this war. But today is a day for you to catch your breath for a few moments and congratulate yourselves and each other for a job well done.

And I wanted to take a few minutes this morning to personally congratulate each one of you."

This time, when he finished speaking, the applause came broadly and spontaneously. Calvin allowed himself a broad smile as he nodded a couple of times to the audience, and then shook Mr. Jenkins' hand.

The crowd began to disperse, and a few of the managers in the front near where Calvin McKinnon had been speaking waited to shake his hand and exchange a few brief words. The secretaries headed back to their desks, since the conclusion of the remarks had been timed perfectly for the start of the normal work day.

Angela retrieved the stack of papers from her "to be typed" box left over from yesterday and skimmed through them, rearranging them in the order that she would tackle them. From the corner of her eye she noticed this Mr. McKinnon headed in the direction of her desk, stopping at each of the other desks along the way to exchange a few words – and a smile – with some of the other secretaries. Figuring that he would likewise stop at her desk, Angela quickly selected one of the handwritten pages and rolled a fresh sheet of paper into her typewriter. I might as well appear to be as hardworking as possible when this bigwig reaches my desk, she reasoned.

"Well, my congratulations to you for all of your hard work, Miss DeLuca."

The words interrupted Angela's concentration as she was adjusting the margins on her typewriter before beginning to type an indented paragraph. This Mr. McKinnon was obviously taking note of the metal nameplates on each secretary's desk, and making a point to address each of them by name.

"Thank you," Angela replied, and then was unable to help herself from correcting him:

"It's Mrs. DeLuca."

"Mrs. DeLuca," the man repeated and then halted.

"Oh! You're Elizabeth's sister-in-law, aren't you?"

Angela felt her mouth fall open, and she was so shocked at this stranger's fantastically unexpected words that she couldn't muster a response. Finally, noticing that this man was still staring at her, smiling, and apparently expecting an answer, she squeaked out:

"Uh-huh."

Uttering those two syllables seemed to have cleared the logjam in Angela's confused thoughts, because after a second's pause she continued, her eyes narrowing warily as she inquired:

"You know my sister-in-law?"

This Mr. McKinnon's smile broadened even more.

"Oh my, yes," he replied pleasantly. "I know her quite well; from the Witherspoon Club."

Angela's brain was instantly processing this information (Hmmm...I suppose the Witherspoon Club makes sense; but "quite well"?...) when she heard him add:

"And also from supper with her at her parents' lovely home in Highland Park."

Angela was powerless against blurting out:

"She's had supper with you at her parents' house?"

Angela realized as the words were leaving her mouth that her tone was highly accusatory; not so much disbelieving of this man's words, but simply because the message behind those words was the furthest thing in the world from she should be hearing from this total stranger!

Angela's tone wasn't lost on Calvin McKinnon, but he seemed to take no offense.

"Yes I have," he confirmed in a manner that conveyed to Angela that he had clearly picked up on her skepticism and suspicion, but that Angela should take no misunderstanding at all from what she had heard.

"It's been a little while," he added, "but perhaps again soon. Though that estrangement with her parents..."

He left the sentence hanging as he pursed his lips and slowly shook his head with exaggerated sorrow, the radiant smile instantly vanishing as his eyes remained locked with Angela's.

McKinnon looked up from Angela and then back at her, smiling broadly once again.

"Well, I should continue my round of thank-yous before I depart for a meeting downtown. Once again, Mrs. DeLuca, my thanks to you for all of your hard work in helping us get to this point in the war, and I'm sure you'll continue to do the same until victory is at hand."

With those words Calvin McKinnon departed the area near Angela's desk and continued his way to the next secretary's desk, leaving behind a stunned Angela DeLuca.

*   *   *

The rest of the workday was a nightmare for Angela. She was so distracted by that brief, disturbing exchange with the WPB big shot that she made mistake after mistake in her typing. By the end of the day the wastepaper basket next to her desk was overflowing with crumpled-up typewriter paper. Worse: Angela barely made a dent in the stack of documents in her "to be typed" box by the time 5:00 rolled around, meaning that tomorrow would not only be filled with catch-up work, but also irritated WPB managers, angry that Angela hadn't finished one particular typing task or another.

Throughout the afternoon strange, disturbing notions floated in and out of her thoughts. On the one hand, it seemed highly unlikely that Angela's worst inferences from what that Mr. McKinnon had said could possibly be true. As far as Angela knew, Elizabeth hadn't stepped foot inside the Witherspoon Club for the longest time: about a year and a half, going far back to that hoity-toity Christmas party near the end of '42. Elizabeth was home at the DeLuca house in time for supper almost every evening…unlike when Carmela was carrying on her affair and would come and go so unpredictably.

Was it even remotely possible that Elizabeth was carrying on with this man? Angela was helpless against reading between the lines of what Mr. McKinnon said and coming to the conclusion that there was far more to the story. He had casually and confidently declared that "I know her quite well" in response to Angela's startled initial question. Then that business about having dinner with her at her parents' house…when in the world had that occurred? Maybe it had been long ago, before Elizabeth moved out and came to live at the DeLuca house at the end of '42. Or had such an occasion occurred more recently, perhaps in the aftermath of some quiet partial reconciliation with her mother that Elizabeth was holding close to her vest? Had there been an evening in the recent past when Elizabeth had quietly diverted to her parents' house, and Angela simply hadn't taken notice?

Maybe a less complicated, but still highly troubling, scenario was what had actually happened: there had been some quiet hanky-panky between Elizabeth and this man more than a year and a half ago, but for some reason that illicit relationship had cooled by the time Elizabeth moved into the DeLuca home. So something *had* been going on, but it was over now and had been for a long while.

But then Angela thought about what Mr. McKinnon *didn't* say as the conversation ended: specifically, something along the lines of "please say hello to Elizabeth for me." Those words would have implied that he hadn't seen Elizabeth for a long while, and thus would have been the natural, almost clichéd, declaration to include.

Conversely then, did the absence of that sentiment mean that the opposite was true; that it *hadn't* been a long while since he last saw Angela's sister-in-law?

* * *

During the streetcar ride home, contemplation of the backstory – if there was one – to her brief conversation with Calvin McKinnon continued to weigh on Angela.

At the very least, Elizabeth had held back a secret that for some reason she had decided not to share with Angela: specifically, that at some point after marrying Carlo, she had engaged in at least a couple of social interactions with this young, handsome WPB man.

Suppose that Elizabeth somehow knowing Calvin McKinnon was perfectly innocent. Maybe he somehow did business with Elizabeth's father, or even her brother William before his arrest and then being sent off to the Army. Perhaps supper at the Buchanan home and drinks at the Witherspoon Club and whatever else might have occurred had all been totally innocuous, and had occurred many months ago; and Elizabeth's presence had been happenstance.

Then why would Elizabeth have not have said anything at all to Angela about this man...not *one single word?* The pair had spent hundreds, if not thousands, of hours together for more than two years now, ever since their respective weddings one week apart back in the spring of '42. They had discussed so many things about their husbands and their occasional frustrations with their mother-in-law. They had commiserated over the endless trials of wartime rationing and other hardships. They had shared their fears and nightmares about Tony and Carlo fighting against the Nazis and the Japanese, and most of those discussions had been accompanied by plenty of tears. They had gossiped about Carmela's belatedly revealed affair, and what the aftermath might be when – or if – Tony DeMarco returned after the war.

In fact...maybe that was it! In retrospect, for many months Carmela had all but flaunted the fact that she was having an affair with her brazen irregular comings and goings from the DeLuca home. Perhaps Elizabeth, fully aware of what Carmela had actually been doing right under their noses, was simply being much more careful with her own affair.

Angela contemplated how each day since Elizabeth began working at the shoe and boot war plant, she took a morning streetcar to the Monongahela River edge of downtown Pittsburgh. Elizabeth would then would briskly walk across the Smithfield Street Bridge to catch the Monongahela Incline up to Mount Washington. She would then reverse the direction of the journey after work. Her total travel time took about forty-five or fifty minutes each way, which was a good fifteen to twenty minutes longer than when Elizabeth worked in Oakland at the OPA and accompanied Angela to and from work most days.

But in both directions Elizabeth passed through downtown…where Calvin McKinnon worked. Maybe she dawdled in the morning, or more likely in the late afternoon, remaining in downtown long enough to rendezvous with that man. Maybe it wasn't even to sleep with him; at least not all the time. Maybe she met him for coffee some mornings or a drink occasionally after work, where they would hold hands and laugh and enjoy each other's company for a few brief minutes at a time until it was time for her to catch the streetcar home to Morningside.

Or maybe, on some days, Elizabeth hurried down from Mount Washington during her lunch hour and the two of them would quickly check into some inexpensive hotel along Carson Street for a noontime rendezvous before she hurriedly took the incline backup the mountain to make it back on the production line just in time. Was that even possible?

Whether Angela's mind was only engaging in lurid fantasies about some secret life her sister-in-law was leading, or if a more mundane and even understandable explanation for how Calvin McKinnon knew Elizabeth was the truth, *something* was out there that Elizabeth had deliberately withheld from Angela.

And Angela wanted to know what that "something" was.

*   *   *

Why is she looking at me that way?

Every time Elizabeth looked across the supper table at Angela that evening, her sister-in-law was staring at Elizabeth so fiercely that someone else might think Angela was mightily trying to peer into Elizabeth's very soul! Curiously, Angela was never the one to break the eye contact. Her gaze remained grimly locked onto Elizabeth as if she were a scientist resolutely studying a laboratory subject. Uncomfortable at being under a proverbial microscope, Elizabeth would look away...only to gaze back at Angela moments later and be subjected to the same intense scrutiny.

Elizabeth did her best to distract herself with the suppertime conversation. However, discussing the day's news about the invasion of France and the Marines dangerously moving inland on Saipan, and the Americans and British still fiercely engaging with the Germans in northern Italy...all of that hardly what was needed to provide any sort of calming counterbalance to whatever Angela's problem might be.

Elizabeth was so out of sorts about her sister-in-law's strange behavior that she went up to bed as soon as *The Lone Ranger* finished at 8:00, even though it was a good two hours before she was able to finally fall asleep.

Angela, however, stayed up after her in-laws and Carmela all went upstairs. She half-listened to the *Stage Door Canteen* program until 11:00 that night, at which point she sighed heavily and trudged upstairs to the troubled, restless semi-sleep that she knew awaited her.

Chapter 27

One week later, Elizabeth hurried from the bottom of the Monongahela Incline across Carson Street, past the Pittsburgh & Lake Erie Railroad terminal, and then quickly across the Smithfield Street Bridge. She checked her watch: 5:23. If she made it to the other side of the bridge and the streetcar stop within the next five minutes, she would have time to grab a fresh copy of the afternoon *Pittsburgh Press* to read on the way home.

Elizabeth was desperate for war news from the Pacific, to see if any new information had come out of the fight for Saipan since she had scanned the morning *Post-Gazette*. On weekends, whenever she was home, Elizabeth stayed glued to the radio to catch the news throughout the day, mostly from Mutual or the NBC Red Network. During workdays, however, war news was prohibited at the plant other than during lunch; the idea apparently was to keep all the workers' minds focused on the tasks at hand and not be distracted by bulletins or even regular news reports from the various theaters of operations.

Elizabeth arrived at the newsstand and was digging in her pocketbook for either the exact four cents needed or a nickel when she heard:

"Elizabeth! Elizabeth DeLuca! How *are* you?"

She turned around at the sound of a man's voice that was both familiar and unfamiliar at the same time. It took a millisecond for Calvin McKinnon's face to register with her memory. She hadn't seen the man in person in a year and a half, yet that very same face was still uncomfortably in her dreams on occasion.

"Mr. McKinnon," she responded hesitatingly. "I'm f…"

"Uh-uh," that familiar broad smile immediately appeared on his face as he good-naturedly wagged his left index finger at her. "Calvin or Cal, remember?"

Elizabeth was powerless against returning the smile.

"Okay, Calvin," she began again. "I'm fine. I'm so surprised to see you!"

"The same here," Calvin answered. "Are you downtown shopping?"

Elizabeth stepped back from the newsstand to allow a harried-looking businessman to grab a copy of the city's other afternoon paper, the *Sun-Telegraph*, and quickly be on his way. Elizabeth suddenly realized that because she had become engaged in this conversation, she almost certainly would miss the next streetcar. Oh well, she told herself; she would simply grab the next one in about twelve minutes later, as she often was forced to do coming home from work.

"No, I work up there," Elizabeth nodded backwards over her left shoulder, in the direction of Mount Washington. "At a war plant that makes shoes and boots for the Army."

"Ah, I didn't know that," Calvin nodded, his smile subsiding for the moment. "Though I suppered with your mother at the Witherspoon Club last summer and she did tell me that," Calvin's voice lowered, "after that matter with your brother, you were no longer working at the OPA."

Even as she began responding, a portion of Elizabeth's thoughts traveled back in time almost one year to the day to that surprise letter her mother had written to her while Elizabeth had been at Camp Lejeune; the letter that brazenly informed her daughter that she and Elizabeth's father had leisurely dined at the Club with Calvin McKinnon and that the young WPB big shot looked forward to seeing her at the next Witherspoon Club Christmas Party (that Elizabeth of course hadn't attended).

"It was so unfair," she blurted out, to which Calvin sympathetically replied,

"I agree; most unfair."

The broad smile reappeared.

"So you're done working for the day, I presume?"

Elizabeth nodded.

"I just finished up at 5:00, and was going to get a copy of the afternoon *Press* when you saw me. I read the war news on the way home on the streetcar."

"Do you know where your husband is? In the war?" Once again, the smile slowly disappeared as McKinnon shifted the conversation in a more serious direction. Elizabeth couldn't help but notice that his facial expressions reminded her of a puppet's movements, so carefully and precisely controlled by some out-of-sight force.

Elizabeth sighed.

"I don't know for certain, but I believe he's on Saipan."

Calvin pursed his lips.

"Tough going there; but it sounds like they're making progress, according to the papers and the radio."

Elizabeth was suddenly very uncomfortable with this conversation.

"I'm not sure that you know," she replied, "but back during the Christmas Party at the Club, the one in '42 when we…" she struggled for the right words, "met each other, Carlo had been wounded a couple weeks earlier, on Guadalcanal. I never knew until I got a telegram after New Year's."

"I did hear that from your mother," Calvin nodded. "I'm glad he recovered."

Elizabeth was just about to say something when Calvin continued.

"I remember that Christmas party very well. You and I had such a pleasant conversation."

Elizabeth's discomfort ratcheted upwards a few notches.

"And as I recall," he continued, "that was the same week that your mother invited me to your house for supper, which was also a lovely evening."

"I don't live there anymore," Elizabeth quickly responded. She was about to elaborate with a bland explanation – something along the lines of "my mother and I had a falling out" – when Calvin instantly responded.

"I did hear that, when I saw your parents at the Club not long after that. That's a shame, but I'm sure it will all blow over in time."

Elizabeth was about to reply with some version of "I wouldn't be so sure about that" when, once again, Calvin steered the conversation in the direction that he apparently wanted to take it.

"That was such a pleasant conversation," he repeated what he had said a few moments earlier. "The Christmas party, I mean. In fact, if you're not in a hurry, we should have a drink somewhere nearby and catch up. It's been far too long."

Elizabeth hurriedly shook her head.

"I need to get home," she quickly responded.

"Oh, it's Friday night," Calvin rebutted. "Just one or two drinks to unwind from the week. I'm sure you can use that as much as I can."

"No, thank you," Elizabeth again shook her head. Her thoughts were now churning. This was something different than a Christmas party conversation at the Witherspoon Club...a lengthy discussion that at the time Elizabeth thought had begun spontaneously but which she later found out had been orchestrated by her mother. Even taking her mother's noxious meddling into consideration, the setting for that single earlier conversation had rendered it benign...mostly.

This, though...*this* was a man persisting in asking a woman whom he knows is married to have a couple of drinks with him on a Friday night; the exact same setting that, according to Angela, had been one of the slippery steps leading to Carmela's sorrowful affair.

More disturbing: the man standing a couple of feet from her who seemingly wouldn't take "no" for an answer all of a sudden seemed to be an entirely different person than the cheerful, pleasantly demeanored young Georgetown man she had met a year and a half ago, and who had surprised her a couple minutes earlier by noticing her and calling out to her.

This man, the one whose broad smile suddenly didn't seem quite so amiable, reminded Elizabeth of a bird of prey who had been circling over its intended quarry for a long, long while, patiently waiting for the exact right moment to make its move.

"I'm sure I'll run into you again," Elizabeth began to disengage herself from this now-unsettling encounter.

"Here in downtown," she clarified. "I don't go to the Witherspoon Club anymore."

"I see," Calvin McKinnon nodded, taking a half step backwards and apparently finally accepting Elizabeth's rejection of his proposition.

"Yes, I'm sure I'll see you again," he added as he slowly turned to his right to begin to walk away. Suddenly he halted and turned back to Elizabeth.

"Please tell your sister-in-law Angela hello."

Elizabeth couldn't help it. Her eyes widened and her mouth fell open. Calvin McKinnon remained poker-faced but Elizabeth was all but certain that he was taking a great deal of pleasure in the obvious shock his words had just caused.

"You…you know my sister-in-law?"

"Oh yes," the broad smile appeared once again. "I just met her last Friday, in fact. I went up to the WPB offices in Oakland to give a short speech of appreciation for all the hard work everyone did now that the Europe invasion seems to be a success. I noticed her last name on her desk nameplate and, sure enough, she turned out to be the sister-in-law you had mentioned."

To her credit, Elizabeth told herself probably a dozen times during the streetcar ride home, she once again instinctively fell back on that all-important lesson from her debutante days after this sudden shock: the importance of maintaining outward grace in all situations, even when one might be so very uncomfortable in one's own mind. Elizabeth so very much wanted to quiz Calvin McKinnon, to press him to find out just exactly what he had told Angela about…well, about anything.

Elizabeth wouldn't give him the satisfaction, though. She said her goodbyes and walked calmly and purposefully towards the streetcar stop. Only after she arrived there did she realize that she had forgotten to buy a copy of the afternoon *Press*. She wondered if Calvin McKinnon noticed that as well; and if he did, she also wondered if he would be enjoying the tiniest bit of satisfaction in having rattled her enough to make her forget to buy her newspaper.

The lack of a copy of today's *Pittsburgh Press* didn't matter, though. The headline could have read "WAR OVER: NAZIS AND JAPS SURRENDER!" and Elizabeth's thoughts the entire ride home still would have been consumed by this troubling encounter.

So that was why Angela had acted so strangely last Friday! God only knew what Calvin McKinnon had said to her! Elizabeth realized, however, that even if he had only mentioned that he knew her briefly from the Witherspoon Club Christmas Party a year and a half earlier, Angela would almost certainly be reading far more into that encounter than there was.

The entire streetcar ride home was an apprehension-filled slog for Elizabeth as she contemplated this revelation. Elizabeth couldn't shake the feeling that even though she had done nothing wrong at all, somehow this was going to all blow up in her face!

* * *

"Can I talk to you?"

Elizabeth had done her best throughout supper to slowly build her internal strength and be able to ask Angela that simple question. The two women had just finished helping Carmela and their mother-in-law wash and dry the supper dishes and cookware.

"Me?" Angela peered back at Elizabeth.

"Uh-huh," Elizabeth nodded.

Angela shrugged. Chances are Elizabeth had finally mustered the courage to demand an answer for why Angela had all but given her the cold shoulder for the past week. The two women had barely exchanged a couple dozen words since last Friday night. Even Carmela had picked up on the tension and had privately asked Angela what was going on with Elizabeth. Angela's non-committal

"Nothin'" didn't shed any light on the situation for Carmela, nor did Elizabeth's earnest "I have no idea!" response when Carmela asked her.

Elizabeth nodded towards the living room, where their father-in-law had already plopped himself onto the sofa with his traditional Friday evening after-dinner bottle of Duquesne. Angela followed Elizabeth through the doorway leading from the kitchen. When they were out of earshot of Rosalia DeLuca and also Carmela, Elizabeth lowered her voice and said,

"Let's go for a walk."

Angela cocked her head at Elizabeth's unexpected and unusual request. The two of them rarely walked together around the Morningside neighborhood, and when they did it was usually because some serious topic needed to be discussed without being overheard by any of their DeLuca in-laws. More than a year had passed since the most recent such occurrence.

"Sure, okay," Angela shrugged. The truth was that she was tired of this past week's chilly standoff with Elizabeth. If Elizabeth insisted on pressing for the reason her sister-in-law was acting so apprehensive, Angela was going to come right out and spill the beans, no matter where that might lead. After all, it was Elizabeth, not Angela, who had some explaining to do.

Earlier in the day thunderstorms had rolled through the Pittsburgh area, but they had dissipated by the time both women made their way home from their respective workplaces. The late June evening skies were threatening again, though, with the distant rumbling of thunder, but Elizabeth was determined to clear the air. After telling their father-in-law that they were going for a quick walk and then poking her head into the kitchen to relay that same information to Rosalia, Elizabeth led her sister-in-law outside.

Just say it already! Elizabeth's brain commanded her vocal cords to overcome the fear that now totally enveloped her. The temperature was a balmy 76 degrees outside, but Elizabeth was consumed by the ice cold chill of sheer terror.

"I heard that last Friday you met someone I know; a man named Calvin McKinnon."

There! The agonizing words had floated free, and there was no turning back now!

For her part, Angela was stunned into silence at what she interpreted as Elizabeth's brazenness. The only way Elizabeth could possibly know this was if she had been with this McKinnon man sometime during the past week, and he had told her. Even as she started to reply, Angela felt her heart sink. All week long, despite keeping her distance from Elizabeth, she had hoped that her worst imaginings were wrong. She might eventually learn that there was some innocent explanation behind Elizabeth's familiarity with that man; that indeed Elizabeth hadn't seen him for the longest time, despite Mr. McKinnon's insinuations (or at least what Angela took as intimations).

Elizabeth, though, had just now all but bluntly declared that she had been with that man sometime in the past week.

"How do you know that?" Angela decided to challenge Elizabeth.

"I ran into him at the newsstand, downtown near my streetcar stop: this afternoon, a couple of hours ago. Right before he walked away he told me that he knew you."

"Actually," Elizabeth amplified his answer, "he was walking away and then he turned back and said something like 'tell your sister-in-law Angela that I said hello.' I was so stunned I just stood there with my mouth open like an idiot, but then I finally asked him how he knew you, and he told me about his visit to the Oakland WPB office last Friday."

Elizabeth's eyes narrowed.

"In fact," she bluntly challenged, "now I know why you've been acting so oddly towards me ever since last Friday. He told me exactly what happened, how he saw your name on your desk and asked you if you were my sister-in-law. Right?"

Angela had been totally unprepared for the direction the conversation had taken, and could only muster a hesitant "uh-huh" in response.

Elizabeth's cold fear had vanished, and was now replaced by rapidly growing anger. She halted and turned towards Angela, who likewise stopped walking. Her tone was as accusatory as her words.

"And no doubt you assumed that I was having an affair with him or something like that, which was how he knew me. Am I right?"

Not one to shy away from confrontation, Angela demanded:

"Well? How *do* you know him? He certainly seemed to know enough about you, with your Christmas party conversations and supper at your mother's house! If that's all so innocent, then why did you never mention *a single word* about him to me!"

Angela's equally accusatory rebuttal immediately tamped down Elizabeth's wrath. Elizabeth sighed heavily, then looked directly at Angela.

"Let's walk," Elizabeth sighed, "and I'll tell you the whole story."

"Not that there's really any story to tell," Elizabeth quickly added. "If you think I'm having an affair like Carmela did, you're wrong. Until a couple of hours ago, I hadn't even seen him in more than a year and a half. And way back then, at the end of '42, it was only the Christmas party when I met him and then when my mother ambushed me by inviting him to dinner."

Realizing that she was getting way ahead of herself, Elizabeth took a deep breath and started from the beginning. She told Angela about the Witherspoon Club Christmas Party and how Calvin McKinnon had seemingly appeared out of nowhere with the offer to refresh her drink. Elizabeth described how later on she had learned that her mother had orchestrated that encounter. She continued the tale into a detailed recitation – as much as she could recall a year and a half later, anyway – of her conversation with him, and why she had abruptly ended the conversation when she suddenly noticed her mother's victorious, malicious smile.

Elizabeth told Angela about arriving home from the OPA that Friday and her shocked surprise at finding Calvin McKinnon ensconced in a chair in the living room, sipping Scotch with her father. She related all the details she could recall about supper that evening and the after-dinner drinks, and how she had marshaled all of her strength to remain outwardly calm throughout the evening even though she was boiling inside.

"That was the same evening I decided I could no longer live there – with my mother – and the next day was when I moved in here."

Angela cocked her head. She had let Elizabeth tell her tale without interruption, and it all seemed…plausible, Angela supposed. Still, she sensed there was more to the story. Maybe it was all related to this last utterance.

"You mean because of your mother surprising you by inviting him to dinner? I thought you moved out because you were upset over your father paying off those draft board men to give your brother 4-F status."

Elizabeth sadly shook her head.

"That's just what I told you," she replied. "And everyone else, including Carlo."

"Well, I could see you being angry with her for inviting him without you knowing…"

"It wasn't that," Elizabeth interrupted. "Well, not totally about her inviting him to supper, that is actually part of it. It's what she said afterwards that was so…"

Her voice trailed off. Elizabeth had decided on the spot that in the interest of sisterly harmony she would tell Angela *everything* about Calvin McKinnon, including what she hadn't yet gotten to in her narrative: why she hadn't mentioned anything about him way back then, or at any time during the past year and a half. It hadn't occurred to her, though, that her revelations would wander into those repulsive and unforgiveable words her mother had spoken.

It was too late, though. Elizabeth's account had meandered its way to that point, and there was no turning back now. In the distance a protracted rumble of thunder made its presence known, serving as the perfect backdrop to this part of the sorrowful tale.

"After he left – Calvin I mean, my father drove him back to his hotel – my brother left also, and just my mother and I were alone. I immediately started yelling at her for inviting him to dinner. I think I accused her of trying to force him between Carlo and me, or something like that; honestly, I don't really remember, from that point on that whole night was a total blur."

She paused for a moment and looked over at Angela as they continued their aimless evening walk, the thunder still rumbling in the distance.

"She started telling me that I should get my marriage annulled because I should be with a man like Calvin, not Carlo. She said all these horrible things about Carlo: how he would never have a good job after the war, and that everybody would understand if I got an annulment. She told me that we would tell everyone that I only got married with all of the war craziness going on, or…I don't even remember the exact words. She did mention you and Carmela, though, that I had made the same stupid mistake that both of you did. I told her to stop saying that, and she kept arguing that it was the only sensible thing for me to do; that I would be wasting my life, and bring shame to her and my father, if I didn't get an annulment."

"Oh my God!" Angela blurted out. "I can't believe it!"

By this point, tears were glistening in Elizabeth's eyes.

"That's such a horrible thing to say!" Angela continued, followed up with a reprise of:

"I can't believe it!"

Elizabeth sniffed as tears began streaming down her cheeks.

"You want to know what the worst thing of all is?" she asked Angela, her voice choking.

Angela was instantly consumed by trepidation as she squeaked out: "What?"

"Part of me wanted to listen to her," Elizabeth sobbed.

*   *   *

The rumbles of thunder had grown louder and longer, and the girls were now inside Bruno Antolini's lounge – Del's – that had been only a half block away from where they had been when the rain suddenly started. Ordinarily this rough neighborhood bar on a Friday night, filled with steelworkers and railroad men and other laborers getting a start on their weekend drinking, wouldn't have been the best place for two attractive, unaccompanied young women…married or not. But inside Del's, no one dared even look in the direction of the two women as they continued their painfully personal conversation at a corner table. Angela had already called home to the DeLuca house to let their in-laws know where they were, and not to worry; they had just ducked into the bar to get out of the weather, and when the storm passed they would head back home.

Bruno Antolini's eyes narrowed as he brought two Fort Pitts to the table. Even in the darkened interior of his lounge, he could tell that Elizabeth had been crying.

"You all right?" he gruffly asked. "Somethin' wrong?"

Elizabeth sniffed and shook her head, but it was Angela who answered.

"It's okay, Daddy. It's nothing serious."

"Your husband all right?" Bruno continued questioning Elizabeth. "He didn't get wounded again or nothin', did he?"

Elizabeth shook her head again. This time she replied, her voice surprisingly steady.

"He's fine...well, as far as we know. I think he's over on Saipan and there's a lot of fighting going on. But I haven't heard anything...you know..."

Angela's father nodded.

"Okay, I'll leave you girls alone. I'll keep an eye on you, but..."

He gazed around the bar and then looked directly at his daughter.

"...if anybody starts botherin' you and I don't see it right away, you come get me and I'll take care of it, okay?"

"Okay, Daddy, we'll be fine," Angela assured him before he strolled purposefully back towards the bar area. Angela noticed that he stopped at a table filled with four or five youngish men, all of whom looked like burly steelworkers, and said something to then as he glanced back towards his daughter and Elizabeth. Angela didn't recognize any of them as boys from the neighborhood whom she knew. Probably a group of men who somehow happened to be in Morningside for this Friday evening, Angela figured. No doubt he was preemptively warning them against even thinking about coming over to try to make time with his daughter and her sister-in-law.

By the time they had made it to the lounge and gotten settled, Elizabeth's tears had subsided. So when she continued her story, she did so in a much steadier voice than how she had ended the first part only a short while earlier, outside on the sidewalk.

"You remember a couple of months ago back in March," Elizabeth began, "that same day that the Red Cross reported that Mr. Coleman's son was a prisoner but still alive? That night you and Carmela and I were all sitting in the kitchen, talking after dinner. You remember?"

Angela half-nodded.

"Yeah, I think so."

Then she added:

"That's right. I went out for Saint Patrick's Day with Francine and Abby after I told them the news and came home right when dinner was finished."

"We were all talking about how even though it was such wonderful news that your friend Abby's guy was alive," Elizabeth reminded Angela, "things were complicated now for her because she was seeing someone else from work."

"That's right," Angela confirmed.

"Carmela started talking about her affair," Elizabeth continued, "and how she would sometimes think that if her Tony didn't come back from the war, things would be a lot less complicated for her. And then she said – and I'll never forget it – that if she could turn the clock back to when she and her Tony got married, right after Pearl Harbor, she wouldn't have. And not only that, she wouldn't have even gotten engaged. You remember her saying that?"

"Yeah, I do," Angela quickly replied.

"And then she asked both of us how we felt; if knowing what we know now, if you would have married Tony and if I would have married Carlo."

"I remember," Angela sighed as she lowered her eyes towards her beer.

"Neither one of us really wanted to answer her; do you remember that?" Elizabeth reminded Angela. "And then she directly asked you, almost like she was demanding an answer."

"Well, I said that I would still have married Tony," Angela responded defensively.

"And then I said that I would have still married Carlo," Elizabeth reiterated what had been said among the three sisters-in-law. "And then we all went into the living room to listen to the radio."

Elizabeth sighed and took a sip of her beer.

"You have to promise to keep this just between you and me," she continued hesitatingly. "This is all related to this whole business with Calvin McKinnon, and I guess why I never said anything at all about him to you."

Elizabeth stared at her sister-in-law.

"Do you promise?" she repeated.

"I swear I won't say nothin' to nobody," Angela replied.

Elizabeth steeled herself for what she wanted so desperately to share with Angela...with anybody!

"If I had been totally honest, my answer to Carmela's question would have been 'I really don't know; maybe not.'"

She paused to see if the expected reaction was forthcoming from Angela: a sudden horrified, shocked look perhaps, or perhaps just complete disgust. Strangely...no. Angela's facial expression didn't change a bit in response to Elizabeth's words.

"That Christmas party when I was sitting there talking to Calvin right after I met him," Elizabeth continued, "for that hour I felt...I don't know, wonderful! Here we were at the Witherspoon Club, all dressed up, and..."

Elizabeth struggled for the right words. For as many times as she had struggled with these difficult emotions, she was now putting those sentiments into words for the very first time...and the words were not coming easily.

"Remember back in high school when you would meet a new boy for the first time, and you felt all happy? And then when you go on that first date?"

"Sure," Angela replied.

Elizabeth sighed.

"Well, this was something totally different. It was...I don't know, more...powerful, maybe? Whatever it was, this was nothing like when I first met Carlo and became

322

interested in him, or Billy Lennox, or any of my other boyfriends back at Peabody."

She sighed – again – before continuing.

"I know this sounds horrible, which is why you have to promise me that you won't *ever* say anything to anybody…"

"I swear I won't," Angela interrupted.

"For that hour, talking to Calvin, I almost forgot that I was married to Carlo. He had been gone for seven months and well…um…it was like he was more of a dream than reality. I honestly felt as if because of the war, I wasn't really married, despite the wedding ceremony and everything."

"That's what Carmela said about her Tony and why she had the affair," Angela interjected.

"I know."

"You girls doin' all right?"

Angela and Elizabeth both looked up at Bruno Antolini, who was purposefully marching towards them.

"Fine, Daddy," Angela said. "Maybe another two beers?"

Angela's father's eyes narrowed.

"You sure 'bout that?" The unspoken addendum: are you two trying to get drunk for some reason?

"Uh-huh," Angela nodded.

"Don't worry," she added, apparently reading her father's thoughts, "these will be our last ones and we'll be fine. We're just talking about…things, and we're waiting out the storm."

As if to provide cover to Angela's explanation, just that second the loudest thunderclap yet shook the inside the bar.

"Okay," Bruno Antolini agreed, but then he wagged his stubby right index finger at his daughter and Elizabeth: "The last ones, though."

Both Angela and Elizabeth nodded. Even if this were a different occasion and they were committed to getting drunk this evening, it certainly wasn't going to happen in Bruno Antolini's establishment!

Elizabeth waited until Angela's father returned with two fresh Fort Pitts and departed just as quickly before she continued.

"When my mother was saying to me, that night that she invited Calvin to supper, that I would be better off with someone like him with an important war job and a good education and a bright future after the war, it wasn't what she said that got to me. It's that even by then, I was so lonely, every single day. And it's only gotten worse since then. Even when I was with Carlo at Camp Lejeune, I was lonely. So when she said that I should get an annulment, part of me wanted to say that maybe she's right, because this isn't at all what being married was supposed to be like."

Elizabeth paused to take her first sip from the fresh beer, and Angela did likewise.

Elizabeth went on: "After that night I didn't give what she said much thought because I was so angry with her, and I moved out. And then a couple of weeks later was when I got the telegram that Carlo had been wounded. So it's not like I sat there for weeks or months thinking something like 'maybe I really should give some consideration to what my mother said about getting an annulment and then start to see Calvin because I'm lonely and I have no idea when I'll see my husband again.'"

"But you know what?" Elizabeth continued. "That feeling has never totally gone away. And I *hate* myself for feeling like that!"

Elizabeth's eyes started to fill with tears yet again.

"Carlo is probably over on Saipan, and for all I know, right this very second could be face-to-face with a Jap soldier in hand-to-hand combat, about to be killed. Or maybe he *was* killed, five minutes ago or earlier today. Or maybe tomorrow is the day that he'll get killed. I'm a terrible person for feeling this way, but I just can't help it!"

Tears were once again streaming down Elizabeth's cheeks, and now Angela's eyes were teary as well.

"You're not a terrible person," Angela tried to comfort Elizabeth, reaching her right hand across the table and soothingly laying it on top of Elizabeth's left one. She continued, "Do you remember that night when Tony was on furlough and we all went to the Crawford Grill?"

Elizabeth nodded as she continued quietly weeping.

"Later that night and for months afterwards, I kept thinking how the war had cheated me; cheated me and Tony. We had that one normal night together where we had dinner and then went out dancing, and then came home and we...well, you know. But that was all! It was like God was being really mean and teasing us with that night, and then going 'well, that's it until after the war; sorry!' *That's* what married life was supposed to be like; not...well, not like with you and Carlo, and me and Tony, and Carmela and her Tony, and probably millions of other girls."

"I just never thought it was going to be like this," Elizabeth concurred with Angela's declaration. "I don't know what I thought, to be honest. I knew that Carlo was going away to war, but there was something…I don't know, romantic about getting married right before he went away. And I knew it would almost certainly be a long war, but I just didn't have a grasp on what two years almost totally apart from each other would actually be like. And that's so far; if the war lasts another year or two, and if Carlo makes it through alive…"

Elizabeth and Angela both knocked on the wooden tabletop at the same instant.

"…it'll be the first three or four years of our marriage that we didn't spend together. And we'll never get that time back!"

"That girl Francine Donner at work?" Angela inquired. "The one who is engaged to Jonathan Coleman? The brother who didn't get shot down, the other one?"

Elizabeth nodded but added, "I've never met her, but you've talked about her."

"Well," Angela continued, "she's engaged and hasn't seen Jonathan for a year and a half since he was home for Thanksgiving furlough back in '42. There's something…I don't know, different about her being engaged while we're married, even though she's alone at home every night just like we are. But it's like Francine could get tired of waiting and being alone, and break things off if she really wanted to, and it wouldn't be a mortal sin. It would almost be normal, and people would understand. Does that even make sense?"

Elizabeth shrugged. Her tears were slowing once again, but then she remembered something else that had been troubling her since last week.

"There's something else," she began. "At that Christmas party, I thought Calvin was the nicest man, and that was a big part of the reason that those horrible things my mother said even made a dent in my thoughts. But then, when he showed up at my parents' house for dinner…I don't know, even though we all had a nice conversation over dinner and then afterwards, there was something about him that made me feel uneasy; like maybe he had something in mind for me, even though he knew I was married. And maybe if I had stayed living at my mother's house and went to the Witherspoon Club all the time, and my mother kept inviting him over for supper, he would have eventually tried to…well, you know."

Elizabeth sighed.

"Then," she continued, "when I saw him earlier today, the conversation started off…I guess nice, like seeing an old friend who you haven't seen in a long time."

Elizabeth's eyes narrowed.

"But when he kept asking me to have drinks with him and didn't seem to want to take no for an answer, it was almost like he turned into a different person who wasn't anywhere near as nice as I thought. And when at the very end he was walking away and turned back to tell me to say hello to you, I swear it was as if he was saying 'okay, you rejected me, but I have something on you…and I'll be back.'"

She paused to take another sip of her beer.

"Let's say that way back in '42 right after the Christmas party, or sometime in early '43, and also if Carlo hadn't been wounded so he stayed out in the Pacific instead of coming home, I wound up having an affair with him because I was lonely and because of what a nice guy I thought he was. So not what my mother wanted me to do with getting an annulment, but having an affair with him because I was attracted to him and I hadn't seen Carlo since right after the wedding. Well, maybe Calvin *isn't* such a nice man after all, and I would have thrown away my marriage for somebody who turned out to be very different than I thought."

"Well, that's just like with Carmela," Angela agreed. "She thought that…"

"Exactly!" Elizabeth interrupted. "That's exactly it! I never made the connection before, but it's just like with Carmela. She thought that guy was so nice that she was willing to have an affair with him, and then he turned out to be a total snake when he slipped out of town over the weekend without telling her. I might have ended up just like her, and wound up ruining my marriage over a man who turned out to be very different than I originally thought!"

Angela pursed her lips and then offered:

"Well, let's hope that Carmela didn't ruin her marriage, and that when her Tony comes back…"

Yet another round of wood tabletop knocking for good luck.

"...she can make it all work out, and nobody finds out about the affair."

Angela looked across the table and locked eyes with Elizabeth.

"How come you never told me about any of this? We spend so much time together and we're so close..."

"I was ashamed," Elizabeth interrupted. "I felt guilty for thinking for even a single moment about anybody except for Carlo, especially when he was away in the Pacific. I was afraid that you would think I was a terrible person, just like I said before."

Angela lowered her eyes to the tabletop and then looked back up at Elizabeth.

"Just like you asked me to keep this all a secret, you need to do the same for what I'm saying. Because I feel almost exactly like you do. I didn't meet anybody at a fancy Christmas party, but I keep daydreaming over and over that I'm at a lunch counter and I meet an interesting man and we begin talking, and then...well, things just happen."

Elizabeth instantly recalled Angela saying much the same thing during their post-midnight diner discussion the night Angela had picked her up at Penn Station after Elizabeth's return from Camp Lejeune. At the time, Elizabeth had wondered if Angela's description of meeting a man at the drugstore lunch counter was just some random musing in light of Carmela's affair, or perhaps something deeper. Now, here was that sentiment being verbalized once again.

Angela paused to take a sip of her beer before continuing.

"*Everything* that you said about how you feel, I could have said right back to you, including how awful and guilty you feel sometimes, wishing you hadn't gotten married. It's not Tony's fault; he didn't do anything wrong, which is why I feel so guilty. I'm being cheated out of what it's like to be married, but I'm not single, so I can't go out and meet somebody and go on dates. I just go to work and then go home for supper, and wash the dishes, listen to the radio, and then go to bed. Day after day after day; it's all the same. We go see movies on the weekends sometimes, but it's not like we can go down to the Crawford Grill to go dancing on Saturday night, or go out with girls from work to a nightclub. It's all just…"

Angela let out a deep sigh.

"This is all so depressing. I'm tired of talking about it, aren't you?"

Elizabeth nodded.

"I'm sorry for thinking the worst of you," Angela continued. "I should have known better. It's just that Mr. McKinnon caught me by surprise when he mentioned you, and since you never told me about him, I just…you know…"

"From now on," Angela went on, "no more secrets between us. I'll tell you everything, and you do the same. We'll be able to get through the rest of this war that way, however long it lasts."

Angela reached her right hand out again and laid it on top of her sister-in-law's left one.

"Deal?" Angela said as she squeezed Elizabeth's hand.

"Deal," Elizabeth nodded as she squeezed back.

*   *   *

"I had a miscarriage," Elizabeth blurted out, freezing Angela in her tracks. The rain had stopped, probably for the rest of the evening, and they were slowly walking back home.

"Down at Camp Lejeune," she added.

"Oh my God!" Angela's eyes were wide open and her left hand flew to her mouth as she spoke.

"Nobody knows except Carlo," Elizabeth continued. "I didn't want anybody else…I don't know, it's just so personal. So that's why I didn't write you about it or tell you when I got home. I just wanted to forget it ever happened."

Angela remained glued to the wet sidewalk.

"Back there you said 'no more secrets between us' and I agreed, so that's why I'm telling you. *Please* don't say anything, even to Tony in a letter, okay?"

She waited for Angela's hesitant nod.

"If it had happened here at home instead of down there everyone would know, but it's almost as if by happening at Camp Lejeune it was something I could leave behind when I came home. Maybe someday after the war we'll tell Carlo's parents and everyone else; I don't know. But if we ever did, I didn't want you to be all upset that even though we agreed no more secrets, I still kept that from you. But please don't tell anyone: Carmela, Ma and Pa DeLuca…even Tony. Okay?"

Angela could only respond with a tearful:

"I just don't know if I can make it through another day of this war."

Chapter 28

December 6, 1944

Elizabeth shed her overcoat the moment she stepped off of the Monongahela Incline. Whereas the morning temperatures had hovered in the mid-twenties, by the end of the business day the mercury had risen above fifty degrees! Rain threatened, but by this point in the calendar every rare warm day – or half-day – was to be cherished.

"Elizabeth? Elizabeth!"

At the unexpected sound of her name, Elizabeth was certain she would turn around and once again be face-to-face with Calvin McKinnon. The Witherspoon Club Christmas Party was upcoming this Saturday evening. No doubt he had decided to stake out her homeward route to pressure her to attend this year, unlike last year's soirée that had been sans Elizabeth Buchanan DeLuca. Even as she was pivoting into the direction the sound had come from, though, Elizabeth was also thinking that the voice didn't sound quite like that of Calvin McKinnon.

Three or four seconds passed until Elizabeth recognized the weary face of the Army man who had called to her.

"William!"

A smile appeared on the face of Elizabeth's brother as she hurried over to give him a fierce hug.

"Oh my God! William! I can't believe it!"

"It's great to see you," Elizabeth's brother murmured as his sister held him tightly. "I'm also glad that you're happy to see me; I wasn't sure you would be."

Elizabeth was about to reply when she was suddenly aware of something metallic scratching against her cheek as she held onto her brother. She pulled her head back slightly from his shoulder and saw a single gold bar. She released him, slid backward half a step, and eyed him with a surprised look on her face.

"You're a lieutenant?" she said incredulously.

William Buchanan arched his eyes as he let out a half chuckle.

"Who would believe that, huh?"

Elizabeth's face held the same incredulous look.

"How did you become an officer?" The last Elizabeth knew, of course, her brother was being dragged off from the federal courthouse to be unceremoniously and immediately drafted into the Army as a lowly private.

"Battlefield commission," came the hesitant response. "Normally only college boys are officers, but if you do something…I don't know, I guess special in combat, and if they need somebody to take command, sometimes they promote you directly to second lieutenant."

Elizabeth's face shifted from shocked to apprehensive.

"So you were a combat hero?"

William shrugged.

"Something like that," he echoed, his thoughts so apparently far away for an instant as he spoke.

"Anyway," he pulled himself back to the here and now, "they brought me back to the States for the new War Bond Tour, so I get to come home for a couple of days because of the big rally tomorrow night at Forbes Field. I stopped by the DeLuca house and Carlo's mother told me that you were working up there" – he nodded up towards Mount Washington – "and how you got home, so I figured I'd come try to find you."

A pained look suddenly appeared on William Buchanan's face.

"I just wanted to see you and, well…"

The last word came with great difficulty.

"…apologize."

*　　*　　*

William insisted that instead of the Tic Toc restaurant inside of Kaufmann's department store or one of the many downtown diners, he would treat his sister to a splendid supper meal at the William Penn Hotel.

"I make officer's money now," he said with a smile, "and while I'm on the War Bond Tour, I can't lose my dough in a crap game. So I might as well spend it, ya know?"

The brisk walk from the bottom of the Monongahela Incline to the William Penn was just under a mile, and in the twenty minutes it took Elizabeth and her brother to cover that distance, the conversation had mostly been about what had transpired since the moment he had been extricated from the federal courtroom and handed over to the United States Army that very same evening. William's tale had been related chronologically, and just as they arrived at the William Penn he had gotten to the point where he had been put on a train for the West Coast and then a troop ship headed for the Pacific.

They hurried inside out of the cold darkness. Elizabeth searched for a pay phone to let her in-laws know that she would be having supper with her brother and wouldn't be home until later, while William headed for the hotel's elegant restaurant. The maître d' was only too happy to offer a choice table to this Army lieutenant back home from the front, one whose service uniform was decorated with an impressive collection of campaign ribbons and badges. Elizabeth was escorted to the window-side table a couple of minutes later when she had finished with her phone call and made her way to the restaurant after a restroom stop. After William ordered two whiskey sours, he picked up his tale.

"The Army sent me to the 147th Infantry Regiment, which has been out there in the Pacific since '42 right alongside the Marines. They fought on Guadalcanal before I got out there, and when I arrived we were training to go right along with the Marines for the whole next series of invasions."

"Were you on Saipan?" Elizabeth interrupted.

"Yeah, that's what I was gonna tell you," William replied. "We went in alongside the Marines there, and then again right after at Tinian."

"Carlo was on both of those islands," Elizabeth interjected. "I finally got a stack of letters from him last month that he wrote over the summer and fall. He didn't say too much because of the censors, but he did say it was rough there."

William's eyes took on a distant look, even though he was gazing directly at his sister. Elizabeth was suddenly convinced that he was looking past her, thousands of miles to the west.

"Yeah, it was," he sighed.

"Here's the thing," William continued, but he was interrupted by the waiter's appearance to take their orders. William insisted that Elizabeth order the most expensive steak on the menu, which – after several unsuccessful attempts to demur – she finally did. Her brother ordered the same, and the waiter departed to leave them alone with their drinks…and whatever William had on his mind.

"Over there," he began again, "on Saipan and then on Tinian, I was doing a lot of thinking. Not when I was in middle of combat, but in between patrols and fights against the Japs; whenever things were…I don't know, calmed down for a little bit, I guess. You make it out alive from a firefight that lasted a couple of hours, maybe longer, and you just collapse and can't help starting to think a lot."

"Think about what?" Elizabeth asked.

"For one thing, your buddies who you already know didn't make it out alive with you," was Williams's quick, somber response. "Or the ones who got wounded and carried back from the line, and you don't know how bad they got hit and if they're gonna make it."

He exhaled a pained breath.

"Sometimes you wonder if you had taken a different turn at some jungle path if things mighta turned out different. Maybe some of the guys in your squad wouldn't have been killed if you had done something differently; that kinda thing."

"The thing is," William continued, "even way back in basic training I started doing a lot of thinking. At first I thought this whole thing was such a raw deal."

He lowered his voice to make sure that he wasn't overheard.

"Father paid all that money to get me 4-F status, and just because I had the bum luck to get pinched, and that no-good Stanley Croft ratted me out to save his own hide, here I was headed off to the Army, anyway. That's the way I saw things, and I kept thinking about ways to still get out of it. I figured maybe I could be a total goof-up at basic training and not be able to do anything right, and the Army would have no choice but to kick me out, or at least keep me stateside."

He paused for a healthy slug of his whiskey sour before continuing.

"But even from the beginning, there was…I dunno, something about being in the Army with all those guys from all over, knowing that most of us would be fighting the Nazis or Japs before too long. It felt like you were part of something bigger than just yourself."

He sighed.

"I don't even know if that makes sense. I'm not sure I can really explain how I started to feel. And it kept growing stronger and stronger, and then by the time we hit the beaches at Saipan and then the next month at Tinian…look, I don't want to make it sound like I enjoyed being in combat or anything like that, because it's total hell. But being part of something right alongside all those other guys…there's something special, something proud, about that."

Elizabeth stared back across the table at someone who spoke like a total stranger. These words never would have come forth from the mouth of the brother she had grown up with!

William paused his soul-bearing narrative while the waiter placed a beautifully constructed dinner salad in front of each of them, along with fresh whiskey sours.

"What I'm going to say may sound terrible, but I know that you and Mother aren't on speaking terms, and I heard that you don't see Father anymore, either."

"I wouldn't know where to find him," Elizabeth immediately and defensively replied. "It's not that I'm not speaking to him, but other than the house, I don't know where he might be."

A pained look immediately enveloped her face.

"And I just don't want to go over there."

"I don't blame you at all," William quietly replied. "Like I said, I've been doing a lot of thinking for a long time now. And the more I think about it, the more I realize what terrible things they both did – not just Mother – and not just to you."

William's pained look now matched that of his sister.

"To me also. The whole time we were growing up, Mother especially, but even Father too, made sure that we thought we were special; that rules and laws didn't apply to us. That's why I cheated on that math exam at Pitt, the one where I got caught and expelled."

A half-bitter chuckle escaped.

"And let me tell you," he continued, "that wasn't anywhere near the first time I cheated at Pitt; it was just the first time I got caught. And the same with high school; I cheated my way through just about every class at Peabody."

William shrugged and took a bite of his salad before continuing.

"Then all the black market dealings with booze and sugar, and a whole lot of other things you probably know nothing about…it was the same thing with all of that, they both made me think that laws didn't apply to me, so what did I have to worry about?"

William leaned back in his chair.

"But in the Army," he went on, "all the way from basic training out to the Pacific and especially on Saipan and Tinian, I knew that I was nothin' special; at least the way that Mother and Father made me think. I kept looking around at all these guys, some of them who became good buddies of mine, and I couldn't believe that I had let Father pay off the draft board men to give me a 4-F. Honestly, I felt sick that I woulda been perfectly okay letting those guys go invade Saipan and Tinian, and who knows where next, while I was back home stealing sugar and selling it on the black market or running booze from Ohio."

He edged forward, his elbows now on the table, and leaned towards his sister.

"I hated myself for how I used to be, and I swore that I would make up for it."

*   *   *

"I wasn't very nice to you, either, and that's what I need to apologize for," William Buchanan told his sister after he seated himself at the table again following a quick restroom trip. He came back to the table with another two whiskey sours, even though Elizabeth was only halfway through her second one. William had finished his own second one awhile back; apparently the rigors of the Army and the horrors of the Pacific Theater were reason enough for him to have not changed at all from the heavy drinker he had turned into long before his arrest.

"You didn't really do anything to me," Elizabeth retorted.

"Well, yeah," William shrugged, "that's exactly it. I saw the way Mother treated you after you got married and Carlo went away, and I shoulda said something. But I didn't. I was too wrapped up in black market schemes to care one way or another. Father also should have stepped in, but he was like me."

He took a healthy slug from his fresh drink and sighed.

"We both let her get away with treating you like dirt just because you married someone she didn't approve of, who she felt was beneath you. I feel terrible about it, but I also thought the same thing, that you shouldn't have married Carlo because he was just some Italian from Morningside. So I just sat there and let her get away with all the nasty remarks and all that. Then after Carlo went away, right after your wedding, I knew that I was all set with 4-F status, and I remember saying some nasty things to you about him being far away in a jungle while you were back home; something like that, and what kind of marriage was that really?"

William let out a half-snort as he gulped the rest of his third drink.

"In fact, I don't even know if you remember, but one time we were sitting there at supper and I was giving you a hard time about him being away in the Marines. I think it might have been the same day he got on the train not too long after your wedding, now that I think about it. Anyway, you said something back to me like 'maybe you'll wind up in the same jungle next to him and you can personally tell him how much I miss him.' It was something like that."

William Buchanan sighed.

"Who woulda thought that your words would actually come true; that we really would both would wind up on the same islands out there in the Pacific two years later? I woulda bet a million dollars that never woulda happened, but you were right on the money. Anyway, every so often on Saipan we would run into the Marines there, and I kept looking for him in case he was there. I didn't know if he was, but I figured there was a chance. And if I came across him, I was gonna do exactly that."

Elizabeth was just about to ask William what "that" meant, but even before the words could be formed, she suddenly knew. William confirmed that she had indeed understood what he meant.

"I was gonna tell him that you missed him."

Elizabeth felt tears begin to form. As much as her brother's words pained her, she also knew that this confession was difficult for him as well. But the main reason for her tears was because of the contrite soldier sitting across from her, the one who apparently had sought her out specifically to apologize and explain himself.

This wasn't her brother! Or, more accurately, this wasn't the self-indulgent, amoral William Buchanan she had grown up with. *This* William Buchanan had belatedly discovered his moral center despite how he had been raised. The soft young man who had once eagerly let his father pay off the draft board to keep him safely out of this all-consuming war had found the resilience and courage to prevail in vicious combat, even seeming to embrace the very idea of putting his life on the line for his comrades.

Elizabeth would have given anything in the world to have grown up with this William Buchanan as her older brother instead of the selfish and arrogant young man who, as he himself acknowledged with his own words, had been largely created by their mother.

*   *   *

The next night – three years to the day since the attack on Pearl Harbor, that fateful Sunday that had set into motion one surreal year after another – tens of thousands of Western Pennsylvanians crowded into Forbes Field for the War Bond Tour entertainment show and rally. Elizabeth was accompanied by both of her sisters-in-law, as well as Angela's friends from work, Francine Donner and Abby Sobol. They had secured seats along the baseball park's third-base line, within reasonable viewing distance from the makeshift stage that had been erected fifteen or twenty yards behind where second base normally would be.

The program was scheduled to begin at 7:30 sharp. Forbes Field was a short walk from the Oakland WPB building, so Angela, Francine, and Abby headed over right when they were done with work to claim the seats. Carmela had hopped onto a streetcar from Morningside right around 5:30, while Elizabeth had altered her normal going-home route to head directly to Oakland instead of home. By 6:00, the five were all seated.

Originally Carmela had offered to bring a picnic basket filled with sandwiches and thermoses of hot coffee, but the event's organizers had publicized that all concession proceeds would go directly towards the war effort. So just as if the girls had gathered at Forbes Field on a warm summer evening for a Pittsburgh Pirates baseball game, they munched on hot dogs and peanuts as they awaited the start of the big event.

None of them had ever been to a War Bond Rally before, and until Elizabeth's surprise encounter with her brother the night before, tonight's event hadn't been in the plans for any of the women. However, when Elizabeth pulled from a reluctant William that he would not only be in attendance but would be introduced onstage at some point amid the spectacular Hollywood entertainment, she instantly made plans to attend. When Elizabeth returned home later that evening after supper with her brother, she told Angela and Carmela about her intentions for the next night. Both of her sisters-in-law immediately insisted on joining Elizabeth. The next morning Angela shared her plans for that evening with Francine and Abby, who likewise asked about tagging along.

At 7:30 almost to the second, the Forbes Field lights – which had been turned on at half strength – suddenly blazed to their full brightness. Anyone who had been staring at the lights at that moment reflexively squinted and looked away, but still saw spots for several minutes afterwards. The Pittsburgh Symphony Orchestra swung into "God Bless America" and none other than Kate Smith herself strolled purposefully onto the stage, belting out her signature anthem. Everyone in the crowd (other than the infirm) rose, and remained standing as an ensemble of Hollywood and Broadway entertainers came on stage and joined together to sing "The Star-Spangled Banner."

Following the conclusion of the national anthem, most of the entertainers exited the stage, except for Broadway star – and Pittsburgh native – Gene Kelly. The singer and dancer was beginning to make his mark on Hollywood, but was still best known for his starring role in the smash Broadway musical *Pal Joey*.

"Hello Pittsburgh! It's great to be home in the city whose steel is winning the war for us!"

The crowd roared its approval of the actor's sentiments, and it was a good thirty seconds before Kelly could continue.

"Today marks three years to the day of the dastardly surprise attack on Pearl Harbor. In the immediate aftermath of that terrible day, this nation and our armed forces faced tremendous adversity all around the world. But we all pulled together, and it wasn't just the men and boys in uniform who have turned the tide of the war in our favor…"

He paused for effect as he looked from one side of the baseball park to the other.

"…it's been every single one of you!"

Another roar came from the crowd, with many of the attendees again rising to their feet as they applauded and cheered.

"Five times previously this nation has reached out to all of you here in Pittsburgh, and *everyone* across this great land, to ask for your aid and your sacrifice to help us win the war. Every single time, our great President Franklin Roosevelt and our magnificent Secretary of the Treasury Henry Morgenthau set ambitious goals for total sales of war bonds; each one greater than the previous War Loan Drive. And you know what?"

Kelly paused again for effect, leaning forward and cupping his right ear. Overlapping shouts of "we did it!" and "we bought the bonds!" and simple cheering sprung up from all over Forbes Field.

"During *each* of the previous five War Loan Drives, we wound up selling – *you* wound up *buying* – billions of dollars more than the original goal! And because of your tremendous sacrifice and patriotism, we've done it! We've turned the corner on the war, and even though our brave men and boys still have many tough battles ahead of them, we have the enemy on the run!"

Many of those in attendance could barely make out the latter part of what Kelly said because the cheering and applause from all over the park had grown to a ferocious roar. More than a full minute passed this time until the actor was able to speak again.

"Tonight, here at our very own Forbes Field, all of you will have the chance to do your part for the Sixth War Loan Drive. We have an all-star cast of performers here for you tonight, along with some of the brave fighting men who have been winning the war for us. So let's get started, okay?"

More applause and cheering.

"You probably know that several years back I was in a little show in that city…what's the name of that city again?"

Scattered laughter along with more than a few people shouting out "New York!"

"That's right, good old Broadway out there in New York. The show was called *Pal Joey*, and here to join me in a couple of numbers from that show is one of your very own: a young actress who you'll be seeing on the screen more and more frequently. So I'm pleased to introduce Pittsburgh's own Carla Colburn!"

The swell of music began as the actress came out to join Gene Kelly, and yet another round of applause and cheering rang out. Over the racket both Angela and Elizabeth heard Francine Donner cry out,

"Oh my God! That's Charlene Coleman!"

They both looked in Francine's direction, immediately to their left.

"Jonathan's sister!" Francine stammered.

"Jonathan's sister is a Hollywood star?" Angela asked incredulously. "You never said anything about that!"

"I didn't even know," Francine replied, even though she still seemed to be in shock. "Well, I knew she went out to Hollywood last year after she graduated, and Jonathan wrote that she was going to get a couple of small parts in some upcoming movies. But I didn't know that she had a stage name and everything, and was in the War Bond Tour!"

Gene Kelly and this actress whom Francine Donner apparently knew as her fiancé's little sister launched right into "Bewitched, Bothered, and Bewildered," one of the signature songs from *Pal Joey*. When they finished they continued right over the hearty applause into another number from that show, "I Could Write a Book."

"Wow! She's really good!" Angela said to Francine.

Francine hesitated before replying.

"Yeah, I guess so," she answered in noncommittal tones.

The thought came instantly to Angela: she's jealous! But Angela could immediately see why. Here was her fiancé's younger sister, barely out of high school and already in the movies, up on stage singing alongside a Broadway star in front of perhaps 20,000 people. Of course that would be any Pittsburgh girl's dream come true! Francine might be thinking "why not me?" or "how did this girl get so lucky?" Or perhaps Francine was thinking ahead to Coleman family gatherings after the war when Carla Colburn – Charlene Coleman, apparently –

would be present and overshadow every other girl in attendance.

For a brief moment, Angela was piqued at her friend. Her fiancé was risking his life flying dangerous bombing missions, now against Japan according to a letter Francine recently received from him. *That* should be top of mind to Francine Donner, not petty jealousy over Jonathan's sister's apparent success at such a young age.

But then again, Angela realized, Francine was human just like they all were. Putting herself in Francine's place, Angela could see that if, say, Carmela DeMarco were an up-and-coming Hollywood starlet instead of – well, instead of basically the same as Angela – that she herself might be resentful of Carmela's success.

Angela's musings about Francine's reaction were interrupted by the applause and cheers at the conclusion of "I Could Write a Book." Carla Colburn curtsied and waved to the hometown Pittsburgh audience and exited the stage, leaving Gene Kelly alone once again.

"Before we bring out more of our star-spangled Hollywood entertainment for you, it's my pleasure and my honor to introduce to you several of your hometown Pittsburgh boys whose heroics on the battlefield have helped bring us to this point where victory might still be a ways ahead, but it's squarely in sight."

"Do you think this is where they will introduce William?" Angela nudged Elizabeth.

Elizabeth suddenly felt the butterflies, as if she were the one soon to be introduced to this crowd of at least 20,000 people.

"I guess so," she replied nervously.

"Our first hometown hero for the Sixth War Loan Drive here in Pittsburgh is Army Air Forces Staff Sergeant Paul Elias from right here in Oakland."

Gene Kelly waited for the initial round of applause to fade before continuing.

"Sergeant Elias is a B-17 waist gunner with the Eighth Air Force" – the entertainer had to pause once again for a round of applause – "and during our massive air raid on Berlin last March, his aircraft was attacked by numerous enemy fighters just after they dropped their bombs right onto Hitler's head! Even though he was seriously wounded by enemy fire, Sergeant Elias still manned his machine gun and helped hold off the Luftwaffe fighters until the B-17 was back within range of our P-51 Mustangs to escort the crippled bomber back safely to its base. For his heroics, Sergeant Elias was awarded the Silver Star. Sergeant Paul Elias, everybody!"

Every person present at Forbes Field, except for some scattered elderly and infirm men and women, rose to their feet to give the Oakland boy a standing ovation. When that round of applause died down, Sergeant Elias moved to one side of the stage and Gene Kelly resumed his introductions.

"Our next Pittsburgh hero for the Sixth War Loan Drive is United States Army Second Lieutenant William Buchanan from Highland Park...a Peabody High boy, just like yours truly here!"

Angela, Francine and Abby, Carmela...they all quickly looked over at Elizabeth, who had already brought both of her hands to her mouth and was staring straight ahead, her eyes as wide as they could possibly be.

"Not that long ago, Lieutenant Buchanan was Sergeant Buchanan, out there in the Pacific on both Saipan and Tinian, with the Army's 147th Regiment that has fought alongside our brave Marines since Guadalcanal. On Saipan, Sergeant Buchanan's company commander and all of the company's platoon leaders were unfortunately killed or severely wounded by the Japanese during what was reported to be the enemy's largest banzai charge so far in the war. Sergeant Buchanan didn't hesitate to take command not only of his platoon, but his entire company. Sergeant Buchanan organized his remaining forces to fight off the banzai charge and hold their ground, while killing more than four thousand enemy soldiers!"

Wild cheering and applause burst forth once again; yet curiously, Elizabeth didn't share the elation of nearly every other person here at Forbes Field this night. Her mind instantaneously traversed both time and space, and for a few brief seconds she *was* her brother, terrified at what was unfolding all around him: this horrific, seemingly endless enemy charge that could very likely lead to his own death, yet steeling himself to take command and fight to the very end, if necessary.

At the same time, though, another part of Elizabeth's mind likewise negotiated time and space to fuse with that of a Japanese mother whose son was being cut down by the American rifles and mortars and grenades. These soldiers were the enemy, yet there was something tragically sad – even appalling – about the idea of applauding and celebrating the recitation of so much death and sorrow, no matter where it was to be found.

"Sergeant Buchanan was wounded not once; not twice; but *three times* during the attack," Gene Kelly continued, "and still he managed to coordinate the furious efforts of what was now his company. Fortunately, his wounds weren't too serious and he was ready to go once again when the 147th accompanied the Marines to Tinian. For his bravery and his leadership, just before the invasion of Tinian, Sergeant William Buchanan became Second Lieutenant William Buchanan by virtue of a battlefield commission. Well done, Lieutenant!"

Gene Kelly turned towards William and executed a smart salute, which was returned by William after a brief hesitation.

"Did you know about all that? What Gene Kelly said?" Angela asked Elizabeth. "You didn't say anything last night after you came back after dinner with him."

Elizabeth shook her head and raised the volume of her voice to be heard over the roar of the crowd, even though Angela was sitting immediately to her left.

"I didn't know; not all the details. I kept asking him how he had gotten a battlefield commission, and he never really answered me."

Elizabeth leaned even closer to Angela, not sure that her sister-in-law had even heard what she had just said.

"He wouldn't tell me," Elizabeth yelled. "I knew it had to be something like what Gene Kelly just said, but he kept changing the subject every time I asked him."

Angela shook her head a couple of times before offering her own thoughts.

"Last year, before he was...um, you know, arrested...if you had told me that your brother would do what Gene Kelly just described, I never in a million years would have thought that it could be true. I just never woulda seen it from William."

*   *   *

Elizabeth tossed and turned in bed until close to 4:00 in the morning, mulling over everything she had heard and seen hours earlier at the Forbes Field War Bond Rally. Once again, Elizabeth mourned the brother who had been introduced as a hero not being the same older brother with whom she had grown up.

She wondered if her parents – her mother, in particular – had been in attendance, and if so, how her mother felt at the recitation of her son's heroics. Almost any mother would be immensely proud that her son had, in the most trying circumstances one might imagine, risen to the occasion and had demonstrated not only unwavering bravery but also steadfast leadership.

Somehow, though, Elizabeth wondered if Katherine Buchanan would see things that way. After all, William Buchanan was now putting his life on the line alongside boys and men like Carlo DeLuca and his three brothers whom Katherine had time and again dismissed as blatantly inferior to her precious, privileged son. Elizabeth could actually see her mother being ashamed – well maybe not ashamed, but definitely not bursting with motherly pride – in the aftermath of her son's combat heroics.

Maybe not, though. Elizabeth couldn't help but feel a little ashamed herself that even after all this time, she was helpless against automatically imagining the absolute worst about her mother's actions and thoughts. Still, though...

Even beyond these revelations about her brother, Elizabeth contemplated the upbeat mood of the War Bond Rally. Maybe, just maybe, victory really was in sight! Paris had been liberated back in August, and the American Army showed no signs of slowing down as they raced across France. They were now on the doorstep of the Reich at Saarbrücken, on the French border, and all indications were that the Germans were about to fall back another sixty miles or so all the way to the Rhine River.

Over in the Pacific, Army Air Forces B-29s flying out of Tinian – the island formerly occupied by the Japanese but which was now in American hands – were now bombing Tokyo. The Philippines were under attack once again, but unlike three years earlier, this time it was the Americans who were on the offensive. Much more fighting was ahead, and one might argue that even though triumph in the Pacific seemed farther out than in Europe, a roadmap towards victory on all of the war fronts was clearly in sight now.

That was the bigger picture: the perspective of the war as a whole, related through the newspapers and the radio. From a personal standpoint, though, Elizabeth still feared for the safety of her husband – and now her brother William as well – just as Angela worried about Tony, and Carmela worried about her Tony, and millions of others worried about their loved ones. Many more American men and boys would die, even with the tide turned in their favor; that was a tragic reality. For Carlo – and his brothers, and his brother-in-law, and millions of others – the war now became a race of time against fate.

Chapter 29

December 20, 1944

Angela and Elizabeth both exited their bedrooms at the same early morning moment. After locking eyes for a few seconds, Angela went to use the bathroom first, and when she was done Elizabeth quickly followed. Angela waited for Elizabeth and they both tiptoed down the stairs. Angela opened the door and was immediately blasted by the single-digit temperatures. She bent down to quickly retrieve the *Post-Gazette* and shut the door so rapidly she came close to slamming it. Her father-in-law would be up soon anyway, but Angela didn't want to be the one who accidentally woke the entire household with an ill-timed door slam.

The paper's headline was everything she feared.

NAZI BREAKTHROUGH THREATENED

"What does it say?" Elizabeth anxiously asked, but Angela only half-heard her sister-in-law as her eyes wandered to the secondary headline.

Hodges Rushes Men and Tanks to Meet Danger; Desperate American Resistance South of Monschau Halts Flank Attack

Instead of uttering the terrible news that she was reading, Angela handed the paper to Elizabeth, who quickly absorbed the headlines. Elizabeth also noted that on the more positive side, the middle of the first page declared that "Jap Headquarters on Leyte Captured" – so at least this troubling turn of events in Europe wasn't being echoed in the Pacific.

"Oh my God! This is all so terrible!" Angela was already near tears. What in the world had happened? Mere days ago the American and British offensive in Europe was relentlessly churning forward, throwing the German Wehrmacht back farther almost every single day. The thought that the Germans would be capable of launching a massive counteroffensive that would now have the Allies retreating was all but unimaginable! The widespread, uplifting optimism of the War Bond Rally less than three weeks ago, the hope that a victorious end of war was finally on the horizon, had vanished. Poof!

Details about this colossal German counterattack along the Western Front were scarce. Angela mustered the strength to read the *Post-Gazette's* front-page story, which noted that "a full and truthful account of the reverse on the First Army front" would be forthcoming "at the earliest moment consistent with military security." Days could pass before any details beyond the horrifying headline-level news would be released.

Christmas would again be a dreary affair, both Angela and Elizabeth realized. Even without this sudden reversal of battlefield fortunes in Europe, war still raged across the globe, taking so much of the joy out of the holiday as had been the case the past two years, even as the American forces steadily forged forward. But unless this sudden, surprise Nazi counteroffensive was blunted, this Christmas could well resemble that terrible one back in '41, only weeks after Pearl Harbor, when the war effort appeared to be all but hopeless.

Angela glanced over at Elizabeth, and their eyes shared that they both felt exactly the same at this very moment: how could they possibly stand one more day of all of this?

* * *

That afternoon's *Pittsburgh Press* headline boldly declared "NAZI OFFENSIVE 'DENTED' YANKS COUNTER-ATTACKING." The news on both Mutual and the NBC Red Network that night after Elizabeth and Angela returned home from work was far less optimistic, though. Details were sparse, and they both knew by now – as did nearly every other American – that blurrily told tales from the war front usually meant bad news. Throughout that entire evening Angela and Elizabeth, along with their in-laws and Carmela, half-listened to the *Mr. and Mrs. North* mystery melodrama, the *Carol Bruce Show*, and then Eddie Cantor's program, just waiting for NBC Red to break in with a war bulletin. No bulletins were forthcoming, however, which only served to heighten everyone's anxiety.

* * *

Each morning's headlines were more ominous than its predecessor. Thursday, the 21st: "GERMAN ATTACK GAINS IN FURY; FRESH TROOPS HIT YANK

LINES." The next morning: "NAZI OFFENSIVE ROLLS FARTHER INTO BELGIUM AND LUXEMBOURG." For some reason, though, each afternoon's *Pittsburgh Press* headline did its best to put an optimistic spin on the Western Front occurrences: "NAZIS STOPPED IN BELGIUM" on the 22nd, followed the next afternoon by "CLOUDS OF ALLIED PLANES BLAST NAZIS IN BELGIUM."

The most ominous headline of all, though, was when the *Post-Gazette* proclaimed on the morning of the 23rd:

NAZIS 10 MILES FROM FRANCE

Christmas, 1944, would be a melancholy occasion.

Chapter 30

December 31, 1944

My darling Carlo,

Once again I'll begin with the same words that I've written to you the last two New Year's Eves: I can't put into words how much I miss you on this New Year's Eve, as I do every single day. In some ways, this New Year's Eve is almost the same as last year. I don't know exactly where you are, and I hope and pray that you're alright. If you're still fighting somewhere, please stay safe. If you're finished for a while, then I hope it's a long, long time until you have to fight again.

I don't know how much war news from Europe you get out there, and I'm sure by the time this letter reaches you the news will be old anyway. And, I pray, the news will be better. The Germans launched a surprise offensive about a week before Christmas, and it seemed that many of the gains ever since the invasion of France would be lost. But yesterday General Patton sent 100,000 of our soldiers into the battle, and radio bulletins have said that might be enough to halt the

German offensive. We can only hope and pray that comes true.

I really can't write any more war news to you. It's all so depressing. So I'll tell you again that I miss you so very much, and I pray that by next New Year's Eve this awful war will *finally* be over and that you're home for good. Please write me soon.

All my love to you,

Elizabeth

1945

Chapter 31

The schizophrenic atmosphere continued for most Americans through the early months of 1945. By late January the massive German Christmas counteroffensive that became known as The Battle of the Bulge had been blunted, and the Allies resumed their ruthless push into Germany from all sides. In the Pacific, at the same time the tide in Europe was again turning in favor of the Americans and their allies, the unrelenting assault against the Japanese in the Philippines mercilessly and methodically proceeded. By the end of February, both Bataan and Corregidor had been retaken. The fall of Bataan and then Corregidor to the Japanese back in early '42 had marked the low point for the United States in the Pacific Theater, and their recapture was seen by most Americans as long-awaited revenge for the suffering and humiliation that the hated enemy had inflicted three years earlier.

Elation and growing confidence in response to the headlines, though, was tempered by the ever-present dread that loved ones fighting on the war fronts might not live to witness victory and the resultant peace.

*   *   *

A tiny island in the Pacific only 750 miles from Tokyo became a household name when the Marines invaded Iwo Jima on February 19th. One more vicious, iconic battle in the Pacific was underway. Reports that the Army's 147th

Regiment was once again alongside the Marines on Iwo Jima caused Elizabeth DeLuca to fearfully fret almost every single waking second. She knew that her brother had returned to his same unit following the War Bond Tour, and she now had two loved ones over in the Pacific to worry about. Elizabeth wasn't certain if Carlo was among the Marine invaders, and thought that he might very well not be. Unless something had changed, Carlo was still with the 2nd Marine Division, which was not reported to be among the American forces initially engaging the Japanese on that island.

Sure enough, on Saint Patrick's Day, 1945 – one year exactly to the day that she had relayed word to Angela that her friend's former beau had been reported alive – Elizabeth received a letter from Carlo that had been written on March 1st. In the letter he gave no indication that he was fighting for his life on Iwo Jima, and he vaguely mentioned "training" several times. No doubt the 2nd Marine Division was elsewhere in the Pacific, readying for yet another prong of MacArthur's and Nimitz's suffocating series of assaults, each one getting closer and closer to Japan itself. Carlo might be out of danger for the moment, but Elizabeth was sorrowfully certain that his respite from combat wouldn't last much longer.

Later that same Saturday afternoon, however, terrible news insisted on invading the DeLuca home.

*   *   *

Angela collapsed onto the floor into a sobbing mess, the telegram tightly clutched and now crumpled in her grasp. None of the others in the DeLuca living room with her – Elizabeth, Carmela, Giuseppe, or Rosalia – had yet read the words on the telegram, so each one instantaneously assumed the very worst.

Elizabeth was the one who finally, gently pried the telegram from Angela's grasp, being careful not to tear the paper lest they be unable to learn whatever the horrific news was that had been delivered to Angela without having to piece the telegram back together. Elizabeth blinked back her own tears and quickly read the telegram.

THE SECRETARY OF WAR DESIRES ME TO EXPRESS TO YOU HIS DEEP REGRET THAT YOUR HUSBAND STAFF SERGEANT ANTHONY DELUCA WAS WOUNDED IN ACTION 1 MARCH 1945 IN EUROPE IF FURTHER DETAILS OR OTHER INFORMATION ARE RECEIVED YOU WILL BE PROMPTLY NOTIFIED=

J A ULIO THE ADJUTANT GENERAL

Elizabeth choked off what she instinctively wanted to say to Angela: "He'll be all right; maybe he was only slightly wounded, like Carlo was on Guadalcanal." Even if that were the case, Elizabeth immediately time-traveled in her mind back to that terrible day in January of '42 when she received the Navy Department telegram about Carlo. If Angela, or Carmela or anyone else, had tried to soothe her anguish with similar words, she would likely have regarded such an effort as nothing short of shallow and unfeeling rather than an attempt to comfort her. Such a reaction would have been entirely unfair, Elizabeth thought when she thought about that moment in the months that followed until Carlo's return; but anyone who had yet to set eyes on such a telegram about a loved one couldn't possibly understand the all-consuming torment.

"I hope we get further news soon," was instead what Elizabeth cautiously said to Angela, choking back her own sobs.

*   *   *

Further news did come one week later:

THE SECRETARY OF WAR DESIRES ME TO UPDATE YOU ON CONDITION OF HUSBAND STAFF SERGEANT ANTHONY DELUCA HE WILL BE EVACUATED FROM EUROPE TO UNITED STATES FOR TREATMENT AS FURTHER DETAILS OR OTHER INFORMATION ARE RECEIVED YOU WILL BE PROMPTLY NOTIFIED=

J A ULIO THE ADJUTANT GENERAL

If possible, this second telegram caused Angela even greater anguish than the first one. How badly had Tony been wounded to require evacuation back to the States? At least he was alive; but unlike Carlo DeLuca and so many other East End Pittsburgh boys whose families received telegrams similar to the first one, Tony wasn't going to be patched up and then sent back to his unit or some other assignment. He would finally be returning home to the States but not as a weary, victorious soldier. "For treatment" likely meant that because of the severity of his wounds, he faced many months of surgery, rehabilitation, and convalescence.

And after that? Angela had no idea, and she was petrified every time she contemplated the many possibilities. Every time she tried to consciously declare "At least he's alive," her mind insisted on meandering from one devastating scenario to another.

Elizabeth was torn between sharing her sister-in-law's anguish and closely following the war news, day after day. That very morning of the Saturday that Angela received this second telegram, the *Post-Gazette's* headline had screamed:

PATTON DRIVES ACROSS RHINE AND SMASHES TOWARD BERLIN

The Russians were also bearing down on Berlin from the east, and were now only about thirty miles away from the German capital. The Nazis weren't giving up without a fight, but confidence that war in Europe would soon be over grew day by day.

Between the horrific news and uncertainty about Tony DeLuca and the fighting still raging in the Pacific, however, elation was the furthest thing from Elizabeth's mind.

*   *   *

"NAZIS IN WILD ROUT" read the afternoon *Pittsburgh Press* headline on Tuesday, March 27th. With Elizabeth's first glance while grabbing a copy at the downtown newsstand, she instantly had the panicky thought that the Germans themselves had launched yet another surprise counteroffensive and were the ones doing the "routing." Her anxiety was alleviated just as quickly, though, by the sub-headline directly below: "Enemy 'Whipped' – Eisenhower." She paid her four cents and hustled to the nearby streetcar, only seconds before it pulled away.

Settling into one of the few open seats where she would read the paper until the streetcar's arrival in Morningside, her eyes were drawn to another front page story on the left side of the page. "Million Dollar a Week Meat Black Market Flourishes in District," this headline read. She began reading how black marketeers flaunted the ration restrictions on meat in an "almost foolproof" manner, according to the article. Of course, reading or hearing anything about the area's black market operators made her think about her brother William. The Battle of Iwo Jima had been declared victoriously concluded weeks earlier; yet reports filtered in that even as the Marines were redeployed for future invasions elsewhere, the Army's 147th Infantry Regiment was still locked in guerrilla warfare against stubborn Japanese holdouts. Chances were, then, that her brother was still in danger on that already-iconic island, day after day.

Elizabeth's worries were compounded by yet another front-page *Press* article. "Okinawa Foothold Seized, Japs

Say" read that headline. Admiral Nimitz's mighty American Pacific Theater forces made no attempt to masquerade their intentions, landing and securing the Kerama Islands a few miles away from Okinawa while continuing to bombard Japanese forces on Okinawa itself. Carlo may not have been sent to fight on Iwo Jima, but he almost certainly was sitting on a Navy transport somewhere off of the Okinawa coast at this very moment, awaiting the order to hit the beaches.

That Sunday, Angela and Elizabeth accompanied Carmela and their in-laws to Saint Michael's for Easter Mass. Angela had to be all but dragged from the house, insisting that someone needed to remain at home in case a telegram was delivered with updated information about Tony's whereabouts and condition. Finally, Carmela and Elizabeth convinced her that the chances of a telegram being delivered on Easter Sunday were slim at best; or if one would be awaiting her, most likely it would be delivered later in the day, after Easter Mass services around the city were concluded.

The mood inside of Saint Michael's reflected the massively conflicted feeling of Pittsburgh and of the nation as a whole. Victory in Europe was all but a foregone conclusion by this point. Yet so many Pittsburgh men and boys were still engaged in deadly combat, day after day, on the road to Berlin and also on other battlefronts against Nazi divisions scattered throughout the European continent. Meanwhile in the Pacific, victory was also in sight, but that path to triumph ultimately went through the Japanese homeland. If the vicious battles and heavy losses on Guadalcanal, Tarawa, Saipan, Iwo Jima, the Philippines, and dozens of other islands over the past three years were any indication, the worst was yet to come.

"Almighty God," Father Vincente intoned five minutes or so after the Mass began, "we beseech you to show mercy on our loved ones who are now engaged in the climactic battles against those who had once sought to conquer and subdue us. Hard days of fighting are ahead for those of your flock whom you have selected to be your warriors. Bestow them with the strength and courage that they require to carry out your will and end this terrible global war and bring peace to a weary world."

Elizabeth and Angela both glanced around Saint Michael's as the priest spoke. Each took note of more than a few Morningside families who had lost a son sometime during the past several years. Elizabeth and Angela had both known most of those young men. Several of them – Dante Alghetti, Terry Fisher, Stephen Ball, Vinnie Leonardo – had been contemporaries at Peabody High School. All of these young men had been alive three and a half years earlier when the country was dragged into this dreadful war on another Sunday morning, in a very different America.

This Easter Sunday morning, Elizabeth and Angela seemed to be thinking as one. They both continued gazing around the church and each took notice of dozens of other Peabody High girls. Some were their classmates from '41, while others had finished up high school a year or two either before or after the sisters-in-law had graduated. Many of them had married their sweethearts during the early days of the war, just as Elizabeth and Angela – Carmela also – had done. Some had taken wedding vows later in the war years, back in '43 or sometime last year, while a few were still enduring years-long engagements, apprehensively waiting for a fiancé to return from war...if he indeed would make it back home before his number was up.

What had happened to all of them? High school graduation was now in the past, and the midpoint of the 1940s was at hand. Years that should have been filled with movie dates, Sunday drives, and the occasional special evening at a glamorous nightclub had been cruelly replaced by screaming newspaper headlines, NBC Red war bulletins, and unwelcome daily lessons in world geography. A few of these young women who had become furlough brides had become pregnant and given birth, and for now were raising their children on their own while their husbands were still away at war. For most of the others, however, babies and strollers and family picnics in Schenley Park were nowhere in sight, heartlessly traded for the ever-present fear that one day a terrible telegram would callously bring word that those joys were not to be.

* * *

"Turn the radio on," Giuseppe DeLuca asked his daughter when the family trooped into their house after Easter Mass had been concluded. Carmela walked over to the Admiral and flicked the dial. The radio finished warming up just in time for the middle of a Blue Network war bulletin.

"...landing by the American 10th Army, under the command of Lieutenant General Simon Bolivar Buckner, comprised of United States Marines as well as Army soldiers. United Press is reporting that two Japanese airfields on Okinawa have been captured. Stand by for further bulletins. We now return you to your regular local programming."

Elizabeth's legs weakened as she slumped onto the sofa. So it was starting. She knew – they all knew – that the invasion of Okinawa was immutably forthcoming; yet there was something about an ominous Blue Network bulletin bearing the actual news that the landings had begun that suddenly turned the situation all but unbearable.

Elizabeth sighed painfully as she gazed downward and struggled to keep from bursting into tears. She desperately needed a cigarette and looked up to see where she had placed her purse. As Elizabeth glanced around the living room, she caught the eye of Giuseppe DeLuca. Carlo's father's eyes glistened as he did his best to fight back his own tears.

Chapter 32

Angela had abruptly quit her job at the WPB following the news that Tony had been wounded. She anxiously waited at the DeLuca home, day after day – minute after minute – for the promised "further details or other information" about Tony's return to the States. Ordinarily, she would have been carefully following the latest coal miners' strike that had grown daily since the beginning of April…not only in the newspapers and on the radio but also at work. The lack of production coal was having an immediate and devastating impact on steel production, so in her secretarial job at the WPB she would have been typing one panicky letter after another. Even though Angela still read the newspapers every day and saw the stories about the rapidly slipping steel production and the impact on the war effort, her mind simply rebuffed almost every detail about the war or the home front.

Elizabeth read the same newspaper stories and heard the same radio news reports about the growing steel production problems. She tried her hardest, but with each new report she couldn't help but envision Calvin McKinnon smack in the middle of the troubles. Was he calm and collected as he did his best to get the mines going again so the steel plant blast furnaces could resume? Or was this the crisis that finally unwound his cool demeanor? Each time Elizabeth would involuntarily ponder these questions until she was able to force her mind elsewhere.

Because Angela refused to leave the DeLuca home, her mother came there early each morning and spent many hours each day with Angela, Rosalia DeLuca, and also

Carmela. For more than a year and a half, ever since that fateful Monday morning when Carmela learned about the stealthy departure of Patrick Doyle, she had remained at home; she hadn't taken a new war plant or other home front job. Angela and Elizabeth had pondered more than once how their sister-in-law could possibly stand the monotony of being home day after day. It wasn't as if Tony DeMarco was now back home from the war and off working each day, while Carmela remained at home raising their children and taking care of their house. Day after day, Carmela might accompany her mother to the grocery market or the butcher's or baker's, and she would help her mother prepare meals and clean up afterwards. But the woman who had been the brassiest of the family's furlough brides back in early '42 now seemed to be a shell of her former self, exhibiting little enthusiasm for anything.

One time awhile back Elizabeth had raised the possibility to Angela that perhaps Carmela was afraid to take a new job, lest she fall victim to temptation once again. By remaining safely ensconced at home, accompanied by her mother much of each day, she would be buffered from the Patrick Doyles – and perhaps the Calvin McKinnons – who might be out there waiting for a lonely furlough bride who hadn't seen her own husband for years now.

If Carmela hadn't been around, Elizabeth might well have also quit her job to stay home with Angela. But since Carmela was able to be by Angela's side almost every minute of the day, Elizabeth continued her own small contribution to the home front's war effort.

* * *

On Wednesday, the eleventh day of April, Elizabeth returned home shortly before 6:00 that evening. Just as had been the case last year when she was convinced Carlo was on Saipan, she was ravenous for the latest news from Okinawa. This afternoon's *Pittsburgh Press* had frustratingly devoted almost all of its front page news coverage to the European Theater, with the headline screaming "63 MILES TO BERLIN!" This was certainly all good news, but Elizabeth's thoughts were firmly out in the Pacific, on Okinawa.

Elizabeth was barely through the front door when Carmela excitedly rushed to meet her.

"Tony is back in the States!" Carmela breathlessly declared.

"My brother; Angela's Tony," Carmela clarified, though Elizabeth knew which Tony Carmela had meant. "In Philadelphia; the Valley Forge General Hospital, it's a military hospital there."

"Already?" Elizabeth questioned. She had done the mental calculations when word came that Tony would be evacuated from Europe. Based on Carlo's journey from the Pacific two years earlier, she had figured it would be late April at the earliest, and likely well into May, before his troop ship docked anywhere along the East Coast.

"They brought him back on a C-54," Carmela confirmed. "Straight to Philadelphia. He's already been admitted into the hospital."

Elizabeth would occasionally ponder how odd it was that nearly everyone on the home front, male and female alike, could now rattle off different names and designations and types of military machinery, vehicles and weaponry. Before Pearl Harbor, Elizabeth would have been hard-pressed to distinguish an Air Corps pursuit plane from a bomber. Now, after more than three years of war, she – as well as Carmela and Angela and nearly everyone else they knew – could quickly identify a plane flying overhead as a B-17 or a B-24, or a B-25 or some other bomber. They all could somehow work battleships and cruisers and destroyers into a conversation, even if they weren't quite sure of all the particulars and distinctions among those navy vessels. The same manner in which girls and young women could rattle off Hollywood starlet names such as Ginger Rogers and Mae West and Joan Crawford – and Carla Colburn – had somehow been shifted to military weaponry after more than three years of all-consuming war.

So when Carmela related that her brother had been flown stateside in a C-54, Elizabeth needed no further explanation to associate that Air Forces plane designation with the transport planes that were also used for medical evacuation. Later they would all learn that the criteria for medical transport via C-54 rather than troop ship or some other means was that patients who were expected to require three to six months of stateside medical care were being transported from the war theaters via these workhorse cargo planes.

"Angela is upstairs packing," Carmela continued.

For a couple of seconds, Carmela's words didn't register with Elizabeth. Finally:

"She's going out there?"

Carmela nodded.

"Tomorrow afternoon," Carmela confirmed. "She hasn't gotten her train tickets yet, but she already checked the train schedule."

Carmela looked back towards the kitchen, and satisfied that her mother was still in there cooking, she whispered to Elizabeth:

"I'd really like to go with her, to keep her company. But that would leave Ma at home all by herself during the day, doing nothing except worrying about all of my brothers. Do you think Ma would be okay by herself? I know you and Pa DeLuca are here in the evenings after work, but all morning and all afternoon she'd be alone…"

Carmela's voice trailed off. Elizabeth immediately realized that her sister-in-law was torn about who needed her more for moral support: her mother or Angela.

"I don't know," Elizabeth replied, also in a whisper. "Like you said, I'm here in the evenings and Pa DeLuca also, but you're right about her being alone all day. Does Angela have any idea yet how long Tony will be at…where did you say?"

"Philadelphia," Carmela answered. "That's what…about six or seven hours from here?"

"I guess so," Elizabeth shrugged. She only knew that Philadelphia was on the other side of the state, but wasn't quite sure how far from Pittsburgh that actually would be. But regardless of a more accurate approximation of the distance or driving time, the salient point was that Angela would be nowhere near Pittsburgh. She would be with Tony, but how much time each day would the hospital let her visit with her husband? Suppose he needed an operation, or more than one? She would be far away, all by herself, with no family at all. Carmela was right: Angela did need someone with her.

Yet at the same time, Elizabeth could put herself in Rosalia DeLuca's place. Her other three sons were still facing off against the enemy as the war in Europe appeared to be reaching its climax and, over in the Pacific, the horrifying invasion of Japan seemed to be next. How could a mother cope by herself with hour upon hour of uncontrollable fear?

"I have an idea," Elizabeth quietly said to Carmela.

*   *   *

"But what about your job?" Angela asked Elizabeth. "You can't just quit!"

Elizabeth shrugged.

"Mr. Coleman should be able to find someone to take my place pretty easily," she replied. "Besides, with the war in Europe almost over, they'll probably be cutting back on military shoe and boot production, at least a little bit."

Elizabeth sighed before continuing.

"It doesn't matter, though. Carmela is right; you really need someone with you out there, but also Ma DeLuca needs someone here. Those are the most important things. This way Carmela can stay with Ma DeLuca like she does all the time anyway, and I'll be out there with you."

Angela offered a weak smile as she reached out to take her sister-in-law's hands into hers.

"Thank you so much," she whispered as her tears began to flow. "I can't tell you how much this means to me."

Elizabeth began to quietly weep as well.

"You'd do the same for me if it were Carlo out there in the military hospital," she responded. "We've been through so much together; this entire war. We'll see it through to the end..."

Elizabeth choked out a sob along with her final word.

"...together."

Chapter 33

April 12, 1945

The next morning, a half-hour before her shift was scheduled to begin, Elizabeth stood in Mr. Coleman's office, nervously awaiting his response to her news. Fortunately the near-sleepless night, churning stomach, and pounding tension headache were all for naught.

"Of course," the supervisor replied. "I understand completely. To tell the truth, if you had come to tell me that you were leaving immediately, I would understand, given the circumstances. But especially since you will be finishing out the week, we will be just fine."

Gerald Coleman then confirmed what Elizabeth had conjectured to Angela.

"We'll be cutting back production very soon now," he told Elizabeth in lowered tones. "Between the two of us, your leaving us means that one less person will have to be let go. So it's not that I'm not sad to see you leave, but everything here will be changing a great deal, very soon."

"I can't tell you what a relief that is," Elizabeth sighed. "I was up most of the night worrying about quitting and leaving you in a bind. I'm so glad to hear that's not going to be the case."

Gerald Coleman smiled.

"It's most important that you keep your sister-in-law company out there in Philadelphia. Now, is this the girl who used to work here back in '42 and '43?"

Elizabeth shook her head.

"That's Carmela; this is another sister-in-law, Angela. She's married to Carmela's brother, he's the one who was wounded in Italy and got flown back. But both their husbands' names are Tony – Carmela's husband, and also her brother who is married to Angela."

"I see," Mr. Coleman nodded, though Elizabeth had the impression he was unable to keep all of these Italian family members straight. However, he didn't press for further clarification, so Elizabeth let the subject drop.

"I haven't asked you lately, but has there been any word about your son? The one who is a German prisoner?"

Gerald Coleman shook his head as a cloud of concern dropped over his face.

"We found out last week from the Red Cross that the German prison camp he had originally been in was taken by the Russians back in January, but the Nazis had already evacuated all the prisoners and moved them somewhere else. We haven't had any word from him, or any other Red Cross updates, for months now."

"I'm sorry," Elizabeth offered.

"We're hoping that any day now, with the war almost over in Europe, we'll get some word."

"How about your other son? Jonathan?" Elizabeth changed the subject.

"As far as we know," Gerald Coleman replied, "he's still flying B-29s out of Tinian. Every time I see a newspaper headline or hear on the radio news about a massive B-29 raid over Japan, I know that he most likely is up there."

The cobbler-turned-supervisor sighed.

"He survived all of those B-17 missions in Europe, and now he's flying even more missions over Japan in that new bomber. I can only hope that the war is over soon…"

Mr. Coleman's unspoken addendum to his sentence: "…before his luck runs out."

"I know," Elizabeth nodded. "That's the way I feel about my husband. Guadalcanal, Tarawa, Saipan, Tinian, and now probably Okinawa…I'm praying the war out there, in the Pacific, is over soon; just like you said."

Elizabeth DeLuca's unspoken addendum was identical to that of Gerald Coleman, and they both knew it.

*   *   *

As Elizabeth had promised Mr. Coleman, she would finish out the work week before heading to Philadelphia over the weekend to join Angela. Despite Mr. Coleman's assurances, Elizabeth still had the feeling she was leaving the shoe man in a bind; so she was determined to throw herself into her work with every ounce of her energy today and then again tomorrow. The workday passed quickly, and at 5:00 Elizabeth departed the plant and hurried over to the Monongahela Incline. She stepped into line, her thoughts now seeking out Angela somewhere around the middle of Pennsylvania, where her eastbound train should be right now. How was her sister-in-law holding up? Had she solved how to get from Philadelphia's train station to the Valley Forge hospital...something that had yet to be determined when Elizabeth left for work this morning? Would Angela be able to see Tony tonight after arriving?

"...can't believe it..."

"...don't know what to say..."

"...for so long, I swear I can't remember anybody else..."

All around her, people were speaking with a sense of distressed urgency that instantly made Elizabeth extremely nervous. She also noticed that more than a few people were wiping away tears.

"Did something happen?" she anxiously asked the man directly in front of her in line.

The man turned around slowly, revealing glistening eyes.

"Roosevelt died," he stammered, barely able to squeak out just those two words.

Elizabeth felt her heart jump into her throat, and for a second or two felt as if she wouldn't be able to continue breathing.

"About an hour and a half ago," the man choked out. "The radio said a cerebral hemorrhage; somewhere down in Georgia, that's where he was."

Elizabeth was unable to speak. She wanted to ask this man who was going to be president now. The vice-president, obviously, but who was that? Garner had been

FDR's VP during his first two terms, and then was followed by Wallace. But Wallace hadn't run with Roosevelt last year; someone else had. Given the shock of the moment, Elizabeth simply couldn't recall the man's name.

Regardless, they would all suddenly have a new president. But how could that be? Roosevelt had been the President of the United States almost as far back as Elizabeth could recall. Of course Hoover had preceded FDR, and Elizabeth remembered a little bit about him from her girlhood. But FDR had been in the White House for more than twelve momentous, history-making years…through most of the Great Depression and then all these years of the war. How in the world could he have died when victory was finally in sight?

* * *

Angela's train pulled into Harrisburg just after 6:30 p.m. The train would remain at the station for fifteen minutes, and passengers were allowed to briefly disembark if they desired. Angela decided to step off the train to stretch her legs and grab a copy of that city's evening paper to read during the remaining couple of hours until arriving in Philadelphia.

She headed to the station's newsstand and immediately noticed an exceptionally large crowd gathered around the stall. She eased her way through the people, picking up tidbits of conversation as she made her way inward.

"…twelve years, but it seemed like forever…"

"…I heard at seven o'clock tonight he'll be sworn in…"

"…never even heard of Truman before, even though I voted for Roosevelt…"

Even before she saw the oversized-print headline on tonight's extra edition of *The Evening News*, Angela had a good idea what had happened.

THE PRESIDENT IS DEAD

The headline sat atop a large black-bordered photograph of the only President of the United States whom Angela could clearly remember.

Even with victory in Europe seemingly at hand any day now, Angela felt as if they had just lost the war.

Chapter 34

"But it took me almost two hours to get here from the train station!" Angela protested, but the front desk nurse was unmoved.

"I'm sorry, Mrs. DeLuca, but visiting hours were over at seven o'clock, and it's almost ten o'clock right now. You can visit your husband tomorrow morning; right now he needs his rest."

"But I came all the way across the state!"

"I'm sorry," the nurse shook her head once more, "but we are required to adhere to these rules by the Army. They set the policy for all Army hospital visiting hours in Washington, and we *must* follow them."

The nurse was getting irritated now, but Angela's frustration was about to boil over. The stern-looking woman, probably in her late thirties, wore the gold oak leaf of an Army Major on one collar of her starched white nurse's uniform, but Angela wasn't intimidated.

"All I want to do is see him!" Angela was just about yelling now. "I need to find out how he's doing!"

"You can speak with a doctor tomorrow morning," the nurse testily replied. "I'm very sorry, but rules are rules in a hospital…and *especially* in an Army hospital."

Angela realized that she wasn't going to win this argument.

"Can you at least tell me how he's doing?" Exasperation had quickly given way to fighting back tears.

The last thing Angela wanted was for this battle-axe nurse to see her crying!

"You can speak with a doctor tomorrow morning," the nurse repeated. "I'm afraid that all medical information about patients to their families must come from a doctor."

Angela finally acknowledged defeat. She would simply have to wait until the morning to see Tony with her own eyes, and to learn from one of the Army doctors just how severe his wounds were. She wordlessly turned and shuffled fifteen or twenty feet to a bank of chairs and several wooden benches, where she supposed she would have to spend the night. Angela was arranging her belongings and had just slumped onto one of the hard wooden benches when the nurse asked her:

"Are you planning on spending the entire night here in the waiting room?"

Angela felt her eyes narrow. So now this biddy was going to tell her that she couldn't even stay in the waiting area?

"I don't have any choice," Angela replied through clenched teeth. "I told you, I'm not from Philadelphia, I came here all the way from Pittsburgh to be with my husband."

The nurse seemed to contemplate what Angela was saying.

"How long are you planning on staying here? In Phoenixville, I mean."

The Valley Forge General Hospital had turned out to not to be in Valley Forge at all, but rather in nearby Phoenixville, about five miles away in another community outside of Philadelphia. That geographical curiosity was one of the reasons Angela had arrived at the hospital so late, after embarking on a streetcar route bound for Valley Forge and then having to redirect once she realized her error.

The question took Angela by surprise. The truth was, she had no idea how long she intended to stay, and hadn't thought that far ahead. From the moment she had heard Tony had made it stateside, she had been singularly fixated with reaching him and being by his side. She hadn't given the matter of where she would stay, or how long, any consideration. She supposed that it would all work out somehow once she made her way to him.

"I don't know," Angela finally answered the nurse's question. "I suppose until he's ready to come home to Pittsburgh."

The nurse eyed Angela.

"So you're planning on camping out in the waiting room every single night? You don't have a place to stay?"

Again, Angela's reply was offered through clenched teeth.

"No, I don't." She was just about to demand how that was any of this nurse's business anyway, when the other woman said,

"There's a house about a half-mile from here where an older couple lives, and they have several rooms that they make available to our patients' family members who are from out of the area, like you. Their name is Stroskovich. They only charge three dollars a week, to pay for their boarders' meals; it's very reasonable. I believe they have a room available now, and I can call over there for you."

Angela was stunned into silence. This unyielding, unpleasant nurse whom Angela had quickly come to intensely dislike had suddenly changed her tune. Finally Angela replied, much more contritely than her last couple of statements,

"Yes, if you wouldn't mind. Thank you."

No more than five minutes later, the nurse handed Angela a sheet of paper on which she had scribbled an address and a hastily drawn map.

"It's safe around here for you to be out at night," the nurse told Angela. "It's about a ten-minute walk from here. Just make sure to watch for the street sign for Buchanan; it's easy to miss."

At the mention of a street that shared her sister-in-law's maiden name, Angela instantly thought about Elizabeth about to make the same journey from Pittsburgh.

"My sister-in-law is coming here Sunday," Angela informed the nurse. "Do you think they'll have a room for her?"

The nurse's testy demeanor apparently wasn't to be kept at bay any longer.

"You'll have to ask either Mr. or Mrs. Stroskovich," she snapped. "I'm not their hotel clerk."

* * *

Phoenixville, Pennsylvania, seemed like a quiet little town; not all that different than Pittsburgh's Morningside neighborhood, Angela thought to herself as she followed the nurse's map. She kept shifting her suitcase from her right arm to her left, and back again. She had been carrying the suitcase her entire trip, but other than making her way from the Pennsylvania Railroad platform to the nearby streetcar stop, Angela hadn't had to wrestle with the luggage. Now, though, both of her arms ached terribly. She was bone-weary, not to mention achingly frustrated that she couldn't see her husband until the following morning.

Angela made one more turn, and according to the map's directions, the Stroskovich house should be on her right, four more homes down. As she got closer, she noticed a tired-looking red brick home with the porch light illuminated, and decided even before counting buildings that must be the one. She steeled herself for the home stretch of this half-mile walk that – because of lugging her suitcase – seemed ten times as long of a distance.

Angela reached the sidewalk in front of the house and wearily turned towards the front porch. The very first thing that caught her eye was the red-bordered service flag in the front window with four stars embroidered on it, just like the one that hung in the front window of the DeLuca's Morningside home.

Unlike the DeLuca's service flag, though, with its four blue stars, the Stroskovich's banner displayed three blue stars, along with a solemn gold one.

*   *   *

"Come in, come in," Mr. Stroskovich urged Angela as he reached to take her luggage. "You must be bone-tired from such a long journey!"

Angela managed a "thank you" as her left arm was freed of the suitcase that now seemed to weigh a thousand pounds. She followed the man inside the house, taking note of his stooped-over, slight build. He appeared to be close to seventy years old, and when Angela found out later that night that he wasn't yet fifty, she immediately thought, that's what losing a son in the war must do to you.

Angela was barely inside the door when Mrs. Stroskovich appeared. This hefty, matronly woman was every bit as welcoming as her husband had been moments earlier.

"Can I get you a cup of coffee, my dear? Something to eat?"

Angela shook her head.

"No thank you," she replied.

"Are you sure?" the woman persisted. Thinking that perhaps refusing this offer of hospitality might be construed as being standoffish or rude, Angela relented.

"Well, a cup of coffee would be nice," she nodded.

Apparently satisfied that this young girl would partake of her hospitality, Mrs. Stroskovich hurried off into the kitchen.

"Please sit down," the husband told Angela. "I'm sure that you're exhausted, but you should sit down for a few moments to relax a bit from your travels before we show you where your room is."

"Thank you," Angela replied as she sunk into the living room sofa. All she really wanted to do was collapse into a bed, but given that her other alternative for the evening had been sleeping upright on the wooden bench at the General Hospital, the least she could do was respond to these folks' hospitality.

"I'm sure you heard the terrible news about the President earlier today?" Mr. Stroskovich said.

"I did," Angela replied. "It's just awful." She proceeded to tell the boarder how she had learned of the tragic news at the Harrisburg train station.

"I don't know anything at all about this Truman fellow," Mr. Stroskovich offered. "But we can only hope that he has a steady hand and cool head, with victory in Europe so close at hand."

"I know," Angela acknowledged.

"So tell me about your husband," the man asked. "I don't mean to pry, but we always like to know a little bit about the loved ones of those who stay with us, so we can pray for them."

"He was wounded in Italy," Angela answered. "I don't know anything yet about how he was wounded, or exactly what his injuries are. The Army evacuated him from Europe and he just arrived here yesterday."

Mr. Stroskovich seemed to measure his words carefully.

"Wasn't he able to speak when you visited with him just now?"

"They wouldn't let me see him!" was Angela's suddenly animated reply.

"What? After coming all this way?"

"I know! I argued with the nurse, but she kept saying over and over that it was Army rules and hospital rules, and that there wasn't anything that she could do!"

Angela was about to launch into a long complaint about the nurse's demeanor, but then she realized that despite the woman's insistence on rules above compassion, she had been the one responsible for Angela being here in the Stroskovich home right now rather than stiffly attempting to sleep in the hospital's waiting area.

"Well, you'll get over there first thing in the morning to visit him."

"And to find out from the doctors how he is," Angela added. "I still don't even know anything at all about his condition."

"That's terrible," came Mrs. Stroskovich's voice as she appeared in the doorway leading from the kitchen, carrying a tray bearing three cups of coffee. Angela immediately rose from the sofa to give the older woman a hand, but Mrs. Stroskovich just as quickly said,

"Oh no, no, please sit down, I know you're tired."

Mrs. Stroskovich took a half dozen steps across the living room to where Angela was now standing in front of the sofa. Angela reached for a cup of the coffee, and then waited for the older woman to serve her husband and then sit herself before slumping back onto the sofa.

"You said that your husband was wounded in Italy?" Mrs. Stroskovich asked.

"Yes, he was," Angela replied. "But I don't know where; just some place in Northern Italy where all the fighting has been since spring."

"Our son Milan was killed at Anzio," the husband flatly stated. "You probably noticed the gold star on the banner in the window when you came up the porch stairs."

"I did," Angela quietly replied. "I'm so sorry."

"He was our third son," Mrs. Stroskovich chimed in. "The other boys are all over in Europe also, all of them in the Army. Our oldest boy, Peter, is a paratrooper with the 82nd Airborne, and the other two are in the infantry, like Milan was."

Angela thought for a moment before responding.

"Tony – my husband – was at Anzio also. He had been in North Africa and then Sicily, and then in Southern Italy. Then his unit was pulled for the Anzio landing."

Mr. Stroskovich sighed.

"Everything we heard about Anzio and what those boys went through afterwards was just terrible," he said. "Our poor Milan didn't have much of a chance."

Realizing what he had just said to Angela, Mr. Stroskovich added, "Your husband was one of the fortunate ones, to make it through that one."

"I suppose," Angela agreed uneasily as she sipped her coffee. Eventually Tony's fortune had taken a turn for the worse, though, and here he was.

Suddenly she realized just how exhausted she was after a long day of travel and frustration. She rubbed her eyes and then looked at Mrs. Stroskovich.

"My sister-in-law is coming to be with me while I stay with my husband," Angela said. "Would it be all right if she stayed here with me? She can stay in the same room and we can pay extra…"

"Of course that's fine, my dear," Mrs. Stroskovich interrupted. "She can stay as long as you are with us, until your husband is ready to go back home."

"Thank you very much," Angela nodded and then took another sip of the coffee. Suddenly she couldn't keep her eyes open.

"I hope you don't mind," Angela said as she placed the now-half-empty coffee cup on the end table next to the sofa, "but I'm exhausted. I can barely keep my eyes open, and I need to get up early and go right to the hospital."

"Of course, of course," Mr. Stroskovich answered this time. "Come with me, I'll take your suitcase upstairs and show you where you'll be staying."

"Good night," Mrs. Stroskovich said pleasantly as Angela rose to follow the older woman's husband upstairs, echoing the "good night" as she did.

Upstairs, directly across the tiny hall from the top of the staircase, was the room that Angela was apparently being given.

"This was our son Milan's room," Mr. Stroskovich said quietly as he opened the door and headed into the room. For a second or two, Angela froze, not quite certain that she wanted to follow the man into his dead son's childhood bedroom. She gathered her wits, though, and walked inside. The room looked very much like Tony's room at the DeLuca home, with a few sports trophies and boyish books resting on a tiny bookcase. Tony's brothers' rooms looked like this, too, and for a fleeting moment Angela wondered if perhaps every young soldier's childhood room happened to be nearly identical to all the others.

"The washroom is down the hall on the left," Mr. Stroskovich advised Angela. "Tomorrow I'll introduce you to the others who are staying with us in the other two bedrooms. There's a nice couple from Cincinnati who are about the same age as Mrs. Stroskovich and me, around fifty, and their son was badly wounded at the Battle of the Bulge. Then there is another girl a few years older than you who is also here for her husband. He was an Air Corps P-51 pilot and was wounded when he had to ditch in the English Channel. He was in a British hospital for a short while until he stabilized and then they sent him back here."

Mr. Stroskovich seemed to feel the need to put Angela's mind at ease.

"Everyone else is very nice," he assured her.

"I'm sure they are," Angela replied as they said their good nights.

*　　*　　*

"Mrs. DeLuca, I'm Dr. Benson," the exceptionally tall man told Angela as he offered his right hand. Angela noticed as she shook the man's hand that he was wearing a colonel's eagle on his white coat's collar.

"Doctor, when can I see my husband?" Angela hadn't meant for her first words to sound so frustrated, but she couldn't help herself.

Dr. Benson cocked his head slightly.

"You mean you haven't seen your husband yet?" he asked.

Angela was unable to contain the look of surprised irritation at the doctor's words.

"No, I haven't! Last night when I got here they wouldn't let me see him. The nurse said it was after visiting hours."

Angela then quickly added:

"She wouldn't tell me anything about his condition, either! They said all patient information had to come from a doctor, and I had to come back in the morning."

The Army doctor seemed as if he was about to say something, but apparently decided not to. Later, Angela concluded that he had been about to sympathize with Angela and agree that she had been unfairly kept at bay by that battle-axe nurse. Apparently, though, the doctor didn't see the point in criticizing one of the Army nurses to a patient. Angela hoped, though, that in private the doctor gave that biddy a piece of his mind!

"Well, before I take you to his room, let me fill you in on his condition."

Angela involuntarily gasped in response to the doctor's words, but he shook his head.

"No, I'm not trying to alarm you. His condition is actually much improved from not too many days ago. The field hospital did a marvelous job with him, and considering the incredibly unique wound that he suffered…"

Angela let out another gasp, and the doctor offered a small, tight smile.

"I'm sorry, I keep alarming you. But I must say that your husband's situation is one of the strangest I've ever seen or heard of. For that matter, that *any* of us have seen or heard of."

Angela was ready to scream: tell me already!

"Your husband was shot in the heart," the doctor bluntly stated, and Angela immediately dissolved into tears.

"Actually, he was shot through his left lung and then the bullet lodged in his heart," the doctor continued. Now Angela wanted to shout: stop! I don't want to hear any more!

"Normally the wound would have been a fatal one," the doctor continued, slipping into a clinical recitation of this peculiar case as if he were delivering a journal paper at a medical conference. "But the bullet shredded his lung tissue, which then somehow wrapped around his heart and dramatically slowed the blood loss. The medics had to take him fifteen miles away to the closest field hospital, and it took them more than four hours. However, because the lung tissue was curtailing the bleeding, he survived long enough to make it onto the operating table at the field hospital."

"Oh my God!" Angela was weeping uncontrollably now, but the doctor seemed too wrapped up in the recitation of this one-in-a-million case to notice.

"That wasn't the only strange part. The bullet wound up dropping into a large vein and made its way to his groin area. The doctors at the field hospital had to operate a second time once they realized this, to remove the bullet. But in the meantime his heart and lung wounds were patched up."

Angela's sobbing began to slow down, until the doctor added:

"Oh, they did transfusions totaling fifteen pints of blood."

Angela's weeping went right back into high gear. The doctor seemed puzzled – almost irritated – that this soldier's wife apparently didn't appreciate the medical uniqueness of what he had just described to her.

"Let's go see your husband," the Army doctor finally told Angela.

*   *   *

He died! That was Angela's first reaction at the sight of her husband prone in the hospital bed, his eyes shut. *That nurse wouldn't let me see him last night when he was alive, and this morning he's dead! I'm too late!*

Just as Angela's rational mind was doing its best to shove aside that wild, unfounded idea, Tony DeLuca's eyes slowly opened. He slowly turned his head to the left, towards the hospital room door.

"Hi doll," he croaked.

At the sound of his voice – and also that term of endearment that she had last heard from her husband almost three years earlier – Angela burst into tears yet again.

"Oh my God, Tony," she managed to squeak out in between sobs. She instantly took several quick steps towards the hospital bed, wanting so very much to fiercely hug her husband. Suddenly she froze and looked over at Colonel Benson.

"Can I touch him? Am I allowed to?" Angela asked.

The Army doctor, so used to wives and mothers urgently rushing towards his patients' beds at first glance without any thought for their condition, was slightly surprised at Angela's question.

"It's good of you to ask," he nodded towards this young Army wife from Pittsburgh. "Be careful around his chest area, but you can give him a welcome home kiss if you'd like," the doctor added with a slight grin.

Angela continued towards Tony. The top portion of his hospital bed was elevated, so she didn't have to lean down very far to do exactly what the doctor had just suggested.

"I'm so glad you're home," she was able to declare, staccato-like, until her sobbing totally overtook her and she was unable to say anything else.

"It's okay, doll," Tony mumbled, his voice apparently still very weak.

He mustered his strength to continue, looking first at Angela and then at Colonel Benson.

"I'm back here now, and they're doing a bang-up job patching me up. Right, sir?"

"I was telling your wife about your miraculous wound, Sergeant," Colonel Benson nodded to Tony.

A groan from the other side of the curtain to the right of Tony's bed caught Angela's attention, and for the first time she realized that Tony wasn't alone in this hospital room. A second, louder groan caught Dr. Benson's attention, who strode by the foot of Tony's bed and past the edge of the hospital curtain.

"How are you doing there, Captain?" Angela heard the Army doctor ask whomever the other patient was.

"An Air Forces pilot," Tony said quietly to Angela, referring to the patient on the other side of the dividing curtain. He managed a weak grin as he added:

"I guess I'm important enough to be sharing a room with an officer, huh?"

Later that afternoon, Angela would learn that the other patient – Captain Donatelli, a P-51 pilot from nearby Allentown – was the husband of one of the other boarders at the Stroskovich home.

"So I guess you heard about my miracle wound, huh?" Tony weakly asked his wife, causing yet another burst of sobs from Angela.

"Come on," he added, "don't cry. I'm gonna be okay, that's what the doc says."

"I figured my number was up back in Italy," he continued in a near-whisper. "But I made it, and I'm back now."

Tony managed a weak chuckle.

"Probably for good," he added.

* * *

That first full day of Angela's stay, she was able to manage four short visits with her husband, each one about ten to fifteen minutes. She would have camped out besides Tony's hospital bed nonstop, slipping away only for an occasional bathroom break, and only when she couldn't hold it any longer. Given Tony's still-touchy condition, though, hospital policy dictated short-duration visits only for the time being. And, as Angela had found out the previous night, policy in an Army hospital was sacrosanct. Each time a nurse showed up to usher her out of Tony's room, she would reluctantly depart to take up residence in the closest waiting room area. She didn't even take time to go to the small hospital cafeteria for lunch, and by suppertime she was famished. Angela was allowed to sit with Tony while the nurse fed him his tiny portion of some bland, mushy-looking substance that apparently was all he was able to stomach. Angela finally noticed how gaunt he looked, and figured that he was probably twenty pounds lighter – maybe even more – than when she last saw him back in the summer of '42.

After Tony's meager supper, the nurse and an orderly shooed Angela away once again so they could change the dressings on his wounds and surgical incisions. Angela finally headed to the hospital cafeteria just before 6:00 p.m., selecting an unappetizing plate of meatloaf and mashed potatoes from the food line and then finding a seat. Despite being nearly ravenous, Angela picked at her food. The evening news on Philadelphia's Mutual Network affiliate played through several speakers haphazardly placed around the smallish eating area, and Angela learned that the Red Army had captured Vienna after a week-long siege; United Press was reporting that more than 125,000 German prisoners had been taken.

What was to become of all of those prisoners? Angela wondered how they would be treated by the Russians, the same as so many German soldiers who were being captured on the other side of Europe, day after day, as the Americans and British closed in on Berlin. Considering how many of these Allied soldiers' comrades had been killed by the Germans – or had been put into hospitals such as this one because of severe war wounds – she wondered if the prisoners would be treated harshly, or perhaps even brutalized as revenge for the killings and injuries that they had inflicted.

"Are you eating by yourself?" The melodious voice interrupted Angela's troubled musings, and she looked up at the woman who had just asked the question. She appeared to be a few years older than Angela, but otherwise nearly a spitting image of Angela herself.

"No…I mean yes, I am, but you're welcome to sit down if you'd like," Angela replied.

The woman smiled as she offered a "thanks" and then placed her cafeteria tray, bearing the exact same dullish meal that Angela had selected, onto the empty place directly across from Angela.

"Is your husband here?" the woman asked.

"Uh-huh," Angela replied. "I just arrived last night and I got to see him for the first time today."

The woman seemed to measure her words carefully before asking her follow-on question.

"How is he doing?"

Angela hesitated before answering.

"I don't really know," she replied truthfully. "He's able to talk and they just fed him dinner, so he's able to eat a little bit. But he was shot through the heart and lungs and…"

"Oh, Sergeant DeLuca?" the woman interrupted. "You're his wife?"

"Uh-huh," Angela nodded.

"I'm Maryann Donatelli," the woman offered. "My husband is in the other bed in your husband's room. I had to go home to Allentown this morning and just made it back here a little while ago; that's why we didn't run into each other in their hospital room."

Angela offered a tight smile.

"It's nice to meet you," she said, and then realized that she had better ask, "How is your husband doing?"

Mrs. Donatelli shrugged, and a worried look suddenly appeared on her face.

"He's better the past week or so, but until then the doctors weren't sure that he would be able to walk again. He had to ditch in the English Channel – he's a P-51 pilot – and…"

"Are you staying at the Stroskovich house?" Angela interrupted, the woman's story bringing back recollection of Mr. Stroskovich's brief narrative last night.

The woman seemed surprised at the question, and hesitated a second or two before responding.

"I am; how did you...oh, you must now be in the open room they had," she realized. "Mr. Stroskovich is a very nice man, but he does talk up a storm about everyone!"

Maryann Donatelli chuckled.

"This is a small world, huh? Our husbands are in the same hospital room, and we're staying at the same house."

"I guess so," Angela agreed.

* * *

The two women went together to their husbands' hospital room for a final visit that night before both were abruptly kicked out at 7:00 promptly by the same nurse with whom Angela had battled the previous night. On their walk back to the boarding house, Angela told Maryann Donatelli about last night's encounter.

"The same thing, pretty much, happened to me a couple of weeks ago when I first got here, right around ten o'clock also," she told Angela. "The same nurse. Since we're from Allentown, about forty miles away, I just turned around and drove back home and then came back the next morning. But she was very unpleasant."

"Well, at least she told me about the Stroskoviches," Angela suggested. "She could easily have left me sleeping in the waiting room on the hard bench all night."

"True," Maryann Donatelli agreed.

*   *   *

The next morning Angela accompanied the Air Corps pilot's wife to the hospital, and they each more or less repeated what Angela had done the previous day, and what Maryann Donatelli had been doing almost every day since her husband was flown back to the Army hospital from England. Tony seemed slightly stronger than he had the day before, but the ward nurses still permitted Angela only the same four short visits she had been granted a day earlier.

Angela's spirits improved slightly throughout the day, though, as she became accustomed to Tony's condition and the belief that the worst was behind him. Several times during the day, when Maryann Donatelli was visiting her husband and Angela was out in the waiting room (the nurses wouldn't permit both wives to visit their husbands at the same time except at the end of the visiting day, claiming that simultaneous visitations would cause too much commotion in the room), Angela found herself wondering exactly how much Tony would recover. With bullet wounds in one lung and his heart, and the aftermath of three surgeries – so far – would he ever be able to chase their yet-to-be-born son around a tiny front yard at some cozy house they would move into someday? Would he be able to play catch with that son for more than a few minutes before tiring and needing to quit? Someday far in the future, would he be able to walk his daughter down the aisle at her wedding?

Each time, Angela forced those thoughts away when she found her fears threatening to spiral out of control. The future would take care of itself, she would tell herself; she had best concentrate on the present and doing whatever she could to help her husband heal.

Later that Saturday evening, shortly after 9:00 p.m., Angela was sitting in the Stroskovich living room along with Maryann Donatelli and the Trammels – the couple from Cincinnati also staying at the makeshift boarding home – discussing President Roosevelt's funeral procession that had taken place earlier that day. The Stroskoviches had both listened to the Columbia Network radio broadcast of the procession, while the others had been more focused on visiting their loved ones at the Valley Forge General Hospital and hadn't been in the vicinity of a radio during the broadcast. Mrs. Stroskovich was relating how FDR's body would soon be on its way by train to his beloved Hyde Park, where he would be buried tomorrow morning, when several knocks on the front door interrupted her.

Mr. Stroskovich rose to open the door and then reach for Elizabeth's suitcase just as he had done for Angela's upon her arrival. Meanwhile, Angela was already across the living room like a shot, reaching to hug her sister-in-law.

Releasing Elizabeth, Angela turned towards the others.

"This is my sister-in-law Elizabeth," she said, and then proceeded to introduce each of the others to Elizabeth.

"Her husband is a Marine," Angela added when the introductions were finished. "He's probably on Okinawa now," Angela continued before realizing that bringing up Carlo's likely danger to Elizabeth might not be the best idea. In fact she did notice Elizabeth flinch slightly at the name of the Japanese island, so she shifted her narrative.

"Elizabeth was fortunate enough to go with Carlo – that's her husband – to Camp Lejeune for a couple of months back in '43. He was assigned there as an infantry instructor."

"That must have been wonderful," Mrs. Stroskovich offered. Elizabeth thought to herself, "wonderful" wasn't quite the right word, but she figured that the older woman meant well, and didn't want to make a stink by critiquing the woman's choice of phrasing.

Elizabeth joined the conversation for a brief while, but her cross-state journey had been every bit as wearying as Angela's several days earlier. She and Angela said their good nights – Maryann Donatelli did as well – and headed upstairs.

Angela proceeded to tell Elizabeth about Tony's condition: his terrible but miraculous wound, and how he seemed now. Elizabeth listened intently but couldn't help her drooping eyes, and she was soon asleep.

Chapter 35

Over the next couple of weeks, Tony's condition seemed to improve a little bit each day, despite requiring one additional surgery. He soon was allowed – in fact, ordered – to undertake short walks up and down the hospital ward's hallways. Angela made sure that she accompanied him every single time, and Elizabeth also did so about half of the time. Elizabeth realized that Angela wanted some time alone with her husband, and these brief shuffling strolls presented the perfect opportunity for that to occur. Other times, though, Tony seemed to especially welcome his sister-in-law's company. Perhaps being with both of the girls together gave him a sense of family that he had missed for so long now, both Angela and Elizabeth thought.

Maryann Donatelli's husband was released from the hospital about a week after Angela's arrival, and sent next to a rehabilitation hospital near their home in Allentown. The pilot would likely be discharged from the Army Air Forces soon, so being closer to home was a blessing. Angela was sorry to see Maryann depart. Even following Elizabeth's arrival, Angela and her near-look-alike had developed something of a bond. Angela and Maryann exchanged addresses and promised to write each other about their husbands' respective recoveries. Perhaps they would encounter each other again someday, Angela thought. Even though Allentown was on the other side of the state from Pittsburgh, it wasn't that far away, so anything was possible.

Angela and Elizabeth both followed the war news as April drew to a close. By the end of the month the once-invincible Nazi government was in shambles. Heinrich Himmler, the dreaded S.S. Reichsführer, was reported by the United Press to have offered unconditional surrender to the American and British forces if the Russians were excluded from the surrender terms. ("No dice" was the immediate reply from the Americans, even though frantic surrender overtures reportedly continued.) Berlin's Nazi defenders had been "virtually wiped out" by the Red Army, according to newspaper headlines and stories. Rebels in Munich radioed an appeal to American forces to support an overthrow of the remnants of the Nazi government there.

Mussolini was caught trying to escape from Italy and was shot, his body subsequently hung upside down and desecrated by Italian civilians and partisans. Days later, it was Hitler's turn: Hamburg Radio reported that Hitler had fought to the death defending Berlin. American authorities were skeptical of the report, and rumors began to circulate that Hitler had escaped – or was in the process of escaping – Berlin. General Eisenhower himself weighed in on the controversy, postulating that Hitler had perhaps died of a stroke rather than fighting to the death. Regardless, it seemed that the hated Führer, the murderous tyrant who had begun the European side of this global war that had cost tens of millions of lives, was suddenly no more.

The peace feelers kept coming from Germany. On May 2nd, the German Armies of Northern Italy and Western Austria formally surrendered. Peace in Italy had finally arrived...too late for Milan Stroskovich and Tony DeLuca and hundreds of thousands of other wounded and dead Allied soldiers from the Italian campaign, but still mercifully welcome.

Two days later, still more German surrenders occurred in Holland, Denmark, and Northwestern Germany. Reports began filtering out of Berlin that Hitler had, in fact, committed suicide. Meanwhile, over in the Pacific, the Marines were reported to be within one mile from Naha, the capital city of Okinawa. This report – heard by Elizabeth after supper that Friday evening via an NBC Red bulletin – reminded Elizabeth (not that she needed reminding) that despite the collapse of the once-unstoppable Nazi forces, war still raged in the Pacific, and Carlo was right in the middle of that fight.

Day after day, a victorious halt to the fighting in Europe edged closer and closer. Finally, on Monday, the long-awaited word came that the following day – Tuesday, May 8th, 1945 – would be proclaimed Victory in Europe Day with the last remaining Nazi forces surrendering unconditionally.

*   *   *

"Oh my God! Look at this!" Angela was reading the Saturday edition of the *Philadelphia Inquirer* back in Tony's room. The hospital typically took delivery of a dozen or so copies of the local paper each day, which were shared back and forth among patients and their visitors.

She first handed the paper to Elizabeth for a fleeting second to show her sister-in-law what had caught her attention, and then handed the newspaper to Tony, who was now able to sit for short stretches in a chair in his room.

AFRICA-EUROPE VETS OUT OF WAR, the headline read, followed by: "Soldiers in Two Campaigns Not Going to Pacific."

"That's you!" Angela excitedly said to Tony as he absorbed the headlines and began reading the story. Many of the three million military men – women also, since nurses and other servicewomen were included – currently in Europe were scheduled to be shifted to the Pacific, now that victory in Europe had been secured. However, General Eisenhower had decided the previous night that anyone who had fought in *both* North Africa and Europe was to be excluded from what was being called "R-Day," for Redeployment Day.

"That means you don't have to go to the Pacific! You were in North Africa also!" Angela joyously exclaimed to her husband.

Tony slowly nodded as he continued reading. The truth was that for the moment he was in no condition to be sent anywhere near a combat zone, even if General Eisenhower personally dictated otherwise. All Tony was focused on was getting well enough to get out of this Army hospital; anything beyond that was simply on the other side of the horizon for him.

Wounded or not, though, Tony was still an Army man, and until he became otherwise, his fate was in the War Department's hands. If he became well enough to be released from the Army hospital, then quite possibly he would have been susceptible to being sent to the Pacific for the inevitable invasion of Japan.

Not now, though. Regardless of the speed of his recovery – or lack thereof – the fighting days of Staff Sergeant Tony DeLuca, United States Army, were apparently in the past forever.

Tony let out a heavy sigh as he handed the *Inquirer* back to his wife.

"Vinnie and Michael are probably going, though," he shook his head. "Neither of them was in North Africa; only Europe."

Tony looked over at his sister-in-law.

"Carlo also, he's still out there," he said to Elizabeth, shaking his head again.

Elizabeth gazed at Angela's husband, almost positive that she could read his thoughts:

If all three of my brothers have to take on the Japs until the bitter end, then I should be with them, not sitting it out back here in the States.

*   *   *

The rest of May and the first weeks of June passed at a snail's pace; both Angela and Elizabeth could feel it. There was something very strange about the war in Europe being over after so many years, while schizophrenically the fighting in the Pacific raged on. The newspaper headlines and radio news reported the relentless bombing of Tokyo and other Japanese cities, day after day, along with the fighting on Okinawa nearing its inevitable victorious conclusion.

What then, though? For the past three years, ever since the United States Navy sank four Japanese carriers and carried the day at the Battle of Midway, there had always been *something* next up in the Pacific Theater. Guadalcanal, New Guinea, New Georgia, Tarawa, Bougainville, Guam, the Philippines, Saipan, Tinian, Iwo Jima, Okinawa…every one of those Japanese strongholds and dozens of others needed to be taken along the lengthy, torturous road to Japan. Then, after each success, either MacArthur's or Nimitz's forces would clock ahead to their next objective.

Now, however, the road to Japan had taken the Army and the Navy and the Marines to Japan itself. No other stepping-stones remained. Okinawa was about to be secured, and now all that was left was the Japanese homeland. It didn't matter that Army Air Forces General Hap Arnold was quoted as declaring that next year, more than two million tons of bombs would be dropped on Japan and "there shouldn't be anything left of Japan by the end of 1946." Elizabeth and Angela – and the rest of the nation – knew that plenty of death and misery was directly ahead…and not just in Japan.

*   *   *

As Tony slowly regained his strength, Angela was permitted much longer visits with him. She relished every moment, even though Tony was frequently moody. He accepted the painful physical therapy he was required to undergo with few complaints. Instead, his sullenness seemed to surface when he was required to be back in his room, either sitting in the chair or resting in bed.

He began encouraging Angela to take a break every so often from being entrenched hour after hour at the Army hospital. "Go see a movie with Elizabeth," he would frequently say to his wife. "Get outside and get some fresh air for a little bit. It's summertime."

Angela felt highly conflicted about these requests. On the one hand, she felt extremely disloyal strolling about the small Phoenixville downtown area with her sister-in-law, peering into the windows of shops, as if the two of them were spending a leisurely afternoon in downtown Pittsburgh. She felt duty-bound to be by her husband's side; after all, why else had she raced to the other side of Pennsylvania upon receiving word that Tony had been returned to the Army hospital there from Europe?

At the same time, however, more than two months now of monotonous hospital-sitting, day after day, was taking its toll on Angela. They had been given a vague "sometime in July, probably" date for when Tony might be well enough to be discharged from the Valley Forge General Hospital. Tony still didn't know what was in the works for him afterwards. A new military service discharge points chart was due to be released any day now, and chances were that Tony would then have enough points to qualify for immediate discharge from the Army, coinciding with his discharge from the hospital. Should that be the case, he could then start looking forward to returning to Pittsburgh with Angela. Until any official word, however, neither Tony nor Angela dared give that possibility any credence. If there weren't an Army discharge in his future, then he likely would be given stateside duty at an Army post somewhere; so returning home after the completion of this lengthy hospital was by no means a foregone conclusion.

One Sunday afternoon in late June, Angela did slip away from the hospital with Elizabeth just as Tony began his two-hour physical therapy session. They strolled to the nearby Colonial Theater in Phoenixville's quaint downtown area, a distance of slightly less than a mile, just in time to catch *Flames of the Barbary Coast*, the new John Wayne movie.

The newsreel before the movie began with – of course – a title card stating "YANKS BATTLE FOR OKINAWA!" The newsreel was slightly dated, showing the invasion itself and also solemnly reporting the waves of Japanese kamikaze attacks that had wreaked havoc on the U.S. Navy's ships ever since the beginning of April. In fact, the Battle of Okinawa had been declared concluded last week, and all eyes now turned towards Japan...even as mop-up operations against stubborn holdouts continued, the same as on nearly every previous island.

Something about the newsreel made Elizabeth extremely uneasy. She could barely concentrate on the movie, and was anxious for the film to be over.

"Are you all right?" Angela asked her sister-in-law as they exited the theater. "You look...I don't know, strange; worried."

Elizabeth sent a troubled glance in Angela's direction as a reply.

"I guess I'm okay," she said. "It's probably that Okinawa newsreel. I haven't heard anything from Carlo in a while, and even though they said the fighting is almost over, I won't feel better until I know that he's safe."

"For now," she added.

* * *

Angela and Elizabeth arrived back at the hospital a little bit past 5:00. Tony should be receiving his supper right about now, Angela figured. She always enjoyed sitting with him while he ate. Now that his rations were more like a normal meal, and he could sit and eat by himself rather than be fed by a nurse in his bed, watching her husband eat was…well, if not enjoyable, at least doing so was no longer heartbreaking.

They arrived in Tony's room and, sure enough, his meal had been delivered a little bit early tonight. He was already about halfway through his meatloaf and mashed potatoes, so Angela and Elizabeth settled in to keep him company. Elizabeth always felt as if she was intruding when she sat with Angela while she in turn sat with Tony, but neither of them seemed to mind.

"Mrs. DeLuca?" Both Angela and Elizabeth turned towards the door at the sound of their shared name. Major Lereaux – that same battle-axe nurse with whom Angela had clashed that first night back in mid-April – stood in the doorway. In the intervening months, the Army nurse had proven to be much more accommodating; even pleasant on occasion. Angela occasionally felt badly about her own harsh feelings about the woman. Her job couldn't be an easy one, Angela realized. The nurse saw and was personally involved with more than her fair share of pain and tragedy and death. Angela wondered how she would fare in such a position rather than, say, the WPB secretary she had been up until several months ago. Each time, Angela gained a little bit more empathy for the woman.

"May I see you?" Major Lereaux stared directly at Angela as she spoke, seeming to take great pains to keep her tones even. For a split second, Angela was certain that she was about to be scolded for something, and she could feel her temper starting to flare. Noticing the look of measured concern on the Army nurse's face, though, Angela immediately thought otherwise.

The nurse nodded towards the hallway, indicating that she wanted Angela to follow her. Angela looked over at Elizabeth and then back at the Army nurse, and then reluctantly rose to follow the woman. What could she want? Quite possibly something to do with Tony's treatment, Angela worried. She was suddenly anxious that perhaps Tony had suffered some sort of setback; maybe one that even he didn't know about. Here he was, though, in the chair in his hospital room happily chowing down on his Army hospital meatloaf with the same gusto that he might enjoy a choice steak in a swanky hotel dining room.

Elizabeth also thought it was likely that whatever the nurse wanted, it had something to do with Tony's condition. The second Angela stepped out of the room to follow the nurse, Elizabeth did her best to engage Tony in conversation.

"The movie was swell," she offered, even though she already could recall very little of the story. "I'll bet you can't wait until you can go with Angela to the movies, huh?"

"Yeah," he replied. "It's been…what, almost three years since I took her to the movies, you know that? Way back in '42 when I was home on furlough. We went and saw *Men of Texas* with Jackie Cooper."

Tony let out a heavy sigh and lowered his fork to his plate.

"Wow, I can't believe I even remember what movie we saw; that seems like a hundred years ago," he softly said.

"I know," Elizabeth agreed after a slight hesitation.

Elizabeth's brother-in-law looked at her.

"You know what I was thinking the other day? I didn't want to say nothin' to Angela, but...well, I dunno...just don't say nothin' to her, okay?"

Elizabeth nodded.

"Not long after that furlough was when we invaded North Africa," Tony DeLuca continued. "Do you know I was the last one left from our unit? From all the original guys in North Africa? I know it was more than two years, but every other guy either bought it or was wounded bad enough to get sent home. A few of them went to other units somewhere along the line, I guess, but they were gone, also. A lot of the guys got killed or wounded in North Africa or Sicily, and then even more in Southern Italy. And then from the time we all hit the beaches at Anzio and went straight into that slaughterhouse in Northern Italy..."

Tony DeLuca shook his head, so very obviously trying to force away unwelcome images and memories.

"I was the last one," he muttered again. "I remember about a week before I got hit I was looking around at all the other guys there, and I felt like this...I dunno, like I was a ghost still hanging around some old house where I once lived when I was alive, even though new people had moved in and were just going about with their lives."

He looked over at Elizabeth, and she could see that his eyes were beginning to water.

"I just felt like I shoulda been gone with all the other old-timers; that's where I belonged. I was a part of the past, not the present."

Elizabeth was about to offer what she hoped were comforting words to Tony. She was about to tell him that no doubt, Carlo felt the same way; probably Vinnie and Michael, too. They were all old-timers as far as this terrible war was concerned. Millions of American men and boys had been pulled into this war over the past three and a half years, but there was something special about those like Tony and Carlo and their brothers, and Tony DeMarco and so many others, who had answered the call so early in the war when everything looked so bleak; almost hopeless. As Tony had just reflected, too many of those who were on the front lines in that first year of war were gone now. Yet Tony *was* still here; he had survived, even if so many of his comrades hadn't. Was there a reason? God only knew, and maybe someday Tony would be enlightened. Perhaps even someday Tony would be reunited "up there" with all of his long-lost comrades; though in Tony's case, unlike those who had been killed in combat, any such ethereal reunion would hopefully take place after a long, full life.

Elizabeth wanted to share all of these thoughts with Tony, but she didn't have a chance. She heard a shuffling behind her and looked toward the hospital room door. Angela had halted in the doorway; her eyes were red and watery.

Elizabeth tried to speak, but was unable to do so. She could only wait helplessly for her sister-in-law to muster the strength to say something, which Angela finally did.

"It's your brother," Angela was able to manage before dissolving into uncontrollable sobbing.

Chapter 36

Mop-up duty.

The phrase, so widely adopted by the newspapers and press bureaus and radio newscasters, implied that the brutally difficult work of taking an island from the Japanese had already been victoriously completed. A few stubborn enemy holdouts might still be out there; but the conquerors would simply, at their leisure, root out those who foolishly had not surrendered and then pick them off, one by one.

Mop-up duty: the phrase brought to mind a grocery market stock boy retrieving his mop and bucket from the storeroom at the end of the business day to clean the floors – to mop up the floors – and eradicate any dirt and spills and muddy footprints.

Dirt and spills and muddy footprints were, however, passive entities. Japanese soldiers steeped in a code of fighting to the death rather than facing the shame of surrender were anything but passive. "Mopping up" a just-conquered enemy island such as Iwo Jima or Okinawa was a ludicrous concept, if one really thought about it. Mop-up duty in war was accomplished with rifles and grenades and flamethrowers and mortars, just the same as "actual" combat was.

William Buchanan's 147th Infantry Regiment was regularly assigned mop-up duty in the latter stages of these iconic island battles. They became the ones responsible for clearing the caves and remaining pillboxes, and conducting sweeps from one end of an island to another, in search of

Japanese soldiers still determined to inflict pain and death on the American Marines and soldiers, refusing to accept the mortification of defeat.

The final days of battle on Okinawa were costly ones to the American forces. Simon Bolivar Bucker, the Army three-star general who had led the invasion, was killed by enemy artillery only days before the island was declared secured. Two hours later, a patrol led by Lieutenant William Buchanan was ambushed, with nearly every American soldier in the patrol killed or wounded. William Buchanan would receive a second Silver Star medal for his bravery as he led his men against the remaining enemy who needed to be "mopped up."

Unlike his first Silver Star, the one conferred to him for his bravery on Saipan, this second one would be awarded posthumously.

* * *

There would be no funeral.

William Buchanan had already been buried on Okinawa. Much later his remains would be disinterred and returned to Pittsburgh for reburial in Allegheny Cemetery. But in the summer of 1945, while the Second World War still raged in the Pacific, returning the remains of dead soldiers and sailors, Marines and airmen to the United States simply wasn't practical.

Elizabeth returned to Pittsburgh the day after receiving the terrible news of her brother's death. Tony was recovering, and would most likely be returning home soon to Pittsburgh. Angela didn't need Elizabeth with her any longer. If anything, Angela wished that she could accompany Elizabeth back to Pittsburgh. Who did she have back there? Her mother, with whom Elizabeth hadn't spoken for two and a half years? Angela shuddered when she thought about the upcoming "reunion" of mother and daughter. She felt for Elizabeth; Angela could *feel* how awful everything would get when Elizabeth came together with Katherine Buchanan in the aftermath of William's death.

*   *   *

Elizabeth dreaded the encounter. She had covered the three-quarters of a mile from the DeLuca home in Morningside to her parents' home in neighboring Highland Park as slowly as she had ever walked in her life. At least three times along the way she had actually turned around and begun walking quickly in the opposite direction, only to force herself after a few steps to pivot and resume slowly striding towards this inevitable reunion.

She could put it off no further. She arrived in front of the stately home in which she had been raised, and slowly climbed the four porch stairs and then shuffled to the front door. Her father's Packard Twelve was nowhere to be seen. Maybe they're both somewhere else, Elizabeth hopefully thought, before acknowledging immediately thereafter that if her mother weren't home, that still did not absolve Elizabeth of the inevitable encounter in the wake of her brother's death.

She knocked on the door and waited. After nearly thirty seconds had passed Elizabeth was ready to pivot and all but flee the front porch; but then she heard the click of the deadbolt lock. The front door slowly opened, and Elizabeth was struck by the appearance of her mother. Two and a half years had passed since the last time the two women laid eyes upon each other. That long duration, now coupled with the death of Elizabeth's brother, made Katherine Buchanan appear to have aged two decades. The stately woman who had always ensured that she was impeccably dressed with full makeup and lipstick, even around her own house, now looked more like Rosalia DeLuca than someone who would regularly dine and socialize at the Witherspoon Club.

"I was wondering when you would get around to coming here," Katherine Buchanan proclaimed. Just from that single sentence, Elizabeth could tell that her mother had been drinking heavily. Not that Elizabeth blamed her; losing a son to this war was certainly reason enough for anyone, man or woman, to hit the bottle.

"I was in Philadelphia, with Angela," Elizabeth replied. "Her husband – Tony – was badly wounded in Italy, and they flew him back to an Army hospital there. I came home as soon as I heard about William. Carlo's father called out to there after Father called him, looking for me to tell me about…"

"Of course you were out there," Katherine Buchanan interrupted. "That's your family now; those Italians."

"That's not fair!" Elizabeth immediately protested. "I just said that I came back as soon as I heard. My train got into Pittsburgh around one o'clock this morning, and I came over here as soon as I woke up!"

Elizabeth's mother's only response was a shrug as she opened the screen door and said:

"Well, come in anyway."

Elizabeth was ready to turn around and leave, but she was determined to be the bigger person. She followed her mother into the house and asked:

"Is Father here? I don't see his car."

Katherine Buchanan halted and turned around to face her daughter.

"He's probably down at the Witherspoon Club, listening to everyone tell him how sorry they are that his hero son was killed. I'm sure he loves the sympathy."

The nasty tone of her mother's words took Elizabeth by surprise.

"I haven't heard anything about how William was killed on Okinawa, but I did hear all about what he did on Saipan. He *was* a hero!" was her rebuttal.

Another infuriating shrug was Katherine's response.

"Sit down," she said to her daughter, and then nodded her head towards the makeshift bar area in the corner of the elegant living room. "Would you like a drink?"

"It's not even ten o'clock!" was Elizabeth's automatic, astonished response even as she realized that the mid-morning hour was apparently not a restraint on her mother's grief-stricken drinking.

"As I understand it, a Gold Star Mother, which I now am, is permitted to partake at any hour of the day or night, with no restrictions."

Her mother's half-slurred words suddenly caused Elizabeth to realize that when she had hesitatingly walked onto the front porch, she hadn't seen a service flag in the window. Possibly there had been one with its single blue star, and upon word of William's death it had been quickly removed while waiting for a replacement with a gold star. Somehow, though, Elizabeth didn't think that was the situation at all. She was all but certain that there had never been a service flag adorning the window of the Buchanan home.

Elizabeth asked, "Did you go to the War Bond Rally at Forbes Field last December? When William was introduced as a hometown hero?"

"Of course not!" was Katherine's immediate bitter reply. "He never should have been in a position in the first place to be a 'hero.'" She spat out that last word, her disdain for the idea so very evident. "He was meant for much more, and now he's gone!"

Katherine glared at her daughter.

"Your father went to that rally. He insisted on going. I told him – your father – that he was disgracing his good family name by encouraging this war hero nonsense!"

Elizabeth's mouth dropped.

"I saw William the night before the rally," Elizabeth retorted. "He came downtown to find me, and we had dinner together. He told me all about how he felt; how proud he was fighting alongside all the other soldiers. He was scared, but he was also brave. I was there at the rally, and you should have heard Gene Kelly describe what William did, and how they gave him a battlefield commission. You should be proud of him!"

"That's *not* how I raised him! He wasn't meant to be some anonymous soldier, whether he was killed or not. He was every bit as important as Calvin McKinnon, and should have had some important war job, not crawling through the mud in some godforsaken jungle thousands of miles from here!"

"William told me," Elizabeth replied through clenched teeth, "that all the while they were getting ready to invade Saipan, it made him sick to think that Father had paid to buy him 4-F status so these soldiers who were now his friends could risk their lives instead of him. William is dead and it's terrible, but he died a better man than when he spent all of his time cheating on exams and making black market deals and then getting arrested!"

Elizabeth was on the verge of continuing with what William had painfully told her – that he largely blamed his mother and his upbringing for his selfishness and always looking to somehow beat the system – but she caught herself. As angry as Elizabeth already was with her mother, she realized that Katherine Buchanan had still lost a son.

Katherine glared back at her daughter.

"I'm not surprised that you see it that way. I wouldn't expect anything different from you after you turned your back on this family. Now I have no children left at all."

"That's a terrible thing to say! I'm right here; right in front of you!"

Katherine Buchanan seemed as well-rehearsed for her response as she had been back in December of '42 in the aftermath of Calvin McKinnon's surprise dinner invitation, fending off Elizabeth's inevitable challenge to Katherine's maneuverings with her pleas for her daughter to get her marriage annulled.

"Oh really? You're 'right here'? I haven't seen you in two and a half years. You've gone out of your way to shame me…"

"Don't start that again!" Elizabeth was furious. "You're the one who refused to accept my marriage to Carlo, and did your best to ruin it by sending Calvin my way! I didn't shame you in any way at all, and I'm tired of hearing you say that! You sound like a broken record!"

Katherine Buchanan was unmoved.

"I should have had a son like Calvin McKinnon, or a son-in-law like him."

She again scowled at her daughter.

"Or both."

Elizabeth had never sat down, given that her mother had launched into her attacking words the moment they walked into the living room. She turned towards the door but paused to lock eyes with her mother.

"Look," Elizabeth sounded defeated. "I don't want to fight. My brother – your son – is dead, and I came by to see you since there's not going to be a funeral. I know it hurts. There's a lot more of this terrible war ahead once we invade Japan, but hopefully it will be like Europe, and then after a year or two we'll win there, and the war will be over once and for all; and life can get back to normal."

Elizabeth paused for a second, her mind racing, wondering if she should continue with what was on her mind.

What the hell, she thought to herself; why not?

"If Carlo comes back safely, then we'll have your grandchildren to bring over to you. If we have a boy we'll name him after William, and I'm sure that with time..."

Elizabeth intended to continue painting a picture of a life after war that would no doubt be radically different than if so many years of war had not occurred, but hopefully would be at least somewhat returned to what prewar life had been like in Pittsburgh and across America.

She didn't have the opportunity as her mother interrupted.

"Well, maybe your precious Carlo *won't* come back; did you ever think of that? Then maybe you can marry Calvin McKinnon, or someone like him. *Then* you can bring my grandchildren over to visit. You've wasted all these years, but maybe it's not too late for you."

Elizabeth was stunned into silence, but her mother wasn't yet finished.

"In fact, even if your Italian husband does come back, I'm sure he'll be interested to hear that you had eyes for Calvin..."

"I did not! I talked to him at a Christmas party almost three years ago, and then *you* invited him here for dinner. That was all! In fact, I saw him downtown last year, a little bit after D-Day; and the more I thought about it, the more I think that he's really a creep, if you want to know the truth. He kept asking me to have drinks with him, even though I told him that Carlo was fighting on Saipan at the time."

Elizabeth's anger was now all but uncontrollable.

"How dare you lie like that and try to make something out of absolutely nothing! You have this horrid obsession that I need to marry someone like Calvin, and you told me that I should get my marriage annulled. I'm married to Carlo, and that's the end of it!"

Elizabeth stomped towards the front door, hearing her mother say behind her:

"Then I guess we'll see what your husband thinks if he comes back, won't we?"

* * *

Elizabeth endured a long string of terrible dreams that night. Each one was some variation of her mother either embellishing that long-ago holiday party conversation into something much deeper, or seeking out Carlo and flagrantly lying to him that Elizabeth had engaged in an affair with the government man. The light of day brought an end to the nightmares, but Elizabeth endured a restless morning and afternoon, fretting over something that she had no control of. She was now convinced that in a year or two, should Carlo return safely from the invasion of Japan, her mother would do everything in her power to destroy her daughter's marriage, merely because William was now dead, and Carlo DeLuca was not Calvin McKinnon or someone else whom Katherine Buchanan found acceptable to be the male heir in the Buchanan family. Elizabeth now deeply regretted not fully confiding in Carlo during that long walk back in the spring of '43 when she gave him an abridged, censored version of the schism with her mother. She could only hope that should her mother's threats become a reality, Carlo would believe his wife rather than the poisonous lies.

What was her mother's fixation with Calvin McKinnon? The young Georgetown man might indeed have held an "important stateside government job" for the past several years and thus have been exempt from military service. But as year after year of war came and went, Elizabeth began to look at this particular military exemption with a different eye than she had long ago when engaged in deep conversation in the midst of the Witherspoon Club Christmas Party. Each one of President Roosevelt's own sons, who surely could have wrangled "important stateside government jobs," was serving in the military during the war. Their distant relative –Theodore Roosevelt, Jr., son of the earlier President Roosevelt – had been the only general to land with his men by sea in the first wave on D-Day, earning the Medal of Honor for his leadership and heroics at Utah Beach. Teddy Roosevelt, Jr., was also surely capable of landing an "important stateside government job" if he had chosen that path; instead, he had been the oldest man hitting the beaches in the entire D-Day invasion, despite his ill health that led to the heart attack that took his life only days later.

Elizabeth fully realized that important stateside war jobs in the WPB, OPA, National War Labor Board, and many other agencies indeed needed to be filled by capable men who were as much a part of the war effort as those in uniform. Where she differed so greatly from her mother, though, was her mother's insistence that these home front government men were somehow "smarter" and "better" than their military counterparts simply by virtue of being able to avoid a uniform, and thus should be given first consideration as prospective marriage partners by girls such as Elizabeth.

*   *   *

For the rest of her life, Elizabeth Buchanan DeLuca would endure the overwhelming guilt that upon receiving word early that evening of Katherine Buchanan's drunk-driving death, her immediate reaction was instantaneous relief. Katherine Buchanan rarely drove, and no one would ever know where she was headed that afternoon. The Pittsburgh papers would soft-pedal the story, focusing instead on the angle of the grief-stricken Highland Park semi-socialite sadly dying not long after her war hero son, leaving behind poor Spencer Buchanan to deal with the tragedy of so much loss in such a short period of time.

At her mother's funeral, Calvin McKinnon approached Elizabeth – seated next to her father – to pay his respects. Elizabeth coolly gazed at him, waited for him to finish what he was saying, and then replied:

"Thank you, Mister McKinnon; that's very thoughtful of you."

Chapter 37

August 6, 1945

"Elizabeth! Elizabeth!"

Elizabeth was resting in the tiny backyard, her mind a million miles away as she enjoyed a touch of sun now that the thunderstorms earlier in the day had cleared. She looked up and saw Angela rushing through the kitchen door that led to the backyard. Angela and Tony had been back in Pittsburgh for three weeks. Tony – Army discharge fresh in hand, thanks to the new separation points schedule – was still undergoing medical and rehabilitation treatment at West Penn Hospital, all fully paid for by the Army.

Elizabeth looked up at Angela, immediately fearful that terrible news had just been received, probably delivered by telegram. Instantly, though, Elizabeth recalled how her sister-in-law had looked back at the Valley Forge General Hospital after Major Lereaux told Angela about the emergency phone call from Giuseppe DeLuca, and Angela had to deliver the terrible news to Elizabeth about her brother's death. The look on Angela's face now was nothing like that.

"We dropped an atom bomb on Japan!" Angela excitedly declared. "On Hiroshima!"

Elizabeth had no idea what an "atom bomb" was, and was vaguely aware that Hiroshima was a Japanese city. She wondered what all the excitement could be about a single bomb.

"Come listen! Hurry!"

Elizabeth was apparently too slow in rising from her chair, because Angela repeated:

"Hurry!"

Elizabeth quickened her pace, and made it inside the house and into the living room where her mother-in-law, Tony, and Carmela were all gathered close to the Admiral radio.

"...world will note that the first atomic bomb was dropped on Hiroshima, a military base." Even as she listened to President Truman's words, Elizabeth couldn't help but think how undistinguished his voice sounded when compared to the regal tones of the late President Roosevelt. "We won the race of discovery against the Germans. We have used it in order to shorten the agony of war in order to save the lives of thousands and thousands of young Americans..."

"It's some special kind of bomb," Tony said to nobody in particular. "Something about atomic energy, and being equivalent to a thousand regular bombs."

Elizabeth and Angela looked at each other, still uncertain what an atom bomb actually was but apparently sharing the same thought: did this mean that the end of the war might finally be at hand?

*   *   *

That afternoon's *Pittsburgh Press* provided plenty of additional information. "SECRET ATOM BOMBS TO

WIPE OUT JAPAN" the headline screamed, followed by: "Quit or Die, Truman Warns."

Much of the newspaper's front page was dedicated to not only the details of this surprise new weapon and its use on Hiroshima, but also unveiling the closely held details of what apparently had been years of incredibly expensive, top-secret development. One of the stories even postulated how the heart of this new weapon – Uranium-235 – might be harnessed for ultra-efficient peacetime energy usage.

All of this news, along with one radio bulletin after another throughout the afternoon and evening, was captivating. To Elizabeth, as well as every one of her in-laws, it all came down to the sudden realization that not only might the war end soon – *very* soon – but also that its conclusion might come without the terrible invasion of Japan that everyone had been dreading.

*   *   *

Three days later, the second atomic bomb attack, this one on Nagasaki, brought the war even closer to a victorious conclusion. Japan waffled back and forth for several more days, not exactly in a strong negotiating position, yet in many ways emulating the last gasps of Nazi Germany back in late April and early May, struggling for a few crumbs of self-destiny in the face of overwhelming military defeat.

On Wednesday morning, August 15, 1945, Elizabeth was the first one in the DeLuca home to awaken. She raced downstairs and hurriedly opened the front door, and then leaned down to retrieve this morning's *Pittsburgh Post-Gazette*. She unfolded the paper and was overjoyed at the oversized bold-typed headline:

WAR IS OVER

Carlo would be coming home now, and their married life could finally begin, and they could now start a family. First she would inform Angela, who was walking down the stairs at this very moment...

Chapter 38

December 18, 1945

Elizabeth DeLuca awoke to the instant realization that today was finally The Day: Carlo was finally coming home! At 3:00 this afternoon she would be waiting for him – along with his family, of course – at Penn Station, and she would rush into his arms and greet her husband with the biggest kiss imaginable.

For four months now, ever since Truman's announcement of the Japanese surrender, Elizabeth had waited impatiently for Carlo's return. Each passing day was agonizing, especially with wave after wave of servicemen now arriving back in the States from Europe and even the Pacific. The official Japanese surrender ceremony on September 2nd made it all official, which was a relief to Elizabeth. For several weeks after Truman's mid-August announcement that peace was finally at hand, she had endured nightmares almost every night that despite what the President had said, the enemy had changed their mind and had decided to fight on...and that the massive invasion of Japan would be necessary after all. Finally seeing the newsreel footage of the signing ceremony in Tokyo Bay when she, Angela, Carmela, and Tony went to the Fulton to watch *Wonder Man* with Danny Kaye, convinced Elizabeth that the peace was real, and her nightmares ceased.

During October, word came that both Vinnie and Michael were slated to be part of the occupying force in

Europe, and neither would receive a discharge before mid-1946. Giuseppe and Rosalia DeLuca were both terribly disappointed; this news meant that regardless of when Carlo returned home, the entire family would definitely not be together once again for either Thanksgiving or Christmas this year. What neither parent, nor anyone else in the family knew yet, was that both Vinnie and his youngest brother had actually volunteered to remain in the Army and in Europe, even though both had enough points for a discharge. Vinnie had an English sweetheart, while Michael had become bewitched by a French girl. Victory was sweet and home awaited, but neither of the unmarried DeLuca brothers was in a hurry to leave Europe.

Tony DeMarco did arrive home from Europe in late October, and Carmela moved with him to his parents' house. Elizabeth and Angela privately wondered how their marriage would hold up, given Carmela's affair back in late '42 and '43. Both girls kept waiting for some sort of falling-out, but apparently enough time had passed for Carmela to put the whole affair behind her as if it had never happened. Tony and Carmela were frequently over at the DeLuca home for supper or Sunday visits, and they appeared to be happy enough.

In early November, Elizabeth finally received a single V-mail letter from Carlo, the first in a long while. She was certain that he had written others; but if anything, the sudden peace in the Pacific made overseas mail traffic slower and more erratic than ever. Hopefully, other letters would eventually arrive in Pittsburgh. Elizabeth sank down onto the sofa and began reading. Ever since the Japanese surrender the military censors had gotten very lax, and parts of Carlo's letter that surely would have been excised before the peace had been left alone.

October 2, 1945

Dear Elizabeth,

I just received a whole stack of V-mail letters today from you dating back to July. They took a while to catch up with me since we were staging for Okinawa over on Saipan, then went to Okinawa, and then back to Saipan to train for the invasion. Then they sent some of the 2nd Division to occupy Nagasaki, and I was there until last week. You should see how that place was leveled. I can't believe that just one bomb did all that.

I'm so sorry to hear about your brother, especially since he was killed on Okinawa. Everything you told me about him in all the letters you wrote since late last year tells me that he was a good man, no matter what he had done before. May he rest in peace.

I'm sorry also to hear about your mother. I know you two had that falling-out a while back and you didn't say if you had a chance to see her after you got back to Pittsburgh, before she died. This war has been rough on you, I'm very sorry.

I never fought on Okinawa. I was there, but the 2ⁿᵈ Marine Division wound up being a diversionary force. We made a couple of feint landings - basically, fakes to keep the Japs off guard - but the 1ˢᵗ and 6ᵗʰ Divisions, plus the Army, did all the fighting.

I was relieved at not having to fight the Japs on one more island, because honestly I thought my number might finally be up. I know that's not what you want to hear but that's the way I felt. At the same time, though, there's something about knowing that the other Marine divisions, plus the Army, were doing all the fighting and we were just sitting there offshore being the decoys. It didn't feel right. Anyway, I'm glad it's all over.

I said above that I was in Nagasaki until last week. Here's the big news - they told me that I'm being discharged, and right now I'm in the Philippines until I'm scheduled to come back to the States. They tell me I should get home right before Christmas, and I'll keep letting you know what I hear. Since letters take so long back and forth, though, I'm not sure when you'll see this letter or any of the others that I've written. For all I know, I could be home before you even get the letters. But anyway, I think I'll be home for Christmas, and I can't wait. When I get stateside I'll send you a telegram to let you know when I should be back in Pittsburgh. So if you don't get this letter, you're in for a big surprise when you get that telegram.

Tell Tony I said hello and I hope his recovery is still going good. Is there any word about Vinnie or Michael yet? Write back and let me know.

Love,

Carlo

Elizabeth took a moment to absorb what she had just read, and then shouted to anyone else in the house who might be able to hear her:

"Carlo is coming home! Maybe by Christmas!"

*   *   *

Today was the day. The minutes ticked by all morning and early afternoon at quarter-speed until it was time to leave for Penn Station. Elizabeth, Carlo's parents, Tony, and Carmela all squeezed into Carlo's Packard Six that had become the family car during his long absence. The *Gotham Limited* was scheduled for a 2:55 p.m. arrival, and this close to Christmas numerous trains were bringing back servicemen to Pittsburgh from all corners of the country. Penn Station was packed, and Giuseppe DeLuca had to let everyone out of the car to head inside while he circled to look for a parking space to open up.

The main part of the station was packed with uniformed servicemen hugging loved ones. Heading down to the platform where the *Gotham Limited* would be arriving, the scenes of tearful greetings were repeated time and again.

The moment was almost here, and Giuseppe DeLuca arrived on the platform just in time for the first signs of the train chugging slowly into the station. Elizabeth burst into tears; she didn't need to wait for the sight of her husband. Suddenly, she had the strangest feeling that Carlo wasn't even aboard this train; he had somehow been held up in Chicago or Fort Wayne or somewhere else along the line, or had simply missed getting on board. Carlo had sent a telegram from San Francisco the moment he received his travel orders and itinerary, but something might have happened since then. She felt foolish to be already crying, especially if the tears turned out to be for nothing.

Elizabeth needn't have worried. The train slowed to a stop and the passengers – about three-quarters of them in uniform – hurried off the train cars, most eyes searching for a familiar face. A minute or so later a Marine Staff Sergeant with a weary but familiar face stepped onto the platform. Carmela was the one who spotted her brother first.

"Carlo! Carlo! Over here! Carlo!"

Somehow, Carlo DeLuca was able to hear his sister above the deafening noise, and he looked in the direction of the sound until he spotted her; his parents; his brother; Angela…and his wife.

As if they were recreating a scene from a corny war movie, Elizabeth burst into a full-speed run at the same instant that Carlo did, coming from the opposite direction. Each one expertly weaved through the throngs of people on the platform between them, just as an all-star college halfback might do. They collided, and everything that had happened since they reluctantly said goodbye to each other on this same platform, more than three and a half years ago, abruptly melted away.

* * *

"This is a buddy of mine, Jack Leonard," Carlo introduced another Marine staff sergeant who wandered up to the group. "Second Marines also; we go back to Guadalcanal together."

"He went to Schenley," Carlo added, referring to one of the rivals to their own Peabody High.

Tony was the first to shake his brother's friend's hand, and as Jack Leonard proceeded to shake hands with everyone else in the DeLuca family, he said to Tony, "Carlo tells me you were wounded in Italy."

"Yeah," Tony replied. "They sent me back to the States on a C-54, and while I was at the hospital near Philadelphia, I got discharged."

"Yeah," Jack Leonard replied, "I got hit on Guadalcanal, and then again on Tarawa and Saipan."

"Geez," Tony DeLuca replied. "Carlo got hit on Guadalcanal also; but I guess you know that."

Jack Leonard nodded.

"Yeah, all three of us." He paused to look around. "But we made it, huh?"

"Yeah, we did," Carlo chimed in, his left arm clutching Elizabeth tightly.

The group slowly moved from the platform to the main area of Penn Station. Elizabeth's tears had slowed slightly, but she could still feel freshly formed ones slowly trickling down her cheeks. She still couldn't believe that everything happening around her, at this very moment, was true. She had endured so many strange, disturbing dreams throughout the war that she fully expected to suddenly awaken and find that the war was still raging, and that Carlo was actually still somewhere out in the Pacific.

"Hey," Jack Leonard said all of a sudden, "I see a football buddy of mine from Schenley. I'm going to go over and say hello to him."

He turned to Carlo DeLuca, his fellow Marine combat veteran, and the two locked eyes for a few seconds.

"I'll see you around the city, huh?" Jack said.

"Yeah, guess so," Carlo said. The two shook hands and simultaneously reached out with their respective left hands to give the other a squeeze on the arm. There was something about watching her husband and his friend, two Pittsburgh boys who had been forced to grow up way too fast and who had survived so much during the past few years, that brought a fresh outbreak of tears to Elizabeth.

The two Marines finally, reluctantly, released their grips.

"My buddy over there was an Air Corps pilot and wound up as a German war prisoner," he explained to

Carlo as he began to turn away. "Looks like he made it back; I hope he did okay."

As Jack Leonard hurried away in the direction of his high school buddy, both Angela and Elizabeth simultaneously had the same strange thought. Surely there were more than a few Army Air Forces German war prisoners returning home to Pittsburgh. But could Jack Leonard's friend possibly be Joseph Coleman, who both girls recalled had gone to Schenley High School?

Maybe they would find out someday. In the meantime, Elizabeth clutched Carlo's left arm as tightly as she could. Giuseppe DeLuca offered to carry his son's seabag so Carlo could be unencumbered as he walked arm-in-arm with his wife through Pittsburgh's Penn Station, the same as Tony and Angela were doing.

Exiting the train station out into the glorious late afternoon sunshine of a crisp mid-December day, Giuseppe and Rosalia DeLuca trailed slightly behind their sons and their wives – Carmela also, who kept pace with her brothers and her sisters-in-law – and took in the sight in front of them. Nearly four years ago these three children of theirs had all hastily married high school sweethearts during the earliest, darkest days of the war. Instead of summer cookouts and boisterous family Christmas dinners and even struggling to pay the bills – and of course welcoming babies – they all had been forced to endure year after year of fear and separation and loneliness.

What would be the toll of the years lost to war on Carlo and Elizabeth; on Tony and Angela; and on Carmela and her Tony? Time would tell, and both Giuseppe and Rosalia DeLuca each said a quick prayer that their children's immense sacrifices would somehow be repaid in the years ahead.

Epilogue –December 31, 1945

"Are you almost ready?"

"Almost," Elizabeth answered her husband's question, even though she was still vacillating between the two dresses hanging in front of her.

Sensing that his wife wasn't being fully honest in her reply, Carlo added:

"We better get there soon if we want to get a table; the joint's gonna be jumping."

"I know," was Elizabeth's near-automatic reply, her attention still focused on deciding between the green dress versus the red one. Both were new – the green one a Christmas present from Carlo, and the red one from in-laws – and neither had been worn yet. Either would be perfect for what was planned this evening: New Year's Eve at the Crawford Grill along with Tony and Angela, Carmela and her Tony, Rocky and Tina Santucci, and several other couples.

"Elizabeth…"

Realizing that Carlo was getting impatient, Elizabeth looked back at Carlo, only a few feet away in the tiny bedroom, and asked:

"Could you please look in my jewelry box for my pearl earrings?"

Carlo sighed. He realized that years of being a Marine, when someone would demand "Jump!" and the only acceptable response was an immediate "How high?" were now over. Elizabeth was his wife, not one of his platoon members, and Carlo needed to relearn the concept of patience.

He opened Elizabeth's oversized jewelry box, and the first thing he saw was an envelope with his name handwritten on the front.

"What's this?" Carlo asked, looking back at Elizabeth as he picked up the envelope.

"Open it," was her response after a brief hesitation.

Carlo did as she asked and began reading.

December 31, 1945

My darling Carlo,

Three years in a row, I sadly wrote you a New Year's Eve letter telling you that I couldn't put into words how much I missed you, as I did every single day; and shared the hope that next year would finally be the year that the war was over and we would be together. Finally, I no longer have to write you from thousands of miles away, nor do I need to tell you that I miss you. You're here now, for good, and not only will we spend our New Year's Eve together, we can finally spend our lives together.

All my love to you,

Elizabeth

Carlo looked up from reading, and saw that Elizabeth's eyes glistened with tears…the same as his eyes now were. He took a deep breath and said in a choked voice as he looked back at the letter:

"New Year's Eve, and I'm not in a Navy hospital or sitting on some island out in the Pacific…God, it feels strange."

He paused for a second before continuing.

"But it feels good, I gotta tell you."

"I have all of those other letters, you know," he continued, still gazing at the letter in his hands. "Not just the New Year's Eve ones, but every letter that you wrote me over there."

Carlo finally looked up at Elizabeth and smiled despite his watery eyes.

"Come on, decide on a dress already," he gently chided, his voice still choked. "It's time for us to get going."

Author's Afterword

Several footnotes to our tale are worth mentioning.

1. Tony DeLuca's "unique wound" – being shot through his left lung and his heart, with his shredded lung tissue miraculously wrapping itself around his heart to slow the blood loss – is based on an actual reported wound from World War II. "Shot in Heart Fails to Kill Greensburg Yank in Italy," read the headline of Page 1 story in the April 11, 1945, edition of the *Pittsburgh Press*. The Pittsburgh-area soldier – Private Ray Shaffer, Jr. – suffered a wound exactly as described in our novel. The story was unusual enough to make the first page of the afternoon newspaper, and I felt compelled to use it as the basis for Tony DeLuca's war wound, which also occurred in Italy.

2. Even though the Sixth War Loan Drive took place between November 2nd and December 16th, 1944, the Forbes Field War Bond Rally on December 7th, 1944, described in the story is a fictitious event. In fact, the occasion described with dozens of Hollywood and Broadway celebrities participating in a single song-and-dance (and comedy) extravaganza would have more accurately described a USO show, which were common occurrences not only overseas, but also on military installations across the United States throughout the war years. War Bond Rallies (more precisely, the First through Eighth War Loan Drives, held periodically from late 1942 through late 1945) tended to be prolonged "multi-media" campaigns: special traveling live performances of popular radio shows; newspaper and radio advertising; radio broadcast speeches from President Franklin Roosevelt;

newsreel appeals in theaters before movies, made by military leaders such as General Eisenhower and celebrities such as Bugs Bunny (seriously – see https://archive.org/details/U.s.WarBondsCommercial); and so on. The legendary Kate Smith, who kicked off our fictitious Forbes Field Rally with a rendition of "God Bless America," did indeed devote much of her wartime efforts in this direction…and is considered to be the World War II War Loan Drive champion, selling more than $600 million in war bonds. (Source: https://www.britannica.com/biography/Kate-Smith)

3. One of the characters in this novel, William Buchanan, served in the United States Army's 147th Regiment. Iconic Pacific Theater "island hopping" battles on Guadalcanal, Saipan, Tinian, Iwo Jima, and Okinawa are typically associated with the United States Marine Corps. Yet the only American military unit to fight on *each* of those five islands was the Army's 147th Regiment. (Different Marine Corps Divisions were assigned to the various islands. For example, our character Carlo DeLuca's 2nd Marine Division did not fight on Iwo Jima.) The Army's 147th Regiment is often overlooked in the history of the Pacific War's island hopping campaign in light of the accomplishments of the Marines on those islands, and incorporating the 147th into our story is an attempt to bring to light their service and sacrifice.

4. *The DeLuca Furlough Brides* features several crossover characters from one or more novels in my "An American Family's Wartime Saga" series (*The First Christmas of the War* and its sequels). Gerald Coleman, Francine Donner, Abby Sobol, Charlene Coleman, Jack Leonard, and (by reference)

Jonathan, Joseph, and Tommy Coleman all appear in this novel. Those of you who have read one or more of these other novels can get a sense of the backstory to plotlines such as the saga of Joseph Coleman and Abby Sobol.

Likewise, Carmela and her husband Tony DeMarco are crossover characters from my Pittsburgh-set novel *Unfinished Business* that takes place in the early 1950s. In novel-writing terms, all of these tales – and other forthcoming ones – take place in the same fictional "universe" of World War II-era and postwar Pittsburgh. Watch for additional crossovers in the upcoming sequel to this novel *The DeLuca War Brides – Book 2: The Ones They Brought Home.*

The saga continues.

The DeLuca War Brides
Book 2: The Ones They Brought Home

Late 1946.

Vinnie and Michael DeLuca finally return home from Europe, each of them bringing along a new addition to the family. Join the entire DeLuca family as they pick up their lives after years of war and embark on a journey through postwar America, and learn to embrace the surprise additions to the family: the DeLuca War Brides.

Coming soon!

To be notified when *The DeLuca War Brides* is available, contact us at info@alansimonbooks.com.

Also by Alan Simon

An American Family's Wartime Saga

The First Christmas of the War – the sudden attack on Pearl Harbor brings about a troubling Christmas like none other for the Coleman family...

Thanksgiving, 1942 – Jonathan and Joseph Coleman return home on furlough for a brief, bittersweet family holiday before heading off to war...

The First Christmas After the War – World War II is over, and new journeys begin for the members of the Coleman family...

The First Winter of the New War *(available soon)* – Tommy Coleman is caught up in the tide-turning enemy counterattack that quickly turns General MacArthur's optimistic proclamation of imminent Korean War victory by Christmas into an ominous "entirely new war"...while his family digs out from a ferocious Thanksgiving blizzard and anxiously waits for word of Tommy's fate...

Please visit your favorite online book retailer to buy in either eBook or paperback.

Then: stay tuned as the Coleman family's "home front holidays" saga continues into the 1960s and 1970s with upcoming titles in the series. If you would like to be notified when the next title is available and also stay up to date with other titles from author Alan Simon, contact us at info@alansimonbooks.com to be added to our mailing list. You can also visit our website at www.alansimonbooks.com to learn more about our books.

A *USA Today* Bestseller

GETTYSBURG, 1913: THE COMPLETE NOVEL OF THE GREAT REUNION

July 1-3, 1863: The famed Battle of Gettysburg turns the tide of the Civil War, but not before approximately 50,000 soldiers from both sides become casualties during those three terrible days of carnage.

June 29-July 4, 1913: To commemorate the 50th anniversary of The Battle of Gettysburg, more than 50,000 Civil War Veterans ranging in age from 61 to more than 100 years old converge on the scene of that titanic battle half a century earlier in an occasion of healing that was known as the *Great Reunion*.

Abraham Lincoln had incorrectly surmised in his famed Gettysburg Address that "the world will little note nor long remember what we say here" four months after the battle itself, but those very words could well be said about the Great Reunion that occurred half a century later. At the time the 1913 gathering was a well-known, momentous commemoration with 50,000 spectators joining the 50,000 veterans, but the grandest of all gatherings of Civil War veterans has been all but forgotten in the 100 years since that occasion.

Until now.

GETTYSBURG, 1913: THE COMPLETE NOVEL OF THE GREAT REUNION: Available in both eBook and paperback from online bookstore.

About the Author

Alan Simon is the USA TODAY bestselling author of several historical novels set in the mid-20th century: **The First Christmas of the War, Thanksgiving, 1942, The First Christmas After the War, Unfinished Business,** and now **The DeLuca Furlough Brides.** He is also the author of the USA TODAY bestseller **Gettysburg, 1913: The Complete Novel of the Great Reunion** about the magnificent 1913 "Great Reunion" that was held exactly fifty years after the Battle of Gettysburg and which was attended by more than 50,000 aging Civil War veterans, both Union and Confederate.

Alan is also the author of the memoir *Clemente: Memories of a Once-Young Fan - Four Birthdays, Three World Series, Two Holiday Steelers Games, and One Bar Mitzvah,* published in honor and memory of the fortieth anniversary of baseball Hall-of-Famer Roberto Clemente's tragic loss on a humanitarian mission.

Also in the works, in addition to upcoming historical novels, is a series of contemporary novels. He is a native of Pittsburgh (where many of his novels are set) and currently lives in Arizona.

Visit www.alansimonbooks.com for more information.